THE DARK DREAM

KAYE DOBBIE

Acknowledgments

My heartfelt gratitude to my agent, Selwa Anthony, and to my editor, Julia Stiles, for their help and support – thank you!

Thanks also to the Bendigo City Library and the Bendigo Historical Society for their assistance in researching this book.

WINTER ON THE ROAD

KAYE DOBBIE

CHAPTER 1

———◆———

*S*HE WAS ALONE IN A *clearing and the dark forest was all around her. Like a great soundless wave. And she was frightened. But even as the fear beat at her, she knew, as if it had all happened to her before, that there were people searching for her. And if she stayed here in the clearing, if she stayed quite still in the darkness, she would be found.*

The wind made the tree tops billow like sails at sea. She breathed in the sharp scent of pine and tilted her head far back, gazing up. The moon was directly above her, floating in a deep blue sky. It seemed benevolent, a watchful friend. She sensed movements and sounds out in the darkness. Voices calling, calling her name. Burning torches flared through the thick branches. They were looking for her. She heard her own voice calling back. She stretched her hands out towards the darkness ... and her fingers sank into it. Soft and horrible. Like mud.

———◆———

From somewhere outside the dream, she recognised that it really was mud. The awful feel of it forced her into consciousness. She opened her eyes. There was a throbbing pain in her head and her vision was cloudy, but she saw enough to know it wasn't night-time and she wasn't in a pine forest. She was lying on her stomach, her head lower than her feet and only inches from where water lapped. The mud was under her cheek too, warm against her skin. She could smell it, musty and faintly rotten with dead vegetation.

The thought brought her jerkily to her knees, scrabbling backwards despite the shivers of nausea and the drumming in her head. Low, scrubby bush covered the slight slope that ran up from the water, but a spindly sapling had raised its head above the rest She grabbed it and used it to pull herself to her feet. Looking back, she realised she was by a sort of lagoon or, worse, a swamp. The water lay still and sullen and there was no sound apart from her own breathing.

As in the dream, she was all alone.

The light has gone strange, she thought fuzzily, and then realised the sun, low on the western horizon, had begun to set. The green of the trees had become greener, the brown of the mud browner, and the water was now shadowy and secret. She shuddered and put her hand to her head. Her hair was stuck down on one side with mud and when she tried to free it she felt a large lump on her scalp. Pain shot through her in sickening waves.

Had she fallen over? Or had she been hit? A sudden sharp memory of hurt and terror, gone as swiftly. It was only then, as she tried to recall the thought, that she realised everything was gone.

Everything.

The shock of it froze her. Everything that had been and was and would be, all gone. It was as if her life was a blackboard and someone had come and washed it clean. She was nothing, she was newborn, she had come to life here by the water, in the mud.

With a gasping cry she pulled herself further up against the thin trunk of the sapling, feeling it bending under her weight, seeking some comfort from another living thing no matter how unfeeling it might be. A bird on a last foray before nightfall scolded her, rustling amongst the leaves and twigs. It fluttered up into the branch above her head and gave a harsh call. The beady eye blurred ... became two ... four ... She squeezed her eyes shut, trying to clear them. When the waves of dizzy faintness had at last receded she looked again. The bird had gone and she was alone.

Desperately she tried to remember *something* ... but there was nothing. Her mind had closed up, taking all her memories with it. Her childhood, her family, her *life,* all gone.

'There must be someone,' she told herself in a shaking voice which was meant to be reassuring. 'Someone must be looking for me ...'

A breeze rustled the leaves, replying to her whisper, and she felt chilled. The skin on her arms rose up in tiny bumps, and as she rubbed them she knew with sudden certainty that she owned a cloak, a new dark red one. She could the heavy weight against her shoulders, the swing of it against her skirts. She looked down, fully expecting to see it, and saw instead her gown, dark of colour and now grubby with mud. Her feet were bare and streaked with dirt.

She looked like a pauper! She might well be one, except that she knew, again with a certainty that could not be ignored, that she was not. She knew she was used to being well cared for and well loved, and while the doubts circled her like cruel children taunting, she clung on to that knowledge.

Then why am I here? she asked herself, holding her aching head. No one answered her. Only the terrible quiet. A great wave of fear and loneliness gripped her, and she slipped and almost fell, clinging wildly to the smooth-trunked sapling. Behind her a sudden gust of wind rippled the surface of the lagoon, as if someone was running swiftly across it, running after her. She felt the terror rising, and knew in a moment she would lose what common sense she had left and disgrace herself by screaming hysterically.

That was when she heard the sound.

At first it was just a whisper, like a vibration in the air. And then the whisper gained a rhythm – the sound of a horse galloping. With a cry, she began to push and pull her way through the scraggly bushes on the slope, towards the top. There must be a track of some sort up there and someone was coming. Someone who may be able to help her!

The dull striking of the horse's hooves was getting louder. She reached the scrub edging the bank and burst through at a run, and the beast was upon her.

It was a brown horse. An ugly creature, she thought, even as she screamed. It veered to the side, missing her by a breath. She covered her eyes with her hands like a child. The rider was shouting 'Whoa!' and pulling at the reins. The horse whinnied, rearing half-heartedly on broad haunches. But it required effort to play up, and the horse was tired. It tossed its head a few times just to show its displeasure, and then stood still.

Slowly, she spread her fingers and peeped out. The rider was staring at her as if he could hardly believe his eyes. He was so thin, his clothing flapped on him. He wore a dusty felt hat over his wild black hair, and his beard was the same colour only streaked with silver, and his dark eyes were sunken in a gaunt face. He said some words she was sure she had never heard before - was he a foreigner? But then she realised he must have been swearing, for he went on in a gravelly voice, 'Are yer hurt?'

Was she hurt? She tried to clear her thoughts, but the scramble to the track had brought back the dizziness and she suddenly felt very peculiar. 'I've hurt my head,' she managed. Her voice sounded soft and clear and educated, completely at odds with her appearance.

He gawked at her. If she had been an African lion he couldn't have looked any more astonished.

She swayed, almost fell. That had him off his horse, but slowly, looking about him as if he expected someone else to pop out. She saw his hand slide across his waist, and noticed that he had a pistol there, tucked into his belt. He came closer, but still with caution.

'Who are yer?' he demanded.

Suddenly she was very tired; her mouth trembled. 'I don't remember who I am. I don't remember anything. I woke up just now, down by the water, and I don't remember anything.'

He stared at her, wide-eyed. 'Down by Seaton's Lagoon?'

She nodded.

He came closer, frowning. 'Blonde, blue eyes,' he muttered to himself. 'And pretty ... under the dirt.

Hey!' His eyes widened. 'I found some shoes lyin' in the middle of the track about a mile back. I put 'em in me saddle bag. Maybe they're yours?' Then the frown deepened and he put out a hand and touched her temple. When he took it away, there was blood on his fingertips, dark and sticky, like jam.

'Yer hurt,' he said blankly. And then, scowling, 'Come on. I'll take yer back to me friend.'

Back to his friend? she thought. But her head was spinning too much to ask questions.

'You shouldn't go off on yer own,' he was muttering. 'Ain't safe these days. There're thieves in these parts'd do yer in for a penny!'

She let him prattle on, as he lifted her up into the saddle. He seemed concerned for her and that was comforting. Surely a man wasn't concerned for you if he meant you harm?

'You must take me to the nearest town,' she informed him, trying to be heard above the hammering in her temples. The order sounded familiar – she was used to giving them.

But he wasn't having any of that. 'I'll take yer to Adam,' he replied firmly.

Who was Adam, she meant to ask. But the horse was moving uneasily, disliking the stranger on its back, and she had to concentrate on staying on. The man climbed up behind her.

'Come on then. It's not far,' he said in a soothing rumble. He dug his heels into the horse's flanks and set it to a trot, back the way he had come.

Her head was coming off. She kept expecting it to roll over her shoulder and bounce along the track behind them. The image made her smile to herself, although she knew she must be out of her senses to be imagining such things.

The horse was stubbornly slow, resenting its double load. The journey seemed to go on and on. Her head drooped in pain and exhaustion and she was almost asleep when a flying beetle blundered, whirring, against her face. She felt the scratchy legs on her cheek and cried out, pushing it away. The thought of it tangled in her hair made her shudder. After that, she stayed awake.

The man spoke to her occasionally, perhaps to satisfy himself she was still conscious, and every time he spoke his breath puffed like white smoke in the frozen air. He told her his name was Harvey, that he had had some bad news and was on his way to an inn to drown his sorrows – he said he had almost forgotten the taste of rum. Somehow, she got the impression that he worked on a farm with sheep, a lonely place. She remembered him saying, 'Nearly there,' a couple of times. And once, 'Yer'll be safe with Adam. He'll know what to do for yer.'

And the confidence in his voice instilled confidence in her.

It was beyond twilight now, but the moon was up enough for them to see their way. The track was a pale, narrow ribbon curling into the darkness, and the trees were black shadows bending over them with evil intent. She stared about her, shivering, half delirious. Perhaps I am dead, she thought. Perhaps I died back at Seaton's Lagoon, and this man who calls himself Harvey is Death, and he's taking me to Heaven ... or Hell.

She tried to turn her head, to see if beneath the wild black beard was a smooth white skull. But although his face was gaunt, it was not frightening. He gave her a reassuring grin and she realised he had hardly any teeth. And then the horse took a curve in the track and suddenly there was a camp site immediately before them.

She blinked. The flare of the campfire threw strange shadows among the trees. She hardly noticed the cart drawn up under their shelter, or the horse cropping nearby, or the dog barking. Her eyes went to the man squatting beside the fire, his head up, watching. As the horse trotted, puffing, towards him, he rose slowly to his feet, and the light of the fire coloured him red and orange, as if he too were burning.

Harvey called out in a loud, gruff voice. 'Adam!' And then added in that soothing rumble, 'Here's Adam. Yer safe now.'

The horse came to a standstill, too tired to complain as the dog circled it, still barking. Harvey swung down, turning to help her to the ground. But as her bare feet came into contact with the hard earth her knees buckled. He grabbed her awkwardly under the arms.

'Wolf!' Adam called the dog to heel. And then, 'Is she hurt?'

'Someone's clobbered her all right. Bushrangers, I reckon. Hit her and threw her into Seaton's Lagoon ... or near enough. She'd just crawled back up to the track when I found her. Nearly ran her down.'

'Do you know her?' Adam asked.

'Sounds Scotch to me, but I've never seen her before around here.'

She lifted her head with a mighty effort, drawn

by the need to see as well as hear what was going on. Harvey was frowning at his friend, but Adam was looking at her. He was of medium height and strongly built. Fair hair straggled unkempt over his shoulders and a beard covered most of his face. He was younger than the other man, but he looked just as rough and grubby – like a tinker, she thought. And his eyes were a tinker's eyes, dark and liquid and very intelligent.

He seemed to take in her situation with one hard look. 'I'll see to her head,' he said, and slipped his arm around her, taking her weight from the older man. For a moment her sheer helplessness frightened her and she struggled in the stranger's grip, but he murmured low in her ear, 'I won't hurt you,' and she subsided, leaning against him.

'Yer'll need to wash it,' Harvey said in a matter-of-fact voice. 'Salt'll do, if you've nothing else. Don't like treatin' head wounds meself. Never know what the damage is inside, where yer can't see. Might be better to take her to a quack.'

Adam barely glanced at him. He helped her over to the campfire, gripping her arms as he set her down beside it. The warmth was immediate – she had not realised until now how cold she was – and she gave a great shiver. He moved a billy of water onto the coals to boil, then went over to the cart and came back with a blanket to wrap around her.

'Can yer cope, boy?' Harvey asked. He had been watching, moving from foot to foot restlessly.

'Aye, I'll take care of her. She's in your debt for this, Harvey.'

Harvey murmured something, looking bashful. 'I'll get on to the inn then,' he added, more loudly.

'I've been lookin' forward to a drink, and I don't reckon I can wait for mornin'.' He licked his lips to prove it.

She straightened her back and struggled to find her voice. 'Thank you, Mr Harvey.'

Harvey smiled back at her gummily. 'Yer a lucky man, Adam,' he said.

The comment seemed strange. Surely no man would consider himself lucky to be lumbered with an injured woman who had no memory of her past. She closed her eyes. The two men were speaking, but in voices so low they were inaudible. The dog, Wolf, brushed against her, sniffing curiously at her skirts, and then sank down by the fire with a sigh. She heard the sound of Harvey's horse moving away into the darkness, quickening to a gallop. She heard the tinker – Adam – step closer, and realised he was removing the boiling water from the coals.

She opened her eyes a slit, all she could manage, and watched him. He was adding what looked like salt to the water, swirling it around to dissolve it. 'To clean your wound,' he explained without looking up. Then, with a quick glance, 'Did Harvey give you somethin' to drink?'

She shook her head and he went over to a rolled bundle of blankets on the ground – his bed for the night. He came back with a water bottle and held it out to her. She put the opening to her mouth and swallowed the cool, brackish liquid. It was heavenly, but when she tried to gulp more he removed it from her.

'That's enough for now. Too much and you might bring the lot up.'

He set the bottle down and returned to the cart. Wolf heaved himself up and trotted after him. She let her eyes wander to the fire, mesmerized by the colours and the way in which they were constantly changing. Gold and orange, then flaring up into angry red as the chill breeze caught them. That same breeze whirled the smoke into her face and she coughed, eyes stinging.

'Are these yours?'

His voice startled her. She blinked and tried once more to focus properly. Adam was holding something else up, and she realised that it was a pair of shoes.

'I don't know,' she whispered. 'Where did you find them?'

'Harvey found them along the track,' he told her evenly. 'You must've dropped them ... or someone else did.'

'I don't remember,' she admitted at last. 'I don't remember anything.'

He stared at her blankly. 'You mean ... nothin' at all?'

'Nothing. Not even my name.' The thudding in her head was getting worse and she had to close her eyes tightly to ease it

'Not even your name!' he repeated to himself. And then, gently, 'Here, try these shoes on.' He knelt at her feet and slipped one shoe on. It fitted perfectly, as only an old pair of shoes can, as if the leather has moulded itself to the contours of the wearer's foot and become almost a second skin.

'They mine.' Her voice was strange and high, like a child's.

The tinker was looking at her and suddenly his

eyes were glinting with laughter. 'Maybe we've found a name for you, Cinderella.'

Bemused, she stared back at him. His face was slowly beginning to turn, which was very odd, she thought. And then she realised that the whole world was turning, around and around and around. She was spinning towards the dark forest she had been dreaming of while she lay by the lagoon. She was among the straight trunks, the moon sailing above, the smell of pine filling her head.

And then there was nothing.

———◆———

Her fingers moved, twitching, feeling. But this time it was cloth beneath them and not mud. It was warm and soft, and it covered her entirely, keeping out the chill. And this time it was not the smell of decaying vegetation but smoke, catching at her throat and making her want to cough. It overlay other smells, unfamiliar smells of earth and bush and dog.

She opened her eyes and found that she was lying on a blanket. There was another blanket tucked over her and, close by, the fire had burned down to glowing coals. Wolf lay at her side, his rough grey fur making him look remarkably like his namesake. She lightly touched his head and he opened one brown eye, watching her with drowsy contentment.

It was very late. She could tell by the fire and the stillness. There was a breathtaking chill in the air outside her cosy nest. She moved, stretching cramped muscles. Her head felt different and when she put her hand up she realised her wound had been cleaned and some sort of makeshift bandage wrapped around it.

'Are you thirsty?'

The voice was unfamiliar. She turned her head towards it and felt the throbbing pain return. He was a few steps from where she lay, a shadow half risen from the ground. At her movement he stood up and came towards her. Wolf thumped his tail. She remembered him then; the fair-haired tinker with the dark eyes. What was his name? Adam, that was it. The tinker called Adam.

'I am thirsty,' she said. An understatement: her throat was dry as dust.

He stooped over her, helping her to sit up and sip from a mug. The water was still brackish and she gagged. He stayed kneeling beside her, watching her closely, as if expecting her to say or do something. Or, she thought wryly, expecting her to be sick.

The water hovered in her throat a moment and then mercifully slid down. She breathed a deep sigh of relief - she didn't want to be sick in front of him. She wished she wasn't so dirty and dishevelled, with her hair all down and her legs showing. It made her feel even more vulnerable than she was.

She lifted her chin and croaked politely, 'Thank you.'

He was silent, still watching her. Her head was pounding now as if someone were jumping up and down in it.

'That will be all,' she murmured, hardly aware of what she said, only wishing the thumping in her head would go away.

He gave a startled crack of laughter. 'No, that's not all, Cinderella. I have to see you safely first.'

Slowly, carefully, she forced her eyes back to him. 'Do you?'

'I feel it as an obligation,' he added quietly.

'My head hurts,' she complained.

He sat back with a smile. 'So it should. I don't suppose it helps for me to tell you it could've been worse?'

She grimaced, and that hurt more. 'No, it doesn't'

'There'll be a doctor somewhere along the track,' he added. 'You'll just have to make do until then.'

The dark eyes surveyed her from the shadows of his face. She remembered the impression she had had of him from the first ... that he was a tinker. She asked him if he was.

He took his time in answering. 'I've bought meself a horse and cart, and I intend to make money selling goods on the Bendigo diggings. I suppose that does make me a sort of tinker.' He smiled. 'I've got blankets, boots, clothing, cloth, pans, picks, nails, flour, salt, sugar, raisins, salt-fish, tea and half a dozen good sized cheeses.' He winked. 'All the things that make money on the goldfields, Cinderella.'

'Goldfields?' she repeated softly.

He chuckled. 'You must've hit your head hard! The gold rush, Cinderella, that has this place turned arse over. Ballarat and Mount Alexander and Bendigo. They're the main fields, although there've been other smaller rushes. Melbourne's empty of all but the women and children, and the harbour's full of empty ships. Every able-bodied man has up and left for the diggings to make his fortune. Every week, it seems, there're more wild stories. I've heard you can pick gold nuggets up off the ground like potatoes.' But he looked skeptical. 'Everyone's on the move. You can't have forgotten that?'

'No,' she said slowly, cautiously testing her memories as she might the first steps on a shaky, swinging bridge across some bottomless ravine. 'I believe I do remember the gold rush.' She was so pleased and grateful to have remembered, she beamed up at him.

He smiled and patted her shoulder in a gesture at once comforting and congratulatory. His sleeves were rolled up to his elbows and there was a blur of colour on his brown forearm, a dazzle of blues and greens. A tattoo, she thought. He has a tattoo. Briefly, it seemed as though that meant something to her.

On impulse she reached out and caught his hand in hers so that she could have a closer look. The tattoo portrayed a mermaid, curled sinuously across the width of his forearm, waves of fair hair snaking over but not quite covering her naked upper body. Beneath her curving fish tail was a date – 1849.

The mermaid was beautiful, but so much naked-ness ... she was taken aback. And yet the face was somehow familiar. She spoke her thoughts aloud. 'I know her, don't I?'

Adam had lost his smile. 'It's you,' he said. 'Or near enough as makes no difference.' Her eyes widened in surprise. She realised that she was still holding his hand and dropped it.

'But you don't know me,' she whispered. 'Do

you?'

Adam shook his head. 'Never met you before in me life, Cinderella.'

She spoke again, more sharply, to hide her embarrassment. 'What year is it now? Is it still 1849?'

Laughter danced in his eyes as if the serious moment had never been. 'No, it's 1852. Winter, 1852.'

She nodded slowly. The year meant nothing.

'Could I be travelling to Melbourne? Are we far from there?'

He frowned. 'About twenty-five mile. But the road over the Keilor Plains is already a quagmire from the rain and all the traffic headin' north. We can't go back there. It's bad enough up ahead from what I hear. In good weather it takes about a week to get from Melbourne to the Bendigo Creek but if this rain keeps up, it'll take that long to get one mile.' He paused. 'As I say, I'm bound for the Bendigo diggings, but I could leave you at one of the inns along the way.' But he looked dubious, and she felt a sharp jab of loss at the thought of being left with strangers. Already this tinker had become someone to cling to in a world of confusion.

'Maybe I was travelling to the goldfields, too,' she said quickly.

'Well ... perhaps. It's possible you were taken by bushrangers. It happens. There are plenty of 'em around, lookin' for easy pickings. It could be your husband wrote and told you he'd struck it rich. Sometimes miners do that, send for their wives and families. Do you wear a wedding band?'

She lifted her hand and looked at her fingers. There was no ring but on the third finger of her left hand there was a pale circlet on her flesh where a ring had been. She stared until her eyes began to ache but it was no use. Her mind simply refused to divulge any of its secrets.

'Stolen probably,' he said, with a grimace.

'Well, at least we've discovered you're *Mrs.* Cinderella and if you've a husband somewhere out there he'll likely come lookin' for you. I know I would.'

She hardly heard him. She felt so weary suddenly. 'You can't keep calling me that,' she murmured, and closed her eyes. 'That's not a proper name.'

Somewhere there were people who loved her, somewhere there was a home she knew well. It did not seem right that she should be here with this stranger, in the silent, lonely bush. Perhaps, she thought, in the morning everything will be all right again.

'Cinderella suits you.' His voice came through the rising tide of sleep. 'But for now I can call you Mrs Seaton. That's where you came from, wasn't it? Seaton's Lagoon ...'

Cinderella Seaton. It was a name, and would do as well as any other. His voice faded to nothing. Beneath the warmth of her blanket, she slept.

CHAPTER 2

———◆———

WHEN SHE AWOKE IT WAS dawn and her head did not hurt so much. Sleep had been deep and healing, preparing her for the day to come. She lay a moment, knowing that contrary to her hopes of the night before this was not a dream. She really was alone, with no memory of her past. The reality was still daunting, but not quite so terrifying as it had been last night. The morning had brought new hope. She glanced around her with awakening curiosity.

The clearing was bathed in pale sunshine, though white fingers of mist still caressed the shadows. The tinker moved about, keeping the fire crackling while a pot of water boiled over the flames. He wore the same clothing as yesterday – she doubted he had any others – moleskin trousers, a blue woollen shirt and a thick jacket. His boots, too, looked as though they had seen good service. She noted how quietly he moved. Although he wasn't tall, there was a breadth of shoulder and chest and hip which spoke of great strength. Self-contained, too; his thoughts his own unless he chose to share them. A bit of a loner. And yet he had been kind to her.

'Hungry?'

His voice interrupted her thoughts. Was she hungry? A rumble from her stomach answered the question. He turned and grinned at her over his shoulder. Sun and hardship had put lines around his eyes and the beard gave him a certain maturity. It was hard to tell his age but she thought he was somewhere in his twenties.

'I've some Johnny cake,' he told her, 'and some mutton.'

Upon inspection, Johnny cake turned out to be pan-fried damper. 'Thank you,' she said, trying to sound grateful.

'How's your head this morning?'

Carefully she put a hand to it. Beneath the bandage she could feel the painful bump. It hurt, and the headache was still there, but much improved from last night.

The tinker was holding out a mug towards her and she took it, burning her hand. When she finally got the mug to her lips, she found the tea hot and strong, and closed her eyes with pleasure. The silence settled around them, broken only by birds singing and the horse cropping. They might have been alone in all the world, the tinker and her.

Tinker, she thought irritably. I must stop calling him that.

She opened her eyes and realised he was watching her. His gaze travelled slowly over her muddied skirts, pausing at her bare ankles. She wriggled self-consciously, tucking them up under her hem so that only the toes of her shoes showed.

'I haven't even thanked you, Mr... er, Adam,' she said uncomfortably.

He looked up, and she noted again the intelligent gleam in those dark eyes. 'It's just Adam.'

'That's all? Adam?'

'Yes.'

She repeated it, in case it meant something to her. It didn't. She squared her shoulders and held out her hand. 'How do you do, Adam?'

He looked at her hand and then at her, and slowly reached out to engulf it with his own. His fingers were callused, the nails ringed with grime. Hers were little better.

'How do you do, Mrs Cinderella Seaton?'

'A bit of a mouthful, isn't it?'

He smiled. 'Aye, it is that. Maybe we can call you Cinders.'

'Oh no!'

He laughed at the revulsion in her voice. 'Ella, then. Is that better?'

She thought about it a moment, and then nodded. 'Yes, much.' His friendly smile disturbed her with its familiarity; he was a stranger and a lowly tinker, after all. Surely he should show her more deference ... more respect?

She made her voice coolly polite. '*You* must address me, however, as *Mrs Seaton*, Adam.'

He bowed his head in acquiescence. His expression was suitably respectful now, Ella couldn't fault him on that. It was the gleam in his eyes she mistrusted.

The food filled her up, but that was about the only good thing she could say about it. The Johnny cake was dry and hurt her gums, the mutton was old and tough. While Ella surreptitiously fed most of it to Wolf, she tried to visualise what she usually dined on. For an instant there was a flicker of something ... a white-clothed table with silver cutlery and fine crockery, a blaze of candles ... but it was gone as suddenly, and she was left with the suspicion that her mind had merely conjured up what she wanted to see.

After breakfast Adam set about harnessing his mare to the cart and packing up his few belongings. Ella had no brush and although she longed to take the tangles out of her hair, she could not bring herself to ask for Adam's comb - always assuming he owned one. He had suggested in an offhand way that she might want to go into the bushes for a bit, and although she wanted to relieve herself desperately, it had embarrassed her to have Adam know. Well, she told herself as she squatted in the leaves, difficult and embarrassing as it was, she would just have to put such niceties aside while she was travelling with Adam.

When she returned, he was ready and waiting. He held out his hand to her, pulling her up onto the seat beside him. It was narrow and hard, but she made herself as comfortable as she could. Adam flicked the reins and set the mare into motion. The cart started with a jolt before settling into a sort of bumpy roll.

They moved along the track, traversing the same ground Harvey and Ella had covered last night.

'We'll be on the Bendigo road by noon,' Adam told her.

Ella shifted on the hard seat. 'Why did you leave the Bendigo road in the first place?' she asked him, and then answered her own question. 'I suppose you were visiting your friend Mr Harvey.'

Adam smiled at the mare's ears. 'Harvey calls everyone his "friend". But, aye, we are friends. Harvey was keen to be off to the inn, so he went on ahead while I camped for the night.' He cleared his throat. 'I was visitin' a girl I know. She works on the same sheep station as Harvey. That's why I was off the Bendigo road.'

He seemed embarrassed, and Ella thought it prudent to change the subject. 'Is Mr Harvey going to the goldfields, too?'

Adam shrugged. 'He'll spend all his money on rum, sleep it off, and then go back to shepherding or starve.'

The scorn in his voice made her curious. 'Have you ever been a shepherd?'

'No,' Adam said emphatically.

'Tell me about Bendigo,' she asked after a moment.

'I've never been there,' he admitted with a wry smile. 'But I've heard the Bendigo field is big – about 50,000 miners on it. First place they found gold there was in the Bendigo Creek, but that was last year. They say a woman found it, the wife of a sheep station foreman. There was a big rush, but after the first excitement things settled down. Now they've found gold at another place on the Bendigo, called Eaglehawk Gully. Everyone's headed that way: the Vandemon lads, the farmers, the shepherds, them with their feet still wet from the boat. Everyone. I hear Ballarat's nearly empty, the same at Forest Creek. They all think there're fortunes to be made at Eaglehawk, one way or another.'

Ella thought about this for a moment. The Bendigo goldfield sounded like a place of bustling hysteria and excitement and possibly danger. Perhaps it would be more sensible and safer to return to Melbourne. And yet, if the road really was as bad as Adam had said ... Suddenly she cringed at placing herself in yet another stranger's safe-keeping. If Adam was going north, then so was she!

Another thought occurred to her. 'Will there be a policeman on the way to Bendigo?'

He gave her a speculative look. 'Could be.'

'I need to report what has happened to me.'

'There are a lot of things go on these days without much hope of findin' out who did them and why. A life doesn't count for much on the goldfields, Cinderella.' He rolled the name off his tongue as if he enjoyed saying it, irritating her.

'What am I supposed to do then?' she asked crossly. 'I want to find out who I am. I want to find out where I was going, and why.'

'I can do some askin' for you,' he said matter-of-factly. 'Leave it to me.'

Her headache was getting worse. 'I still think I should tell someone.'

He shrugged as if it were a matter of indifference to him.

She narrowed her eyes. 'Are you a wanted man, Adam?'

He laughed at that. 'I'm thinkin' of you, Cinderella. You don't realise what sort of world you've dropped into.'

'Maybe not, but I still need to report this to someone.'

Adam nodded solemnly, as if he agreed whole-heartedly, and yet she wasn't at all sure he did.

'And please, call me Mrs Seaton. Anything else is most improper.'

She sounded irritated – she *was* irritated! Maybe

it was petty, but she knew in her soul that never had a man of Adam's lowly station called her anything but 'ma'am'.

For a long time they were silent. The cart moved slowly along the track, while Wolf trotted beside it. Occasionally the dog would wander off into the trees on its own business, returning at regular intervals to supervise the journey. They were travelling through a forest of rough-trunked trees with narrow grey-green leaves, which Adam called box. The quiet and the shifting light could have been lovely, but there was a cold wind which went right through Ella's thin gown. She thought again of the cloak she was certain she had owned, and shivered.

'Here.' Adam handed her something that looked suspiciously like a horse blanket.

She opened her mouth to refuse it, and then changed her mind. It was better than nothing, she thought grimly, as she draped it around herself like a shawl. It smelt strongly of Bess the mare, and Ella bit a suddenly quivering lip. She was certain that never in her entire life had she worn a horse's blanket. It was almost worse than eating Johnny cake and riding on a cart!

They had rounded a bend in the track, and suddenly the passing scenery had a strange familiarity. Ella cried, 'Stop!'

Adam drew Bess up with a 'Whoa!' and a startled glance sideways. But Ella was staring towards the spindly growth at the track's edge and a thin sapling which rose, like a spear, above the scrub.

'This is where Mr Harvey found me,' she said quietly. She felt her body quivering. 'There's a swamp down there – '

'Seaton's Lagoon,' he cut in, and somehow his voice soothed her fear. 'I'd better take a look in case you've left somethin' behind.' Then, softly, 'Do you want to come down too?'

But Ella shook her head.

Adam handed her the reins without another word, and vanished over the bank. He was gone a long time, and Ella waited impatiently. She was tempted to follow him down, but she knew she didn't want to see that place again. Wolf snuffled in the bushes, head down and tail up. At last, Adam reappeared.

'Well?' she asked him more sharply than she meant.

He shrugged. 'No luggage, Mrs Seaton. Sorry. But you weren't alone down there. I found foot-prints. Three men, I'd say. They left their horses up on the track and climbed down. Must o' thought you were dead, or near enough, when they left you.' He paused. 'Looks to me like they were in a hurry - perhaps they heard someone else comin' along the track. It's busy enough some days. Might explain why you weren't hurt worse.'

'Worse!' she burst out. 'How much worse could it be?'

He scratched his beard. 'Well... you could've been raped, Mrs Seaton.'

He sounded indifferent, as though he were tell-ing her the time of day. Ella shivered under her blanket, her eyes fixed on his. He glanced away. 'We'd better get on,' he muttered. Ella said nothing, still shivering. After a moment Adam added in that same even tone, 'I don't believe in hurtin' women.'

There was a glitter in his eyes that hadn't been

there before and it took a moment for her to place it. Anger, that's what it was. Adam was angry because of what had been done to her.

'Harvey said that these things happen all the time,' she whispered.

'Not when I'm around they don't.' His words were comforting, and gradually the shivering stopped. After a few more miles, Ella had to admit that the warmth of the blanket was worth the indignity. Why, she thought, there were probably women who would envy her this blanket, and the cart! Slowly the warmth and the rocking of the cart soothed her. Her head nodded and she slept.

———◆———

It was day and sunlight shone in soft beams. She walked on the pine-needle covered ground, soundless. She knew, without being told, that she was no longer a child as she had been in the dark dream, but was now a woman. I am here to make a decision, she thought. A decision which will change my life. The sunlight streamed onto her face, but she felt dejected. There was an invisible weight upon her shoulders.

In her head her father reminded her: 'A woman must wed and it is past time you made your choice.'

'But he is not my choice.'

Her mother was puzzled by her resistance - what else was there for a woman but marriage? 'He is an important man, he has wealth and good looks. He may not be "quite a gentleman", but you can smooth out any rough edges. Isn't there a sister, too?'

'Yes ... in Sydney.'

'Well, he seems quite devoted to her. There, now, surely

a man who has such feeling for a sister will adore his wife!'

'I don't love him.'

Her father's outrage shrivelled her. 'Love? How can you speak of love? You are no longer a foolish child! You are a grown woman of four and twenty. You should be grateful for any offer … and such an offer!'

Her mother was softer, wheedling. 'We never hoped for such an offer for you. We are not wealthy but none can dispute our social standing. You are the laird's daughter! You have looks, but beauty on its own is not enough, and you can be so distant, so offputting, my love. I had begun to despair … you are almost on the shelf! And now, to receive such an offer! If you can't think of yourself, you must think of your sisters and your brother. You must think what you can do for them.'

'But I will have to leave my home. I will have to go across the seas to another country.'

Her cry fell into silence. They wanted her to do her duty. And she knew, even while she pretended to decide upon the course of her life, that the decision was already made. She must think of her family. They would all benefit from such a marriage. Her husband-to-be was a rich and powerful man and if, as her mother said, he was not quite a gentleman, such things could be glossed over. It was childish to believe in marrying for love. Marriage was a duty one performed for the good of others.

So when her heart cried out within her, she reprimanded it, and repeated to herself all that her parents had said. And yet … and yet there was something so cold in his eyes. As cold as her heart. And it made her afraid.

Ella woke suddenly, confused and full of fore-boding. She had dreamed, but the sense of it had already gone back into the blackness of her past. She moved, easing cramped limbs, and found that she was curved against something solid and warm, while a firm hand rested in the hollow of her waist. Befuddled, she opened her eyes and realised that she was sleeping against Adam, held there within the safety of his arm.

Horrified, she jerked away from him so quickly her head spun. 'I do beg your pardon,' she managed in a gasp, pushing her tangled hair out of her eyes. 'I must have fallen asleep.'

'No need.' He gave her a look she could only describe as quizzical. 'It's been a long time since a woman slept in me arms.'

Ella widened her eyes at him, doubting she had heard him aright. He laughed. 'I said slept, Cinder-ella. I've had women in me arms for other reasons.'

He was coarse, she thought, and rough and ill-mannered. A tinker, not a gentleman by any means. Ella was affronted by his words, and insulted that he would think so little of her respectability as to utter them aloud. But she was also intelligent enough to realise she couldn't judge Adam by her own standards – he came from another world. She must make allowances.

He had been watching her, eyes alight with laughter, waiting to hear what she would say to his outrageous comment.

'Are you married?' she asked him quietly, regain-ing some composure.

'No,' he said easily, 'that's something I'm not.'

'I wonder where my husband is?'

'Could be you're a widow,' he supplied.

Was that it? Was her husband dead? Did that explain her wandering alone on the roads? She tried to feel grief, but there was nothing but that terrible blankness.

Ella felt Adam watching her, reading her thoughts on her face. He didn't say anything; he was clever enough to know there was nothing he could say. She sat quiet, swaying with the movement of the cart, staring ahead at the track as Adam did. The silence was like the silence around the lagoon yesterday. If she hadn't met Harvey, what would have happened to her? Would she have wandered through the bush until she died? What would happen when they reached the inn? Would Adam go off and leave her there? She fought down her panic. Someone must be looking for her. Someone must be missing her. She must believe that!

Adam tightened his grip on the reins and Ella saw the beginnings of the tattoo where the jacket sleeve had ridden up. 'Why do you have 1849 on your arm?' she burst out, as much to block out her own growing fears as because she wanted to know.

'I was over in California in 1849,' he said. 'I'm a forty-niner, Mrs Seaton.'

'Oh?' she frowned.

'The Californian gold rush,' he mocked her, but gently.

'I'm sorry. You'll have to explain it to me.'

'Well, it was the first big gold rush ... and a great adventure. Like now, here in Victoria, men thought they could make a fortune by just picking the gold off the ground. And they made the journey from all over the world – England, France, Spain, Ireland ... everywhere. Yankees travelled around the coast from the east – it took some of 'em eight months. I came by sea from Sydney and I got there quicker than them!' He laughed, his dark eyes shining at the memory. 'San Francisco was a village of a couple of huts and señoritas with brown eyes and sharp smiles and dogs running in the streets. But San Francisco was only the beginning of the journey for us would-be miners. We had to make our way inland, down the rivers, to find the gold. The country was wild, and so cold in winter it froze the breath from your mouth. It weren't for the weak, Mrs Seaton.'

He glanced at her, as if to assure himself he had her attention before going on. 'I was at Sacramento first – the mosquitoes were big enough to carry you off. That's where I found Wolf. A dirty ball of fur he was, but he had strength enough to lick me hand.' He grinned at the memory. 'Then I made my way up the Yuka to the foothills of the Sierra. It was hard work. I was young and strong, and I thought I'd make a fortune in a day and leave.' His own naivete amused him. 'I was far from home, a stranger. They hated strangers, and after a while I learned it was best to keep me mouth shut. The Yankees didn't much like their own countrymen, but they hated anyone from outside it. They hated us Sydney Ducks, as they called us. We were all felons to them, and they'd hang us as soon as look at us.'

Adam glanced at her again, but she was silent, listening intently. She didn't even notice that it had begun to rain lightly. 'At night the miners fought and gambled and drank. I found a partner – a

Frenchy. We ate pork and beans because it was all we could afford. Frenchy swore that one day he'd be havin' oysters and champagne.' Adam laughed without humour at the memory. 'He probably did have them at that.'

'Surely being a ... forty-niner you would have a head start on the other miners going to Bendigo,' Ella declared. 'Is that what you intend?'

Adam shook his head. 'I've no intention of mining, Mrs Seaton. If I learned one thing in California, it was that there are easier and quicker ways of making money than digging for it or standing in freezing water up to your waist! You see, at every new rush the storekeepers and traders'd come in and set up and feed off us miners like leeches. And it'd be them who left with all the money – rich men every one! So I made up me mind that if there ever was a next time, I'd be one of the leeches!'

Ella glanced at him sideways. Adam met her look and smiled blandly. 'It's early days yet. Give me a year or two and I'll have a store and a whole string of wagons, and more money than I know what to do with.'

The quiet way he said it made her think he was serious about it.

'I might even be a moleskin squatter!'

She blinked. 'What is a moleskin squatter?'

He winked. 'An ordinary man who's made good, Mrs Seaton. Good enough, anyway, to buy himself some land and call himself a squatter. Whether his neighbours invite him to tea is another matter.' His voice had an ironic note to it. Ella tried to picture Adam in a frock coat and a top hat and failed.

'Did you actually find any gold in California?'

His mouth, which seemed to be made only to smile, turned down at the corners. 'I found gold all right but that was my bad luck. I found it and lost it again, all in the same day. And nearly lost me heart with it.'

'Your heart?' she laughed, thinking he was joking.

'Frenchy tried to cut it out.'

Ella gasped. 'What did you do?'

'By the time I was meself again, he'd gone, and the money with him. I made me way back to San Francisco ... I hardly recognised the place. There'd been a big fire and it was all new built. The Yankees were wild to rid the place of the Sydney boys – they blamed them for the fire. And then news arrived about the gold rushes at Summerhill Creek and the Turon in New South Wales, and Clunes, here in Victoria. It seemed the right time to come home.'

But Ella had fallen silent. One of the words Adam had spoken had given her further cause for alarm.

Money.

Despair dripped into her heart, slowly rising like a black tide. Money was something she didn't have. Even her wedding ring was gone, and if she had had any other belongings, they must also have been stolen by her attackers. She swallowed, trying to think. What could a woman do, who had no husband and no means of support? The answers that came to mind were not pleasant.

I won't think of it, she told herself quickly. I won't worry about it until I have to.

There didn't seem anything more to talk about after that, and she was glad when Adam decided they should stop for something to eat and drink. Afterwards they moved on again, at the same slow and steady pace. They had reached the Bendigo road now, but it was not much better than the track. Heavy traffic and wet weather made it slow going. Bess pulled them up an increasing incline towards Aitken's Gap. Even Wolf had given up his rambling, and had jumped up onto the back of the cart, making himself comfortable on top of the tarpaulin.

Her head aching, Ella dozed. At length two stooped figures appeared before them on the road and as the cart gradually gained upon them she realised that they were loaded down with mining gear. Each man had a very large bundle on his back which she assumed contained his bedding and blankets, as well as tools for mining and a few odds and ends for cooking.

'New chums,' snorted Adam under his breath. 'Haven't learned to keep their loads light yet.'

'New chums?'

'New to Victoria, new to the goldfields,' Adam explained. 'Now me, I'm what you'd call an "old hand", Mrs Seaton.'

'I'm sure you are,' Ella murmured dryly.

They were abreast the two men now. The pair had stepped aside to wait for the cart to pass them. They were clean shaven, or the next best thing to it, and Ella could see the weariness and exhaustion in their faces as they watched the cart trundle by.

But instead of passing, Adam pulled Bess up. 'Where are you bound?' he called out to them.

'Bendigo,' one of them replied, between wariness and hope.

'Aye, well, we're goin' as far as the Bush Inn,' Adam told him casually. 'I could carry your gear.'

The two men exchanged an uneasy glance, but Ella could see they were sorely tempted. 'How much?'

Adam scratched his beard, considering. 'Thirty shillings.' The men glanced at one another again, this time in dismay.

'It's too much,' the first one said baldly. 'I could buy a gold licence for that.'

Adam appeared astonished by this, and took some time to answer. When at last he did, he reduced the figure by half, but in such a way that it seemed like he was doing them an extraordinary favour. The haggling went on for some moments while Ella watched and listened in amazement. Finally the two miners agreed with ill grace and threw their packs onto the cart. Adam shook the reins and Bess plodded on, the two miners trailing behind.

'I can see why you gave up mining,' Ella said.

Adam grinned at her.

There were more miners on the road now. Mostly they travelled in small groups; perhaps two or three or four. Some had purchased horses or bullocks and carts to carry their equipment. Adam pointed out with contempt that this equipment often included feather mattresses and crockery and other heavy but useless articles.

'A miner needs to travel light or he's tired out before he gets to the diggings.'

Ella supposed he was right, but couldn't help a wistful, 'But the ground is so *hard* Adam. And tea tastes so much better from a china cup.'

He laughed at her, but again she noticed that his

eyes were kind.

As the afternoon wore on, the sky grew darker and rain began to fall steadily. They would have to spend another night camping, Ella supposed, and was not looking forward to it. Her head was hurting, and now her back had joined in. But quite apart from the physical discomfort, she was becoming increasingly aware of the awkwardness of travelling alone with Adam.

It was true that he was taking her to help and shelter. She did not dispute that, and she was grateful … but it wasn't proper. She should not be alone with him, or indeed with any man who wasn't her husband or a relation. She might have lost her memory, but she knew the rules of the narrow polite society in which she lived.

One of the miners accompanying them had even referred to her as Adam's 'missus'. Stunned, Ella had waited for Adam to correct him and when he didn't, she opened her mouth to do so, only to catch Adam's sharp warning look. As she had hesitated, he had leaned towards her. 'If you look about you, Mrs Seaton, you'll see it's almost entirely men going to the gold rush. It's safer if you're somebody's missus … Even if that somebody is a tinker like me.'

Ella had looked about her and realised the truth of it, and she had made no protest the next time the miner called her Adam's missus.

Adam glanced at Ella. 'Are you all right?'

'Is the rain ever going to stop?' she muttered crossly, and pulled the blanket closer about her. Her hair was so wet it clung to her head, and the bandage was sodden. She was sure she had never felt so miserable in her life – she would have remembered misery such as this.

'We'll be there soon.'

'At the inn?' With a gasp of pleased surprise.

But he laughed and shook his head. 'No, the Gap. We can camp for the night.'

Camping for the night was too awful to be contemplated, and Ella shuddered without replying.

The sun was sinking, hidden by the clouds. Darkness settled around them, growing thicker by the moment. Bess's ears twitched as if she heard something that Ella could not, and Wolf ran ahead to investigate. Slowly, Ella became aware that the silence was being invaded. Voices, just a murmur, and then the smell of wood smoke mingling with someone's supper. Ahead was a large camp site. Tents and makeshift shelters were set up by the roadside and among the trees. Pale, weary faces peered out at them from inside dim calico caves and from under carts and drays. Horses stood, heads hanging, while bullocks roamed, the bells around their necks clanking rhythmically. All around water dripped.

To Ella it looked like a wet version of hell.

'Here we are,' Adam said with satisfaction.

She just stared at him.

He smiled, sensing her outrage. 'The country around here's riddled with bushrangers, Mrs Seaton. That's why travellers camp together – for safety.'

Ella felt too numbed with cold and weariness to do more than sit huddled by the cart as Adam made camp. It was only when he had the fire burning brightly – a miracle in the steady rain – and had placed a hot mug of tea in her hands that she began to return to life.

The Gap, as Adam had called it, was so busy it could have been a town on market day. Despite the crush, teams of bullocks were still pulling up, their drivers calling to each other and swearing foully at their beasts. There were carts like Adam's as well as drays, gigs, and even hand barrows pushed by bedraggled miners. Others had settled for the night and were preparing their meals or laying out their bedding in whatever shelter they could manage.

Ella realised that Adam had already done all this, moving about silently, waiting upon her as if she were his invited guest rather than an uninvited stranger. Suddenly she was ashamed of her own inadequacy.

'I'm not much use to you, am I, Adam?' she said quietly.

He glanced at her but this time didn't smile. 'I don't expect you to be, Mrs Seaton. I know you're a lady, even if you can't remember your name. I couldn't ask you to light me fire and cook me mutton. Wouldn't be right.'

His words touched her, and humbled her when she remembered how she had looked down on him. 'Nevertheless,' she replied at last. 'You must tell me how I can help you. I don't want to be more of a burden than I am already.'

Now he did smile. 'You can help me by eating what I cook and pretending it's oysters and champagne.'

Ella even managed a smile back.

'What's 'appened to yer missus?' a voice interrupted. She glanced to the side and saw an interested row of faces over the flicker of a neighbouring fire.

Adam continued to fry the piece of meat and didn't answer.

'Bushrangers, were it?' another voice piped up.

'Could have been,' Adam replied evenly.

The others took this as a 'yes' and shook their heads gloomily. One of them puffed on a short-stemmed pipe, and the air was pungent with a mixture of tobacco smoke, burning wood and damp clothing.

'You goin' north?'

'Aye.' Adam divided the meat and tipped Ella's share onto her plate. She felt his eyes on her, warning of something she didn't yet understand. 'Eat up,' he murmured, 'and then I'll have a look at your head.'

His voice was almost drowned out by a roar of laughter from across the track. The bullock drivers were drinking, passing their bottle around. Ella realised, with a strange quiver inside, that she was the only woman here. The thought of being Adam's 'missus' was suddenly very reassuring.

She ate her meal, and afterwards he took off the bandage and frowned at the bump on her head. His hands were gentle but impersonal, dispelling any embarrassment she might have felt, but it seemed to Ella that everyone at the camp site watched with interest.

Adam winked at her and said, 'You'll do. Climb in under the cart and get some sleep. I'll just check on Bess.'

She moved to obey, thinking of her wet clothing and knowing she wouldn't be able to change out of it. Adam had laid out her bed in the dry darkness beneath the cart, and she pulled the blankets over herself, shivering. The hum of voices and the laughter receded, and she was almost asleep when a stirring near her startled her into wakefulness.

Ella lifted her head, eyes wide, and saw that Adam was stretched out beside her with Wolf in the middle. 'You can't sleep here!' she gasped.

He turned his head and looked at her in amazement.

'You can't sleep here,' she repeated, wondering how he could be so obtuse.

A flicker of impatience lit the dark eyes. 'I'm not sleeping out in the rain, Mrs Seaton. An' I'm not interested in your body. I'm sorry if that's indelicate, but I don't know no other way to put it.' He spoke in a practical manner, but there was mockery in it. 'I feel an obligation to you, that's all. You're a lady not used to taking care of herself. I can see that. So I'll take care of you until you find someone else. There's no more to it than that.'

Long before he had finished, Ella knew she'd erred. Once again she'd applied normal rules to a situation that was anything but normal. She felt her face flaming, and hoped he couldn't see it. She nodded jerkily and lay down. After all his kindness to her! She should have known better. Who was there to see, anyway? Who was there to know what she and Adam had done? Who was there to care?

'No one,' Ella whispered softly. 'There's no one.' She was alone, abandoned, and the rules of polite society no longer applied. The only rule was to survive.

'Goodnight,' Adam murmured, and Ella knew it was a sign to her that he had taken no offense.

'Goodnight,' she whispered back.

At some time during the night, she half woke from her dreams. She was in the dark forest again, and the voices and the torches were coming closer. Ella stared up at the underside of the cart, not seeing it, not knowing where she was.

'I want to go home,' she said in a slurred, sleepy voice. 'I don't like it here. Can I go home?'

A dark shape leaned over her; she felt his warm breath on her cheek. 'You can go home, Cinderella. You just tell me where it is.'

But the dream was already drawing her back. She snuggled closer into her makeshift bed, pressing against the warm bulk of Wolf the dog, and went back to sleep.

CHAPTER 3

THE BUSH INN, ON THE southern edge of the Black Forest, was a large and established hostelry, crackling with frantic life. Ella gazed upon it with weary relief.

The journey from the Gap, though short in miles, had been dogged with rain and ill luck. What should have taken a couple of hours instead took an entire day. The cart wheels had become bogged numerous times, and each time Ella had had to climb down while Adam coaxed Bess to pull them out Sometimes it had meant unloading everything before the wheels would budge, a lengthy and frustrating process. The two miners, whose baggage Adam was carrying, had helped, but it was mainly Adam who did the work.

Ella had stood in the drizzling rain, huddled in her blanket, her shoes sodden and muddy, and thought life could hold no misery greater than this. Even Wolf had looked depressed, preferring to crouch beside Ella rather than explore ahead. Adam had worked on grimly, his fair hair darkened with rain and sweat. And finally the cart would pull free, and they could move forward again. It was late in the day when Adam discovered Bess had thrown a shoe, but there was nothing to be done but continue on until they came to civilization.

Adam had glanced at her now and again, but he said nothing. Neither of them had been in the mood for conversation. All along the road, miners had slogged through the rain, and slow, unwieldy bullock drays had ploughed onward. Sometimes they had passed the wreckages of other vehicles, and Ella had seen the half-rotted corpse of an abandoned horse or bullock.

It had made her even more appreciative of the Bush Inn, its chimneys belching a smoky welcome in a late afternoon already waning to darkness.

The inn was built of brick and timber, a solid piece of architecture in a transient landscape. Travellers could expect hot meals and drinks, for a price. There were private rooms too, but again the price was high. Most of the guests were content to share. When Adam and Ella arrived it was like a town, there were so many vehicles drawn up around it and for an impressive distance before and beyond it too.

New arrivals gazed about in excited amazement, customers spilled from the doors with their drinks and their laughter. Wild-eyed miners shouted to each other about the latest gold finds and new chums told tales of bushrangers in the Black Forest and frightened themselves witless. A small number of women, some with children, attempted to create a semblance of normality, preparing meals on sullen fires and making up beds in their cramped, gloomy tents.

Adam drew Bess to a halt and Ella saw that, besides the inn, there were other buildings – cottages, and one slab hut recognisable as a blacksmith's shop. The bad road and bad weather meant plenty of business, and the smithy and his helpers were fully occupied with several horses to be shoed and a wagon with a broken axle.

The two miners collected their belongings from Adam's cart with murmured thanks and goodbyes. Adam stood and watched them fight their way into the inn; Ella could almost see him regathering his strength, before he faced the smithy.

The blacksmith was clean-shaven with lank grey hair and massive shoulders. He looked up as Adam approached, sharp eyes assessing his worth. Ella watched them confer for what seemed a very long time, until at last Adam nodded his head in a manner more resigned than satisfied. He came back to Ella, his face looking strained and tired. She supposed she looked the same.

'Two shillings for a horse shoe,' he groaned. 'Bloody robbery. And he says he's too busy to do it till the mornin'.' He sighed. 'Well, there's no help for it.'

Ella wished she could say something to soothe, but there didn't seem to be anything appropriate. Adam glanced across at the inn and the crowd gathered about it. 'Wait here,' he said. 'I'll go and ask about a bed for you.'

She was too weary to do more than nod and watch him push his way through the crowd and vanish into the inn. The rain was still falling. Ella saw one miner, the worse for drink, stagger and fall. A roar of laughter went up as he lifted a face caked with mud. Two men on horses galloped past, shouting and waving their hats. 'Melbourne-ho!' they shouted, and the crowd gave way, agog. One of the horsemen drew up briefly, his bearded face streaked with rain and dirt. 'It's raining gold on the Bendigo!' he called. And then his horse had carried him on after his mate.

Ella was aware of the excitement rippling all about her. Despite her own weariness, she felt an urge to get up and move on with the rest, and she wasn't even a gold-seeker! Imagine, she thought, how such sights and sounds must affect the miners. Did they really believe it rained gold at Bendigo? Looking about at their faces she decided that perhaps they did.

At first she was so deep in her own thoughts that the touch on her arm didn't register, and it was only when it changed to a violent tug that she looked down.

A woman's face, drawn and blue-tinged with the cold. 'You won't get no rooms here,' she said. 'Charges gold prices, does this place. You'd be better off goin' home while you still can.'

Ella blinked. 'I beg your pardon?'

'There's nothin' ahead but misery, and plenty of it,' the woman went on, her voice rising. 'I can see you is a decent sort. Beware! The temptations are great on the goldfields. Many a good woman's turned her back on respectability for gold and fine livin'. And many a man's been blinded by his greed and lust.'

Ella tried to gather her wits. The other woman seemed to mean her warning kindly, but there was something fixed in her eyes that was unnerving.

'Tell your 'usband to turn around and take you home,' she went on. 'Tell 'im now before it's too late.'

'I ... he's not my husband,' Ella stammered.

The woman's eyes bulged. Ella braced herself for a tirade, but it never came. Suddenly a man appeared at the woman's side, slipping his arm about her thin shoulders and drawing her back. 'Come on, Mina,' he murmured. 'Come and lie down now.'

The staring eyes blinked and blurred, and the woman bowed her head, as meek as a lamb. The man looked up into Ella's startled face.

'Don't mind my sister, ma'am,' he said quietly. 'I reckon her mind's wanderin' a bit. Her husband ran off on her. I'm takin' her home to Melbourne.'

'Oh. I'm very sorry.'

And she was sorry. For Mina ... and herself. Such an episode made her more than ever aware of how vulnerable she was without family and money. She had been left like poor Mina.

For a moment the immensity of such a thing made her shake, and then she remembered the kind brother who had led Mina away, and she remembered Adam. Even the sound of his name was a sort of talisman against the darkness of her past and the uncertainty of her future. Adam might be a stranger, but just now he was everything to her.

As though her thinking of him had conjured him up, Ella saw that Adam was pushing his way towards her through the drunken crowd, Wolf at his heels. Even before he spoke, she could tell by his face that the news was not good.

'No beds except for royalty.'

'What will we do?' Ella whispered, appalled.

Adam sighed, and then managed a wry smile. 'We make camp, Mrs Seaton, that's what we do.'

Ella had been hoping for a feather bed. She swallowed. 'I still need to speak to the owner of this place,' she went on desperately. 'Someone might know me, or remember me. I may have come this way and stayed the night.'

Adam hesitated, and she read the doubt in his eyes. She realised suddenly that his hesitation was made through kindness rather than obstruction. He didn't want her to raise her hopes and then have them dashed. 'I have to find out, one way or the other,' she told him firmly. 'If you won't come with me, I'll go alone.'

Adam nodded, resigned. 'I'll take you,' he said and helped her down. 'Use your elbows,' he advised her as they pushed towards the door. 'And if that don't work, kick!'

The tap room was an assault on every one of Ella's senses. The combined smells of ale and brandy and sweat took her breath, while the noise of so many voices shouting at once made her ears ache. And the press of bodies ... if she hadn't seen with her own eyes that so many drunken miners could be crammed into so small a space she would never have believed it. She was glad of Adam in front of her. As he shoved his way through the pack, she moved in his wake.

Somehow they reached the front. Adam leaned forward over the bench that served as a bar and caught the arm of the publican. The man swung around, ready for a fight, but when his eyes lit on Ella he changed his mind.

Adam explained the situation in brief, shouted sentences. The man's eyes remained fixed on Ella and she held her breath while he considered whether or not she was familiar. But already he was shaking his head. 'Never seen her before,' he said. He turned and called out through a door behind the bar and in a short time a woman appeared, her face flushed from cooking over a hot fire. She also gave Ella a searching look, but the answer was the same. 'Sorry,' she muttered. She hesitated, sensing that Ella was desperate. Watching her with held breath, Ella could see the moment when the wavering in the woman's eyes switched to indifference. Ella's plight was nothing to do with her; she had her own problems. She turned in a swirl of floury skirts and was gone.

Ella felt a sudden, overwhelming sense of isolation. No one knew who she was, and no one wanted to be burdened with her. She hardly noticed that Adam, protecting her with his arms, was all but carrying her back outside. 'Looks like you didn't come this way, Cinderella,' he said, panting a little.

'No,' she murmured miserably.

Adam patted her shoulder. 'Cheer up, Mrs Seaton. Something'll turn up.'

Ella tried to smile, but she couldn't help but think of deserted Mina and her wild, lost eyes.

'Bess'll be fixed up in the mornin',' Adam added. 'We can move on. At least the road's free!'

Ella said nothing.

'There are plenty more inns between here and the Bendigo,' he went on gently. 'We won't give up yet. Someone'll remember you, Mrs Seaton.' He took her arm and led her back towards the cart. 'Now, let's set up camp, and I'll get some water and boil you up a nice mug of tea.'

Ella wanted to say thank you, but she didn't trust

her voice.

———•———

Ella slept fitfully The noise from the inn kept waking her. The bar, it seemed, never closed. Underneath the cart it was dry, but sleeping in wet clothes was not the best way to stay in good health, and she found herself longing passionately for a hot bath, fresh clothing and a warm bed.

Adam had risen early to take Bess to the black-smith, and was now busying himself making their breakfast – tea and mutton and damper. Ella dragged her unwilling body out into the open and glanced about her, to find the rain had stopped and the sky was a cold, distant blue. The sun shone without warmth onto the unfamiliar scene around the Bush Inn. Some of the miners had simply fallen over where they stood, while others were huddled in their tents. But most of them were breakfast-ing like Adam, preparing to take to the road north, drawn by dreams of gold.

There was a certain grimness, too, prevalent among the travellers. The next stretch of road, run-ning through the Black Forest, was considered by many to be the most dangerous. The Black For-est was twelve miles long, and the home of many desperate bushrangers who made their living by thievery and assault and, sometimes, murder.

'We'll travel in a group,' Adam told Ella. 'It's safer that way.'

'Do you think we'll be robbed?'

His mouth went grim. 'Not if I can help it, Mrs Seaton.'

Startled and unsure, she looked at him. But the truth of his statement was there in his eyes – Adam would do all in his power to protect what was his.

They went to the blacksmith's shop to fetch Bess. The smithy had a new crop of customers and was busy shoeing a black mare while its owner waited glumly nearby. Adam handed over the money while Ella stood back slightly, cupping her cold hands and blowing into them. The smithy glanced up towards her, and away, and then towards her again. His look intensified and then, when she still made no move, he raised his arm in greeting.

'Didn't expect to see you again so soon, ma'am!' he called out in a friendly manner.

Ella's heart gave a great thud.

Adam turned and stared at her. But his face was a blur, Ella had eyes only for the blacksmith. She came forward on stiff, wooden legs and didn't even feel Adam's hand grip her arm, keeping her upright.

'Do you know me?' she asked in a wondering voice.

The blacksmith's smile grew forced. 'You came through here four days ago, ma'am. You and your servant.' His eyes flicked to Adam and back again. 'Is there something wrong?'

'The lady had an accident,' Adam said quietly. 'She's lost her memory. Did she tell you her name?'

The blacksmith's eyes had widened, but he shook his head. 'No. I only said "good day" to you, ma'am. It was your man I spoke with. He was ... well,' and he shifted uncomfortably. 'He was like Adam here, if you get my meanin'.'

Ella was puzzled, but Adam gave a wry smile.

'He means the man with you wasn't no gentleman, Mrs Seaton.'

The blacksmith nodded. 'That's it. He kept lookin' to you before he said yes, like he was your servant. He was Scotch like you, ma'am. Your mare'd thrown a shoe,' he added slowly, as his memory returned, 'and your man's horse was lame. You'd both ridden hard. I shoed yours and sold your man another.'

Ella wanted to sit down; instead she leaned against Adam. 'Where were we going?' she asked huskily.

'You were headin' south. Melbourne, my guess. You didn't stay at the inn, just waited until your mounts were ready. Said you was in too much of a hurry.'

'So we came from the north?' Ella whispered.

He nodded. Others had gathered now, sensing that something interesting was happening, but as far as Ella was concerned they did not even exist.

'Did you hear the servant's name?' Adam asked.

But he hadn't heard, or if he had he'd forgotten. 'You were wearin' a red cloak,' the smith added quickly, 'and it had a hood. I remember that. A real picture you made, ma'am, despite lookin' tired and – ' but he broke off, suddenly uncertain.

'And?' Ella breathed.

'Well,' with a shrug, 'I thought you seemed upset about somethin'. You looked behind you more often than seemed right somehow. As if someone might be followin', or you'd left something behind. And you rode off with your man like it was a race between the two of you.'

Yes, Ella thought. Yes, he's telling me the truth. I sense it, I *know* it. She straightened, pulling away from Adam. 'Thank you,' she said quietly, and walked away.

Her head was spinning. She had passed this way only days before. She had worn a red cloak and ridden with a man who was probably her servant, and who also bore the accent of the Scot. She had come down the Bendigo road, from the north. North. Ella knew now that everything she was seeking lay in that direction.

Adam had caught up with her. He grasped her arm, but she shook his hand off and kept walking. 'Where are you goin'?' he called out after her.

Ella turned around and stared at him as if she didn't know him.

'Cinderella?'

She blinked, and suddenly the present was back in focus. 'Do you think I was riding to Melbourne?' she whispered.

But of course he couldn't know that.

'Something must have happened on the road,' she mused. 'I must have been attacked by bushrangers, just as Harvey said.'

'Seems likely.'

'I wonder what became of my servant?' Her eyes grew big. 'Was he hurt, too? Do you think he might be dead?' Her voice squeaked on the final word, but Adam shook his head.

'Run off, if you ask me,' he drawled. 'He'll keep runnin' until he finds somewhere to hide.'

Ella let it pass. 'What will I do?'

He met her eyes in his direct way, and she could sense his mind turning over the possibilities. 'I think you should keep on north as we planned. Even empty of its menfolk Melbourne is a big place, and we don't know where you were going to once you got there. But if we travel north ... you'll have left a trail, Mrs Seaton – a word here, a glimpse there. We have to follow your tracks until we come to the end, and then we'll know ... everything.' He made a flourish, like a magician, his dark eyes gleaming.

It sounded the right thing to do. 'Yes,' she breathed, and laughed with hope and excitement. 'Let's go then!'

* * *

It was still early, but a straggle of miners and bullock wagons and carts was leaving the inn. Very soon, groups began to splinter off, the quicker ones joining with their like, and the slower ones with theirs. Adam and Ella were in a group of several miners, some on foot and. others with barrows. Most of them were dressed in the digger's uniform of moleskins, woollen shirt of blue or red, scarf and boots. Every man wanted to look like a seasoned miner, even if he had never dug a hole in his life.

The Black Forest was indeed black. Ella looked about at the dark trunks and branches of the iron-bark trees and thought the place was well named. Adam told her a fire had been through the forest, and Victoria, the year before. Lives had been lost and property destroyed, and that day had gone down in history as Black Thursday. The tree trunks were still charred, although new life had been quick to spring forth.

One of the miners in their group, a former shep-herd, had been ten years in the country, and knew many of its secrets. 'Some o' these Godforsaken plants don't even come out o' the ground unless a fire goes over 'em,' he told them.

Some of the other miners volunteered that they were new chums, recently arrived in Melbourne, while three others had left their jobs and families in the capital to travel north to the goldfields. Four, from their dress, were obviously sailors jumped ship, while the final trio had the look of Vandemonians, with hard, cunning eyes and the scars of the leg irons still on their ankles.

The only thing all of them had in common was gold. To Ella's amazement they seemed able to discuss it for hours at a time, delving into all the intricacies of mining. There were disagreements too. The new chums had loaded themselves up with all manner of useless items, gadgets they had brought from home and which they believed would be invaluable on the goldfields. The Vandemonians sneered, arguing that all a miner really needed to find gold was a pan and a pocket knife.

Some of them had heard about the Californian rush and believed that mining involved constructing water races and altering the courses of creeks, as well as building long wooden cradles called Long Toms in which to capture the gold. But Adam shook his head.

'You've got to have the right sort o' country for that kind of mining. I've heard that a lot of the land to the north is so dry you have to carry your dirt to the water, instead of the other way around!'

One of the Vandemonians scowled at Adam. 'You're full of it,' he muttered.

A flash of anger fired Ella. 'He knows more than you, sir! Adam has mined in California.'

Unimpressed, the man gave her a sly look. 'He'll be able to point us in the right direction then, won't he?'

Adam laughed and shook his head. 'The man who could do that hasn't been born. It's luck as much as anything. You can have two claims side by side and one'll be a jeweller's shop, full o' gold, while the other has nothing in it but rocks.'

There was a silence, and then one of the new chums, a fellow called Morris, asked almost diffidently if he'd tell them something of his travels in California. Adam glanced sideways at Ella. 'I don't want to bore the lady ...' he began expectantly.

'I'd like to hear,' Ella replied. It would, she thought, take her mind off her own worries, and Adam clearly longed to talk.

Adam paused a moment and then launched into a story about mining at places called Rough and Ready, and Poker Flat, where the wolves and coyotes howled at night.

He held everyone spellbound, Ella thought, watching their faces. And she couldn't blame them for being caught up in his words. Adam had a way of bringing his stories to life; a few well chosen words and the listener was drawn into Adam's new and different world.

He was making them all laugh now with a tale of how he had had to make a hasty escape from a game of 'monte' in one of the waterfront taverns and, full of 'Tarantula juice', had taken the wrong turn and lost his boots in the sticky San Franciscan mud.

After he had finished his story, and the miners had set off ahead of the cart, Ella said, 'You've led a very interesting life.'

He gave that serious thought. 'Maybe. Some of it through necessity not choice. I went to California to get rich and I came back poor. Now I'm goin' to the Bendigo to get rich and who knows what'll happen there?' His eyes were shining at her. Ella felt a strange quiver in her stomach, as though a hundred butterflies had suddenly taken flight. The feeling startled and confused her. She said the first thing that came into her mind.

'Perhaps my husband will reward you ... when we find him.'

'That would be welcome, Mrs Seaton,' he replied politely. The gleam in his eyes had gone; he was respectful again. The strange moment had passed and Ella tried to forget it.

The new chum, Morris, dropped back again to walk beside the cart. He was a thin man of about forty with a serious smile, and he seemed to have taken a fancy to Ella. He told her he had been a clerk in London when the news of the Australian gold rush took the city by storm. His life sounded safe and dull. Ella wondered what he thought of this place he had travelled so far to reach and whether he wished himself home again, but when she asked him his replies were so lacking in any sense of excitement or anticipation, she wondered why he had bothered to come at all.

After a time his slow, measured conversation grew tedious, and when he began instructing her on what he considered the necessary qualities of a good wife, she retorted, 'Indeed? I had not thought you were married, Mr Morris?'

'I am not,' he replied soberly. 'I have not yet

found a woman who fulfills all my requirements.'

Ella's eyes narrowed, and something in them seemed to pierce Mr Morris's good opinion of himself. He coughed nervously.

'I'm sorry you have not yet found such a woman,' Ella said, mimicking his ponderous tones. 'I fear if you are seeking perfection, you may remain a bachelor until you die.'

'You dismay me, ma'am. Do you really rate your sex so low? Surely some women aspire to more than mediocrity?'

She was speechless.

Thinking her struck dumb by his fine argument, Mr Morris went on. 'I had thought,' and he cleared his throat again. 'When I spoke with you for the first time, ma'am, and heard your sad story, I began to hope that here was the sort of woman I had been – '

But Ella had had enough. 'Then you must prepare yourself for a disappointment! I am not perfect. I have numerous faults, all of them beyond mending.'

'Surely not, ma'am! I had only noted one or two. And all so trifling, I'm sure they could be overcome if you tried sufficiently hard to – '

'You misunderstand me, Mr Morris,' and her voice was even colder. 'I am fond of my faults. I cherish them. I have no wish to overcome them!'

'Then it is a pity, ma'am. A great pity.' Mr Morris shook his head and hastened his step, rejoining his fellows.

'Well, you fixed him all right,' Adam murmured admiringly.

Ella coloured. 'I was rude. I should apologise to

him.'

Adam laughed. 'Rude is the only thing a man like that understands. *Your* mistake was being nice to him in the first place. I was wonderin' there for a while if I'd lost you to him altogether.'

'Unlike Mr Morris,' Ella replied firmly, 'I don't seek perfection in my companions.' And then she blushed when she realised what she had said.

But Adam only grinned at her and retorted, 'Neither do I.'

There were dozens of tracks leading between the trees of the Black Forest, as if everyone who passed through it had made a new one. Ella was sure if she had been alone she would easily have become lost. It was silent, too. As if the birds had stopped singing, hushed by the malevolent spirit of the place. And as they moved further into the forest their voices, too, grew quieter. Ella noticed Adam glancing about him, searching for watching eyes. Sometimes, to their right, she would see the bulk of Mount Macedon peering at them through veils of mist.

'When old Major Mitchell came exploring this country in the thirties, he climbed to the top of Macedon,' the shepherd told them. 'He went all over this country. We're still following the tracks he left, only now we call 'em roads!'

The road they were on was certainly poor. Rain had turned it to sludge, and in some places other travellers had put fallen logs over the worst bits, making wooden bridges. There were potholes and ditches deep enough to break a leg in. Adam shook his head. 'It's bad enough now, but it's passable. Another few weeks of rain and traffic and no one'll be able to get through.'

Poor Bess pulled her load gallantly onward, and where possible Adam took her by more solid tracks around the main route. But he preferred not to diverge too far from the others. Sometimes they had to pause while Bess rested or Adam urged her through a particularly difficult patch, and the group of miners moved on further and further ahead, their voices dwindling into silence.

Ella hated that. She found herself glancing nervously around, expecting at any moment to be confronted by a dozen desperate bushrangers. If Harvey was right, and she was beginning to believe he was, it had been bushrangers who had attacked her and left her for dead at Seaton's Lagoon. And she had no wish to repeat the experience.

The silence hummed in her head. When something rustled suddenly in the leaves, Ella jumped. Adam glanced sharply at her. 'It's only a bird.' Concern mingled with amusement in his eyes. Ella shivered, trying to control her rising fear.

'I was thinking ... I was wondering what sort of men become bushrangers.'

He gave her a brief, searching look before turning back to the muddy road ahead. 'Some are miners who've had no luck at mining, and some are wild boys lookin' for a bit of adventure, and some are ex-convicts, wanting an easy life. You have to agree, Mrs Seaton, it's easier to take gold off someone who's already done all the hard work than to do it yourself.'

'I suppose it is.' Ella shifted uncomfortably, glancing behind her.

'Of course there are other pickings besides gold,' Adam went on. 'Anything that'll make them money. Bushrangers aren't fussy.' He saw her face blanch. 'Now then, Mrs Seaton, there's no need to look so scared! I've heard that troopers patrol the forest now, and anyway I'll protect you.'

But how could one man overpower a dozen armed murderers? Ella asked herself bleakly. The doubt must have shown in her eyes for he answered it, his voice full of confidence.

'I'll get us both to Bendigo, Mrs Seaton.'

And despite all reason she believed him.

They stopped at noon. Ella drank her tea and chewed on the damper Adam had made the night before in the ashes of the campfire. Looking up at Mount Macedon through the drifts of cloud and misty rain Ella thought, I must have come through this way. But there was no memory. What would make a woman like her ride alone with only one servant for protection? The reason must have been a desperate one.

Ella moved restlessly, impatient to be off again. But Adam had his own agenda and wouldn't be rushed. She thought she knew him well enough now to know that. When she had first met him, she had seen only the tinker. Since then she had learned a little of the man beneath. Adam was kind, or at least he had been kind to her. Perhaps he hoped for a generous reward, but she couldn't convince herself that that was the only reason for his kindness.

With a sigh, she reached out to ruffle Wolf's fur,

giving Adam a surreptitious glance at the same time. He was leaning back against the wheel of the cart, eyes closed. He looked completely relaxed, half dozing. She wondered how old he was. Sometimes, when he was telling his stories of California, he seemed young, younger than herself, and then there were other times when he would say or do something that made him older and wiser by far.

Ella moved restlessly. What did it matter? Their paths had crossed, their lives had bisected briefly, and soon they would part again. But even as Ella longed to resume her lost life, she knew she would not forget Adam.

He had opened his eyes and was looking back at her. His face was completely expressionless. How can he make his eyes so unreadable? Ella asked herself. I had thought of them as clear and honest, but really they are opaque. He shuts himself off, showing only what he wants to. Even as she watched, amusement gleamed in them, warm, shining, glowing like a candle flame.

'You're not counting up me faults, are you?' he asked her quietly.

Ella felt her face colour. She turned away. 'I'm sorry. Was I staring? I was thinking of something else.'

He was silent. She glanced at him again. Mischief had come into his eyes now. He said, 'You're not lookin' for perfection, are you, Mrs Seaton?'

'Of course not,' Ella retorted. And for some reason her face coloured again.

CHAPTER 4

———◆———

*T*HE COLD WIND TANGLED HER *hair. She turned her face into it, feeling her bonnet tugging at the ribbon about her neck, feeling the surge of the ship beneath her feet. She felt alive and excited, as she had not felt in months.*

Since the wedding.

She closed her eyes. Leaving her home had been as painful as leaving her heart. Her family had believed they would see her again. A year or two, they said, and you'll be back home. But she knew she would never return.

'Sydney'll be your home now,' her husband had said. 'You'll make your life there as my wife.'

A position of honour and importance - he didn't need to speak the words, she read them in his cold eyes.

The wind tossed her hair. She shivered. She had married him without love but she had expected something. Friendship, warmth, laughter. Not this freezing formality, this coldness. Sometimes when he looked at her she felt that he actually disliked her.

The ship surged again, knifing her bows through the green ocean, Sydney bound.

———◆———

The gunshot woke her, splintering through her dream and bringing her up wide-eyed, blind in the darkness. It took a moment for her mind to begin functioning again. Voices were calling out, slurred with sleep and fear. A horse whinnied, and somewhere a twig cracked loudly underfoot. Wolf began to bark, hackles raised.

Ella felt for Adam with her hand, and made him jump. He swore softly, catching her fingers in his and moving closer. 'Stay quiet,' he whispered against her ear. She watched him crawl towards the edge of the cart, calling the dog. It came bounding back, and he grasped it firmly, holding it beside him. With a gasp, Ella crawled after Adam, and peered out past the edge of the wheel into the camp site.

The trees around them made a dark, impenetrable wall. Within, the fires had burned down very low, but still gave enough light for Ella to see what was going on. Some of the miners were standing about in an odd assortment of clothing, while others were still huddled in their beds. They looked confused and frightened.

'What is it?' Ella whispered. As she spoke, there was an explosion of shouting and whooping. Three horsemen sprang out of the dark forest into the clearing, nightmare shadows against the firelight.

For an instant Ella thought they were troopers on patrol, but the clenching in her belly told her that she was wrong. One of the men lifted a pistol into the air and fired a shot which flamed red against the blackness. Bess, in the trees behind the cart, whinnied fearfully. Wolf growled deep in his throat, but Adam held him firm. Ella felt her own throat go tight. Again Adam took her hand in his, gripping it painfully hard, and repeated urgently, 'Stay quiet!'

Out in the clearing the bushranger who had fired the shot was shouting, 'Drop your guns! We don't want no trouble!' Ella saw with terrified eyes that he held a gun in each hand, waving them as he spoke. 'Just hand over yer valuables and we'll be on our way.'

There were now five horsemen – five that she could *see*. Their leader was resplendent in a coat with big buttons that flashed gold with every movement he made. Wild dark hair hung over his shoulders and a beard covered his face. He towered above the others, even on horseback. Ella tried to keep her breathing soft, but it was more like a gasp.

Terrified by the embodiment of all their fears, the miners forgot any thought of resistance and dropped their weapons.

'Good boys,' the bushranger praised them with muffled laughter in his voice. 'Now I'll have yer cash and yer tickers and anything else yer might have about yer. And then we'll take a look in yer bundles.'

There was a burst of protest, which he halted by firing his gun once more into the air above their heads. The sound was shockingly loud, stunning them all to silence. So riveted to the scene was Ella that at first she didn't realise that one of the bushrangers had walked his horse over towards the cart and was peering suspiciously into the shadows beneath it.

Terror clamped about her like iron chains. Adam had been her protection from the miners, but he could not possibly protect her from these danger-ous, lawless men. Perhaps, and the terror rose into hysteria, they were even the same ones who had attacked her at Seaton's Lagoon ...

Ella closed her eyes and prayed.

'Damned thieves! Take my money if you want it, but I won't *give* it to you!'

The shaking, furious voice startled everyone. There was another terrible silence. Ella opened her eyes and saw that the approaching bushranger had stopped in his tracks. He was looking back over his shoulder into the clearing where Mr Morris had stepped aside from the other miners, his white face set with grim determination.

Adam groaned. 'Bloody fool.'

Morris's words had sounded very much like a challenge. The leader of the bushrangers turned his head slowly until he found the culprit. Beneath his gaze Morris went even whiter, but he stood firm, head held high. Ella could admire his courage even as she deplored his recklessness. She held her breath and tried to hear above her own heartbeat.

'Now, now, boyo,' the bushranger began in deceptively reasonable tones, 'we've got to make a livin' too.'

'By stealing from others!' Morris shouted back. His friends shifted slightly, distancing themselves from him, as appalled as Ella at his foolhardy daring.

Another silence. The bushrangers appeared somewhat taken aback by this turn of events –resistance was evidently something they didn't often have to deal with. They glanced at each other, steadying their nervous mounts.

'Tie him to a tree!' the leader boomed out his order. Tie 'em all to trees. They can stay here until they starve!'

Cries of protest rose from a dozen throats, but the loudest by far was Mr Morris.

'You devils! Would you tie up a defenseless woman?'

The clearing became absolutely still, and into the stillness crept something sly and evil. Ella had the odd sensation that the bushrangers, like wild dogs, were circling her, coming closer.

'What woman are we talkin' about, boyo?' the leader asked softly.

'Oh shit.' Adam groaned as if he were in pain. He looked at Ella - she saw the shape of his face but could not read his expression. 'Stay put,' he told her, 'and hold onto Wolf.'

She reached out automatically to grasp a hank of rough fur. Adam began to crawl out from under the cart. At his movement her panic increased. 'Where are you going?'

He turned and looked at her over his shoulder. 'They know you're here, Mrs Seaton, and they'll look until they find you. I can't let that happen.'

And he was gone, moving swiftly out from the shadows. Horrified, Ella held on to a struggling Wolf and watched as Adam walked calmly towards the horsemen.

'I thought you'd be dancin' on the stars by now!' Adam's voice was loud and carrying, and he kept walking.

The leader swung around, his guns came up. Ella whimpered, knowing that in a moment he would shoot Adam dead. She was out from under the cart without remembering how. Her legs were gathering strength. She felt them preparing to push, to take her running into the clearing.

The bushranger gave a great bellow of laughter. Ella froze.

'Adam! Is it you?'

Adam came to a stop before him and stuck out his hand. The bushranger took it in his, gun and all, and wrung it savagely.

Ella felt the strength running out of her, like water from a leaky barrel. Adam knew this man? And the bushranger knew Adam? Her legs collapsed, and she sat down suddenly against the cart wheel, in the shadows. Wolf, sensing his master didn't need him as much as Ella, pressed against her. As if through a haze she heard their voices.

'You turned to fleecin' miners now, have you, Eben?' Adam growled disapprovingly, but Ella could hear the fondness in his voice. Abruptly, she was angry. Why had he not told her he knew the man, instead of allowing her to think he was walking to his certain death for her sake?

Eben bellowed again, and then glanced around the silent audience with derision. 'Aye, sheep the lot of 'em! But it's surprisin' what sheep hide in their bedrolls. I'm hopin' to make enough to move north, up into cattle country. Far enough away from the troopers so's they leave me alone.'

'You'd die of boredom.'

Eben snorted. 'What about you, boyo? What are doin' in the Black Forest?'

Adam moved closer, and his voice was too low for Ella to hear his reply. But Eben was nodding, and then he flung his arm around Adam's shoulders. His cohorts were looking about restlessly, probably wondering if the troopers had heard the shots. Eben called them over and briefly they conferred. Then, to Ella's amazement, they turned and rode back into the dark safety of the trees, leaving Eben and Adam standing alone by the campfire.

The miners hesitated, plainly confused by this turn of events. Eben watched them a moment and then said in a sneering voice, 'You've struck it luckier tonight than yer ever will on the goldfields. Your bits and pieces are safe for now - go back to bed.' They did so, even Morris, wide-eyed with wonder. Ella watched as Adam and Eben walked towards the cart, the orange light of the campfires flickering on their faces as they passed.

Adam stopped by his own fire, gently teasing it back to life while Eben crouched down on his haunches and held out his hands to the growing warmth. Ella noticed he'd slipped his guns into his belt, but he was still a fearsome sight. She sat perfectly still against the cart wheel, like one confronted by a dangerous animal. Her knees were drawn up to her chest and she tried to make herself as small as possible. But he must have sensed her presence or heard Wolf's puffing breath, because he looked up and saw her.

There was something frightening about Eben. Not just his unkempt beard and hair, but the wild recklessness in the set of his head and the slant of his dark eyes. His teeth flashed white through the beard.

'Well now,' he said in a deep, amused voice. 'What do yer have here, Adam?'

Adam glanced up. For an instant she thought she read a warning in his eyes, and then he too was smiling. 'This is me wife.'

Eben lifted his eyebrows. 'Yer *wife*? She looks like

she needs a scrub.'

Ella felt her temper flare. 'I'm not the only one!'

Eben was momentarily taken aback, and then he laughed. 'She's got a tongue like a razor, Adam. Where'd you find her? Not in San Francisco? I thought you and Nancy were near enough to wed while you were there.'

Adam made a sharp movement. 'Nancy went her own way.'

Eben laughed again. He seemed to find everything very amusing. 'I know that, Adam. Things got a bit close for her in California. They closed up the inn, yer know, and she had to bolt. She was only an hour in front of the mob, and it were only luck that they didn't search her ship when it left the Bay.' He grinned. 'She's here now. Up in a place called Sawpit Gully. She runs an inn, same as before. I visit her now and then. We have an arrangement ... business, of course.' He seemed to be mocking Adam, daring him to protest.

But when Adam spoke again, his voice was even and unruffled. 'What about Rufus? You'll be tellin' me next he's here as well.'

Eben shook his head slowly, the smile turning savage. 'The Yankees hanged Rufus in San Francisco. You remember what they was like? Hang first, ask the questions later. They caught him with money on him he had no right to. He was supposed to go to trial, but the mob got hold of him. And that were that.'

Adam grimaced. 'He died as he lived, Eben. He was a murderer. You know that as well as me. You saw him do it. It was Rufus and his like gave us Sydney boys a bad name.'

Eben turned back to Ella, and seemed to lose interest in Rufus's untimely end. The fire was burning brightly now, radiating warmth, but Ella resisted the urge to crawl towards it. Eben grinned and made himself more comfortable, as if sensing it was his presence kept her away.

Adam had boiled the water and now began making tea. Eben watched him a moment before asking scornfully, 'You always do the work, Adam, while your woman takes her ease?'

Adam smiled blandly. 'Some women are worth more than others, Ebenezer.'

Eben laughed. 'You always were one for the ladies, brother.'

Shock gave Ella back her voice. 'You're brothers?' she demanded hoarsely.

Eben grinned his savage grin. 'We are that, Adam's wife.'

Ella stared, the implications of this new development running wild through her mind.

'Same mother, anyhow,' Eben went on conversationally. 'Adam's father was a sailor off one of the whalers. Mine was an overseer, in town for a spree. That's what she told us, any rate, and if anyone should know, it were her.' Eben took the mug of tea from Adam. He fumbled in his coat pocket and pulled out a silver flask. 'Belonged to a very important gent,' he informed her, holding it up. 'Got his name on it and all.' With a grin, he added some of the. contents to his tea and when Adam nodded, added some to his too.

Eben shook his head. 'You was always her best son, Adam. I was the bad 'un. She gave up on me long ago, but she always reckoned you'd do her proud. Pity she didn't live long enough to see it.' There was no bitterness in his voice, only a sort of amused resignation.

Adam shrugged the comment off. 'I haven't done much to make anyone proud yet. Only made a fool of meself in California.'

Eben snorted. 'We had a bloody good time in California! By God we did.' He sighed, and jerked his head scornfully at Ella. 'And now you'll be settlin' down, with a cottage and a cow and church on Sundays.'

Adam shrugged.

'Ah well,' and Eben finished his tea, scalding as it was. 'I'd best be off before the Joes come, or your brave friend over there decides to be a hero again.' He stood up, his coat flapping around him, the gold buttons glinting dully. 'Goodbye, Adam's wife.'

Ella inclined her head as though he were a guest at a grand ball. He laughed and added slyly, 'Nancy'd be pleased to meet you.'

Adam walked with him back to his horse. They stayed for a long time. Ella closed her eyes, feeling suddenly very weary. So many new things to assimilate. She felt too exhausted to start. The jingle of harness and Ella's eyes snapped open again. Eben was back on his horse, Adam standing beside him, and then Eben waved an arm and the horse shot off with a clatter of mud, gone back into the darkness.

He's probably off to rob someone else, Ella thought.

Adam stood a moment looking after his brother the bushranger, and then he walked slowly back towards the cart, his head bent in thought.

Ella allowed him to reach the campfire before she spoke. 'Why didn't you tell me?'

Her voice was loud in the silence. He turned to look at her. It seemed to Ella that he was choosing his words very carefully. 'There wasn't time to go into me life story.'

'He really is your brother?'

'Aye, he really is,' he mocked her softly. 'After Ma died, we travelled to California together to make. our fortunes. Eben was a miner for a while, but then he found out it was easier to take what he wanted off others. There were some bad ones in San Francisco, and Eben has always been drawn to scum. The Yankees thought we were all convicts anyhow. Sydney Ducks, that's what they called us – I think it was somethin' to do with the clothes we wore. For a time they tolerated us, and some of the ducks were payin' the law to look the other way. But men are greedy animals. It got so the Yankees couldn't ignore us any more. They caught one of the boys, Rufus his name was, stealin' and hanged him without a proper trial. San Francisco had one of its big fires not long after that, and they blamed the Sydney boys for it. Said we started it for revenge. I don't know the truth of it; I was laid up in the north from Frenchy's knife. Anyway, after the fire, the Yankees turned nasty. Those of us who could, left.'

'But *you* didn't do anything wrong. Did you?'

She was surprised how important his answer was to her.

Carefully Adam placed more wood on the fire. 'There was a whole pack of 'em in San Francisco, in a place called Little Chile and on the waterfront.

There were taverns there, people I knew from home. I ran with them ... for a while.' He hesitated. 'I didn't kill anyone, if that's what you mean. I knew men in Little Chile who'd cut throats for a dollar. Me and Eben weren't like that. I was lookin' to find gold and go home, and Eben ... he was wild, but there were things he wouldn't do.'

'And now he's a bushranger in the Black Forest.'

'Aye.' He glanced at her. 'I don't agree with what he's doing, Mrs Seaton. Don't think that. But he's still me brother.' He came and sat down beside her, making himself comfortable. Wolf nuzzled his hand. 'I asked him whether he'd heard of a woman and her servant riding through here four or five days ago. He hadn't. He didn't know anything about you being attacked at Seaton's Lagoon either.'

Ella watched him curiously. 'Why did you say we were man and wife?'

Adam leaned back against the cart wheel and stared into space. 'Eben's me brother, and I know him well. I knew he'd not touch me wife, so that's what you had to be.'

How do I know you're not just as dangerous as Eben? Ella asked silently. You talk of cutting men's throats and having a different father from your brother, as if it were something common to everyone. Perhaps you're lying to me, perhaps you're like a snake gliding through the grass ...

But even as the doubts were gathering force against him, Ella was reminding herself of his kindness towards her during the past few days. Adam had taken her on when no one else wanted to. He had looked after her without complaint and with no expectation – at least that she could see –

of reward. And finally, if it hadn't been for Adam being Eben's brother, Ella might now be tied to a tree. Or worse.

She shuddered violently.

Adam's hand found hers; it was very warm. His voice was quiet and soothing. 'Tomorrow, if Bess and the road hold up, we'll be out of the Black Forest. We'll be on our way to Bendigo. And there are plenty of places along the way to ask about you, Mrs Seaton. Think of that. Maybe we'll know who you are by this time tomorrow night. Maybe I'll have that reward right here, in me pocket.'

Ella tried to laugh, but her body was shaking too hard. He made a sound like a groan and wrapped his arms around her, squeezing her tightly, his warm body against her cold one. He smelt of the fire and the earth, and he was warm, so very warm. And gradually his warmth filled her, and the shaking stopped. The instant it did, he moved away. 'Get some sleep,' he murmured brusquely. 'It'll be dawn soon.'

Alone now, Ella nodded, and obediently crawled back to her bed. She closed her eyes, but it was a long time before she felt Adam lie down beside her, and a long time before her thoughts would stop rattling in her head so that she could sleep.

CHAPTER 5

———◆———

THE REST OF THE JOURNEY through the Black Forest passed without incident. Although if Adam had expected gratitude from the miners for saving their possessions and their dignity, and possibly their lives, he was mistaken. Eben's visit had altered their attitude to him. They eyed him now with unease and murmured to each other in hushed voices. The respect they had felt for him when they learned he was a forty-niner had turned to mistrust. As soon as they reached the safety of Five Mile Creek, they prepared to leave Adam and Ella behind.

Five Mile Creek was a hamlet which had sprung up at the northern end of the Black Forest, around the Wood End Inn. A bridge spanned the creek and it was here that Adam drew up the cart to rest Bess. In no time he was coaxing a fire out of some damp kindling, and Ella carried a bucket down to the fast-flowing water. She found a relatively solid bit of bank to stand on and was filling the bucket when she heard a footstep behind her.

She looked up, alarmed by memories of Eben and the Black Forest, but it was only one of the miners. Indeed, it was the courageous Mr Morris. He hesitated, but only because he was uncertain of the muddy ground. As he started forward down the bank, his boots sinking, Ella could see he was determined to speak to her about something.

'Ma'am, may I have a word?'

Ella nodded, made uneasy by the stubborn way Mr Morris was jutting his chin.

He stopped before her, grimacing at the state of his boots. 'Ma'am, I feel I must speak. I don't know what this man Adam is to you, but I must set you on your guard against him.'

Ella felt her cheeks flame. 'My ... my guard?' she gasped. 'What can you mean? Adam very possibly saved our lives. If he hadn't been ... acquainted with that bushranger, we would probably still be tied to trees in the Black Forest, if not worse!'

Morris's brow creased and he shifted nervously, but his chin remained set. Ella could see he would never accept Adam had saved them for that would mean admitting he had failed. He hurried on. 'A man such as Adam is not suitable company for a lady such as yourself.'

If Ella had been bemused and amazed before, now she was angry.

Morris plunged on regardless. 'I must insist that you travel with us, ma'am.' He flushed at her surprised look. 'I would ensure you were quite safe.'

He was so sure of himself it made her want to scream, but at the same time she supposed his intentions were good. Ella gritted her teeth.

'Thank you for your concern, sir, but I am perfectly safe with Adam.'

The chin jutted even further. 'You should not be alone with him, ma'am! He's a ruffian of the worst kind. He'll take advantage of you – '

Ella's anger swelled beyond stopping. 'I see I must

be plain with you, sir,' and her voice was icey. 'I'd rather keep company with a ruffian, if that's what Adam is, than all the gentlemen in Victoria! He has been kinder to me than you can know, and I will hear no more on the subject.'

Morris looked taken aback. For the first time he had doubts that Ella would bend to his better judgment, but still he could not quite accept it. 'Ma'am, I must ask you to reconsider.'

'I will not, sir.'

He stepped back. She glared at him, daring him to say more. 'I cannot believe – '

'What believe, Mr Morris, is of no interest to me whatsoever!'

He closed his mouth in a stubborn line and turned away. Ella watched him climb back up the bank, his back stiff with hurt pride.

Now that he was gone, she had some doubts. Should she have agreed to go with him instead of Adam? But she shook her head decisively – No. The thought of placing herself in Mr Morris's hands made her shudder; Adam may be a 'ruffian', but she trusted him with her life.

Slowly Ella made her way back to the fire. The rain had sharpened the smells of earth and eucalyptus, mingled now with the wood smoke. There was meat sizzling, too. Adam had shot a couple of birds early that morning and was cooking them on spits over the fire.

He looked up at her with a smile that erased some of the tiredness from his eyes. 'Everythin' all right?'

'Aye,' she replied, and he laughed at her mimicry. 'We should reach Carlsruhe tomorrow. If the weather holds.' He turned the meat deftly as he spoke. 'There's a mounted police station there. We can ask if they know anything about you.'

'What about your brother?'

Adam's eyes narrowed at her, but it could have been the smoke. 'What about him?'

'I meant ...' She shifted uneasily. 'If they ask about bushrangers ... if someone has reported ... Oh! Should I pretend it never happened, if the police ask me?'

He grinned. 'I'd be grateful,' he allowed. 'Now ... are you hungry?'

The meat was delicious, and Ella ate her share, piece by succulent piece, finishing by sucking on the bones. She didn't think she could ever have enjoyed a meal quite so much. Adam gravely accepted her compliments, but she saw the warm gleam of pleasure in his eyes.

They made camp by the creek. A few other travellers arrived and set up their own camps nearby. The soft sounds of talk and laughter lulled Ella. She watched the mist creeping up from the water like ghosts. Wolf's eyes gleamed in the firelight, and she knew he'd rather be out in the dark, hunting, than sitting passively by the fire. But Adam kept him close: he said a good guard dog was as important on the gold-fields as a pick and shovel.

The fire crackled and Ella yawned. Soon, she would curl up in her blankets and go to sleep. And perhaps tomorrow, at Carlsruhe, she would discover who she really was.

Carlsruhe consisted of the Mount Macedon Police Station, a horse changing station for the new gold escort, a post office, and the usual rough slab huts and calico tents to serve passersby. Adam had high hopes. Surely, he said, someone *here* would know something of the woman in the red cloak!

But when they arrived, the troopers were in the middle of a crisis. The man in charge, a Lieutenant Moggs, ushered them impatiently into his office. To Ella he seemed impossibly spick and span in his uniform, a gleaming sabre clipped to his side and boots like mirrors. This was no rough and ready soldier, recruited to the undermanned Victorian police force. This was a young gentleman who for reasons of his own had chosen to make a career for himself with the hated 'Joes'.

Lieutenant Moggs informed them in a clipped and educated voice that there had been yet another robbery in the Black Forest, and he and his men were at this very moment preparing to ride out to investigate.

Ella kept her eyes carefully from Adam's as he expressed his concern. Lieutenant Moggs began to move impatiently and Adam came to the point.

The man's eyes flicked from Ella to Adam. 'I haven't seen anyone of that description in the past six months,' he informed them, his impatience growing.

'Are you sure?' Adam went on doggedly. 'Mrs Seaton doesn't remember where she came from. She doesn't know who she is! The lady needs official help.'

Lieutenant Moggs frowned. Obviously eager to be about his duties, he was finding this nothing more than an irritating setback. He eyed Ella's grubby clothing and tangled hair with distaste; she could see that he had already formed his own opinion of her and was not about to change it.

'I can't do anything now, I have other more important matters to deal with. But if she wants to stay until my return, perhaps I can arrange an escort back to Melbourne.'

Ella felt her stomach drop. She had not realised she might have to remain here at Carlsruhe waiting until Lieutenant Moggs found time to send her south. And what then? She glanced anxiously at Adam and saw he was also looking doubtful. 'What'll happen to her down there?' he asked.

The lieutenant eyed him coldly, clearly of the opinion Adam had no business to be asking *him* questions. 'There's a hostel in which she can stay until we decide who she is and what to do with her. Or someone decides to claim her.' But from the look on his face he considered the last option unlikely. His face grew suspicious. 'I thought you said she'd forgotten her name? Why do you call her Mrs Seaton?'

Adam sighed and explained, but the lieutenant had stopped listening. He wasn't interested. He was itching to be off after the bushrangers and a misplaced woman was of no importance to him. 'Leave her here,' he snapped. 'I'll deal with her when I've a chance.'

'I think I'd prefer to go on to Bendigo,' Ella said quietly but firmly. 'Thank you all the same.'

Lieutenant Moggs's rather cruel face relaxed with relief. 'Well! That's probably best. The Commissioner there may be able to help you ...er, ma'am.'

Ella knew that he had forgotten her as soon as he turned his back.

Outside, Adam shrugged. 'We tried.'

Ella tried to smile. 'I seem to be too much trouble.'

He gave her a quick look. 'Aye well, that's the way of the world.'

'Do you think I'm too much trouble, Adam? You were hoping they'd take me on, weren't you? I should have realised ... I'm holding you back.'

His smile mocked her. 'It's the road and the weather holding me back, not you.' He hesitated. 'It was a close call in the Black Forest. It could've turned out different. I've been thinking that you'd be better off with someone else, someone official. An escort, like the lieutenant said. I'm not the proper person for a lady like you to be travelling with.'

Ella wondered whether Adam had also had benefit of Mr Morris's insights into her character. 'I wish you'd told me this back at Five Mile Creek,' she murmured.

'You what?'

But she shook her head. 'Adam, you've looked after me like a baby. You've probably saved my life - certainly my virtue and my dignity. I don't care any longer what people say - I mean look at me!'

He laughed. 'You do look a bit rough.'

She took a deep breath. 'Can I stay with you, Adam? Until we reach Bendigo?'

She sounded humble; she didn't dare look up at him. He patted her shoulder in a brotherly fashion. 'Until Bendigo then,' he promised.

The relief made her dizzy.

———◆———

After Carlsruhe, the road seemed to improve. They made better time and were soon passing through the little farming community of Kyneton.

Kyneton had grown fat. The farmers in the area had a ready market on the goldfields for there was never enough food to feed the diggers and what there was often cost a hundred times more than it should have. In California Adam had lived on pork and beans and dreamed of oysters and champagne; here in Victoria the miners ate mutton and damper but their dreams were the same.

Beyond Kyneton the road was dotted with 'coffee' tents. 'They're really grog shops,' Adam told Ella. 'Bloody awful stuff some of it. They mix their own ... you're lucky if your head's still fastened on in the mornin'.'

But such places sold more than just grog. They served tea and coffee, hot meals, and often supplied a corner in which to sleep out of the rain. Now, because of bad roads and bad weather, the bullock drays that brought goods from Melbourne were late or had not arrived at all. Supplies were running low and Adam was able to wrangle a good price from desperate proprietors for some of his own wares. After one such session, he came back with a big grin on his face.

'You made a profit,' Ella guessed.

Adam laughed. 'That I did.'

At another of the coffee tents a group of miners had gathered, complaining loudly about the thirty shillings a month needed to buy a gold licence. Ella learned that every miner was required to purchase one and carry it with him at all times.

'Most of them don't find enough gold to cover the cost of the licence,' Adam explained. 'But Charley Joe La Trobe reckons he needs the money to run the goldfields and won't hear of stopping it.'

Sir Charles Joseph La Trobe was the Governor of Victoria, and the miners disliked him heartily. The police who enforced his gold licence law were disliked even more, and were known as Joes or Charley-Joes after their master.

Ella and Adam's northward journey took them down from the higher country - the mountain range which divided Victoria. The bleak, bone-freezing winds they had experienced ever since Kyneton gave way to more moderate though still cold, conditions. The creeks they crossed were swollen with rain and although there were usually bridges or punts to ferry them over, often Adam had to unload the cart and bring the contents separately.

He seemed remarkably good humoured despite the setbacks. He was, thought Ella, a remarkably amiable man. Only once, when he sank down beside the fire dripping and cold from a dunking in the water, did he mutter, 'I should've stayed home in Sydney.'

Ella eyed him curiously. 'What did you do there?'

He shrugged. 'Bit of this and that. When I was seven I ran messages for one of the hotels in George Street. Later I drove a cart for a timber merchant and then I was on the docks. That's how I heard about the rush to California - I was there when the ship bringin' the news sailed in.'

'How old are you now, Adam?'

He raised his eyebrows, amusement making his eyes shine like polished mahogany. 'If me mother's to be believed, I'm twenty-five, Mrs Seaton.'

Younger than she had thought. Perhaps the surprise showed in her face, because he added, 'I reckon I've already done more in them twenty-five years than some men do in their entire lives.'

'You're probably right.'

There was an awkward silence. Adam gave a great shiver, and Ella realised with concern that he really was soaked.

'Perhaps you should take off those clothes and dry them,' she suggested. 'You can't drive on like that.'

'I'll be all right,' he began, but another great shudder stopped him and he smiled wryly.

'We're a long way from a doctor,' Ella reminded him uneasily. 'And I don't think I'd make a very good nurse.'

Adam needed no further prompting and began to strip off his jacket. Ella took it from him, arranging it near the fire. He pulled his woollen shirt over his head and handed it to her, and then bent to remove his boots. Ella tried not to look but her eyes wouldn't obey her. His back and chest were wide and browned from the sun, though mottled now with cold. A life of physical work had built up hard, curving muscles on his arms and his shoulders were big and broad.

I should find such obvious strength comforting, Ella thought. Why, then, were her pulses quickening? It was as if her blood had begun to sing a song she had never heard before.

Adam had finished with his footwear and stood up, hands going to his moleskins, ready to peel them down over hips and thighs. Ella's eyes lifted nervously, and widened. There was a scar running across his ribs on the left side, all the way from his nipple right down to his waist. It was a long slashing scar, made by a vicious, murderous blade. Whoever had attacked him had meant to kill him. Ella imagined that smooth brown flesh laid open, bleeding and torn, and she shuddered. She had an intense desire to run her fingers over the wound, as if by doing so she could somehow heal his remembered pain.

Adam had not moved, his hands still resting on the waist of his moleskins. Ella looked up and met his eyes. There was something quizzical in them. He had evidently noted the direction of her gaze because he touched the scar himself.

'I was asleep,' he told her softly. 'I heard him just before he came at me, and put up an arm to knock the knife away. The blade went across me ribs instead of through 'em.'

'You were lucky.' Her voice sounded odd even to her own ears. She dragged her eyes away and stood up abruptly, turning her back. 'I'll fetch you a blanket,' she said, and walked quickly over to the cart.

The wood was smooth and warm under her fingers, like flesh. She closed her eyes. 'No!' the word, though stifled, was a violent denial. Adam was her travelling companion, her friend, but no more. She must not allow herself to feel more. The attraction had been a violent thing, taking her completely by surprise, and no doubt it would vanish just as suddenly. She mustn't let Adam sense it, for both their sakes. I'd just be using him so that I could feel close to someone ... anyone, she told herself. Because my life is so empty, because I'm so alone.

Ella opened her eyes. Adam was cold. She would fetch the blanket she had promised and put everything else from her mind.

But he had forestalled her.

'Here, I'll get it.' He had come up behind her and now he reached past for the blanket. His bare arm brushed hers. 'You sit down,' he suggested kindly. 'I'll make you a hot cup of tea.'

'No,' she managed hoarsely, and cleared her throat. 'I can do that.'

His expression was doubtful.

'I can manage,' she assured him in firmer tones.

He sat silent, watching her while she boiled the water and added the coarse dried tea leaves. The process of doing something helped to steady Ella to the point where she began to wonder how she could have allowed herself to be thrown off balance by a man such as Adam. How could she, even for a moment, be attracted to him in such a hot, trembling way? It wasn't like her — or the woman she assumed herself to be. Was her image of herself so mistaken, so wrong?

'You learn quick,' Adam said, when she handed him his mug.

'I'd have to be silly not to be able to make tea!'

'Well,' he eyed her sideways, 'you're not that.'

Ella felt her smile go awry. 'But what am I, Adam? That's what I would dearly love to find out. What am I?'

He stared pensively into the dark brew in his mug. 'Have you remembered nothin' at all?'

She frowned. 'Sometimes I think I remember things. I have dreams ... there's a forest and I'm lost. But when I wake, everything's foggy and confused. The harder I try to remember the worse it becomes.'

He nodded as if he understood.

Suddenly it was as though she needed her own opinions of herself reinforced. 'Tell me, Adam, what do you think I am? Apart from a lady,' she added quickly as he opened his mouth.

He smiled. 'Well,' he began slowly, 'I think you've been to a fine school, Mrs Seaton. You know things. And I think that maybe you've suffered, because you're kind when you could be cruel. But you don't like people like Morris telling you what to do; you like to run your own race.' He thought again. 'You've been used to living well and this life on the road is hard for you. But you've got courage, that's for sure, and you don't give up.'

There was warmth in his eyes. He looked, Ella thought, like an Indian chief, with his hair straggling about his shoulders and the blanket clasped around him. She saw the tattoo snaking up his arm and a triangle of bare chest. Her eyes slid up to his again, and now there was something new in them, something she didn't dare explore.

Ella turned away. She wondered, with a sick feeling in the pit of her stomach, whether he had read the need in her own eyes after all.

'It's getting dark,' Adam said quietly, evenly. 'We can camp here for the night and be on our way in the morning.'

Ella took a deep breath and nodded. 'Very well. I can cook supper – '

'No.'

She turned sharply. 'Adam, please, I know perfectly well how to fry chops!'

He grinned. 'I didn't mean that. I saw a travellers' rest just up ahead. We'll see what they're serving. Wolf'll guard the cart.'

The thought of sitting down to a meal other than mutton and damper was too tempting to resist. Ella agreed with alacrity.

The travellers' rest was actually a slab hut with a calico roof and smoke dribbling from a barrel chimney. The cook was a short, plump woman with a big smile, her partner a large, red-haired Irishman. Ella suspected that, as Adam had previously warned her, they sold liquor on the side. But she didn't care.

The food was hot and filling – stew and dumplings with a plum pudding for afters. They ate on a makeshift bench – knocked up from three logs in five minutes, according to their host – with several other travellers. The smoke stung Ella's eyes but she was content to sit, slightly squashed, with the wall on one side and Adam on the other, and listen to the talk.

They were discussing gold again and a loud argument ensued between the Irishman and a little Cornish miner over the best shape to dig a hole. Hot toddy was passed around, but one sip was enough for Ella and she refused more. Her head nodded with weariness. She felt Adam's hand reach up, pressing her down onto his shoulder. Sleep crept over her.

Her last thought was: my toes are warm. They haven't felt warm for days and days and days …

———•———

Sydney was still and humid. She felt a drip of perspiration roll down her spine and wisps of hair clung to her brow. They were staying overnight in a hotel on George Street with a grand staircase. Their room was large and light, a bowl of roses scented the air. He strode back and forth, her husband, as if he couldn't breathe.

'I'll have some food sent up,' he said.

'You're not staying?' she asked, knowing he wasn't. The anxiety that had become so much a part of her began to beat in her chest.

The cold eyes slid over her and away, as if there were something wrong with her. 'I have an engagement.'

'But we've only just arrived,' she began, her voice sounding ineffectual even to her own ears.

'There are matters to attend to,' he replied. 'Tomorrow I'll take you to meet my sister. Perhaps you should prepare yourself for that.'

'I am looking forward to meeting her,' she replied, and truly she was. She hoped to make a friend of this unseen sister of her husband's.

'You would do well to befriend Catherine. There is much she could teach you.' His cold eyes warmed.

She sighed, relieved she had said something that pleased him. So often she seemed to annoy him with her conversation. At home she had been considered rather intelligent, if proud. Her coolness had not made her a great many friends - people considered her haughty - but no one had ever found her tedious. No one had yawned while she was speaking, as her husband did, and said, 'I didn't marry you for your opinions, woman. Confine yourself to your stitchery.'

That was when she realised that he had a shallow mind. Oh, he was bluff and handsome, and cunning enough to make himself a rich man. But he was also shallow and vain and mean. His ideas of wedded life, too, had come as an unpleasant surprise to her. He did not look for her company, her presence did not please him, he never touched her in affection - their night-time couplings were rough and mercifully swift. His hands kneaded and prodded her body in the darkness ... he always smelled of peppermint - he chewed it to disguise the odour of bad teeth.

And every month he had asked her that same dreaded question:

'Are you with child?'

But she never was, and his cold eyes would flash his annoyance. She tried to please him, indeed she had no choice, but it was a rare moment when she did.

'Please don't,' she whispered now, the scent of roses filling her head and her eyes bright with tears. 'Please don't go ...'

———◆———

'We've got to go.' Adam's warm, amused tone soaked into the aridity of her dream, like rum through a sponge cake. He was looking down at her, the glow from the fire reflected in his eyes. He was very close.

Ella blinked.

'We've got to go,' he repeated.

She sat up. The tent was quiet now, muggy with smoke and the smell of close humanity. Someone was curled up on the floor in a blanket, like a small animal. The Irishman was leaning back against the wall, snoring with his mouth wide open.

'You've been sleeping.' Adam's breath was sweet with rum. When he smiled his eyes went strangely out of focus.

'There was a man,' Ella whispered, her thoughts still concentrated on the dream.

She saw the little muscles around his eyes contract and narrow. 'What man?'

'I dreamed of a man, my husband. I ...' But it was fading, and although she clenched her fists, trying to hold on to it, the memory slipped away from her. 'It's gone.'

'You're shaking,' he whispered. He helped her up, his arm around her. She realised then that it was more for his support than hers.

'Oh Adam,' she complained. 'How will I get you back to the camp?'

"I'll be all right once I get outside.' And although he reeled a bit when the night air struck him, he did seem to sober up. It was as sharp as a knife, and so cold Ella's eyes watered.

'Perhaps we should have curled up on the floor by the fire, like that miner,' she said through chattering teeth.

'We can curl up under the cart, just you and me together.'

Ella felt herself go still inside with fear and longing. She couldn't think of anything to say.

'It was just a thought,' he went on evenly. 'Maybe it was the rum put it there.'

She wondered what he would do if she agreed, and the possibility made her begin to shake again. But such a thing couldn't be.

Perhaps he thought her silence was a form of

acquiescence, because he leaned forward and kissed her on the cheek. With a gasp Ella began to run, stumbling forward in the darkness. The glow of their fire shone ahead, and Wolf ran to meet her. She sank down, wrapping her arms around the warm, wriggling body, and burst into tears.

She heard Adam behind her, panting from the run. 'I'm a bloody fool,' he muttered, and there was genuine anguish in his voice. His hand touched her hair. 'I never meant nothing, Mrs Seaton. I swear I'd never hurt you ... I'd never do nothing to you, unless you wanted me to do it. Oh Christ, I mean ... I didn't mean ...' He fell silent. She heard him sigh, and when he spoke again he sounded weary. 'Come on. Get some sleep. Who knows? Maybe by tomorrow night you'll know who you are, and I'll – '

'Have the reward money in your pocket.' She mimicked him in a husky voice. She wiped her cheeks with her fingers, leaving dirty marks, and then cleared her throat. 'I'm the one who's sorry, Adam. You deserve that reward, indeed you do.'

He helped her to her feet, his hand light and impersonal on her elbow. 'Goodnight, Mrs Seaton,' he said softly.

'Goodnight Adam,' she replied, in the voice she used with her servants, and crawled into bed and tried to fall asleep.

CHAPTER 6

———————

THE ROAD AHEAD WAS FULL of the usual
straggle of miners, and strewn with their leavings - broken carts and drays, discarded personal
effects that had grown too heavy or were no longer of use. Most people were going north, to make
their fortunes in one way or another, so the traffic in the opposite direction was sparse, consisting
mainly of empty bullock drays. The very first gold
escort from the diggings at Forest Creek galloped
past and everyone stopped to watch it. The troopers, with sabres drawn, carried the gold in bags
attached to their saddles. They rode at a constant
gallop – Adam said they had changing stations along
the route so that they never had to slow down. The
miners who took the precaution of sending their
gold by escort were able to retrieve it when they
themselves reached Melbourne.

A coach and horses thumped past, the body
swaying precariously from side to side while the
passengers inside clung on grimly. After that, Ella
developed a new fondness for Bess and her sedate
plod.

Adam kept asking if anyone had seen a woman
in a red cloak. But no one remembered her. The
rain had begun to fall heavily, soaking through the
blanket and trickling down Ella's neck. It darkened

Adam's hair and dripped off the end of his nose.

The grey misery of it seemed to fill Ella, and at first Adam, sensing her depression, tried to cheer her up. She pretended to be cheered but the pretending got harder and harder. Finally he just took to glancing at her, his expression growing more and more concerned as she withdrew into herself.

Beyond the Coliban River there was a long, steep incline. Ella had to climb down and walk beside the cart to give tired Bess a better chance of hauling it to the top. Adam walked beside her, coaxing the mare, his boots slipping in the mud. The rain struck their faces, stinging and reddening their skin. Ella put up a hand to wipe her eyes and found it so cold she could hardly feel her fingers.

When they reached the top, Adam said, 'There's a place called Sawpit Gully up ahead. A woman I know runs an inn there. They'd likely have a bed for you.'

The words took a moment to penetrate her numbness. 'A bed?' she repeated incredulously.

'Aye, a bed. And a bath, too, I wouldn't wonder. We'll be there by dark.'

'Oh Adam,' she whispered, tears blurring his face. 'Oh Adam ..."

He laughed, and patted her shoulder.

Ella bowed her head and swallowed, grasping her hands tightly together. A bed! She longed for it more than all the gold on the Bendigo goldfield. And a hot bath to warm frozen flesh and wash off the grime of their journey.

And then a doubt caught her, stilled her. 'Is the woman who owns the inn the one your brother mentioned? The one you knew in San Francisco?'

His face was bland, his eyes wide and innocent. 'She was near enough to a stranger to me, Cinderella.'

He sounded offhand, but Ella had come to realise that this meant he didn't want to answer her questions. A niggling sense of unease told her she should delve further, and then she thought: What if I discover something I don't want to know? Something that would prevent me from going to Sawpit Gully? This woman, whoever she is, has a bed and a bath. Does anything else really matter?

To her shame, nothing did.

———◆———

The sun was setting when at last they rattled into Sawpit Gully. The place was a series of narrow gullies, encircled by bush-covered hills. The approaching darkness hid something of its squalor - but not much. Ella looked about her with misgiving. Tumbledown huts and shanties loomed out of the fading light. Candles flickered from the doorways of single-room grog shops and other even less salubrious dwellings, while the occasional lamp illuminated the signs of those buildings bravely proclaiming themselves inns.

Adam had told her that visitors to Sawpit Gully were a mixture of miners in from the diggings to the north and would-be-miners from the south. It was a town which had grown up higgledy-piggledy out of a former timber camp, to supply the needs of lonely men. There were no liquor licences allowed at the diggings themselves, and Sawpit Gully was close enough for a binge. Most of the miners didn't even stop for a bath before spending their gold dust on the various intoxicants of the mind and body that were offered for sale.

It was like another world to Ella. She glanced at Adam, but he appeared not to notice the state of the place, and if he did such sights were nothing new to him. He must, she thought, have seen much worse in his days in California. A villainous-looking man slunk by, and then a woman in skirts so gaudy they glowed in the fading light. Ahead of them in the narrow street, a miner stood smoking, his moleskins caked with clay, the sleeves of his red shirt rolled up as if he were out for a summer stroll.

Adam called to him. 'Mrs Ure? Where's her place?'

The man gave directions, a sneer twisting his bearded face. 'She's a bitch, that one. She'll cheat yer if she thinks she can get away with it. Watch yerself in there.'

But Adam smiled a secret smile. 'She won't cheat me.'

The inn was off the main track, set on rising ground overlooking the town. The building was constructed of vertical slabs, with several thicker pieces of timber propped against one end, presumably to hold it up. Candlelight slunk through the cracks and gaps in the slab walls. The shuttered windows were set crookedly, making them appear as if they were winking. As they approached, the noise from within grew. Someone was playing a squeeze box with great enthusiasm, but even so it was nearly drowned out by the shouting and laughter.

Ella could see the inn sign now, illuminated by

a lamp. It was a rather amateurish depiction of a snarling lion, but all the same it was menacing. She shivered and drew her blanket closer, hoping it was not a portent.

At the front of the inn, horses were tied to a hitching rail made of stringy-bark poles, the bark still hanging off them in strips. A boy loitered nearby, and as Adam drew up, he came forward. Ella thought his clothing looked borrowed, the trousers too big and the shirt too small.

'I'm lookin' for Mrs Ure,' said Adam.

The boy cleared his throat. 'This is 'er place 'ere. 'Old yer'orse?' he offered.

'Can we go around to the stable, boy? I don't want to leave me goods out in the street for any man to pick over.'

The boy nodded and set off at a trot around the corner of the building, leading the way. Adam flicked the reins and manoeuvered the cart through a narrow gateway into the quiet darkness of the stable yard. The back door to the inn stood open, lamp light and appetising smells spilling out

Adam jerked his thumb towards it. 'Nancy'll be inside. Wait a moment while I settle Bess and I'll take you in.'

Ella took a breath. 'Will you have to tell her we're man and wife? As you did with your brother?'

He hesitated. 'Not this time. But I want you to go along with everything I say. And be sweet to her. Sweet as sugar, Mrs Seaton. Can you do that?'

'Why?' Ella demanded.

He winked, dark eyes gleaming with humour. 'If you want a bed tonight, just let me do the talking.'

What was the point in standing in the cold arguing with him? 'Very well, Adam.'

He grinned and set about unharnessing Bess. The boy moved to help. The stable yard smelt of mud and horse dung and straw; Ella's empty stomach quivered with revulsion. She rubbed her eyes, swaying in the darkness. She had not realised until now how tired she was. Above her, the stars were clear and bright in the cold sky. She gazed up at them, her breath like smoke from her lips. It was as if the heavens were turning in a great arc above her head. Their movement made her feel dizzy, or perhaps it was she who was moving ...

Adam's hand closed on her elbow, steadying her. 'Come on then,' he said, his breath warm on her cheek, and with Wolf on one side and Adam on the other, Ella stayed more or less upright as they walked towards the inn.

She tripped on the two bricks that formed the step, and then they were inside. The warmth enclosed her, delicious smells embraced her. She saw, blinking like a possum, that it was a kitchen. A fire glowed in a brick hearth, while pots boiled and bubbled, splattering hissing water onto the coals. There was a spit upon which a large leg of mutton crackled, dripping grease.

Ella felt faint. Sensing it, Adam's fingers tightened on her arm. And then the door opposite banged open and two women entered, their shoes tapping like impatient fingers on the hard earth floor.

'Round to the dining room, if you please!' one of them snapped, with a brief glance at their dishevelled state. 'And get that mongrel out of here!' with a longer glance at Wolf. She was thin with steel grey hair and black eyebrows soaring above bold black eyes. Her mouth was pursed, probably from discontent, but it gave the impression of a pout

Adam hadn't moved. The woman looked up again, and the black eyes narrowed. 'You deaf or somethin'?' she demanded, and Adam laughed. Slowly, the woman's expression changed, grew full of wonder.

'Adam!' She shrieked so loudly that Ella jumped.

'Hello, Nancy,' drawled Adam, his dark eyes gleaming.

Nancy smiled a smile so broad it threatened to split her narrow face in two.

The second woman had paused to stare, blue eyes big and curious. She was young and pretty, a girl rather than a woman, with chestnut brown hair wisping about her flushed face. Adam pulled out a stool and with a murmured 'Sit down', pushed Ella's tired and aching body onto it. The smells of the room were so exquisite her mouth was watering, and she had to swallow several times. A neatly framed quote hung on the wall beside the hearth. 'If any would not work, neither should he eat.' It seemed to rock gently before her eyes.

'You said to look you up when I got back,' Adam was saying to Nancy Ure.

Nancy wiped hands, which shook visibly, on her apron. 'Aye, but I never thought you would.' And then she came forward in a rush, black eyes swimming with tears, and threw her thin arms around him in a savage hug. 'Oh Adam, it's so good to see you!'

Adam returned the embrace, laughing, and lifted her feet clean off the floor.

'Pffft, you stink!' Nancy gasped, and as suddenly

as she had embraced him, pushed him away. She stood, eyeing him a little suspiciously.

'What have you been up to, Adam? Why are you here?'

Adam leaned back against the corner of the fireplace, not at all put out by being told he stank. Nor, thought Ella, by Nancy's emotional welcome. 'I've been working here and there,' he said with a grin. 'You know how it is, Nancy. I had enough left from California to fit meself out with a cart and horse and something to sell when I get to the goldfields. I heard you were here and thought I'd drop in and see you on me way north.'

A pleased flush rose in Nancy's cheeks. 'I thought you'd head back to Sydney.'

Adam shook his head. 'The ship was bound for Melbourne. I reckoned the gold was as good here as anywhere, so I stayed.'

'Well,' and she smiled at him, 'I'm glad you did.' She took a breath, settling her emotions, and suddenly her eyes alighted on Ella. It was an unfriendly stare, and the thin face hardened. 'Who's this then?' she snapped, biting out each word as if she resented the inconvenience of speaking it. 'You've not got yourself a wife at last, have you, Adam?'

Adam smiled blandly, innocently. Like a child. 'She was lost, Nancy. I just happened to find her. Can you put her up for the night? She needs a bed and maybe a doctor, if you have such a thing in this place.'

Nancy was glaring at Ella now with fierce suspicion. Ella stared back coldly and it was only when Adam nudged her that she was prompted to give the sweet smile she had promised.

It had no effect on Nancy Ure.

'Who are you, girl?' she demanded. Then, in a vicious aside to Adam, 'Is she simple?'

'Her name is Seaton.' Adam told the lie easily. 'Mrs Ella Seaton.'

Nancy flashed Adam a look of sour amusement 'Hasn't she got no tongue neither?'

He laughed. 'Aye, she has a tongue, but she's about done in. Can you see her right for a bed tonight, Nancy?'

Mrs Ure raised her dark brows until they disappeared into her grey hair. 'This isn't no posh 'otel, Adam. Where's she from?'

Thinking it was about time she spoke up for herself, Ella found her voice. 'I don't know where I'm from. That's the trouble. I've lost my memory.'

But Mrs Ure was unsympathetic. 'I've got enough to be getting on with,' she said coldly. 'I don't want invalids cluttering up the place. What if she's light-fingered?'

Adam laughed loudly. The pretty girl stirring the pots stopped and watched him with interest. 'You're worried *she's* a thief?' he retorted. 'An' you're as pure as snow, are you, Nance?'

Nancy's expression softened and she smirked. 'Well, you know what I mean.'

Ella bit her lips to stop them wobbling with a combination of misery and weariness and anger. What sort of place was this? What sort of people had she fallen in with? Bushrangers and grog shop owners! What next – murderers, cut-throats? Even Adam had deserted her ... indeed, seemed a part of this scene! She shouldn't be here. Why didn't someone come and rescue her and take her home?

'Oh all right then.' Nancy Ure's sharp tones interrupted Ella's thoughts. 'But I expect a favour in return.'

'I knew you had a heart of gold,' Adam said blandly. 'Now, what about a doctor? Do you have one?'

Mrs Ure sighed. 'Aye, if you can call him a doctor.' She turned to the other girl, who was eavesdropping openly while she stirred her pots and pans. 'Kitty! Go and fetch Doctor Rawlins. Adam'll give you a guinea.' And she smiled viciously at Adam. 'It costs a guinea to get him out of his hut. He don't come otherwise.'

Adam shrugged and found the money, handing it to Kitty. The girl's red lips curled into a smile, and she gave him a bold look. 'Thank you, Adam.'

'Go on then!' Nancy Ure snapped, and Kitty quickly closed the door. 'I'll get you a hot bath, Adam,' Nancy went on, smoothing out her voice.

Ella realised suddenly that Mrs Ure wasn't as old as she had at first thought – in her early thirties at most. It was the grey hair that had made her seem older.

Adam peered down at himself with a grimace, and then gave Nancy the benefit of his most endearing smile. 'I won't deny it sounds bloody good but – ' and he nodded his head in Ella's direction, 'I think she needs one more 'an me!'

The mockery in his voice was designed to negate any insult Nancy might have felt but it still made Ella flinch. Nancy gave her a searching look. 'Aye,' she said grimly, 'you're right. Where'd you say you found her, in a mud puddle?'

He laughed. 'Somethin' like that.' A sort of cunning came into his eyes, and he spoke again, softly, 'I saw a friend of ours on me way up here.'

'Oh?' Nancy Ure tilted her head to the side.

'Eben.'

She stiffened. 'Don't say that name in here!'

'No one's listening.'

Nancy Ure glanced at Ella, but Adam laughed. 'She won't say nothing. She's lost her memory.'

Nancy's thin mouth tightened. 'Eben's a wanted man.'

'So he said.'

'What else did he say?'

But Adam just smiled.

'From what I remember, you weren't so innocent yourself,' Nancy snapped, but she was uneasy.

Adam leaned back and crossed his arms. 'I'm a changed man.'

Nancy laughed softly, disbelievingly. 'Are you now? Are you now indeed?'

The door opened then and Kitty entered. Behind her trotted a short, rotund man with a moustache so large and curled it was almost bigger than he was. As he came closer, the fumes of some alcoholic beverage wafted over Ella, adding to her dizziness.

'Doctor Rawlins.' Mrs Ure smiled, a brief scornful twist of her lips which made it clear what she thought of the doctor. 'Got a patient for you.'

Doctor Rawlins twitched his grand moustache. 'Indeed, my good lady.' He had the sort of loud, hearty voice that Ella would have expected from a man twice his size. He looked at Ella, head cocked like a little sparrow, and met her eyes with his own muddy brown, bloodshot ones. 'And what's the matter with this young woman?'

'You're the doctor,' Mrs Ure snapped. 'You tell us.'

Doctor Rawlins smiled and nodded, and seemed not to notice Mrs Ure's hostility. 'If I may, madam?' he murmured politely to Ella and, ignoring Wolf's investigation of his boots, bent to take her pulse. He then proceeded to poke and prod her, asking if that hurt or that. Nothing did, until he found the bump on her head. And then he peered closer. 'Well, you've had a nasty knock there, but it's healing. Any headache ... blurring of vision? Well, you'll need to rest up. And maybe a tot of warm brandy and milk at night.'

Mrs Ure muttered something under her breath about drunken fools. But Doctor Rawlins was looking at Adam and again didn't appear to hear her. He obviously felt he'd finished his work and was awaiting payment. Ella felt a stirring of resentment that she could be dismissed so easily, and found her voice. 'I've lost my memory.'

The doctor frowned, twiddling with his moustache. 'Yes. Hmmm. Well. It does happen. Memory loss. Probably come back in time, and with rest. If you allow it to prey upon your mind, it will only make it worse. Just rest up and try not to think too much, and more than likely it'll just pop back.'

'What if it never *pops* back?' Ella asked crossly.

'Hmm. Then I expect you'll just have to do your best without it, madam.'

Ella stared grimly at her grubby shoes, hardly hearing Adam's soft, 'Some may say a loss of memory is a useful thing.'

Mrs Ure laughed loudly, and Doctor Rawlins guffawed.

'And you are, sir?' the little doctor asked, his bleary eyes alight with interest.

'This is Adam,' Mrs Ure answered for him. 'A friend.'

'Ah.' Doctor Rawlins rocked back on his heels. 'Do you intend staying long at Sawpit Gully?'

'I'm on me way to Bendigo.'

'Hmm,' the doctor nodded sagely. 'I've heard of some good finds up there. Hard to imagine only a year ago it was all scrub and wallabies!'

'You'll stay another day though, Adam?' Mrs Ure interrupted. And then, hearing the pleading note in her own voice, snapped, 'Not that it matters to me! I've work to be doing. Have you finished?' to Doctor Rawlins.

Doctor Rawlins nodded. 'Indeed I have, Mrs Ure. I'll mix up one of my cordials for you, young woman. If you'd like to collect it in the morning.'

Adam sighed. 'Aye, all right. What is it, coloured water?'

Doctor Rawlins didn't appear to know whether this was an insult or an honest question. 'Coloured water? Oh! Oh, hmm.' Finally, he gave a rather sickly smile and departed.

Ella felt too tired to take any further part in the conversation. It was all too complicated, and besides, the warmth of the kitchen was having an effect. The stool seemed to be pitching, as if it were afloat on a stormy sea. Her surroundings blurred into mere snatches of words and colours. She felt confused, disorientated. She closed her eyes.

'I'll fetch us a drink. You must be parched, Adam.'

Mrs Ure brushed by Ella, and the noise of the bar struck her like a blow as the door opened and closed. She felt the pretty girl, Kitty, move closer. There was a whiff of something sweet competing with mutton stew. 'You got a woman, Adam?' she asked softly. She sounded bold enough, and yet very young.

A silence.

'It's all right,' Kitty added dismissively. 'She's too far gone to hear us.' Then, 'Have you? Got a woman, I mean.'

'No,' Adam said softly.

Kitty moved again – Ella heard the swish of her skirts. 'No point in goin' out lookin'. If you're lonely, you can come to my room. A shilling and sixpence, all right?'

The dreamlike feeling vanished. Ella froze. Behind her the fire, crackling merrily, seemed terribly out of place. Unable to move a muscle, she waited for Adam's answer.

'It's a good offer,' Adam replied, and there was kindness in his voice. 'But when I said I hadn't got a woman, I didn't mean ...'

Kitty stepped back, her voice became brisk. 'It's all right, no 'arm done.' Then, with a curl of something wistful, 'Maybe another time?'

'Maybe,' said Adam.

CHAPTER 7

—◆—

ELLA WOKE IN A BED.
     There were voices outside and, briefly, the beat of a horse's hooves. Weak sunlight shone gently through plain curtains onto the coverlet, an old quilt with flowers embroidered at the edges. The walls were made reasonably draft-free with mud or clay stuffed into the gaps between the rough wooden slabs, and had been thinly washed white.

Apart from the bed, there was only one other piece of furniture – a squat, badly made chest with a circle cut in the top for the chipped washing basin. A rail fixed into one corner did service for hanging clothes. It was all very bare and plain, but it was clean.

To Ella it was paradise.

Last night she had washed in a hipbath, straight backed with warm water lapping her drawn-up knees, her hair and body lathered with soap scented with rose petals. There had been a white nightdress that floated like a cloud around her. And, finally, the indescribable luxury of a warmed brick at her feet as she climbed beneath the bedclothes. She had fallen asleep with a smile on her face.

And had slept long and deep, and awoken refreshed.

Ella's hand crept out of the covers, smoothing the

worn fabric of the quilt. A sense of serenity still lay over her, but beneath it the doubts were stirring, returning to life.

Her mind moved back, reluctantly, over what she knew of her past. Then she saw again Nancy's sharp, dangerous face and Adam's smiling one. Ella's fingers stilled on the faded flowers. Adam had said that he knew Nancy Ure slightly, but she had realised as soon as Nancy clasped her arms about him that this was not true. Hadn't Eben said something about them being close, and then taunted Adam about his, Eben's, arrangement with her?

Suddenly Ella didn't want to know. She dismissed it from her mind, wriggling her toes and smiling to herself. The bed was wonderful. She felt warm and safe. How long since she had felt like that? Such feelings of security were rare to her these days, perhaps rare even before she lost her memory. Maybe they were rare to most adults, felt only by beloved children.

Quite suddenly an image filled her mind. Another, larger bed with swags of curtains either side and the sun beaming through tall windows. Ella held her breath, holding the picture, leaning forward as if that might help her to see more clearly ...

Someone tapped on the door. The memory was gone, burst like a bubble. Ella groaned, and for a moment was tempted to pull the covers up over her head and pretend she was still asleep.

'Mrs Seaton?'

It was Kitty. There was, it seemed, no escape. Ella gave up and called, 'Come in.'

Kitty wore the same dress as yesterday and her brown curls were pulled back at her nape. She was carrying a jug of water – the steam rose from it welcomingly – a towel, a cake of soap, a comb, and what looked like a bundle of clothing. She smiled as she came in, but her eyes were curious. 'Mrs Ure says you're to get up now and come to breakfast. I've set some aside for you.'

Ella sensed that this was a personal kindness on Kitty's part: Mrs Ure wasn't the type to keep breakfast for someone who'd slept late. She hadn't thought, before, of Kitty being kind; she'd been too shocked by what she had overheard. But now she looked at her with fresh eyes. How old was she? She appeared hardly more than sixteen, with her shiny curls and clear skin. It was her eyes which gave her away, big and blue but not innocent. They looked out on the world with a directness and experience few young girls possessed.

Ella rose and made use of the water. Soap and hot water were things she knew she would never again take for granted. Kitty was busying herself by the bed, and when Ella turned she realised the girl had laid out the clothing. It consisted of underthings and a dark blue dress Ella had never seen before.

'Belongs to Mrs Ure,' Kitty explained, seeing her look. 'Adam bought it off her. He said you couldn't wear rags even though – ' and the smile reappeared, 'even though your name *is* Cinderella.'

'That's not my name, I don't know my real name. But it was kind of him.'

Kitty's blue eyes fixed on Ella's boldly. 'So it's true you've no remembrance of your past?'

'Yes, it's true.'

'Fancy that. Not a one!' The girl shook her head in amazement at such a notion but, unlike Nancy

Ure, there was sympathy in her voice.

Ella smiled. 'Perhaps it will just pop back, as the doctor says.'

Kitty nodded abstractedly, her eyes still on Ella. She hesitated, and her expression became speculative. 'Have you been travellin' with Adam since he found you?'

'Yes, I have.'

Kitty didn't move, and yet Ella felt as if she'd stepped closer. Suddenly her voice was very businesslike. 'I've an offer to put to you, Mrs Seaton. I'd like to come along with you and Adam, as your chaperone.'

Ella stared. Chaperoned by a girl who charged men one and sixpence to visit her room? It was absurd.

Kitty's lips tightened, and a faint flush coloured her cheeks. 'And I know what you're thinkin'! But no one will know what I am ... at least no one at Bendigo. I'm just a woman keepin' you company on the journey. Who's to know when I first joined you and Adam? And it'll help, believe me, Mrs Seaton. I know men, I know what they're like, and your husband, when you find him, won't be no different from the rest. As soon as he hears you've been travellin' with someone like Adam, he'll believe the worst o' you!'

Ella knew she should be angry and indignant – on the surface she was both – but beneath it all a little voice was saying, Well, isn't it the truth, after all? There flashed across her mind a picture of Adam as others must see him: a young man with a ready smile and clever eyes and a smooth tongue. They didn't know him as she had come to know him, they didn't know of his humour and his good temper, his kindness and gentleness, and his perseverance through everything fate had thrown at him. Her husband, when she found him, would see only Adam the tinker.

Ella gave Kitty a narrowed look. 'I don't believe you're doing this simply for my benefit.'

Kitty flashed her smile. 'Oh, I don't deny it'd suit me, too, Mrs Seaton. I want to get out o' this place. I don't like some o' the things that go on here.' And suddenly her eyes slid away, slyly. 'But I don't want to hitch a ride with just anyone. I've been bidin' my time, waitin' for the right moment, and now I think it's come. I know you're a lady, though maybe you don't think much of me.' She lifted her chin. 'I don't go with just any man, you know.'

'But you'd have "gone with" Adam?' Ella murmured.

Kitty nodded slowly. 'Yes, I'd have taken Adam to my room.'

Something in the way the girl said Adam's name made Ella feel uneasy. It's nothing to do with me, she reminded herself sharply. I am only travelling with him through necessity.

'I'll have to think about it,' Ella said at last, coolly. 'I don't know if I want a chaperone.'

Kitty shrugged as if it were now a matter of indifference to her. But as she reached the door she spoke over her shoulder, 'It's Adam's cart. He's the only one can say yes or no to me,' and left Ella staring after her, feeling again that curl of unease in her stomach.

There was no mirror in the room, but Ella was used to dressing without one. The blue dress fitted

her well enough, clinging from neckline to waist
and then flaring out over her hips. It was too long,
obviously meant to go over stiffened petticoats, but
she could tuck it up at the waist, that was easy. Her
hair was the real problem. It was full of knots that
she'd been too weary to comb out last night. Ella
combed it now, ruthlessly, and then braided it in
one long plait down her back.

Her scalp still tingling, she moved to the window,
and looked out into the small, muddy stable yard. It
appeared deserted, apart from a bedraggled rooster
perched on the edge of the horse trough surveying
his domain. At least, she thought wryly, he knows
his place in the scheme of things. I am yet to find
mine.

Outside Ella's door was a short, narrow passage.
There was a door beside her own, and another
door at the end. Ella took a step and noticed that
the closer door was ajar, although not enough for
her to see within. Before she stopped to think, she
had pressed the wood delicately with her fingertip
and the door swung open.

It was another bedroom, but vastly different from
her own. The bed was larger, with a pretty white
and pink counterpane. A delicate-legged wash
stand held an equally delicate bowl and jug. A large
number of dresses hung on the rail in the corner,
dripping lace and ribbons from sumptuous cloth.
A richly decorated nightgown and wrap lay across
a chair, itself covered with brocade.

Surely, Ella thought, this was the sort of room in
which a woman of means resided? And yet it was
ludicrously out of place in this inn. Whose room
was it? What grand lady lived here? Ella glanced

around. And then all such questions fled her mind. For she was not alone. Her heart seemed to rise up into her throat, choking her.

There was someone standing by the window, staring back at her.

It was a woman. A fair-haired woman, with blue eyes and a white face and lips slightly apart. Something about her stance told Ella that the other woman was as frightened as her. She, too, was unmoving, the folds of her dark blue dress swaying as if she were caught in the act of turning to run.

And then Ella gave a gasp of relief as she realised the truth. She was looking into a mirror! And the woman she was looking at was herself.

She leaned heavily against the doorjamb, her relief as debilitating as her fear had been. Silly, she thought. How silly! And yet she realised this was the first time she had really seen herself. Oh, she knew her hair was fair, her eyes were blue, and she knew the shape and texture of her body. She had seen vague reflections of herself in the creeks and rivers they had crossed. But she hadn't really *known* what she looked like, or how others saw her.

Ella straightened and with real curiosity, met her own eyes in the mirror. It was difficult for her to decide upon her age. She could be as young as twenty, but she knew she was older than that. Slowly, curiously, she examined every feature.

The shape of her face was oval, the skin pale and smooth. It was, she admitted, an arresting face. There was honesty and strength in the tilt of her chin and her wide brow, and when Ella felt uncertainty her face reflected that inner turmoil faithfully. Not a face, then, to keep a secret!

Her hair was not corn yellow but very fair, so pale it was almost silver. Her eyes were not deep blue like Kitty's, but paler, cooler, almost grey.

I am a woman without colour, Ella thought in surprise. A grey woman, a woman seen in moonlight with all the brightness washed out. A ghost. She shivered. Only her lips were bright, too bright. Their redness looked contrived, as if she were wearing rouge. There was a certain sensuousness about them that made Ella uneasy.

Outside the rooster crowed and made her jump. She touched the buttons at her throat nervously, and watched her reflection mimic the movement. The blue colour suited her, and the tight bodice outlined full breasts and a trim waist. Who are you? she asked the woman that was herself. Where do you belong?

But the only answer was silence.

Her stomach growled, destroying the seriousness of the moment and reminding her she had had no breakfast. Ella smiled, and cast a final sweeping glance over the elegantly furnished room before she closed the door.

The kitchen was as warm as last night. The young lad who had shown them the way to the stables was standing at the table, peeling potatoes. In a chair by the hearth, a clean-shaven stranger was reading a newspaper, his stockinged feet resting on a stool. At the sound of Ella's step, he glanced around and she saw surprise flash in his dark eyes. He stood up, putting the newspaper aside, and it was only then that Ella realised the stranger was Adam.

He'd washed his hair and he, or someone else, had trimmed it back to a more respectable length.

He'd shaved, too, and she saw that his jaw was strong and his mouth wide – a mouth made for smiling. Only his eyes were the same. Dark eyes beneath dark brows. She could not in all honesty have called him a handsome man, but it was a good-humoured face, an attractive face, a face to draw a second glance.

They stared at each other like strangers meeting for the very first time. And then Adam whistled admiringly under his breath and stepped back as if to take in the total picture. 'Well, Cinderella!'

'You look rather grand yourself,' she smiled. And then, remembering what Kitty had said about the dress, 'Thank you for this ... I believe it was Mrs Ure's?'

Something in his face made her suddenly, intensely aware of herself. 'It looks better on you.'

There was a warmth in his eyes, the admiration she had seen before. With flushed cheeks Ella glanced about her, seeking to change the subject. 'Where is she?'

'Nancy? She's gone to buy eggs.' His voice remained even, natural.

Aware that the boy peeling potatoes was openly eavesdropping, Ella moved closer. Obediently, Adam bent his head towards her. 'You know I can't repay you?' she murmured. 'I haven't any money.'

He shrugged as if it were a matter of indifference to him. 'Aye, well, we can settle up when we find out who you are. Unless,' and he raised an eyebrow at her, 'you've remembered already?'

But he could see she hadn't.

'Well,' he went on easily, 'no doubt it'll happen soon enough.'

Another thought came to her. 'There must be so many people coming and going through Sawpit Gully. Perhaps I could ask around? It would give me something to do.'

His eyes remained fixed on hers, and yet she felt as though something in them had shifted. 'I'll do that for you, Mrs Seaton,' he said quietly. 'You don't want to go out there among that mob. Some of them aren't too respectful when it comes to women.'

Ella gave Adam a doubtful look. 'I'm not afraid of bad language – ' she began.

Adam raised his eyebrows. 'It's not just bad language, Mrs Seaton. People disappear in Sawpit Gully, and they don't get found. There're some desperate characters about. You don't want to walk out alone, not even in daylight.'

A vision of him lying bleeding jumped into her mind. Unconsciously, Ella stepped even closer. 'Adam, you will take care?'

He tried to be suitably solemn, but the ready laughter was dancing in his eyes. 'I'm sorry – ' she began stiffly.

'Don't be. I like it. And don't worry about me. I'm used to taking care of meself.'

He sounded kind. Just as he had been kind to Kitty last night when he had refused her offer. The comparison gave Ella the jolt she needed to pull herself together.

'Kitty said something about breakfast,' she managed in her usual cool voice. Indeed, her head was spinning from hunger. Adam smiled and nodded towards the hearth, and Ella saw the plate there, set to one side. Fried chops and fried bread. She carried it gingerly to the table and set it down. The boy had finished peeling his potatoes and, with a shy glance at her, went out into the yard to dispose of the peelings.

An awkward silence hung over the room, and then Adam said, 'I'll go and see to Bess before I do some asking around.'

'Adam?' She looked up at him, a piece of chop halfway to her mouth. 'Is there someone else staying here besides us?'

He was puzzled. 'Not that I know of, why?'

'I ... it's just that in the room beside mine ... it looks so ...' But she had remembered now that she shouldn't have looked in, and her voice grew cooler as she tried to cover her awkwardness. 'There are a great many pretty things in there. I thought there might be another woman staying at the inn.'

His expression was momentarily blank, and then his mouth went grim. 'You'd be better not looking into other people's rooms, Mrs Seaton. If you saw something, then forget it. Curiosity can get you killed in Sawpit Gully.'

Startled, she put down the knife. 'I was only–'

'Forget it.' And he was gone, the door closing hard behind him.

Ella stared after him. He was angry with her! Just because she happened to notice how finely furnished one of the rooms was. It made no sense. Surely Adam, with his bushranger brother and questionable past, would be the last person to censor her behaviour? She picked up her food thoughtfully and began to chew. Well, one thing was certain, if Adam had hoped to stifle her curiosity with that outburst, he had done the exact opposite!

After breakfast, Ella sat and read the newspaper. It was several weeks old, and the headlines spoke of gold, gold and more gold. Kitty came and went, but said little. Out in the bar, Ella could hear a stirring as the citizens of Sawpit Gully came to life. Tobacco smoke drifted under the door into the kitchen.

Eventually Nancy Ure herself came in from the yard, her thin face flushed from the chill air. She gave Ella a look that was far from friendly, and dumped her basket onto the table. There were a number of eggs in it and a dead chicken, the limp head hanging grotesquely over the side. Ella flinched, sickened, and a smile touched the other woman's lips.

'And how is her *ladyship* today?'

'Much better, thank you,' Ella murmured politely, trying to ignore the sneer in Nancy's voice.

Nancy took the chicken out of the basket and dumped it onto the table beside Ella, laughing softly when she averted her eyes. 'Where's Adam?'

'Gone out,' Kitty answered her. 'Mrs Seaton wanted him to ask around for her, to see if anyone knew her.'

Nancy wasn't pleased with this revelation. Her black eyes gleamed with spite. 'Oh aye? Couldn't you do that for yourself? Or is it beneath you to talk with common folk?'

There was no mistaking the viciousness in her, but Ella was more surprised than affronted. There seemed no reason for Nancy Ure's hatred on such short acquaintance. Dislike, perhaps, would be understandable – Ella had not taken much to

Nancy, either – but not the deep hatred she saw in the other woman's eyes.

Nancy Ure had expected no answer to her question. 'This'll do for the soup tomorrow,' she told Kitty, nodding at the dead chicken. 'Add plenty o' water and it'll stretch to two dozen.'

Ella thought it would be a very watery concoction, but knew better than to say so aloud. Nancy Ure gave her another black glance and went out into the other room. Kitty took up the chicken, holding it by its trussed feet.

'Looks like I feel,' she said.

———◆———

Adam returned at midday, rubbing his cold hands, his hair lank from the wind. Ella noticed his beard was already a dark shadow on his jaw again. He grinned at her as he stripped off his jacket

'I reckon we've struck paydirt, Mrs Seaton.'

'Someone saw me?' She whispered the question, hardly daring to believe.

'Aye, someone saw you. A woman in one of the shanties. She remembers your red cloak. You rode through with your man.'

'I want to see her.'

Adam looked doubtful. 'I don't think that's a good idea – '

'I want to speak to her myself. I must, Adam.'

He pulled a face. 'Aye, well, if you *must*. But it's not the sort of place you'll be used to, Mrs Seaton.'

Ella gave him a wry look. 'I'm getting used to all sorts of places, Adam.'

The midday meal was a thick mutton stew with

potatoes and fresh bread still warm. Afterwards Nancy Ure went to take a nap and Kitty made them a cup of tea so strong Adam claimed he could eat it with a fork. Kitty laughed, deliberately widening her eyes at him. Ella put her hands around the warm mug and ignored her.

'Do you think it will rain again?' she asked Adam.

'Too cold,' he replied. 'I thought we might set off this afternoon, after we've spoken with that woman.'

Ella stiffened. Dismay filled her, her spirits plummeted, and she couldn't hide it. 'Of course,' she said, trying not to sound as downhearted as she felt.

But he must have known. He eyed her sideways and rubbed a thoughtful hand over his scratchy jaw. 'Maybe we can leave it one more day.'

Ella felt like hugging him, but contented herself with a breathtaking smile. He pretended not to notice.

Kitty, who had been watching them like a hawk, cut in. 'I was hopin' you might take me with you both, Adam. I want to go to Bendigo, and I'd feel safer travellin' with another woman.' She gave him a coy, slanting look. 'You know how wicked people's tongues can be when a man and a woman are travellin' alone together.'

There was a long silence. Ella didn't dare look at Adam; she fixed her eyes instead on the mug before her. 'Aye, I know,' he said at last. 'Can you pay your way? And I don't mean on your back.'

Ella was shocked and expected Kitty to be angry. But Kitty just laughed. 'I've some money put by. I can pay my way.' And there was something bold in her voice which was almost a challenge.

The two of them eyed each other warily, and then Adam nodded. 'All right.'

Kitty smiled back, slowly, and now the challenge was unmistakable. There was a tension between them that made Ella feel uncomfortable and out of place.

'How did you meet Mrs Ure?' She heard her own voice, sharp and strange, filling the silence.

Adam turned away from Kitty and met her eyes. For a moment he was a hard-faced stranger, and then all at once his expression slipped back into familiar lines. He smiled, and relaxed. 'Nancy ran an inn on the waterfront in San Francisco. It burnt down twice - San Francisco burned down regularly. When I came back from the mountains, I hardly recognised the place.' The memory seemed to amuse him, and he laughed.

'Where is her husband?'

The dark eyes narrowed. 'He died of a fever. She ran the place on her own after that. She could put the fear of God into the worst of 'em. But the Yankees got sick of us Sydney boys, and Nancy felt it'd be safer if she came home.'

'She hasn't changed.' Kitty's voice was tart. 'Everyone in Sawpit Gully thinks she's a witch.'

Adam snorted.

'You knew her well in San Francisco, didn't you?' Kitty asked him innocently.

Adam glanced at Ella. 'The Yankees didn't like anyone who wasn't one of them, so if you met someone from home you stuck together.'

'Oh? Stuck together?' Kitty mocked. It was as if she were goading him, looking for a reaction.

But Adam ignored her. He was watching Ella,

and suddenly he frowned as if he'd remembered something, and slipped his hand into his pocket. He placed a small blue bottle on the table between them. 'I forgot. Doctor Rawlins sent you this. You're to take a spoonful before bed.'

Ella looked at it a moment, and then at him. 'Thank you.'

'He wants to see you again before we go.'

Ella wondered what point there would be in that, but nodded all the same.

'He calls himself a doctor,' Kitty murmured, 'but no one knows for sure. He's a drinker, and people say somethin' happened to him ... his wife was sick and he made a mistake and she died. He came to Victoria to hide himself away.'

Men with pasts to hide seemed to be thick on the ground, Ella thought grimly. It was ironic, when all she wanted to do was *find* hers.

She cleared her throat. 'Can you take me to see the woman now? The one you said recognised me?'

There was a mocking light behind Adam's smile. 'You're sure about this?'

'What woman?' demanded Kitty.

'She calls herself Red Phebe.'

Kitty gave a crack of surprised laughter. 'Gawd, you're takin' *her*?' with a look at Ella, 'down there?'

'I want to go,' Ella said coldly.

Kitty laughed again, her bold eyes sliding back to Adam. 'She thinks I'm a bad woman,' she told him. 'Wait until she meets Red Phebe!'

CHAPTER 8

———•———

THE SHANTY WAS BUILT OF saplings laid horizontally, one on top of the other, with the bark still clinging to the wood, and bound together with straps of hide and rope. A flag fluttered wildly from a pole just outside the door, and a hand-painted sign offered drinks at good prices.

Adam pushed aside the tattered piece of cloth that served as a door, and Ella followed him inside. The smoke was so thick she could hardly see, and the air was heavy with alcohol, sweat and other even less savory aromas.

Adam gave her a look which she knew meant, 'I told you so'.

'Adam!'

The voice was deep and husky. Ella peered ahead, and made out a group around a table. One of them, a woman, rose to her feet. She was big and broad, and her green skirts dragged on the packed-earth floor, sweeping dust and debris before her.

'I've brought Mrs Seaton,' Adam said, and stepped aside so that Ella had no choice but to stop hiding behind him and come forward. She did so, lifting her chin to disguise a sudden urge to bolt.

Red Phebe had hair a very unnatural shade of red, on top of which was pinned a concoction of lace and ribbons. 'Adam 'ere says you don't remember much, Mrs Seaton.'

Ella found her voice. 'No, I don't.'

Red Phebe searched in the pocket of her dress and took out a short-stemmed clay pipe. She slid it into the corner of her mouth and lit it with a taper from the fire, puffing clouds of smoke up to join the rest. 'I saw you,' she spoke at last. 'You had on a red cloak, and you were ridin' like the devil hisself was after you. It was early, but I was up fetching water.'

Ella held her breath. She had ridden through Sawpit Gully early in the morning. She could see herself through Red Phebe's eyes, a cloaked figure, crouched low over the mare's neck, riding ... Riding where? And where had she come from? It seemed unlikely that she had travelled all night. She must have stayed somewhere close and made an early start. Slowly, she spoke her thoughts aloud.

'Maybe you slept rough,' Adam suggested.

But Red Phebe shook her head. 'Don't look like the sort to sleep rough. Could've stayed the night at Weatherby's.'

Ella turned to Adam. 'Weatherby's? What's that?'

But he didn't know, and it was Red Phebe who answered for him. 'A sheep station. The Weatherbys are squatters. They run sheep and a few cattle, sell 'em to the goldfields. Most of 'em are too old to be anything but string and gristle, but the diggers can't afford to be fussy. They'll eat anything.'

'Where is it?' Ella asked, excitement filling her.

'You go about two miles north along the Bendigo road, and then head east for five.'

'What about the man with her?' Adam was asking. 'What was he like?'

Red Phebe shrugged indifferently. 'Dark hair, skinny … nothin' much to look at.' Her eyes swept admiringly over Adam, the glance saying more than words ever could about her preference in men. Ella tried not to smile. 'He rode a few paces behind her. Could've been her 'usband, I suppose, but he was more like her servant. Not that some men aren't one and the same!' with a guffaw loud enough to shake the rafters. 'Maybe she bought 'im in Bendigo to keep her warm on the journey. Sorry luv,' she added, winking at Ella, and then laughed again.

Adam smiled, but somehow Ella did not think he was amused.

'You stayin' at Nancy Ure's?' Red Phebe went on, her voice dropping another octave.

'Aye, that's right.'

Red Phebe's lip curled. 'It's women like her give this place a bad name.'

Outside, the cold caught Ella's breath, and made her eyes water and her ears ache. It was dark, the bad weather turning afternoon to night. The distant hills rose bleakly to a bleak sky. A few hardy souls were going about their business, but most were huddled inside the shanties and grog shops, seeking oblivion.

'The Weatherbys must know who I am!' Ella gasped, hurrying to catch up with Adam's long strides.

'Maybe. If you stayed there.'

'Red Phebe is quite right, you know. I don't think I'd ever slept rough before I met you.'

He gave a brief, humourless laugh.

'If there was a bed available, I'd have taken it. And if the Weatherbys were known to me I'd be more likely to stay there than at Sawpit Gully or to camp out in the rain.'

'Aye, well, nobody camps out in the rain unless they have to.'

Ella realised then that she might have hurt his feelings, and reached out to grasp his arm. He stopped, surprised, and glanced down at her. 'I didn't mean ...' But he stayed silent, and the words failed her. 'Thank you for finding Red Phebe,' she said at last, awkwardly. 'I'm sure I could never have done it on my own.'

'Aye, well, I'm used to pokin' around in the dirt,' he replied grimly. 'You can buy men like me in any town.'

Something *had* hurt him, but she didn't know what. 'Do you think we can stop at this sheep station tomorrow?' She sounded diffident. 'Is it far out of your way?'

'It's not far out of me way.' Suddenly he put out a hand and touched her nose with his finger. 'You're turning blue,' he told her bluntly. 'Do you want to see the doctor while we're out here? Save us doing it tomorrow, then we can get an early start'

'Yes, all right'

Again he set off with her following.

The sky was getting darker by the moment, and calico and bark roofs flapped and rattled in the wind, despite their anchorings of slabs and stones. Ella kept her head down, picking her way over muddy cart tracks. A few bleary-eyed miners were wandering about in their uniform of moleskin trousers and woollen shirts. Some had on the high boots made popular by the Californians, others more modest gear. Most wore cabbage-tree hats, their hair and beards long and untrimmed.

A woman passed them, her hips swinging in a flashy yellow dress, but when she lifted her hem to step over a mud puddle, her petticoat was old and dirty.

Adam bent towards Ella, his breath like a puff of smoke. 'You can get married in Sawpit Gully for a couple of shillings. An' the marriage lasts as long as your gold lasts.'

'Why not get married properly?' she replied, puzzled.

Adam shrugged. 'There're not enough women here to go around, or the man might already have a wife back home, or maybe he doesn't want a wife to keep.' The expression on her face seemed to amuse him. 'You don't approve?'

Ella shook her head, the cold wind whipping colour into her cheeks. 'No, I don't.'

'Would you be me wife for a day, Mrs Seaton, if I had pockets full of gold?'

The question surprised her. She frowned at his profile as he walked beside her, trying to read his mood. 'No,' she said at last, firmly, 'I wouldn't. I don't believe marriage should be something you buy with gold.'

He turned his head and considered her serious expression. 'What would it take for you to marry a man then, Mrs Seaton? Why did you marry the man you've got?'

'Why?' she repeated. 'How should I know? I've lost my memory, Adam.'

'But a loss of memory don't alter a woman's character. What would a lady like you marry for?'

She didn't know what he was seeking from her,

and she didn't like the way he was doing it. There was something different about Adam today. He seemed less easy-going, his usual smile gone.

'I suppose a lady might marry for position, for duty – '

'Position and duty,' he cut in quickly. 'Isn't that just a clever way of sayin' money?'

Ella made an irritated movement of her hand. 'You didn't let me finish. I meant to add love to the list.'

'Oh, love!' he mocked. 'I thought that was for us lower classes. I thought ladies like you married men picked out by their fathers. Isn't that the way it goes?'

There was a bitterness in his voice she had never heard before. A terrible suspicion was forming in her mind.

'Adam,' Ella asked him quietly, 'do you mean to tell me that if you had pockets full of gold, you'd ask me to be your wife for a day?'

As soon as she said it, she regretted it. She didn't want to know his answer. How would they continue travelling together if he said yes? She would have to leave him and find other transport to Weatherby's station. And how could she do that without any money? She needed Adam's protection and friendship, and she was prepared to give him the same in return. But nothing more.

Perhaps he read the rejection in her face, or perhaps he had only been amusing himself with idle questions after all, for when he spoke again it was to announce in an even voice: 'Here we are.' And looking around, Ella realised they had reached the home of Doctor Rawlins.

It was a hut, built of slabs, although it looked more solid and draft-free than others she had seen. There was a brush fence around it, and a sign hanging from the gate, giving his name and calling. Unnervingly, the hut next to Doctor Rawlins's also had a sign outside, stating baldly: *Undertaker.*

Adam held open the gate for Ella, but didn't follow. 'I'll come back for you,' he murmured, hunching his shoulders against the wind.

'Very well.' Her voice sounded polite but cold. She was withdrawing from him, putting him in his place. Something flashed in his eyes, but he turned away without answering, and Ella watched him go with a sense of relief.

It was only when she had knocked on the door that she remembered what Kitty had said about the doctor being a drinker. She looked over her shoulder, tempted to call Adam back, but didn't. And then the door opened, and the doctor peered out at her. As far as she could tell, he was completely sober.

'Come in and sit down, dear lady.' Doctor Rawlins stepped back, and Ella followed him into the cosy little front room. A fire was blazing, and the tempting smell of coffee drew her closer to the hearth where a pot was heating. While the little man poured the strong brew into cups, Ella warmed her hands and glanced surreptitiously about her.

The room was cluttered, but pleasantly so. Books and papers covered most surfaces, and the unsmiling portrait of a young woman hung in the shadows on the far wall. A sheepskin dangled over a doorway leading to another room at the back – no doubt the doctor's bedroom.

'I regret I have neither milk nor sugar.'

Ella turned and found a cup held out to her. Doctor Rawlins leaned closer as she sipped, eyeing her with a look of professional interest. 'Not remembered anything yet? Well, that's to be expected! One day it'll come back, and then everything will be revealed, eh?'

The coffee was wonderfully hot and fragrant. Ella savoured it a moment before she answered. 'I expect one day I *will* remember everything. Only ...' she hesitated, frowning. It was as if Adam's strange behaviour had triggered something in herself that she was only now able to put into words. 'Only, sometimes, I wonder whether I might be better off not remembering,' Ella blurted out. 'I have dreams, but I don't remember what they're about, not properly. It's like ... well, it's like a perfume lingering in a room long after the wearer has departed. Something similar remains after my dreams, some *feeling* ... And it isn't a nice feeling ...' She shook her head. 'I'm sorry, I'm not making myself very clear.'

Doctor Rawlins leaned back, his stomach bulging under his waistcoat. His little eyes were suddenly very bright. 'Hmmm. Well, have you thought, my dear lady, that your mind does not yet want to remember? Sometimes there are experiences with which the mind is not strong enough to cope, not immediately. Only when your mind is ready will you remember.'

Ella could understand the sense of what he was saying, and yet.... She shook her head decisively. 'I don't care what it is, or how upsetting it might be, I *want* to remember!'

Doctor Rawlins smiled and leaned forward to pat her hand with his plump white fingers. 'In time, in time.' He proffered the coffee pot. 'More coffee?'

She accepted, tempted by the fire and the doctor's company as much as the coffee. It was a relief to be able to relax, away from Adam and Nancy Ure and Kitty.

'How do you find our little community?' he asked her in a conversational tone, stretching his short legs towards the fire.

'I've not seen much of it. And I've met so few people ...You and Mrs Ure and Red Phebe ...'

His eyes popped slightly. 'Well, Red Phebe. Yes. Hmmm.' He hesitated, and suddenly leaned closer in an almost intimate manner. Startled, Ella met his reddened eyes, and saw they were bright with a sense of urgency. 'I wonder if I might give you a word of warning, Mrs Seaton?'

'Do you think I need one, doctor?'

'Perhaps, perhaps. You have a certain innocence, Mrs Seaton. A certain naivete. A rare commodity in such a place as this. I don't wish you to become involved in something that may harm you.'

Colour tinted Ella's cheeks. 'If you mean to warn me against Adam – ' she began. But the doctor forestalled her.

'You should not remain at Mrs Ure's establishment. I'm afraid she is a most undesirable hostess.'

Ella stared. 'I don't understand.'

The little man shifted uneasily in his chair. 'I have contact with the authorities – in short, the police – and she is well known to them. And it is certainly not for her kind heart!'

Ella's eyes widened. 'You mean Mrs Ure is a

criminal?'

Doctor Rawlins straightened his collar. 'I would rather not say more on the matter, other than to advise you to leave as soon as possible. There are plans afoot to put a stop to her activities.'

'But surely, doctor, you can tell me what she is supposed to have done?'

Again the doctor fiddled with his collar. He was frightened. The realisation startled her. 'I believe ...' he began, and gave a little cough. 'I believe there have been several guests who stayed at Mrs Ure's inn who were subsequently robbed or ... simply disappeared.'

'Disappeared?' she repeated loudly.

He jumped. 'Please,' he whispered anxiously, 'there is nothing proved. There is only talk.'

'Does Adam know?' Ella breathed, more to herself than Doctor Rawlins.

But it was the doctor who answered. 'I believe Adam is an old friend of Mrs Ure's. Anyone who is a friend of that woman must be tarred with the same brush, and therefore not to be trusted.'

Ella bit down an urge to argue. The doctor did not know Adam as she did, she reminded herself. But his words had made her uneasy. 'Why did you tell me this?'

The little eyes fixed on hers, and he seemed to be debating whether or not to answer. 'You remind me of someone,' he said at last, and stood up. 'I hear your friend outside.'

He was right Adam's boots sounded on the path, followed by his knock at the door. Ella rose to her feet; she was taller than Doctor Rawlins. 'You didn't examine my head,' she reminded him.

But the doctor smiled. 'I didn't intend to. You are almost healed in body. The rest will come in its own time.'

On the way to the door, she glanced at the portrait It was indeed of a young woman. Fair hair, blue eyes, a wistful expression. There was a slight resemblance to Ella. Was this his wife, she wondered, whose death had sent him running to Victoria? Was this who Ella reminded him of?

Well, whatever his reason for giving it, Ella sensed Doctor Rawlins's warning had been no idle one. And whether it was warranted or not, it had taken courage.

'Thank you,' she said, resting her hand on the latch.

He nodded, his face suddenly yellowy and old. She sensed he wanted her to go now, he wanted to be alone. Perhaps he wanted a drink.

Adam was waiting outside. There must have been something in her expression, for his own became inquiring. Was Doctor Rawlins right? Ella wondered. Was Adam in league with Nancy Ure? Would he really harm her? Perhaps she did have a certain naivete, as the doctor said, because she was finding it difficult to believe he was capable of it.

'Mrs Seaton?' He was holding out a hand to help her down the step.

As she gave him her fingers, Ella had the odd fancy that he could sense the doctor's warning just by touching her. Suddenly she knew she didn't want him to know what had been said. Not until she had thought about it more fully. After all, could she really be sure of his innocence? Could she really make such an important judgment on so short an acquaintance? She pulled away, and brushed by him, setting off towards the gate.

He followed her out. 'What is it?' he asked her evenly.

Ella paused to negotiate a puddle. 'Everything is perfectly all right.' She answered him stiffly, and hurried on. The coffee buoyed her up; she hardly seemed to feel the cold.

'I don't think it is,' he said behind her. 'But if you don't mean to tell me, I can't make you.'

Ella kept walking. No, she thought. No, you can't. She made certain that she stayed just far enough ahead of him to make conversation impossible. When they reached the inn, and Adam left her to go and check on Bess, she avoided his eyes. Adam and Nancy Ure, she thought. How could she trust either of them?

In the kitchen, Mrs Ure herself was dealing with a joint of mutton, bringing the meat cleaver down with savage regularity. Ella tried not to flinch. The black eyes were as vicious as ever.

'How's the doctor today then? Sober?'

'Perfectly. We had coffee.'

Nancy Ure snorted. Ella moved to the fire and held out her hands. What did Nancy do with the guests who had disappeared? Chop them up like that mutton? Ella's hands began to tremble.

The cleaver continued to bang down onto the block.

Ella glanced surreptitiously at the other woman, taking in the hard face and cruel mouth. Suddenly she knew the doctor was telling the truth. Nancy was quite capable of all he had accused her. Ella took a deep breath. Tomorrow couldn't come too soon for her, and she was sure she wouldn't sleep a wink tonight.

When Adam joined them, saying he was hungry enough to eat Bess, Kitty laughed. And monopolised him from that moment on. She hung on his every word, and Ella knew it was not for the content of what he was saying. She could see Adam knew it, too, and it amused him. His words to her earlier seemed unreal ... a dream. She could only conclude that he had been amusing himself then, and now he was amusing himself with Kitty.

When we reach the Weatherbys' tomorrow, Ella told herself, I will stay with them. Even if they don't know me. Surely anything is better than travelling with Adam and Kitty?

'So you'll be off in the mornin'?' Nancy cut short the flirtation.

'Aye,' Adam answered her. 'Me and Mrs Seaton'll be off first thing.'

'And Kitty, too,' Ella murmured, still deep in her own thoughts.

Too late she saw Kitty's furious glance. It was the first time it had occurred to her that the girl hadn't told Nancy Ure of her impending departure. And now Nancy's black eyes were narrowing dangerously.

'What's this about?' She looked from one to the other. 'Kitty's not goin' nowhere.'

Adam said nothing and Ella tried to shrink down into her chair. Kitty had no choice but to brazen it out. 'I'm goin' to Bendigo,' she said boldly. 'You can't stop me. I don't owe you nothin'.'

Slowly Nancy Ure's mouth curled up into a cruel smile. 'You're makin' a mistake if you think you can throw your lot in with Adam. What would he want with a little slut like you?'

'I'm not like that!' Kitty shouted, her face turning bright pink with hurt and anger.

'Anyway,' Nancy went on, ignoring the outburst, 'I don't trust you not to talk out of turn. I want you here, where I can keep an eye on you.'

'No,' whispered Kitty, her eyes bright with tears.

It was too much for Ella. 'Surely,' she heard herself saying in a voice desperately trying to sound reasonable, 'Kitty has a right to leave if she wants to?'

Nancy flicked a look at her that was colder than the wind outside. 'Tell your bitch to shut her mouth, Adam.'

'Nancy,' Adam warned quietly.

'It's none of her business!' Nancy cut in furiously. 'You brought her here, you keep her quiet! Kitty stays until I say different.'

Ella looked at him, expecting him to stand up for her, to stand up for Kitty. But he said nothing. 'Adam?' she whispered, unable to believe he would let such a thing pass without a fight.

'Nancy's right.' His voice was sharp, as it had never been before with her. 'It's none of our business.'

Shocked, Ella said nothing. She knew now, terrible as it was, that Doctor Rawlins must be right. Adam was not to be trusted, he was in league with Nancy Ure, he was as bad as Nancy Ure!

Nancy was smiling, as if she had proved her point. 'Adam never did let his feelings get in the way of business.'

Yesterday Ella would have said Nancy was wrong, but now she was very much afraid Nancy was right.

She couldn't look at him – she felt sick with fear and disappointment. It seemed foolish now, but she had thought Adam better than that.

For supper, Kitty served the watery chicken soup. If Ella had not been so hungry, and conscious that tomorrow she may have no food and no money to pay for it, she would have gladly gone without. As it was she and Adam sat silently at the table, while Kitty moved back and forth, her eyes suspiciously red. Nancy Ure was stirring a hot toddy she had been busy concocting from a number of different bottles and jars. The smell of it was enough to clear Ella's head.

Outside the wind moaned and the trees swayed and groaned. Tonight, the inn was under siege from the weather. Adam went out again to make sure the cart was ready for the morning, and Nancy Ure sent Kitty to serve in the bar. Ella, realising it would be just herself and Nancy, went to rise, intending to retire. She had no desire for a tête-à-tête.

But Nancy obviously had other ideas. Her voice was soft and vicious, like a snake striking. 'You think Adam's your white knight, don't you? But Adam never does nothing without wanting something in return. I wonder what he wants from you?'

Ella gripped her hands tightly together under the table and lifted her chin to show she wasn't afraid. 'You seem to know everything about him, why don't you tell me?'

'Oh, I will!' There was a savage amusement in her

face; she was enjoying herself. 'He looks as mild as soap, don't he? But I've seen him beat a man until he couldn't walk. When I had my inn, in San Francisco, I paid him to deal with any troublemakers. Let's just say he earned his money.'

'This has nothing to do with me, Mrs Ure.' Ella tried to keep her voice calm.

Nancy smiled a slow smile. 'Frightens you, does it? He used to frighten me, too, and I don't frighten easily. He has a vicious temper. That's why I left him.'

Suddenly Ella's revulsion turned to anger.

'Adam has hardly mentioned you at all, Mrs Ure. I'm not interested in his past history.'

'But it isn't the past.' She smiled at Ella. 'I mean to have him back.'

As if on cue the door banged open. Wolf ran in and Adam followed, shaking the rain from his hair with a laugh, his face flushed and alive from the cold. Ella turned to stare at him, still shocked from Nancy's words. She felt a strange sense of helplessness, as if she had no power over what was about to happen.

Nancy Ure moved swiftly to the fire, tipping some of her hot toddy into a mug. She turned and held it out to Adam. As if in a dream Ella saw their eyes meet with a look; a look between two people who knew each other very well. She wanted to get up and leave the room, but she couldn't. Her legs had lost all their strength.

'Adam,' Nancy murmured, her voice softer than Ella had ever heard it She moved closer, leaning against him in a way that was very deliberate. 'I've thought about you a lot since California. Have you thought about me, Adam?'

'I've thought about you,' he replied, just as softly, but with a certain wariness. His glance flicked sideways to Ella.

Nancy laughed, pleased by his answer. 'Remember how it used to be? Remember how we lay in my bed, Adam? Like spoons we were –'

'I remember.' He said it quickly. There was something taut in his stance, as if he were forcing himself to remain still.

'I've been waiting for you to come to me,' Nancy murmured. 'I'm tired of waiting.' And then, deliberately, shockingly, she reached up and pulled his face down to hers, her mouth fastening greedily over his. It was as if she wanted to devour him.

And even worse, thought Ella, sickened, was the way Adam just stood there and let her.

'Well, ain't this a pretty picture?'

The deep voice came from the direction of the yard. Ella realised the dream was turning into a nightmare. Eben stood there, as wild as the wild night, his dark hair plastered to his head with rain, his smile flashing white through his beard. The recklessness Ella remembered was in his eyes.

Nancy Ure didn't even flinch. She finished her kiss and then turned nonchalantly towards the bushranger. 'Have you gone mad?' she remarked coldly. 'Do you know what'll happen if you're seen here?'

Eben came in and shut the door. 'I've come to see me little brother,' he retorted. 'I didn't expect you to be slobberin' all over him, Nance. Not in front of his wife, anyway.' And he grinned at Ella. 'Good evening, Adam's wife.'

There was a deathly silence; even the customers in the bar seemed hushed. And then a log fell in the fire, and it was as if the sound released them. Nancy Ure hissed with fury. 'His wife? This bitch is his *wife*?' Her finger was pointing at Ella like a gun.

Eben's face was almost comical in its dismay. 'What, didn't he tell yer? Oh Adam,' and he shook his head at his brother, 'what have yer been up to?'

'I know why he didn't tell me!' Nancy shouted. 'Because he knew I wouldn't give him a bed! I'd have thrown him out on his arse!'

She aimed a blow at Adam's face, but he ducked and she caught him on the shoulder. Eben was there in two strides, grabbing her wrists and pulling her away.

'Don't upset yourself, Nance,' he was saying.

But she struggled, twisting with rage, her fingers like claws. 'You're as bad as him!' she spat 'Go on, get out the lot o' you!'

'Come on, Nance,' Eben begged, his eyes brimming with laughter. 'You can't throw us out on a night like this. It's not fit for a dog.'

Nancy's reply was so foul, Ella found it incomprehensible.

Adam hadn't spoken since Eben's arrival, but now he did, his tone contrite. 'I'm sorry, Nancy. I should've said. But Ella was done in, and I wanted her to have a bit of comfort. I thought you'd have put all that behind you.'

'You thought!' Nancy spat, her vicious eyes shining with tears. 'You were always the same. You used me, Adam. I don't ever want to see you again. And as for her,' and she spun to face Ella, 'she can get out of my sight before I kill her!'

The hate was there in Nancy's white face and rigid body, a palpable thing. Ella believed at that moment the other woman really did mean to kill her. She stood up, her legs shaking, and felt Adam grip her arm, holding her upright. 'Come on,' he said.

It was quiet in the passage. Adam led Ella into her bedroom and shut the door. He leaned back against it and let out his breath in relief. She stared at him, not knowing what to expect, and saw the gleam of amusement come into his eyes. How could he find humour in a situation like this, when Ella was white-faced and shaking? Perhaps he read the outrage in her expression, for his voice was apologetic.

'I didn't realise she'd still feel like that about me. I wouldn't have come here if I'd known.'

Ella couldn't hide her disbelief. 'Why *did* you come here?'

'I said why. Because of you. I'd never have come near the place otherwise.' Maybe he was telling the truth, but did that cancel out the rest of Ella's doubts?

'Why did you let her kiss you like that? As if she owned you.' She heard the anger in her voice with surprise. She had not realised she felt angry until now.

Adam smiled wryly and looked away. 'She did own me once, in a way. But that wasn't the reason this time. I let her kiss me because Nancy's a very dangerous woman. You don't insult her, not if you can help it. And that's why I didn't argue with her, Cinderella, though I knew you were waitin' for me to stand up and do a Mr Morris. I'd rather Nancy call you names than cut your throat. I'd probably have done more than kiss her, if I had to.'

Ella stared back at him, trying to read his face – the face she had once thought so open and honest. And it was open to her now, his expression a mixture of self-mockery and disgust.

The words came of their own volition. 'Doctor Rawlins warned me against Mrs Ure today. He said that sometimes her guests were robbed or simply disappeared. Is that why her room is so fine? Does she decorate it with stolen goods? Is that why you didn't want me to see it or speak of it?'

'Yes. Dangerous country, Cinderella.' But there was a new alertness in his expression. He took a step towards her, lowering his voice. 'What else did the doctor say?'

'He told me in confidence,' Ella said, staring at her hands twisting in her lap.

He crouched down in front of her and took her hands in his. She let them lie there, loosely, as he gazed at their entwined fingers. 'Tell me,' he said quietly. 'I need to know what he said. You trust me, don't you?' He looked up then, catching her gaze, his own searching. And she knew that she did.

'Yes.' Somehow she got the word out.

'Good.' He squeezed her hands. 'Tell me.'

'He told me that I should leave here as soon as possible. That he had contact with   the authorities and they knew about Mrs Ure. They plan to deal with her, you see.'

Her voice ran out. Adam was frowning at her, but she knew he wasn't really seeing her. 'Sounds like a warning to me. I'd better tell me brother.' Then, in a different tone, 'I won't let anything happen to you. If you can't believe anything else I say, believe that.'

And then he winked at her, and straightened. 'You look tired, wife. Get some sleep.'

'But I thought Mrs Ure wanted us to leave now,' she said anxiously.

'Eben'll talk her around. We'll leave first thing in the morning ... dawn if we have to.' He paused before he closed the door. 'And take your medicine.'

The room was cold. Shivering, Ella undressed and put on her nightdress. She brushed out her hair, running her fingers through it. The fine mass of it felt warm about her shoulders so she left it. She climbed into the bed and pulled the bedclothes up to her chin.

The candle flame dipped and dived, making waves on the walls. Outside the rain fell in a soft, steady patter, like many little feet running. Rain or not, she thought with a shiver, she would be gone from this place in the morning.

Today, she had learned things she had rather not, about herself as well as Adam and Nancy. She realised now that Nancy was right in one respect: she had wanted to make Adam her knight. And in a way, he was. But there was another, darker side to him that had been hidden from her until now.

'I'd probably have done more than kiss her, if I had to,' he had said. Remembering the kiss, Ella shivered again, and suddenly that hot, shaky feeling was back, and in her head it was not Nancy kissing Adam, but Ella.

Angrily, she blew out the candle. The darkness was complete. I won't think of it, she told herself firmly. Tomorrow I'll go to the Weatherbys', and who knows what may come from that. Excitement sparked inside her, and although she tried to damp it down, it continued to grow. The inn creaked and somewhere a dog barked. Gradually the tension left her body, and sleep took her down.

CHAPTER 9

———◆———

*S*HE WAS IN A DARK *place.*
It was long and narrow, like a tunnel. And yet she knew it was no tunnel. Her feet were bare, soft carpet beneath them. Close beside her, hanging along the wall, were portraits in gilded frames. Their faces were frozen, but their eyes watched her passing. Ahead of her light spilled from an open doorway. In its glow she could make out a polished cedar doorjamb, and a section of the carpet runner, rich in reds and greens and black.

She was moving slowly, as if she were pushing through some thick, sluggish liquid. Gradually the doorway drew closer, and she heard voices. They were coming from within the room. Hushed voices. Secrets.

What were they saying? She wanted to hear, she was desperate to hear! But at the same time, she was afraid. There was a sick feeling in her stomach and her palms were sweating. Secrets, so many secrets. Sometimes it was wiser to stop your ears, to close your eyes. Sometimes it was wiser not to remember.

———◆———

A warm hand covered her mouth. The dream shimmered, turning into a whirl of confused colours and sensations. And suddenly Ella was awake, and the hand was real, and someone's warm breath was tickling her cheek in the darkness.

He whispered, 'Don't scream. Please.'

Adam! She blinked up at him, a dark shadow against the paler shape of the window. What was he doing here? Fear went rushing through her body, raising goosebumps oh her skin. Oh please, not that, not that, not from him ...

And then she heard the other sounds, outside in the yard. The rattle of stones, and a footfall beyond the window. Someone whispered, harsh, urgent.

Ella felt her scalp prickle. She saw Adam turn slightly, listening too. 'I'm sorry,' he breathed, 'but it's not what you think, Cinderella.' For a shocking moment, his cold arm brushed against her breast

He laughed softly and a little wildly. 'This is almost worth bein' hanged for.'

Ella tried to shake his hand off her mouth, and when he wouldn't remove it, pulled at his fingers. His face came down so close to hers that she could see the gleam of his eyes.

'You hear that noise, Mrs Seaton? I took a little look through a gap in the wall. There're troopers out there ... mounted police.'

Finally she had his hand free. She swallowed, making her voice small. 'But why? Why are they here? Why – '

'It's Eben,' he cut in. 'They must have followed him, and now they think they have him in his nest.' He hesitated, and then explained. 'He and Nancy are partners. She lets him know when she has guests worth robbing, and he follows them and does the deed. As for disappearing ... I know nothin' of that.'

Ella shivered. Eben and Nancy Ure were of a kind, a bushranger and his accomplice. And Adam ... where did he fit in?

Perhaps he guessed her thoughts, for he said bluntly, 'Nancy and me were living as man and wife in San Francisco. When I met her, she was running an inn on the waterfront. She made me an offer ... I was to make sure she had no trouble and she'd pay me. I needed the money; I did the job.'

A dog barked somewhere in the town and they were both still, listening. After a moment, he went on. 'Her husband was dead by then. She was lonely, and I was there. Well, you don't need me to tell you what happened, Mrs Seaton. But it didn't last. I didn't like what she was doing then and I don't like it any better now. She's a dangerous woman; one you don't cross if you can help it.' His voice was grim. 'There were men crossed her in California, and they're dead.'

It explained Adam's caution when it came to Nancy - if anyone knew of what she was capable, he did.

'Where are Eben and Nancy now? Do they know the troopers are here?'

'They're gone. I told them what the doctor said. Eben wasn't going to hang around after that, and Nancy decided to go with him. She said she'd just about run out of luck here anyway.'

Ella felt him move and again his arm brushed her breast. Her voice came out in a strangled shout: 'Adam, just what are you doing here!'

He cursed softly. They were silent again, listening. A shadow hovered briefly at the window, and then pulled away. Ella took a breath. There was a sense of unreality about the whole situation.

'What are you doing here?' she repeated. 'If they're gone, shouldn't you go too?'

He sighed, and then he said quietly, 'I'm not running with them. I said I'd stay an' take me chances ... hold things up so they can get a good start' She heard a dry note come into his voice. 'Of course there's always the chance they'll find out I'm Eben's brother, and think we were in it together. In that case, they'll take me down to Melbourne and charge me, and I'll be locked away.'

'Adam,' she gasped. 'We should never have come here. Oh Adam, I'm sorry.'

'It doesn't matter,' he murmured. He moved again, easing cramped muscles. He smelled of wood smoke and horse and, underlying it all, Nancy Ure's rose petal soap.

She whispered, 'I'll tell them you're a good man.' And she knew it was true. Somehow Adam had escaped the contamination of his brother.

'You'll say nothing,' he said gently. 'You're not involved in this.'

'But I am! And I won't let you go to gaol.'

He laughed softly against her ear, his lips brushed her skin. The contact produced a tingle that ran all the way down to her toes. 'You're a fine woman, Mrs Seaton.'

She put out her hand to push him away, but he turned his face into her palm, kissing her. Ella knew she should protest, but the feel of his mouth sapped her strength. Even her voice sounded weak.

'Adam, you mustn't.'

'If I'm going to spend the rest of my life in Melbourne Gaol, I want something to remember.' But there was a question in his voice, and Ella knew he would do nothing without her compliance.

It was impossible, unthinkable. The chasm of

class, of their vastly different lives, yawned between them. Ella would not attempt to cross it

'No, Adam,' she managed. 'No!'

He sighed, and moved away from her.

There was no sound outside now, apart from the rain. Perhaps, Ella thought, it was all a mistake, perhaps there had been no one there after all.

'I can't hear the troopers,' she said sharply.

'They're there. They must've left their horses down the track a bit 'cause they came up on foot. I watched them surround the place. They must have been hoping to surprise Eben and Nancy in bed.'

'You should try to get away.'

'No,' he said flatly. 'I'm not shooting anybody and I'm not being shot. I'll bluff me way out of it, if I can. And if not ...'

'But I don't understand! Who is there to say that you are involved with Eben? Kitty won't talk, and with Eben and Nancy gone ...'

He sighed as if she were very obtuse. 'The doctor, Mrs Seaton. He heard Nancy call me her friend. He'll stand in the witness box and swear me life away.'

'But – '

'Hush.'

Ella swallowed her words, though they were like painful lumps in her throat. She couldn't believe there wasn't some way to save him from the fate he had painted. Her mind raced around, going nowhere, while he waited, gathering his own words.

'You must get to Weatherby's,' he told her calmly. 'If they know who you are, then you're safe. If they can't help you, you'll have to go on to Bendigo.

When you get there, go to the commissioner. He'll know what to do.'

She wondered how he could worry about her at such a time. 'Here.' He pressed a rough-textured cloth bag into her hand. She felt the shape of coins.

'I can't,' she gasped, trying to push it back, but he folded her fingers over it and held them there.

'I've got no family ... no wife, I mean. And I promised to see you safe. I still mean to carry out that promise.'

'You've been so kind to me,' her voice was shaking. 'And now you'll be sent to gaol because of that kindness.'

Abruptly, he pulled her against him. She felt the warm, bare skin of his arms; her hands went out to push him away and clung instead. His hair tickled her nose, and his jaw was sharp with stubble.

'It's been a pleasure knowing you, Mrs Seaton,' he murmured, his voice deep and soft.

The door slammed back against the wall so hard that a piece fell off it. Ella screamed. Boots thudded into the room and a lamp shone out, throwing the nightmare shadows of men high on the walls and ceiling. In the room next door there were similar sounds, as if a herd of cattle were reeking havoc amongst Nancy's treasure.

Adam jumped up, his hair wild and his naked chest gleaming. Ella saw that he was wearing his moleskins and nothing else. There were four men, one in a trooper's uniform, the others in civilian clothing. To Ella they seemed like giants.

'Name, sir!' one of them demanded, his voice harsh and unfriendly. Ella held the bedclothes against her like a shield.

'What the – ' Adam began.

But they were unimpressed. 'Get him!' the trooper ordered curtly. Two of the men grabbed Adam and began hauling him across the room. He struggled, but there were too many willing to hold him.

'What the hell is goin' on?' he demanded. 'Burstin' in on Mrs Seaton like this – '

Out in the passage, more boots thumped towards Ella's door. A man's face hung like a pale moon in the darkness of the doorway. 'The bird's flown,' he muttered, rolling his eyes. 'And taken the woman with 'im by the look of it. The lieutenant's come all this way to surround an empty inn.'

There was a silence. Ella glanced sideways at Adam, but he was watching the troopers.

'How in God's name did he get away? Go and look for him! He might be hiding.' The shouted words came from the adjacent room and made everyone jump. The troopers shifted uneasily, plainly uncertain how to proceed. There were more footsteps in the passage, brisk and business-like, and another man entered the room.

He was also dressed in uniform, but his face was flushed with anger, and his hair was untidy where he had been running his hands through it. Ella blinked. It was Lieutenant Moggs from Carlsruhe.

'Right, what do we have here?' He asked the question with all the arrogance of a man who expects an immediate answer. His gaze swept the room as his second in command stammered a garbled account of Adam's resistance. 'Yes, yes, yes,' Moggs snapped impatiently. His eyes narrowed on Ella, and he came and stood by the bed, frowning down at her from what seemed a great height. Ella looked back up at him, feeling not unlike a cornered animal.

'I know you, don't I?' He shot the words at her with all the force of a loaded pistol.

It seemed to Ella that there was a sudden, unnatural stillness. 'Yes,' she managed.

'Name?'

'This is Mrs Seaton,' Adam snarled, finally wrenching his arms out of the grip of the two troopers who held him.

The light of illumination shone in the lieutenant's eyes. 'I remember now. I saw you at the police station in Carlsruhe. You were wearing rags and dripping vermin, and when I offered to take you to Melbourne, you preferred the company of this fellow.' And he nodded at Adam, letting his expression say what he would not.

Suddenly it was all too much for Ella – the insults, his manner, his twisting of the truth. Anger flooded her with a violence that overcame all fear. She sat up, her eyes blazing, too furious to care about the impropriety of allowing the men to see her nightgown. Her pale hair hung about her, and fury stung her cheeks into two bright circles of red, matching the flame of her lips. Every eye in the room fastened on her in stunned surprise and, in all cases but one, admiration.

'You offered to take me to Melbourne, *when* you were finished chasing bushrangers,' her tone was withering. 'And very unhelpful you were about it, too! It mattered more to you that I was unsuitably dressed than I was destitute. If I had fallen dead on your doorstep, sir, I believe you would simply have stepped over my body!'

An awkward pause followed. Some of the troopers smirked, flicking glances at their leader to see how he was taking it. He was not taking it well; he was not used to being spoken to like this. An icy fury hardened Moggs's already hard mouth.

'My job is not to play nursemaid to misplaced females,' he said with savage politeness.

But Ella found that she could be savage, too. 'Oh? What is it then? Surrounding empty inns and arresting innocent travellers?'

One of the troopers laughed. Moggs flashed him a look that froze the culprit in place, and then he leaned over Ella. 'You are pert, ma'am. I think you are in no position to be handing out insults.'

But instead of retreating, Ella leaned forward too, until their faces were only inches apart. 'You forget yourself, sir,' and her voice and eyes were colder than the air outside. 'When I am returned to my husband and family I will describe in detail your behaviour. Indeed, when I reach Bendigo, I will see that the commissioner there ...' A flash of memory came to her rescue. 'Mr Gilbert, isn't it? I will notify Mr Gilbert of your conduct to me and this gentleman.'

'This "gentleman"!' Lieutenant Moggs repeated in disbelief. But she had shaken him. At first he had thought her deranged, but her mention of Gilbert, the Gold Commissioner at Bendigo, made him uneasy. Again he tried to tell himself that she was of no account, only another abandoned woman – there were plenty of them all over Victoria, an unfortunate product of the gold rush. And yet she did not act like the poverty-stricken drab he had thought her to be when they met at Carlsruhe. This was a lady, and even Moggs used caution when it came to insulting ladies. They had an irritating habit of cropping up again in the most inconvenient places, and they always seemed to have influential friends.

He ground his teeth, looking for someone else on whom to vent his spleen. Adam was the logical choice. 'What is your business in Bendigo?' he asked furiously.

'I'm on my way to the diggings,' Adam drawled. 'I'm taking Mrs Seaton to the commissioner, just like you told me to. We stayed here to give her a rest. She's delicate.'

Moggs flicked a glance at Ella. 'Delicate, is she?' he repeated, and there was no doubting the sneer in his voice. 'Do you know the owner of this inn? Her name is Nancy Ure, and she is reputed to be handling stolen goods. I believe she is a friend of yours.'

Adam shook his head, his eyes full of puzzled innocence. 'I'm no friend of hers. I only met her yesterday.'

'That's not the information I have,' was the swift retort. 'You'd better tell me the truth.'

But Adam only shrugged, plainly at a loss.

Lieutenant Moggs was about to launch into another assault when shouting came from outside. Footsteps, running, passed by the inn. Ella could hear the word, 'Fire!' clearly. The lieutenant turned to one of his men. 'Go and see what the devil that's all about,' he snarled and the man clattered out.

The tension in the room had not been eased by the interruption. If anything, it was worse. Adam was still standing between two of the troopers, as though already a prisoner. But he obviously had no intention of making things easy for them.

Ella cleared her throat 'I have no idea what your business is at this inn, Lieutenant Moggs, and frankly I do not care. This, however, happens to be *my* room, and I am requesting you to leave. At once.'

Moggs spared her an impatient glance. 'I'm not interested in whose room this is. I am interested in what this fellow has to tell me. If you like, I will remove him to another room and deal with him there.'

'Deal with him' had an unpleasant ring to it. Ella tried again. 'Adam is my servant You have no right to take him away without my permission.'

'I believe him to be involved in criminal activities, ma'am. I have every right.' He was gloating now, knowing he had the upper hand. Ella felt her power beginning to wane. She searched for something more to say that would sway him into meeting her demands, but she seemed to have run out of ideas.

Boots echoed in the narrow passage beyond the door. The knock was perfunctory. The trooper Lieutenant Moggs had sent to investigate peered in. His face was pink with a combination of the cold and excitement. 'Sir, there's a fire down in the town. I think you should come and take a look.'

'Why would I want to do that?' Moggs asked him impatiently.

The man swallowed, and glanced helplessly at his companions. 'It's Doctor Rawlins's hut, sir. It's well alight And from what I can discover, the doctor's still inside it.'

'What!' Moggs's shock was genuine. He pointed to Adam, ground out, 'Watch him!' and strode out of the room after the trooper. In his wake, his men exchanged significant glances.

Ella didn't notice. Doctor Rawlins was still inside his burning hut. She felt sick. The doctor must be dead. She had spoken to him only hours before, and now he was dead. She had repeated to Adam Doctor Rawlins's warning, and Adam had told Eben and Nancy ... and now the doctor was dead. As if from a long way away, she remembered Adam telling her that anyone who crossed Nancy Ure died.

I killed him. The words were in her head. It's all my fault. *I killed him, I killed him* ... She opened her mouth.

Adam's strong arm slipped around her shoulders, squeezing painfully hard. 'There now, Mrs Seaton, it's all right. It's all a mistake. I'm sure Lieutenant Moggs'll realise that when he comes back.' His voice went on, spilling out soothing nonsense, while the troopers looked on, believing what they saw - the lady was overcome and Adam was comforting her. But it had its effect. Ella was able to pull back from the dangerous urge to tell all.

'Thank you, Adam,' she said at last. 'I'm all right now. I was feeling rather faint.'

He nodded, watching her. Evidently what he saw reassured him, for he let her go. Outside, a dog was barking in the stable, and Ella recognised Wolf's deep voice. Adam's head lifted sharply and he moved towards the door. But the troopers weren't about to let him go.

'Stay where you are,' one of them growled, shoving Adam's chest. 'The lieutenant ain't finished with you.'

'Someone's in the stables,' Adam replied impatiently. 'I've a cart in there.'

'We're searching for the bushranger,' was the answer. 'You stay put.'

'Not that we'll find him,' another of the troopers said. 'Not now. The bird 'as flown.'

'God help us then,' his companion muttered. And, seeing Ella's pale face turned questioningly towards him, added, 'Lieutenant Moggs don't like to be made a fool of, ma'am. He don't like it at all. Prides himself, he does, on his record.'

'And is it a good one, this record?' Ella whispered.

The man grinned. 'It is, ma'am! Only thing he lives for, ma'am. He's gettin' a transfer, too. He won't like it, that his last job was botched.'

'Shut up, you fool!' one of the others growled. 'Moggs'll have our balls if he hears us chattin' with the prisoners.'

An uneasy silence fell, and moments later Lieutenant Moggs returned. His face was grim, but there was a gleam of triumph in his eyes that frightened Ella. 'He's alive,' he said without preamble. 'He happened to be out on a call, and has only just returned. If he'd been inside, he would have been trapped and burned to death.'

Adam's face didn't change, though Moggs was watching him closely. 'Am I free to go now?' he asked evenly.

But Moggs shook his head slowly. 'Very convenient fire, don't you think?'

Adam shrugged. 'The fire had nothing to do with me. Why would I want to burn down Doctor Rawlins's place? I only knew the man 'cause he was treating Mrs Seaton here.'

Lieutenant Moggs moved closer to him, thrusting his face into Adam's. 'You're a liar!' he shouted. 'I'll have you charged with the attempted murder of Rawlins, as well as robbery and murder in this inn.'

Ella had jumped, but Adam didn't even flinch. There was an unruffled air about him that spoke of long practice. 'I was with Mrs Seaton when the fire started, and I have you and half a dozen troopers to swear to it. And before we arrived here in Sawpit Gully, I was on the road up from Melbourne, and before that I was in California. I've never robbed anyone, and I've never murdered anyone.'

Moggs knew the evidence was flimsy – Ella could see it in his face – but he had decided Adam was guilty, and he wasn't backing down. She realised, with dismay, that Moggs was the sort of man who, once set upon a thing, was not easily turned from his path.

'Get Doctor Rawlins,' he said, without taking his eyes off Adam. The troopers looked at each other, and then one slipped out of the room.

'Do you usually conduct your interviews in a lady's bedroom?' Adam asked sarcastically.

Moggs drew back his fist, and with negligent viciousness, struck Adam a blow in the stomach. Adam's breath came out in a whoosh of surprise and pain, and he doubled over. Moggs watched him a moment, satisfying himself that Adam wasn't about to say any more for a while, and then turned to Ella.

She knew her face was slack with shock. It seemed to amuse him. 'I conduct my interviews wherever I have to,' he said coldly, answering Adam's question. 'One cannot always choose one's settings ... or one's companions,' and his mouth twisted with distaste.

The trooper was back, and Doctor Rawlins was with him. The little man looked the worse for wear. His clothes were rumpled and the smell of smoke clung to him, while a streak of soot decorated one plump cheek. But at least he was in one piece. He glanced once around the room, his eyes flicking quickly over Ella in the bed and Adam still doubled over. Then he looked down at his feet. But that one glance had been enough for Ella to see that he was utterly terrified.

'Doctor Rawlins,' Moggs said pleasantly, 'I know you're probably looking forward to a stiff drink and a warm bed, but I need you to help me here. You've been very helpful in the past.'

Rawlins twitched nervously, but didn't reply.

'I want you to look at this man and tell me what you know of him,' Moggs went on.

'I don't know anything about him,' the little man muttered at his feet. 'I told you, I thought he was known to Mrs Ure, but now I don't believe so. I had never seen him until recently, when he arrived with Mrs Seaton.'

Moggs's face tightened, but the smile remained fixed on his mouth, more forced now than reassuring. 'You told us that this man was a friend of Mrs Ure. That she knew him well. That he was involved in Mrs Ure's unlawful activities.'

Ella turned and stared at Doctor Rawlins, but he wouldn't meet her eyes. He looked at his feet, and shook his head. 'I don't remember that. I won't swear to it.'

Moggs's smile had gone. For a dreadful moment, Ella wondered whether he would deal the little doctor the same violence he had dealt Adam. 'Who set fire to your hut?' he bit out.

'It was an accident. The candle overturned.'

Clearly it was a lie, but he said it in a stubborn manner that left no doubt as to his determination to stick to his story. He was badly frightened – by a lucky circumstance he had been away when his hut was set alight and he did not intend to test good fortune a second time.

'Did this man threaten you, Doctor Rawlins?' Moggs's voice had risen in volume, and he jabbed his finger in Adam's direction.

This time Doctor Rawlins looked up, and Ella could see that he was genuinely puzzled. 'Why no,' he croaked, and shook his head, '*he* didn't threaten me.'

Adam laughed, and coughed. He sank down on the side of the bed and looked up at Moggs, his face rather pale. '*This* is your evidence against me? If you take me down to Melbourne on that, they'll throw you out on your arse. You've made a right mess of it, haven't you, Lieutenant?'

Moggs took a step towards him and Ella screamed, thinking he meant to hit Adam again. But instead he whirled around on his heel and grabbed hold of Doctor Rawlins's coat, shaking the little man like a rat.

'You worthless sot,' he hissed. 'I know you're

lying. Don't think you'll get away with it.' And he flung the doctor from him, sending him stumbling and crashing back against one of the other troopers.

The violence appeared to have a calming effect on Moggs. He straightened his cuffs, while his men watched him in awe. Then, when he was ready, he turned and faced the bed. And Adam.

'I won't forget you,' he said slowly. 'One way or another, I'll see you get what you deserve.'

Adam smiled.

To Ella's mind, it was as if Moggs had issued a challenge, and Adam had taken it up.

Lieutenant Moggs pushed by Doctor Rawlins, and was out of the door. The sound of his boots marched away down the passage, and the kitchen door slammed like a cannon shot.

One of the troopers let out a long sigh. 'Now we're for it,' he muttered. And silently, the little doctor huddled between them, they also left the room.

Ella slumped back against her pillow, feeling weak and shaky. Adam was watching her, and somehow she managed to smile. 'Are you all right?' she asked him.

He grimaced and rubbed his midriff. 'I've been better.'

'Do you think Doctor Rawlins will be all right? I hate to think ... he was nearly murdered. That was how I repaid him for his kindness to me.'

'We don't know it wasn't an accident. There's always the chance of a fire in a place like this.'

But he was trying to comfort her, and they both knew it. 'She's an evil woman,' Ella whispered. 'You were right.'

Adam put his hand over hers. 'Thank you for what you said ... the way you stood up for me. I won't forget it.' He grinned. 'Now, I'd best go and find Kitty. You get some sleep, Mrs Seaton.'

Obediently, Ella slid down beneath the bed-clothes and closed her eyes. She felt his fingertip brush across her eyelids, like a caress, but when she opened them again, he had gone.

———◆———

The morning brought a halt to the rain. The sky was a hard, icy blue with white clouds skating across it. Ella tried to ignore the ache behind her eyes as she stood in the yard and watched the troopers loading Nancy Ure's collection of finery onto wagons.

Lieutenant Moggs had at last found an outlet for his pent up fury and he harried his men unmercifully. The inn itself was closed, and already grumbling patrons were being turned away. It was unlikely Nancy Ure would ever show her face here again.

Kitty sat hunched on a box near the wall, sheltered somewhat from the wind. The troopers had questioned her at length last night, but Kitty had had little to tell them. She worked here, she had said, and that was all. She knew nothing of any robbery or murder, she didn't know anyone called Eben. Eventually, in disgust, Lieutenant Moggs had let her go.

'What will happen to her now?' Ella had asked Adam when he explained matters to her.

Adam had replied evenly, 'She's coming with us to Bendigo.'

So Kitty had got her way after all.

Lieutenant Moggs had set his men to search Adam's cart, and Adam had spent much of the morning repacking it. But eventually all was ready for them to leave.

'They say there's nothin' left of Doctor Rawlins's hut but ashes,' Kitty said to no one in particular. 'Any other night he would o' been in there, drunk, but it just so happened one o' Red Phebe's girls was havin' her baby and they hauled him out.' She paused. 'Mrs Ure really hated his guts, didn't she?'

Adam tossed Kitty's bag into the cart and helped the girl up after it. She settled herself on a bag of flour. Ella climbed to her usual spot on the hard seat and the cart set off with a lurch, rattling over the track.

Clouds raced across a sun without warmth, the shadows gliding silently over the land. Mount Alexander lay to their north, a beacon for weary travellers heading to the goldfields.

They drove for a mile beyond Sawpit Gully before anyone spoke. Ella was still too shocked to put into words what she felt, Kitty seemed too tired, and Adam ... he had his own thoughts to occupy him.

'Do you think they'll get away?' Kitty asked finally, wriggling to get more comfortable on her flour bag.

'They've done it before ... got away, I mean,' Adam replied. He glanced back at Kitty. 'You knew what was going on then?'

Kitty pulled a face. 'I looked the other way, but

I knew. She was always wonderin' whether or not I'd tell. That was why she didn't want me to leave with you and Mrs Seaton.' Suddenly she looked far older than her years. 'Maybe she would've finished me off like she tried to finish Doctor Rawlins.'

A strand of hair blew across Ella's face, and she tucked it back with cold fingers. I'm sorry about Doctor Rawlins, she thought. But if I hadn't told, Adam would be under arrest now, caught up in something he had no part of...or maybe even dead, shot in Nancy and Eben's attempts to escape the troopers' net. Either way, people would have been hurt.

'That Lieutenant Moggs really didn't like you, did he?' Kitty was speaking to Adam again.

'He blames me for his failure. Men like him have to have someone to blame.'

'Just as well you were with Mrs Seaton then, when the hut was burned down.' It was innocently said, but Ella knew Kitty was fishing. She gave the girl what she wanted to hear.

'Adam heard the troopers outside and came to wake me.'

Both pairs of eyes were on her, but Ella didn't turn. Her own eyes were fixed on the road ahead. The road to Weatherby's station.

CHAPTER 10

———•———

WEATHERBY'S WAS A LOW WOODEN building with a verandah at the front and smoke rising from the chimney. A stockade type of fence surrounded it and there were fruit trees growing to the side, bare now and barren of fruit A cow was lowing in one of several outbuildings at the back, and two dogs ran barking, warning the occupants of intruders. There was no sign of human life.

However, as Adam drew up the cart, a man came from one of the outbuildings. He was elderly, his walk painfully slow. He peered at them shortsightedly. 'Who is it?' he demanded. 'You're out of your way if you're going to the diggings.'

'We're looking for Weatherby's station,' Adam replied in a friendly voice. 'Is this it?'

The man peered at them again, doubtfully. 'Weatherby's did you say? What do you want with the Weatherbys?'

'We want to talk to someone about a woman who may have stayed here several days ago,' Adam explained patiently.

But the elderly man shook his head as if it were all too much trouble, and waved a hand towards the house. 'I don't know nothing about that. You'd best go and see the missus. She'll know.'

Even as he finished speaking, a woman came out of the house and stood on the verandah. She was young, but her face was already lined from a life of hard work and few luxuries. Her hair was scraped back at her nape into an untidy bun.

'What is it, Marcus?' Mrs Weatherby asked in a harassed voice, eyes going from the elderly man to Adam and back again.

Adam repeated his question with a smile, the woman's lips curving up automatically in response. And then her gaze shifted to Ella, and suddenly her whole face brightened.

'Hello, ma'am!' she said with all the relief of one who discovers a familiar face among strangers. 'Come in, come in.'

As Adam helped the two women down from the cart, Mrs Weatherby came to open the gate, still smiling. 'Marcus is rather deaf,' she excused, as the old man crept back to his sanctuary. 'But he's all I have at the moment. The others are out moving sheep, and my husband and his brother are away at the Forest Creek diggings selling our meat.'

Inside the front room was small and formal – Mrs Weatherby called it the parlour. Ella could see that the best things were placed in it, to impress visitors, and that otherwise it was rarely used. A fire was set but not lit, and Mrs Weatherby soon had flames crackling in the hearth.

'It is very difficult to keep servants these days.' She spoke while she worked. 'As soon as you find someone, they're off to the diggings. We've tried going down to Melbourne and picking them off the boats as they arrive from England. They stay for a time, but before long the gold fever takes them and they're off. Gold will ruin this country, that's what my husband says.'

'You must be making a fair profit selling your sheep at Forest Creek, ma'am,' Adam drawled, and smiled to take the sting from it.

She pushed at her untidy hair, the lines deepening about her eyes as she returned his smile. 'Well, as to that ... you'd have to ask my husband. Now, take a seat and I'll fetch some tea.'

But Ella couldn't wait that long. The polite conversation was like torture to her, and now to sit patiently through a polite tea party ... She burst out, 'Please! You know me, don't you? You *do* know me?'

A look of alarm flashed across Mrs Weatherby's face, but she answered readily enough. 'I know you, yes, ma'am. You stayed with us. You were on your way through to Melbourne with your servant. You were cold and half frozen to death, and we begged you to stay longer, but in the morning you were off again. My husband and I were concerned you'd not manage the journey. I'm glad to see you suffered no ill effects.'

Ella brushed that aside with an impatient wave of her hand. Her voice was shaking so much she could hardly get the words out. 'Mrs Weatherby, please can you tell me my name?'

Mrs Weatherby looked amazed. 'Your name? Why, yes, of course I can! Your name is Mrs Catchpole, Margaret Catchpole.'

A shudder of excitement gripped Ella, and she turned with shining eyes to Adam. There was a strange expression on his face, a cross between surprise and dismay, but she didn't notice. 'Catchpole,' she repeated, tears momentarily blinding her.

The other woman hesitated, and then murmured, 'I'll fetch the tea.' Her quick footsteps faded down the hallway towards the back of the house.

I have a name, thought Ella. I have a name!

She felt Adam move beside her. His voice was gentle, preparing her for bad news. 'I don't think that can be your name.'

The excitement still buoying her up, Ella faced him. Her lips were trembling. 'It must be my name! Didn't you hear what the woman said? "Margaret Catchpole"!' But even as she said it, a dull distant bell was clanging in her mind. The name was familiar to her, but there was something not quite right.

'Margaret Catchpole,' Adam said evenly, 'was a convict, sent out to Sydney for horse-stealin'. She's long dead now, but there was a story ... She dressed herself as a boy and stole a horse and ran away to London.'

The silence grew. There was a lump in Ella's throat, and she knew if she opened her mouth she would begin to cry.

'She died on the Hawkesbury, forty years ago,' Adam added, giving her time to compose herself. 'As far as I know, she never married and never had any children. You must have heard the name and remembered it. But I don't believe it's your real name.'

Ella put up a hand to shield her eyes. She cleared her throat. 'I think you're right, Adam.' She sensed Adam and Kitty glance at each other, and kept her head down. She didn't want them to see the anguish on her face. She had placed such high hopes on this visit She had thought that it could be the end of her journey. Instead, it was only another twist in the road and still she couldn't see ahead to where it was taking her.

'Lots of people give false names,' Kitty remarked.

'But why would *I* give one?' Ella retorted, her eyes on the fire. 'Unless I was running away ... or had done something wrong ..."

There was a thought! Had she committed a deed so foul that she must flee her home and husband, riding – as someone had said – as though the devil himself was after her?

'If that's what you think, maybe you should stop trying to find out who you are, and start trying to hide yourself away,' Adam suggested with calm logic.

Ella shook her head. The tears were back in her eyes, and she blinked savagely to clear them. She felt lost and abandoned all over again.

'All right then,' he amended, 'we keep looking, but we take a bit more care about who we ask. Look at me.' His voice was quiet. Ella lifted her chin, fighting for her cool composure. Adam smiled, and somehow she didn't feel alone anymore. 'We won't give up because you gave a false name. That just makes it a bit more interesting.'

Behind him, Kitty was studying the toes of her shoes.

'Do you think I can trust Mrs Weatherby?' Ella asked diffidently.

'I think you've no choice.'

Mrs Weatherby returned with the tea and some cake, as well as cold mutton and bread and butter. It was a royal feast, and as they partook Ella explained the reason for their visit. Mrs Weatherby listened, her eyes wide, concern warring with the amazement in her face.

'But ... this is shocking news, ma'am! Are you recovered now from your injury?'

'Yes, thank you.' Ella managed a smile. There were so many questions clamouring to be asked, she hardly knew where to begin. 'Did I say where I was going and why?'

'Why, yes! You said you were going to Melbourne. You were taking passage on a ship there ... or perhaps you were meeting someone who had arrived by ship.' She shook her head, 'I'm sorry. You were in such a hurry, you see. I don't think you really explained *why* you were going. You ...' She pushed at her hair again self consciously. 'Your manner did not invite too many questions.'

Adam laughed.

Ella ignored him. 'Where had I come from? Did I tell you that, Mrs Weatherby?'

Mrs Weatherby's gaze slid back from Adam and lost its startled look. 'Well, you said "home". That was all you said. You said you'd set out from home with Ned - that was your servant. You said that your husband couldn't come, and you'd left him behind, but that he'd follow in a day or two. You were agitated, ma'am. I didn't like to pry too much. I ...' Again, she shifted uneasily, as if she felt she should not say what was on her mind.

'Please,' and Ella leaned forward, 'you must tell me everything. I am desperate, Mrs Weatherby.'

Mrs Weatherby nodded, but she avoided Ella's eyes. 'I had the feeling that you were not telling me the whole truth. But, as I said, I didn't like to pry. It was not my place. And you were most generous in your payment for the night.' She smiled sympathetically.

So, thought Ella with a sigh, I bluffed Mrs Weatherby, just as I bluffed Lieutenant Moggs.

Had she told the woman nothing but lies, or was some of it the truth? And "home", where was that?

'It's almost as if you wanted to disappear,' Kitty murmured, intrigued.

'Was she carrying any baggage with her?' Adam asked.

Mrs Weatherby nodded. 'A carpet bag tied to her saddle. She was travelling light. Oh, there was something else!' And her face brightened as she turned to Ella. 'The horse. It was a beautiful animal, a grey mare. You told us it was a birthday present from your husband.'

'A birthday present?' Ella repeated.

'I remember that quite clearly, because my husband was rather impolite - he asked you which birthday was that.'

Mrs Weatherby laughed awkwardly, reliving her embarrassment at the time. 'But you answered him, ma'am. Indeed, I think you weren't really listening to him. You said it was your twenty-fifth birthday.'

Later they took their leave, Mrs Weatherby promising to ask her husband when he returned if he remembered any more. Adam went and found Marcus, but the old man only confirmed that the servant's name was Ned.

As they drove away, Ella repeated to herself: *I am twenty-five years old. I have a husband who gives me presents. My servant's name was ... is Ned*. It wasn't as much information as she'd hoped for, but it was something to cling on to. A life raft on a vast inky sea.

The fork in the road which led off to the Forest Creek diggings was behind them - they had taken the Bendigo road. Ahead lay the Porcupine Inn. The road was still crowded with travellers like themselves. A couple of riders galloped past, and a woman with a baby tied to her breast with a shawl trudged after her husband. Her head was bowed as one foot followed the other.

Ella hardly glanced at them. She felt set apart, isolated. She had hardly said a word since they left Weatherby's station. There didn't seem much to say. Instead of finding answers, she had found more questions. The feeling of dread that had been with her ever since she woke by the lagoon was growing. She remembered Doctor Rawlins telling her that sometimes the mind chose not to recall a memory it could not cope with.

But none of that explained why she had given a false name.

Adam and Kitty had conversed for several miles. The girl brightened under Adam's attention, laughing back at him, forgetting her own troubles. But eventually they had fallen silent and Kitty had curled up on her makeshift bed for a nap.

The sun shone out, drying up the wet ground and giving the journey a much more cheerful aspect. Ella felt its warmth seeping into her. 'Do you think the rain has gone?'

'Maybe.' He turned and smiled at her, as if he were glad to hear her voice at last. Ella felt slightly ashamed for her introspection.

'I'm sorry, but sometimes everything seems so hopeless.' Her voice trailed off.

'Someone's bound to be looking for you,' he said. 'You're a lady, Mrs Seaton.'

'Then why did I use the name of a convict horse thief?'

He rubbed his chin and Ella winced as the dark stubble grated. 'It appealed to you, maybe. It's a romantic tale. Or it was, the way me mother used to tell it. You could've read it in a book.'

'Your mother knew her?' She wanted him to talk. She liked to listen to his voice; it was soothing. And listening meant she didn't have to think.

'So she said.' He winked. 'Maybe it was true and maybe not. She was a convict herself, sent out for larceny.'

Shocked, for a moment Ella could say nothing. 'Larceny?' she managed at last 'What is larceny?'

His smile mocked her. 'She stole her mistress's petticoat and stockings, Mrs Seaton.' The smile grew as Ella's cheeks turned bright pink. 'Aye, that's right. I'm the son of a convict woman and a sailor.' He spoke aloud the thought he read on her face, but he spoke it without bitterness.

'I didn't mean – ' she began, embarrassed.

But Adam wasn't listening. 'One thing I learned from the Yankees,' he was saying, 'every man is equal, no matter who he had for a father and a mother. It's not who you were born that matters, but what you do with your life.'

'That sounds very ... grand,' she murmured uncertainly. It also sounded rather like sedition, but she didn't like to say so.

'Not who you were born, but what you do with your life.' Kitty's dreamy voice echoed his words. 'I like that, Adam.' She laughed, and stretched her arms above her head, suddenly wide awake. 'I dreamed I was on a sailing ship,' she informed them. 'I was startin' to feel sea-sick!'

Adam laughed back at her. Kitty leaned forward and put her hand on his shoulder, and there was something possessive in the gesture. Ella realised then that Kitty and Adam were two of a kind; it was she who was the odd one out.

———◆———

The Porcupine Inn was rowdy with the sort of lawless patronage that had made its name infamous far and wide. Adam had already explained that it had a bad reputation, even worse than Sawpit Gully, and that they would not be staying. Ella gazed wide-eyed as miners staggered about in various stages of drunkenness, shouting and boasting of finds they had made or intended to make. But Kitty looked over her shoulder with something wistful in her face, as the vibrant place vanished from sight.

'It's *her* you're worried about,' she muttered mutinously. 'I know how to look after myself.'

Adam snorted. 'I'm worried about me cart and what's in it. I plan to sell this lot at the diggings, not offer it free to anyone with a loaded gun!'

Kitty sighed. 'It's a pity. Do they have any women there? They're probably old and worn out anyway,' with scorn. 'I could've made myself a fortune.'

Ella felt her face go slack with astonishment She quickly turned to hide it, but not soon enough. Kitty had noticed.

'What else am I supposed to do?' the girl burst

out furiously. 'I don't have any money – Nancy Ure owed me a month's wages – and I can't do nothing else!'

The angry response momentarily stunned her, but Ella rallied. 'I don't believe that. There's always something else.'

'Oh yes? If your husband don't come lookin' for you, you might find out!' Kitty yelled.

'I would never – ' Ella began, in a shaking voice.

'Oh, "never" is it? Well, it's easy to be so high and mighty when your stomach's full and you've got a roof over your head, and someone cares what happens to you!'

Ella closed her eyes. The anger drained out of her. 'Have you really been so alone, Kitty?'

But the girl shook her head mulishly and wouldn't answer.

Ella went on cautiously. 'Perhaps I don't fully understand, but I think I am beginning to. When I am settled again, I may be able to help you to – '

But Kitty wasn't interested in charity. 'Who do you think you are then, bloody Caroline Chisholm? Anyway,' with a narrowed look, 'how do you know it's not you who'll need help, and not me? What if your husband – if there is one! – never comes lookin' for you? What if he don't want you back? What would you do then? Live off Adam's savin's for ever? I reckon he's done more than enough for you already. He's worked hard for his money … what have you done for him but sit and suck off him, like a bloody leech? You turn up your nose at me, but at least I pay my way!'

Adam turned around and gave her a look that silenced her. Briefly, defiantly, she stared back and then the tough exterior cracked. Kitty gave a loud sob and buried her face in her hands, her frail shoulders shuddering.

Ella felt cold. She folded her arms against herself, trying to get warm, but there didn't seem to be any warmth to be had.

What Kitty said wasn't fair, nor was it true. But there was enough truth in it to make her squirm inside. She glanced at Adam, wondering if he really thought as Kitty did, but he was busy pulling Bess up.

'We'll camp here,' he said without expression. Kitty stopped crying and lifted her head. She looked like a child, her face all blotchy and damp with tears, her brown curls hanging damp and limp. There was something very appealing about her misery.

'I'm sorry,' she whispered to Adam, without meeting his eyes.

'It doesn't matter,' Adam teased gently. 'Cheer up, Kitty. You know I won't let anything bad happen to you. Now, I want you to find me some dry wood if you can.'

Kitty gave him a tremulous smile, and jumped down from the back of the cart She brushed out her skirts, her eyes lowered in a manner that was almost shy and, with Wolf at her side, went about her task. Adam unharnessed Bess, setting her to nibble on some green winter grass. Stringy-bark trees screened them from the roadside, the brown bark hanging from the trunks in long, untidy strips.

The sun was sinking, turning the world to gold.

'I can fetch wood, too,' Ella said stiffly.

Adam raised his eyebrows. 'To pay your way, do

you mean?'

'Maybe I do mean that.'

Adam grinned, banishing the seriousness in his eyes. 'If you want to do something for me, Mrs Seaton, then come and make us a cup of tea.'

The fire soon caught, sending out waves of heat to combat the evening chill. They sat around it, and Ella made the tea while Kitty fried the inevitable mutton chops. The girl was quieter since her outburst, and Ella noticed her frequent glances towards Adam. She seemed younger, softer, and the expression in her eyes was almost wondering.

She was in love, and probably for the first time. And Ella didn't need to be told who was the object of her newfound affection.

'I wonder where Nancy Ure is right at this moment,' Kitty thought aloud, smiling to herself.

Adam laughed, as Ella had known he would. 'Far away, I hope.'

Kitty laughed back. 'Maybe she'll turn bushranger, too.'

'I wouldn't put it past her.' Adam watched Kitty turn the chops, his expression indulgent.

Ella sat back, physically and mentally removing herself from the situation. He likes her, she told herself. Perhaps they will stay together. Kitty needs a strong man like Adam, and Adam needs someone who needs him.

They belong together.

'Tell me about yourself, Kitty,' Adam was asking, narrowing his eyes against the smoke.

Kitty hesitated, and Ella knew that if *she* had asked the question, the girl would have refused to answer. But because it was Adam, she half smiled, and said, 'It won't take long,' making a joke to cover the pain.

'My dad made shoes in Bristol, but there was no work. He brought us to Melbourne because he heard he'd get paid well and there was a need for men like him. But Ma was sick, and the change didn't do her any good. She died first, and then Dad. I had a younger brother and sister, but they were sent out to someone down Geelong way. I was the eldest and I didn't fancy being worked to death by strangers. When the gold rush started, I thought if others can make their fortune, why not me? So I set off. But I only got as far as Sawpit Gully ...'

Ella could guess the rest. Kitty would have found herself trapped by need and circumstance at Nancy Ure's inn, dying a slow death. It was lucky that Adam and Ella had come along, beginning the chain of events which set her free.

They ate their meal while the light faded and mist crept up from the gullies. The trees stood dark against the brightening stars, and soon it was time to go to sleep. Only now it was Kitty and Ella who curled up under the cart, while Adam wrapped himself in a blanket and lay by the fire with Wolf.

Ella gazed out at the flickering shadows of the fire. Beside her, Kitty breathed peacefully in her sleep. Somewhere not far away, Ella could hear the murmur of voices. There were camp sites all along the road, excited miners awaiting the dawn so that they could begin the long, slow, haul up the Big Hill, and on to the Bendigo diggings.

She began to drift into sleep, and a picture of Seaton's Lagoon filled her mind. Suddenly she was a bird, flying over the water. She swooped down, gliding closer, closer ... the surface lay still, clear, with scarcely a ripple. She could see the mud at the bottom, and a few fish lazily swimming. And then, floating, a face. Ned's white face, the eyes wide open, the mouth bubbling with words that would never now be spoken.

Ella jumped, awake again. 'No!' she gasped. The gruesome picture began to fade, but all urge to sleep had passed. Eventually she gave up trying and, careful not to wake Kitty, wriggled out from under the cart and crept over to the fire. It was burning low, and she leaned close, warming her hands. Adam lifted his head. He looked rumpled, his eyes narrowed from sleep.

'Sorry, I didn't mean to wake you.'

He rubbed a hand across his face. His beard was definitely growing again, and it gave him an unkempt look. She wished he'd shave it off; she preferred him without it. 'Couldn't you sleep?' he asked.

'Bad dream.' She gave him a wry smile and pushed her braided hair back over her shoulder, gathering her thoughts. 'Adam, when you went down to Seaton's Lagoon, did you find anything? Anything at all?'

He blinked at her, still half asleep. 'Only foot-prints, yours and three others. No carpet bag, if that's what you mean. I would've told you.'

'I know.' She rested her chin in her hands, and stared into the fire. 'I wonder where Ned is. Do you think he's still alive?'

Adam stretched, and then propped himself up on one elbow. 'What's wrong? Have you remembered something?'

She shook her head, and her braid swung back and forth, her fair hair bright against the darkness. 'I dreamed Ned was drowned.' Her eyes shifted, meeting his.

'I saw no body at Seaton's Lagoon.'

He was still watching her and she couldn't seem to look away. 'What if Kitty's right? What if I never find out who I am? What if no one is looking for me, or cares what happened? What then, Adam?' She could hear her own heartbeat, loud in her ears.

'Are you frightened?' he asked, his voice deep and soft

Ella let out her breath on a sigh. 'Yes.'

'You know I won't let anything bad happen to you.'

She smiled despite herself. 'That's what you said to Kitty.' Her smile faded. 'She believes you can work miracles, but I know you're only a man.'

'Aye, well ...' he shrugged. 'I don't plan to go anywhere once I get to Bendigo. Not straight off, anyway. You can stay with me while you sort things out And Kitty can be your chaperone ... remember?'

Ella laughed without humour. 'I'm starting to feel as if I'm the chaperone, not Kitty.'

'She'll forget all about me when we reach Bendigo,' he replied confidently.

'Do you think she's that fickle?'

'I think she's young, and hasn't had much of a life yet. When she starts looking around her without the worry of where her next meal's coming from, she'll see there're plenty of men looking back. Better ones than me.'

Ella shook her head. 'If Kitty's as clever as I think she is, she'll stay with you.'

He said nothing, but his eyes mocked her.

Suddenly awkward, Ella stood up. 'I think I can sleep now. Goodnight, Adam.'

She sounded brisk and impersonal. I'm good at that, she thought. Whenever anyone gets too close to me, I lock myself away somewhere behind a facade. I did it with Mrs Weatherby, and now I'm doing it with Adam.

The blankets beneath the cart were cold. Shivering, Ella wrapped herself in them. Beside her Kitty stirred, sighing, but she didn't wake.

———————

The Big Hill was well named.

It stretched forever, gradually climbing towards the horizon. There was another, easier road to Bendigo that avoided the hill, and was popular in bad weather, but it took longer. Adam had decided to risk the hill.

The rain seemed to have stopped at last, the sky was a hazy blue, and a sharp wind was beginning to dry out the land. Along the road, broken vehicles and exhausted miners formed unhappy tableaus. As the incline became steeper, Adam climbed down to lead Bess and the two women trudged behind.

A small group of miners walked with them, weighed down with their packs. One looked grey with exhaustion, his lips faintly blue. Kitty enjoyed tossing remarks with the youngest of the group, a dark-haired lad with green eyes, and when he mistook Ella for her sister, Kitty laughed uproariously.

'Who'd you think Adam was then?' Kitty asked. 'Me brother?'

The boy put a brave face on it, laughing back at her. 'That or your brother by marriage,' he offered.

Kitty didn't like that. Her eyes lost their warmth, though she kept her smile. 'Why, I've never heard anything so silly!' she retorted. 'Mrs Seaton here is married already.'

The boy said nothing, but Ella could see he was downcast. He would be a fool not to notice Kitty's proprietary attitude towards Adam, and he seemed intelligent enough. When Kitty had quickened her stride, catching up with Adam in front, the boy joined Ella, giving her a shy smile.

'Is your husband waiting for you on the Bendigo diggings, Mrs Seaton?' he asked her politely.

'I hope so.' Ella smiled back. 'What's your name?'

'David Marr. That's my father over there,' and he pointed to the grey-faced man. 'We were supposed to meet my brother at Forest Creek, but he'd moved on by the time we got there. We're hoping he's at Eaglehawk. A lot of miners have moved on there.'

Ella glanced at the father again, but she said nothing. If the man was ill, his son must know it. And if he didn't, Ella feared he would know soon enough.

Despite the fine day, the rain had left its mark. Parts of the road were deep in mud, slippery and smelly. They inched their way onward, legs aching with effort

'Fine strong mare you have there,' one of the group said to Adam. 'How much would you like for her?'

Adam pulled a face. 'I hadn't thought of selling.'

'You won't need her if you're mining. Horses are more trouble than they're worth.'

'I'm not mining,' Adam replied easily.

The man shrugged. 'If you ever change your mind – '

'Too hard for you, is it? Mining?' another voice growled.

'Adam was a miner in California!' Kitty retorted, cheeks flushing with indignation.

Startled, Ella remembered doing a similar thing. It seemed a long time ago. Unintentionally she looked up and met the gleam of amusement in Adam's eyes, as if he had remembered too.

Finally, they were on top. Ironbark trees grew tall around them, and the beginning of the Bendigo Valley stretched before them. Ella heard her own voice joining in a ragged cheer, drowning out the carolling of magpies and the distant ring of an axe.

It was already part of tradition to make camp on top of the Big Hill and congratulate yourself on your achievement while your heartbeat slowed to normal and the muscles of your legs stopped hurting.

Kitty made a fire, her eyes bright with excitement. Ella went to the cart to fetch the billy to boil water. Adam was there, watering Bess and fussing over her.

'Well, we made it, Mrs Seaton,' he said quietly, his back to her. 'Tonight we'll sleep under the stars on the famous Bendigo.'

He looked at her then, and there was no escaping the declaration in his eyes. The thing she had known but hadn't wanted to believe. Adam loved her; for better, for worse he loved her. Ella felt a sudden, soaring triumph. But the feeling didn't last. She wanted to shout at him: 'Don't love me! There can be no happy ending for us!' But instead she just stood there, with the cold wind blowing her hair, and the smoky fires of the Bendigo goldfield rising into the sky behind her.

ON BENDIGO

CHAPTER 11

———◆———

THE DAY WAS ENDING. ELLA gazed below her as the cart creaked its way down the well-worn track towards the diggings. The setting sun gave them a deceptively soft and mellow look, disguising the raw and gaping wounds made by man. She could even picture it as it must have been once, with the pristine little creek sparkling its way along the flat valley floor. Now the water was brown and sluggish, no longer judged on its beauty but on its usefulness to miners panning for gold. Evidence of the rain was everywhere. Water-holes shone like mirrors, reflecting the setting sun, and the ground gleamed greasily from constant traffic. The higher hills and ridges were still thickly wooded and mostly untouched, only an occasional trail of smoke to indicate the advance of the miner, or a bushranger's hideaway.

But down in the gullies and on the flats white tents covered the ground like an erratic fall of snow, and smoke from campfires drifted and hung hazily in the cold, still air. The yellow box trees which had once luxuriated in the rich valley soil were diminishing, cut down by the miners to burn on their fires, or to prop up their tents, or to shore up their mine shafts. But here and there a few specimens remained, tall and stately.

Ella could see miners carrying their wash dirt to the creek in barrows or buckets. Others were crouched, panning in the water or furiously puddling in tubs or rocking wooden cradles. The sheer busyness of the place gripped her. Suddenly she understood how a prospective miner must feel, with the answer to all his hopes and dreams spread before him: quite light-headed with excitement.

Here on the Bendigo diggings one of the world's great adventures was being acted out, and Ella was a part of it.

The track Adam was travelling levelled out onto a wide flat, lined with tents large and small. Flags hung limply outside stores, and Ella could see a smithy and a baker and a tent serving meals. A butcher's stall had sides of sheep hanging from hooks on the front, guarded by a savage looking dog. Wolf bristled, but at a word from Adam pretended indifference. What appeared to be a small detachment of soldiers was mustering outside an official looking canvas tent set apart from the rest, and a sign outside a structure of bark and calico grandly proclaimed it: *An Hotel of the Highest Quality.*

Adam's cart rumbled on. Ahead of them, a bullock dray had tipped over and there were shouts and curses as the driver attempted to right it. Rather than try to go around it, Adam turned off onto one of the many side tracks. This took them through a shallow gully where in all directions campfires were being lit like beacons against the closing darkness.

Music came from one of the tents on the slope, a jig to tap one's feet to. A few solitary miners worked on at their claims – a couple had a lantern hoisted upon a pole – and Ella watched their heads bobbing up and down as they swung their picks. Everywhere earth had been shovelled into untidy mounds and the ground was pitted with holes, some shallow, others too deep to judge in the fading light A little further along, some careless miner had illegally staked his claim right in the middle of the road, so that the traffic had had to make a detour around him. If it hadn't been for Adam's sharp eyes, Bess might have broken her legs.

The road weaved its way around holes and hillocks, the cart wheels slipping and sliding on the soft, muddy ground. They were in yet another gully now, and Adam pulled Bess up while he frowned ahead with the effort to see. The mellow evening light had long ago given way to a uniform grey, while overhead clouds were rolling in to blot out a pale moon.

'I think we'd better camp here and wait for the morning. We've maybe taken a wrong turn.'

Ella peered ahead, too, and saw that this gully appeared less populated than those previously. Tents were fewer, and there were no flags flying. A hole close to the track was half filled with dark water; no one had cared to bail it out. The place had an almost forgotten air to it, as if the bustle of the gold rush had passed it by.

'Do you think there's still gold here?'

Adam shrugged. 'I'd say by the look of it this gully's already been rushed and most of the miners've moved on.'

Ella looked about her again and saw that indeed many of the holes had been abandoned – no one

had considered it necessary to fill them in for
safety's sake. Already low scrub was beginning to
regenerate and a few poor saplings were struggling
to life beside a blackened stump. The gully itself
was quite narrow, the slope on one side sharper
and more severe than the other. Above, at the top
of the ridge, tall dark ironbarks grew, gazing down
at the newcomers with majestic contempt.

Kitty jumped down off the cart and slowly Ella
followed her. She stretched her tired legs and took
a deep breath of Bendigo air – a mixture of wood-
smoke, frying mutton, earth and wet bush. Adam
urged Bess off the track and up the shallow side of
the gully, to a spot that looked suitable for a camp.
Soon he and Kitty had begun to unload the cart,
their voices rising and falling. Ella stood and gazed
out over the scene.

So, she thought, this was what a gully looked like
when it had been 'rushed'.

Adam had explained to her how such things
progressed and Ella felt she had grasped the basics.
First, gold was found above the ground; nuggets
lying gleaming in the sun, to be harvested like
corn. After that the miners would begin digging.
The clay and soil they excavated was puddled –
placed in a tub with water and stirred vigorously
to break the contents up into a thick sludge. This
could then be panned – or worked in a flat-bot-
tomed dish with more water – to tease out the
gold. Adam said it was not as easy as it sounded
and required a certain expertise if one was not to
toss out the gold with the water. Cradles – clumsy
rocking machines – worked on the same princi-
ple, separating the heavier particles from the mud,

so that the gold sank into a removable tray at the bottom.

And so the miners dug deeper, washing their dirt as they went, until the hole was 'bottomed', or they reached the bedrock, and could dig no further. This might be as little as one foot below the surface, or as much as thirty. Sometimes there were nuggets to be found on the bottom, clustered there like eggs, to be removed with a flick of the miner's knife. But more usually the bottom of the hole yielded nothing but disappointment. And when the disappointments grew too great, and the strikes too few, the miners moved on to the next rush.

A gust of wind blew a snatch of song from further afield and Ella turned her head to listen. She noticed then that about twenty yards further along the narrow gully was a group of five miners taking their ease outside their tent. One of them was busy cooking the evening meal, while the rest puffed on their pipes and reflected on the day's work. They were obviously interested in the new arrivals.

'New chums, are ye?' The cook had caught her eye, and took the opportunity to call out to her in a deep, pleasant, Scots-accented voice.

'In a way, yes. Can you tell me what this gully is called?'

The men glanced at each other, seemingly amused at her ignorance. 'This is Paddy's Gully.'

Another member of the group piped up. 'Where are yer from, matey?' And Ella realised that Adam had come up behind her.

'Melbourne,' he replied easily, and strolled over to their campfire. Curious, Ella followed him, Wolf panting at her side.

'Melbourne, eh?' someone else sighed. 'Is it rainin' there 'an all?'

'It's raining all along the road to Bendigo,' Adam said. 'On the Keilor Plain there was mud up to the axles ... and over!'

They mulled over this, puffing on their pipes.

It was quite dark now, apart from the warm light of the campfire. Much further down the gully, Ella saw a tent illuminated with a lamp or candle, the occupants silhouetted in shadow inside it. Suddenly from the same direction a gunshot sounded, making her jump.

The cook laughed. 'Nothing to be afraid o', ma'am. Just someone clearing his gun. It's no' dark enough yet for the candlelighters to be out.'

'Candlelighters. What are they?' she asked, startled.

'It's another name for a thief,' the cook answered her. 'Candlelighters do their mining in secret, at night, in other miners' claims!'

'Yer catch someone around yer tent or yer claim at night, yer shoot first and ask questions later,' another of the group added belligerently.

'What part o' Scotland are ye from?' the cook asked Ella. Then, before she could answer, 'I'd be willing to bet it's north, aye? You've no' the sound of a lowlander.'

'North,' Ella murmured. 'Yes, that's right.'

For a breathless moment she wondered whether he'd go on and tell her the exact location of her birth, but he only smiled and said no more. And she did not see any point in explaining to him her current predicament.

'You'll find all sorts here on the diggin's,' one of

the five butted in. 'Londoners and Cousin Jacks from Cornwall, Frenchies and Germans, even painted men from New Zealand. You'd think it was a bloomin' holiday!'

He pointed his pipe at Adam. 'But we're all of us deadly serious. We want to make our fortunes, just like you do, I reckon.'

There was a pause while they waited expectantly for Adam's answer. Ella felt a sudden, inexplicable tingle of unease.

'I'm planning to set up a store,' Adam replied at last, smiling around in a friendly manner. 'I don't intend to do any digging if I can help it.'

The men laughed in a mocking sort of way.

'I had enough of that in California,' he added quietly.

The effect was not what Ella had expected. The men exchanged a glance that was questioning, almost suspicious. 'Oh aye?' the cook ventured at last, slowly. His eyes showed new interest. 'Do any good, mon?'

Ella opened her mouth, but Adam forestalled her by flinging an arm around her shoulders and squeezing her tight. 'Nothing to boast of,' he answered smoothly. 'Bloody hard work for bloody little! No, I'm not interested in digging for gold this time, boys. Unless it comes out of me customers' pockets!'

At first Ella thought the men were not going to join in Adam's laughter. And then they did, with a roar. Adam was still holding her tight, and when she began to protest, he squeezed a warning.

But the feeling of unease had lifted. Ella sensed her body relaxing, as if some unknown danger had passed.

'Yer'll still need a licence, matey,' one of the men was saying. 'Every man has to have a licence, whether he be a storekeeper or a quack. It's the law. The dancin' master up at the Camp'll send his boys after yer if yer haven't got one. Nothin' they like better than digger huntin'.'

'The dancing master?' Ella repeated, bemused.

They smiled at her, only too pleased to initiate her into Bendigo slang. 'Mr Gilbert, that's his real name. He's the gold commissioner here on Bendigo. Used to be a dancing master or some such thing, so that's what we call him.'

'Actually, Mr Gilbert's a decent enough chap.' The words came from a member of the group who had been silent until now. Ella was surprised to hear such obviously educated tones. A gentleman out to make his fortune? A younger son? Or one of the scorned remittance men -the blacksheep of a well-to-do family sent to the ends of the earth with a yearly remittance to keep him there?

'He's fair, or as fair as any government appointed official can be,' the voice went on. 'But it's true enough, ma'am, about the licence. Your husband will need one even if he doesn't intend to mine. The penalty for not being in possession of a mining licence is a fine of five pounds, or ten days incarceration. My advice is go to the Camp first thing in the morning, before you're questioned by the police. They don't listen to excuses. I'm afraid it's rather a case of *them* and *us*. Jolly unfair!'

'Jolly unfair,' someone mimicked, but it was said in a good-natured way. The gold rush appeared to have brought together an odd assortment of partners.

'*You* know all about incarceration, don't you, Hans?'

Hans, a short, stocky man, nodded gloomily. 'Hans knows the Logs very well!' he agreed in thickly accented English.

'Hans was chained up for two weeks once,' the cook explained to Ella and Adam. 'There's a lock-up at the Camp, but when it's full they chain the prisoners to the trees, or the logs, near it. That's where the name comes from.'

Ella wondered what Hans had done to warrant two weeks in prison, but decided it was better not to ask.

The cook had taken the floor again. 'Where are ye planning to put up your store?'

'I haven't decided.'

'You'll have heard o' the Eaglehawk Gully? There have been fortunes made and lost on Eaglehawk. But you canna get within a mile and a half of the place now ... there's no' room enough to spit, let alone set up a tent!'

'You could try California Gully,' another voice suggested. 'I've heard they've had some good finds around there. Or there's Sailor's Gully. Ironbark, that's rich, they say, and Long Gully's well thought of. White Hills, too. Peg Leg Gully ... well, that's turned out to be another Eaglehawk. You won't get a look in there.'

They were suddenly so helpful. Ella, who had not imagined resident miners would show such concern for new chums, was pleasantly surprised.

'I'm grateful,' Adam said with a grin. He was per-fectly relaxed, leaning back on his heels, his arm loose about her shoulders. Ella took the opportunity to wriggle out of his grip. 'Can you tell me where I'll find the Camp?' he went on.

The gentleman miner pointed towards the far end of Paddy's Gully. 'Straight ahead until you get back onto the main track, and then it's about five miles northeast along the Bendigo Creek. And be prepared to line up at the licensing tent.'

'Bloody unfair it is,' another of the group muttered, banging out his pipe to emphasis his outrage. 'Gold should be free to any man if he's willin' to dig for it. What gives Charley-Joe the right to make us pay for the privilege? And as for that lot up at the Camp, they treat us like criminals. I've 'eard of staunch Queen and Country men turnin' into rebels after a stint at the Logs.'

Ella remembered Lieutenant Moggs with a shudder, and wondered whether the officers at the Camp were all like him. At least Mr Gilbert, the gold commissioner, sounded a reasonable man.

Wolf, who had been nosing about beside her, suddenly lifted his head to stare into the darkness and growled deep in his throat. At the same time a nervous voice called from the shadows.

'Hello there! Hold your dog back!'

'That's just Paddy,' one of the miners reassured them. 'I was wonderin' when he'd turn up.'

Stones rattled down the steep slope on the other side of the gully, and a dark shape crossed the narrow track and stepped into the light of the fire. Wolf growled again, and the stranger hesitated, eyeing the dog uneasily. Ella saw that he was a thin, slight man, sandy of hair and beard, his eyes like dark hollows in his emaciated face.

'Go on then, Paddy,' the cook reassured him. 'Ask your question, mon.' And, in an aside, 'This is Paddy's gully - it's named for him. He asks the same question o' anyone new.'

'You've not seen a man called Mikey O'Halloran?' Irish Paddy asked, peering towards Adam and Ella. 'Mikey O'Halloran?' he repeated. 'I left him at Kilmore six months past. He promised faithfully to come after me, we were to meet here, in this gully. But I've not seen him since.'

'Go on, Paddy!' prompted the cook, as if he were showing off a talented child, 'tell them the look of him.'

Paddy did. 'He was a tall man, and big with it. Dark haired. Dublin-born, like meself.'

Adam shook his head regretfully. 'No, I've not seen him. I'm sorry.'

Paddy sighed but didn't seem surprised by Adam's answer. He hovered, his gaze straying to the frying chops. For a moment he seemed to sway, as though he were floating on the smell of them. The cook took pity and, with a growled, 'Here ye are!', held out a piece of meat. Paddy darted over, snatched it off him, and secreted it within his dirty jacket.

'You've hearts of pure gold, boys,' he told them. The hollow eyes fixed on Ella, and suddenly he grinned at her. 'And here's a pretty one! Hair like the moon, so 'tis.' He stepped closer to her, and for the first time she caught the animal-like smell of him. His voice dropped to a whisper. 'Hair like the moon.' Ella felt her stomach heave as Paddy came even closer and actually put out a ragged nailed finger to caress her hair. She jerked back, unable to bear the thought of him touching her. He stared at her, head cocked to the side, and then with a giggle that was almost childlike, was gone back into the darkness.

The miners were looking at her curiously. One of them murmured, 'Poor bugger – Pardon ladies! – asks everyone the same. We reckon old Mikey's long dead; his throat cut, his bones well picked by now!'

It was probably true, but the picture he conjured was not a pleasant one. Ella glanced nervously about her at the dark gully. Mikey O'Halloran's fate could so easily have been her own.

'There's talk Paddy has a secret claim somewhere up in the bush,' the man went on, still watching Ella. 'But no one's ever found it, and he's too cunning to be followed.'

Behind her, at the cart, she heard Kitty ostentatiously banging the tin plates. 'I'd best go and help,' she murmured, and turned back. If Paddy had a secret gold mine he could keep it to himself! She had no desire to form any close friendships with a man who smelt like an unwashed sheep.

Kitty had made a fire and was cooking their meal. Ella bent to help, ignoring Kitty's sulky look. When she glanced back at the other camp site, she saw that Adam had joined the circle of men, and from the intent looks on their faces, had their full attention.

'Didn't David Marr say he was going to Eagle-hawk Gully?' she asked Kitty. The boy with the dark hair and green eyes, and his grey-faced father, had gone their own way after the climb over Big Hill. But Ella had sensed a certain reluctance in the boy's goodbye.

Now Kitty shrugged as if she didn't care. 'He said his brother was there.'

'I wonder whether we will see him again?'

The meat in the pan hissed and spat, burning Ella's thumb. She made a sound of annoyance, and sucked at it.

'Why should we?' Kitty said behind her, her voice sullen. 'Everyone goes their own way. You'll be goin' yours tomorrow, won't you?'

'Well, I am hopeful,' Ella murmured.

'So am I!' Kitty burst out, as if she couldn't help herself. 'I saw you over there, pressin' yourself all over him! He's mine, do you hear me?' Kitty's blue eyes were furious ... and desperate.

Ella's voice shook with surprised anger. 'I was not pressing myself against anyone.'

'You was! I saw you. And I'd have come over and pulled you off, only-' Suddenly Kitty's voice dried up. She swallowed, and muttered, 'Only I recognised one o' them men from Mrs Ure's inn and I didn't want him to recognise me.'

Puzzled, Ella stared at her down bent face. And then she realised what Kitty meant.

Kitty flashed her an antagonistic look. 'I'm not ashamed of it,' she insisted. 'It's not that I just don't want him to remember in front of Adam ... I don't want Adam to think bad of me.'

'But he already knows.'

'There's a difference between knowing something and havin' your face rubbed in it.'

Ella wondered which of the five men had been Kitty's customer. 'They say they're looking for gold,' she said expressionlessly.

Kitty snorted in disbelief. 'The man I knew

weren't no miner. He were a thief.'

The food was ready by the time Adam returned. He soon restored Kitty to good humour, complimenting her on the meal and teasing her about the admiration of their next-door neighbours.

'They all want to marry you,' he said. 'It's up to you, but I'd take the one with the toffee voice. He's probably royalty.'

Kitty laughed uncomfortably, not daring to meet Ella's eyes, expecting her to spill the truth of the matter.

'As long as you don't choose Paddy,' Ella added with a pretended shudder, and earned herself a surprised and reluctantly grateful look from the girl.

'That reminds me.' Adam turned to Ella. 'What did he say to you when he tried to touch your hair?'

She shuddered again at the memory, sincerely this time. 'He said, "Hair like the moon." Why?'

'Are you sure that's all he said?'

Ella frowned. 'Why should he say anything else?'

'That lot over there,' with a nod of his head towards the five miners, 'think he has a secret claim around here somewhere.'

Ella blinked. 'They cannot possibly think he'd whisper the location of it to me because of the. colour of my hair!'

Adam leaned closer. 'Loneliness does strange things to people.' And then, 'Did you feel there was something not quite right with them over there? That there were things going on in their heads they didn't care to share with us?'

'I did feel something, yes,' Ella agreed slowly. 'Was that why you wouldn't talk about California?'

'Aye.' His dark eyes narrowed. 'Did it strike you as odd, Mrs Seaton, that they took such trouble to convince us this place has no gold, but didn't explain what *they* were doing here? Five big, strong, healthy men ... and no gold.'

It hadn't, but it did now. Suddenly she realised why Adam had smiled and kept his own counsel.

'What *are* they doin' here then?' Kitty asked, all eyes.

Adam rubbed his chin. 'They could be candle-lighters,' he suggested, 'or old lags from Vandemon, come to relieve the miners of their gold.'

Wolf had dropped his chin on Adam's knee and was waiting expectantly, brown eyes begging. Adam didn't disappoint him, caressing the dog's broad head with an expert hand. Wolf gave a deep sigh of contentment.

Adam went on, following his own thoughts. 'The rush at Eaglehawk is still the big one, but Peg Leg Gully is very nearly as rich. Both good places to set up a store.'

'But won't there be plenty of stores there already?' asked Kitty.

Adam winked at her. 'Aye, but with the rain and the bad roads, prices are going up. The bullock drays can charge a fortune to carry goods north from Melbourne and still get plenty of takers. The stores will have to take what goods they can get or go and fetch their own. And the more they pay, the higher their prices. But I don't have to worry about that. I'll charge less and steal all their customers.'

'Is that really fair?' Ella murmured uncertainly.

Adam laughed at her. 'Fair? What's fair about

making money, Mrs Seaton? The important thing is to be smarter than the others. Ollie McLeod taught me that.'

'Who or what is Ollie McLeod?'

Adam's face looked suddenly older. 'Ollie McLeod was a man I knew when I was growin' up in Sydney. He came out to New South Wales as a boy – not a convict, mind, though with some disgrace hanging over him. But he was smart and he was hard, and soon he was one of the richest and most powerful men in old Sydney Town.'

'You sound as if you admired him.' And indeed, there was something in Adam's voice that could have been admiration. But when he looked up and met her eyes, Ella was not so certain.

'I worked for him, off and on,' he said quietly, 'and I learned from him. But I never liked him. No one liked him. He was a bastard.'

Ella felt herself colour at his choice of words, but Kitty leaned closer. 'What were *you* like as a boy, Adam? I bet you 'ad a smooth tongue, even then!'

He smiled at her almost with relief, and Ella knew he was glad to change the subject. 'Aye, I was always good at talking me way out of trouble. Eben didn't bother with talking, he just used his fists. Me ma always said I had the brains. "You'll do better than Ollie McLeod!" she'd say to me. Maybe that's why he's stayed in me head all these years.'

Adam had ambition and determination, and the brains to put them into practice. It was a pity, Ella thought, that such men had to begin at the bottom of the heap. She wondered what he would have been like if he'd had an education, if he'd spoken like the gentleman miner and worn fine clothes and rode a fine horse. Briefly the idea held her spellbound. Adam the gentleman! But it faded, and became ridiculous, and she dismissed it.

'First thing tomorrow,' he was saying, 'I have to go up to the Camp and get that gold licence.'

'Will you take me to see the dancing master?' Ella asked him quietly.

She saw him smile as he bent his head over Wolf.

'The who?' Kitty burst out, but for once Adam ignored her.

'Do you think he'll know you, Mrs Seaton?'

'I don't know,' she murmured. But silently she asked herself the same question. She had remembered his name during Lieutenant Moggs's raid on Nancy Ure's inn. Surely that meant they were acquainted?

Ella's journey may well be coming to an end, too, and Adam must know it.

Kitty was asking again about the dancing master, and Adam was answering her. Briefly Ella allowed herself to remember the look in Adam's eyes on top of Big Hill. The memory made her feel uncomfortable, as if it were her fault. But that was plainly ridiculous. Whatever Adam felt and thought, he was a grown man and could take responsibility for his own actions. At the moment she may seem on the same level as him, but Ella knew she belonged to a different world, one he could never enter. When it was time for bed, Wolf heaved himself up and trotted after Ella. He curled up beside her as if he sensed it might well be for the last time. She cuddled up to his warmth, no longer finding it strange that she should do so, and drifted into sleep. Tomorrow, she thought, Commissioner Gilbert ...

the dancing master ...

She was in a room blazing with candles. Couples danced around and around like exotic moths in a graceful kaleidoscope of colour. She was waltzing, her feet finding the steps effortlessly. Her gown, shimmering green, belled out around her as she turned, and a ruby flashed at her throat. Her partner was tall. She smiled up into his face, but he was gazing straight ahead, lost in his own thoughts.

Gradually, as she danced, her joy in it all began to evaporate. Her eyes strayed again and again towards a far doorway, with an arched and ornate lintel. Birds, carved into the shining wood and painted gold and blue and red, seemed to swoop and dive upon the heads of those passing beneath. She glanced up at her husband - for she knew now that the tall man was her husband - and saw that he was watching the doorway too.

A dark and clammy dread filled her.

Don't come, she whispered to herself. Please, don't come.

But the wish had been made too late. The woman already stood there, poised and still, while above her the wooden birds fluttered.

She was faceless, a dark smooth blank where a face should be, because as yet she had no face. This was the woman Catherine had warned her of. 'He has another woman,' she had said, looking up from her sewing. 'He has another woman.' As if they were discussing the weather.

The dancers stopped dancing. They began to murmur, and the murmur turned into a growl, and the growl into a roar. Her husband released her, vanishing into the taunt-

ing crowd. She turned and ran, bumping into soft bodies, pressing against watts of silk and satin, seeking an escape. And all the while they were laughing at her, amused by her distress.

'He has another woman!'

Someone had stepped in front of her. She looked up, and saw with surprise that it was Adam. But this was an Adam so different she hardly recognised him. He had become a gentleman in a fine black frock coat and a white silk shirt, with his hair trimmed close to his head.

'Adam,' she gasped. 'Help me, please help me. He has another woman.'

Adam smiled. It will be all right now, she thought with relief. Everything would be all right now.

And then Adam took a pistol from inside his fine black coat and shot her through the heart.

CHAPTER 12

———⊱⊰———

THE SCREAM WENT ON AND on, mingling with the echo of the gunshot in her head. Ella struggled up out of sleep. The dream had been so real, it was difficult to shake it off. Half of her was still trapped in the candlelit ballroom. And then Wolf growled beside her and she was back in Paddy's Gully on the Bendigo diggings, and whoever was screaming out in the darkness was not part of any dream.

It came again, loud and frantic, like a razor slashing the tranquillity. 'Help! Help me, for Gawd's sake!'

The shocking cry faded again into the darkness, and the silence it left was almost as terrible. The five miners were stumbling from their tents, mumbling questions. Dogs were barking. Ella crawled out from under the cart and saw Adam silhouetted against the embers of the fire.

'What is it?' she whispered.

But the scream came again. 'I'm down a hole! Help me, help me!'

'What's happening?' Kitty was behind them, her arms wrapped around herself, shivering.

'Sounds like a woman's fallen into one of the old mine shafts,' Adam answered grimly. 'It's probably full of water.'

'Oh no,' Ella gasped, horrified. 'Is there anything we can do?'

He flashed her a grin. 'Aye, we can get her out!' And then he was gone into the darkness, almost instantly lost from sight.

Another scream rent the air, and Ella shuddered violently. A vivid image filled her mind – a woman, alone in the cold, black water. 'Oh Lord, how dreadful,' she whispered. 'Adam said some of those holes are thirty feet deep. What if she drowns before they can reach her?'

Kitty shrugged her shoulders indifferently. 'She should've looked where she was going, shouldn't she?'

Shocked, Ella stared back at her.

'What can *we* do?' the girl declared defensively. 'It's better if we stay here and let 'em get on with it. We've got our own problems, haven't we?'

With a flash of insight, Ella realised that this was how Kitty had survived her harsh life so far, by surrounding herself with a hard, protective shell and not allowing the problems of others to pierce it. But Ella knew she wasn't able to do that – she couldn't go back to bed while someone was drowning. And a woman, too!

There were few enough of the so-called weaker sex on the goldfields, surely it was only right and proper that she go and offer moral support?

Ella took a step into the darkness.

'Where are you going?' Kitty demanded.

'I'm going to see if there's something I can do to help.'

Kitty stared at her blankly. 'You'll probably fall down a hole yourself,' she said, and laughed softly.

Angrily, Ella marched off, in the direction of the call for help. But it took only a few steps for her anger to cool, and to realise Kitty was right. It was no simple matter to make one's way through any part of the diggings at night, but a gully as deserted as Paddy's Gully was especially dangerous.

Ella hesitated, tempted to turn back, but the awful thought of sitting, waiting, and not knowing what was happening decided her. Cautiously, she continued on. The heavy rain had made the ground dangerously slippery. Dips and rises scarred the surface of the gully, and there were plenty of abandoned mine shafts. One wrong step and Ella would be in the same predicament as the woman she was on her way to help.

A night bird called forlornly. Rain, light as mist, swept across the diggings, chilling Ella to the bone. Just ahead of her a single tent offered comfort of a sort, but when she ventured too close, a hostile voice called out from the calico depths, demanding to know who she was and threatening her with violence.

Again she hesitated, about to retreat, when a flicker of light caught her eye. She leaned forward, peering ahead. Did she hear the hum of voices, or was it merely wishful thinking?

But as she picked her way closer, Ella saw that she had indeed reached her destination. The flicker of light was a lantern affixed to a pole, that someone was holding high in the air. A small crowd of men stood in a rough circle and the feeble light shone over them, picking out cabbage-tree hats and bearded faces. The scream came again, shrill with terror, and Ella quickened her step.

'Hold on there, Maryanne!' A gruff voice offered encouragement. 'We'll 'ave yer out, Maryanne!'

Ella had reached them now. She stretched up, anxiously trying to see over the backs of the men before her. When that didn't work, she tapped their shoulders and asked to be allowed through. There were curious looks, and one of them – it looked like the Scots cook – called out, 'Make way now for the lady!'

Suddenly Ella found a cleared passage before her, lined with grinning, bearded faces.

'There yer are, ma'am!' someone boomed kindly. And another, more bold than the rest, 'Fine evenin' for it, ma'am!'

But Ella did not answer, for now at last the full horror of the scene had been revealed to her.

It *was* an abandoned mine shaft, as Adam had said, and it *was* filled with water. And in the lantern light a woman's disembodied face seemed to float in that inky water. She looked small and fragile, a white blur of fear and cold. The water did not reach to the top of the shaft – if it had, the woman would have drowned – but lapped at her shoulders. Ella guessed the hole must have been ten feet deep, for the top of the woman's head was near to five feet below the level of the ground.

A branch had been manoeuvred into the shaft, and Maryanne had hold of it. 'Hold on now, Maryanne.' The voice came from close by. One of the miners was kneeling by the hole in what Ella felt was a rather precarious position.

Maryanne was holding on, she was clinging frantically to the branch. But each time the men tried to pull her out, her hands slipped. Ella realised with a terrible jolt that Maryanne's struggle was sending her deeper and deeper into the hole.

'Get me out, get me out!' The hysterical cry shook them all. 'Eddie, I'm sinkin' in the mud!'

'We will, we will, don't you worry.' Eddie, still kneeling by the hole, was so close now to the edge that the unstable ground gave way and a clod of earth splashed into the water. He didn't falter, although Ella heard the thread of hysteria echoed in his voice. 'We'll get you out, hold on now, hold on.'

It was obvious to everyone that Maryanne was sinking into the slush at the bottom of the hole; the water was already up to her chin. Surely only a few moments remained before that white, beseeching face vanished altogether?

'We need a ladder!' a voice shouted.

'And where'll we get that?' Eddie snapped over his shoulder. Then, his voice softening as he turned back to Maryanne, 'Listen now, lovie. Our mate here is goin' to lean down and try an' catch your hands. You hold onto him. Hold on tight, and we'll pull you out'

Maryanne nodded back jerkily, her teeth chattering.

Ella tried to see around the press of men at her side, to get a glimpse of the rescuer. Someone was indeed stripping off his jacket. His broad chest and shoulders were very familiar ... a tingle of shock went through her.

It was Adam.

She opened her mouth to call out to him, perhaps to wish him luck or to tell him to take care, but there was no time. He was already lying himself down flat on the ground at the side of the hole. Two others had moved to hold his legs, anchoring him. There were some murmured instructions and then the crowd fell silent. Cautiously, Adam eased his way out over the edge of the hole, the upper part of his chest and shoulders leaning into space.

'Oh Gawd,' Maryanne moaned to herself. 'I can feel meself sinkin' ... Oh Eddie, Eddie ...'

Eddie looked as if he wanted to leap into the water with her. Sweat trickled into his eyes and he lifted a hand to wipe it. For the first time, Ella noticed that he had only one arm – the empty sleeve was tucked into his breast – and understood why it was Adam going to Maryanne's rescue, and not Eddie.

Adam had manoeuvred his body further out into space, only his hips and legs now remaining on the precarious ground around the hole. With amazing strength and agility he stretched out over the gap between himself and Maryanne. Another clod of earth broke off, hitting the water. There was a hiss of consternation from the crowd.

Oh, don't, Ella thought. Please, don't ...

'Get me out, get me out!' Maryanne screeched.

'Take me hands,' Adam said.

Maryanne seemed to notice him for the first time and with an ear piercing shriek made a frantic grab for him. Their fingers touched ... and slipped away. The crowd groaned.

'The mud's got me!' Maryanne sobbed, her face streaked with dirt and tears. 'I can feel it sinkin' around me feet. Oh Gawd, oh Gawd!'

She *was* sinking. Ella, filled with a terrible sense of helplessness, watched as the water lapped over her chin. Adam forced himself yet another inch out into nothingness. Sweat dripped off his face, and his arms trembled with sheer effort. If the men holding him lost their grip, if the soil gave way beneath him, he would fall head first into the treacherous slush.

And that would be the end of him.

Suddenly Ella's legs were shaking badly. She dropped abruptly to her knees, impervious to the damp seeping into her skirts. Her eyes were fixed on the scene before her, and she was willing Adam to succeed.

He had stretched out his arms again, the muscles in them standing out. 'Take me hands, woman,' he said in a harsh voice. 'Come on ... take them.'

Maryanne looked up into his face, her own ugly with terror, and it was as if something she saw there steadied her. She reached out, but slowly this time. Her trembling fingers brushed his, caught his ... and held.

Adam gave a smile that was more like a grimace. 'Pull, boys!' he shouted. The men tugged, hauling him in like a big fish. Maryanne came out of the water, but only an inch or two. Her arms were stretched painfully taut.

'It's the mud ...' she moaned. 'It won't let me go!'

'Pull harder!' yelled Adam. The men behind him braced themselves, and others came forward to help. With a shout they began to heave Adam backwards.

For an instant Ella thought Maryanne's arms would spring out of their sockets, so fast was she stuck. And then, with a screech, she came free. The crowd gave a great cheer of relief. Momentarily, Maryanne bobbed like a cork in the inky water, and then, dangling from Adam's hands, she was trawled along to the lip of the hole. Several other hands were reaching out, helping to haul the wretched, dripping woman to safety.

In no time Maryanne lay sprawled on the ground, half drowned and sobbing like a child, while Adam slumped nearby, basking in back-slaps and congratulations. The whole episode could only have taken a few minutes, but it had seemed like hours.

Ella steadied her own shaking legs, and made her way to Maryanne's side. 'Are you hurt?' she asked, bending close. 'Maryanne?'

'Oh Gawd, I were nearly done for then,' wailed Maryanne.

Ella patted her shoulder awkwardly. She was relieved when Eddie, kneeling on Maryanne's other side, lifted the woman into a powerful embrace. The crowd looked on unashamedly. They had suffered with Maryanne and Eddie, they had watched Adam's rescue, and now they felt they had every right to be in at the happy ending.

Ella caught Adam's eyes, her own filling with tears. He looked exhausted, too tired to do more than smile while the crowd lauded him.

'You saved her life,' Eddie was saying in a gruff voice - a rough man unused to showing emotion. He flicked a glance at Adam. 'I don't know what to say to you, mate. I don't even know your name.'

Adam grinned wearily. 'Adam.'

'Three cheers for Adam!'

A shout went up, ringing around the gully. Everyone was smiling. They would have hoisted him onto their shoulders then, but Maryanne forestalled them. She lifted her head from Eddie's chest and fixed great, dark, tear-drowned eyes on her rescuer. 'You saved me life, Adam. I'm that grateful...'

Startled, Ella turned to look at her. This was not how the story was meant to go, surely? Maryanne should be swooning, full of pathetic gratitude. Instead there was something bold and challenging in the woman's eyes, and something definitely inviting in her parted lips. Ella's entire perception of her turned upside-down.

Eddie made a noise like a growl, and pulled Maryanne none too gently to her feet. 'Back to the tent,' he ordered her. 'And next time you go wanderin' around in the dark and fall down a hole, you can bloody well stay there!'

Eddie prodded Maryanne through the laughing crowd. Someone muttered, 'He's got his 'ands full with that one,' and there was more laughter. But the crowd, sensing the drama had come to an end, began to fragment, each going his own way.

Adam shivered and bent to pick up his jacket, easing it on with stiff, tired movements. Wolf, forgotten until now, began to frolic around him, and Adam stooped to ruffle the big dog's coat. Ella, watching him, thought: He doesn't look like a man who's just saved someone's life. And yet that was what he had done. She felt as if these few moments in Paddy's Gully had changed him in some way ... or perhaps they had changed her.

'Are *you* all right?' she asked him quietly.

'Aye.' He smiled at her, and then, as if only just realising what her presence meant, narrowed his eyes. 'What are you doing here? It's dangerous to go walkin' around the diggings at night. The same thing could've happened to you.'

'I thought that I may be able to help,' she replied meekly. 'And I took particular care where I stepped.'

'Oh, did you now? Well, you'd better take me arm this time, just to be on the safe side.' But the anger had gone out of him as quickly as it came, and she saw the shadowy curve of a smile on his mouth as she took his arm. They walked in silence.

'You were very brave,' Ella said softly at last.

'Is that what you think?' His voice was full of pleasure.

'I do. And,' with a teasing note, 'Maryanne seemed most grateful.'

His smile went awry. 'Women like Maryanne are easily won.' There was a certain amount of male derision in his tone.

'Oh?'

'I was never a man to take the easy way. The harder a thing is, the more I want it.'

'Oh,' she repeated coolly. But the coolness was a front; inside she was trembling.

Adam had stopped walking, and his grip on her arm forced her to stop too. She did so, unwillingly, and turned back to him. His expression was hidden in the darkness, and she didn't see his hand reach out towards her, only felt his cold fingers brush her cheek.

Her mind rang a warning. Walk away, it said. You can find your way back to Kitty without him. But the trembling inside her had nothing to do with her mind. She closed her eyes, as if by doing this she could disassociated herself from him. But she could still feel his fingertips against her skin. His thumb brushed back and forth across her lips.

'Mrs Seaton.'

'Adam, you know this is not possible – '

'Shhh.' His breath touched where his thumb had been. Ella felt his warmth reaching out to her, engulfing her. A great longing filled the emptiness within her. There can be no harm in it that reckless demon whispered at her ear. What does it matter if I find some comfort in this man's arms? Who will know? After tomorrow, I may never see him again.

Adam's mouth touched hers, so lightly ... but he groaned as if he were in pain. Her hands slid up over the front of his damp shirt to his shoulders, and clung there. He had been shivering, but now he seemed to have forgotten his wet clothing. He had forgotten everything but her.

'Adam, we cannot.' But was it him she was trying to bring to his senses or herself?

'I love the way you say me name,' he whispered. 'All soft and singing.'

Ella stiffened in his arms, denying the sudden urge to lean into him. She knew that Maryanne's near drowning had filled him with a terrible uncertainty of life ... she knew, because she felt it too. Every moment was precious – a gold nugget to be held tightly in both hands.

'Me mind's full of you, Mrs Seaton.' He admitted it as if he had only just realised it.

'Adam.' She took a breath, seeking for words to break the spell that was falling over them. 'I'm married to someone else – '

'You mean you're a lady, and I'm nothin',' he cut her short roughly.

Was that what she meant? Ella did not need her memory restored to know the rules of the narrow society in which she lived.

'When I look at you, I don't see you as a lady,' Adam was saying. 'I see behind that. I see *you*. I see you, Ella.'

And he kissed her, his mouth hot and strong on hers.

She forgot where she was, and had she known *who* she was, Ella was certain she would have forgotten that too. Her eyes were closed, but she knew if she opened them she would be standing in a clearing in a dark forest with the moon beaming down on her. The moonlight was like fire, a wave of heat encircling her, and it had arms and a mouth and its name was Adam.

He groaned against her lips, and the sound broke the spell. Ella opened her eyes and she was back in Paddy's Gully in the darkness and the rain, and the man she was kissing with such desperate passion was a tinker called Adam.

With a cry, Ella twisted out of his arms. The throbbing was still there, deep in her body, but she ignored it. Her mouth was bruised and sore, but she ignored that too. 'I have a husband!' she gasped. He laughed without humour, and his voice was as breathless as hers. 'That's my bad luck, isn't it?'

Ella felt suddenly awfully tired. Her very bones felt tired. There was an ache, beginning in her temples and travelling all the way down to her toes, that spoke of sleeping in the cold and wet too often.

'I have a husband,' she repeated wearily. 'I'm sorry if I've led you to believe ... if you think I ...' But her tongue refused to form anything like a coherent sentence. 'It can't be,' she ended bluntly. 'It could *never be*.'

He sighed, a sound as soft as the rain. 'You're tempting fate with that word "never" Mrs Seaton.'

But Ella had turned and was walking back to the camp.

CHAPTER 13

THE GOVERNMENT CAMP ON CAMP Hill was the official heart of the Bendigo diggings. It was from here that Governor La Trobe's minions controlled the goldfield, issuing orders and sending out troopers to enforce them. There was a military look about the place that spoke of order and purpose, accentuated by the Union Jack snapping smartly in the breeze.

Tents, big and small, stood to attention. These flimsy structures of calico and canvas were for the men, while the horses were stabled in relative slab and bark luxury.

Ella could see that already a large crowd of miners was assembled outside one of the tents, and guessed this must be where gold licences were issued. A matching pair of troopers, in blue coats and white breeches, rode by on shining mounts. A small group of pensioner soldiers drilled in their green uniforms, the muskets at their shoulders glowing with spit and polish, though sadly out of date.

Opposite the two-rail fence which surrounded the camp, the Bendigo diggings ebbed and flowed. Tent businesses were already shoulder to shoulder down Camp Street, following the line of the Bendigo Creek, and there was also plenty of activity along the narrow gully that ran at right angles to Camp Street, past the camp's upper entrance. By reading the painted signs, Ella could pick out from among the usual number of stores, an apothecary, a solicitor, and the post office.

A small troop of police hurried past. They glanced contemptuously at Adam's cart and its occupants, as if their uniforms somehow made them superior. Ella wondered with a sinking heart if it was going to be like Carlsruhe all over again. Would Mr Gilbert judge her by her appearance, just as Lieutenant Moggs had judged her? She knew her blue skirts were stained with mud from last night, and that her shoes were worse. She remembered again the smart red cloak she had owned, and sighed.

That morning they had breakfasted and packed their belongings, and left Paddy's Gully while the birds were just stirring. The track had taken them down into Golden Gully, which was a great deal more lively than Paddy's, and on through Golden Point. It was here that gold – as legend already had it – was first discovered by Mrs Kennedy, the wife of a sheep station overseer called Happy Jack.

Once more on the main road, they had followed the Bendigo Creek and seen the Bendigo Valley open up before them. Wide and flat, with hills encircling it, the valley stretched seven miles from White Hills in the north to Kangaroo Flat in the south, with numerous gullies spilling into it along the way. In the morning sunshine, the sight of so many men digging, panning and puddling, had been fantastical, while the din they made had been deafening.

There were too many tents to count, some of

them little more than squares of calico strung up with rope over branches. If it wasn't for the occasional slab hut, adding a feeling of permanency, Ella would have found it quite easy to believe that the entire valley could pack up and vanish overnight.

Every second tent along the main route to the camp had flown a flag proclaiming it to be a store. There were signs which read: *Bed and Meals, 20s a week,* and *Picks Sharpened for 2/6d,* and *Hair cut and Beards trimmed.* There were blacksmiths, wheelwrights, butchers, bakers and bootmakers, as well as the ubiquitous coffee shops. Bemused, Ella had noticed that one tent even proclaimed itself a *Lending Library for the Improvement of the Mind.*

A little further on, an auction had been in progress. A sign board had been propped up, announcing: Yankee Charlie, Auctioneer. Yankee Charlie himself was standing on a tea chest, rousing his crowd to a fever pitch of excitement, selling everything from sheets and shovels, to horses and hats, to blankets and buttons. Adam had explained that such auctions usually consisted of the belongings of departing or broken miners.

As they had driven past, Ella twisted around to watch the proceedings, and the auctioneer caught her eye. 'I've just the thing for you, ma'am!' he drawled. 'A tea service, genuine porcelain, ten guineas!'

Adam snorted. 'And you can keep it at that price, Charlie me boy.'

Ella had laughed, and Adam winked back at her.

But despite the easy moment, there was constraint between them. Ella had felt it ever since they rose this morning. If it hadn't been for Kitty's chatter, they probably wouldn't have exchanged more than half a dozen words. It was as if the thread of camaraderie, which had carried them along so far, had snapped.

The beginnings of a headache pounded behind her temples, and Ella rubbed her eyes. She glanced at Adam, wondering whether she had imagined the sensations of last night. He had been fire and light then, engulfing her; now, in the stark light of day, Ella blushed at such fancifulness.

She looked at him hard and saw only a tinker, and a rather desperate one at that! His fair hair was untidy, the stubble had grown longer on his face and his dark eyes were slitted with weariness. Surely there was nothing in Adam to turn the thoughts of a discriminating woman to romance! And besides – with a tug of excitement – she had more important things to consider.

Ella turned to watch the Union Jack fluttering against the cold blue sky. Soon, she reminded herself, she may well know who she was. Soon she may have a name and an identity. Soon she may no longer be a lost and nameless ghost. The dancing master, Mr Gilbert, would help her, and – the hope burst into life inside her – might even recognise her.

Adam found a smithy willing to stable Bess and the cart while they went about their business. As Ella had guessed, it was the licensing tent where the restless crowd of men waited.

'Like,' Kitty sneered, 'sheep for shearing.'

Adam smiled wearily. 'Then I'll just have to join the mob,' he said, and glanced at Ella. 'It doesn't look as if the commissioner's started giving out licences yet, but he should be around here some-where. Do you want me to come with you to find him?'

Ella hesitated. At Carlsruhe, she remembered, Adam had done the talking and Lieutenant Moggs had ignored her petition. Perhaps she would have more luck without him. 'No,' she said firmly. 'I can manage on my own.'

He didn't reply, but he gave her a strange look.

'I'll stay with you, Adam,' Kitty announced.

But Adam wasn't having that. 'You go with Mrs Seaton. I'll meet you both back at the cart.'

'I'd rather stay with you,' Kitty wheedled, sidling closer to him.

'I don't need looking after. And if I do, Wolf can do it.' He was smiling as he said it, but he meant it

The girl pouted, but didn't argue any further. And although Ella wouldn't admit it, she was glad of Kitty's company.

'I'd better get over there with the rest, if I want that licence by nightfall,' Adam murmured. He held out a hand to Ella. 'Good luck, Mrs Seaton.'

She placed her fingers in his. They were so warm and strong ... she wished suddenly that she was wearing gloves. He was looking at her as if he were remembering kissing her, and wanted to do it again. No gentleman would ever look at a lady like that, Ella told herself shakily.

'What was all that about?' Kitty asked suspi-ciously, as he walked away.

'I have no idea,' said Ella breathlessly.

The guard at the door of the licensing tent informed Ella that the commissioner had been delayed on another matter, but was expected shortly. He called out to a passing constable with the curt instruction, 'Gregs here'll take care of yer.'

Gregs gave them a searching look. 'What is it you want? Not from a cat-house, I hopes?' But from the gleam in his eye it was clear he was hoping just the opposite.

Ella didn't know what a 'cat-house' was, but Kitty obviously did. She set her hands on her hips and glared at the man. 'Watch your tongue! This here is Mrs Seaton, and she 'as an appointment with Mr Gilbert. So, quick smart, you take us to him!'

The constable's mouth set mulishly.

Ella decided it was time to step in. 'Please, I must speak with Mr Gilbert urgently.'

The man glanced from Kitty to Ella, and then shrugged. 'I'll take you up there but I don't make no promises he'll see you.'

He led them across the trampled muddy ground of the camp, towards a row of smallish tents, pausing only briefly as a laden wagon groaned its way across their path.

'What's a cat-house?' Ella whispered to Kitty.

'You don't want to know.'

'I do want to know, that's why I'm asking.'

Kitty's look was ironic. 'It's a whore house, Mrs Seaton.'

Ella glared at the constable's back.

Beyond the tents and stables, the extensive camp grounds rose sharply and Ella could see the infamous lock-up set among tall gum trees. The gaol appeared to be built of tree trunks, one piled atop the other. Surely there could be no way out of it once the door was bolted?

'Wait here!'

The constable's voice brought her back from her contemplations, and Ella realised that they had stopped outside one of the tents. If this was the commissioner's private quarters, it was anything but palatial. Indeed, it wasn't even distinguishable from the others. Ella watched Constable Gregs duck his head in through the opening, managing to salute at the same time, and murmur a request. In a moment, another man appeared, youngish and neatly dressed. He frowned at the two women.

'I am Mr Gilbert's clerk,' he announced, with some self-importance. 'Mr Gilbert is an extremely busy man. What is it you want?'

Ella's heart sank at such unfriendliness, but she rallied and stepped forward. 'Sir, I have a request to make.' And she explained her situation as briefly and clearly as she could, while the clerk listened to her in impatient silence.

'Well, that is indeed an unfortunate story,' he said at last, still frowning. 'But I doubt if Mr Gilbert can help you. You may be surprised to know, ma'am, just how many people, men *and* women, are missing on the goldfields. And how many poor creatures die or are murdered without anyone having the least idea of their names.' He cleared his throat, avoiding Ella's anxious eyes. 'However ... wait one moment. The commissioner is presently engaged with one of his officers, but I will speak to him on your behalf.'

And he went back inside the tent and left them to the watchful gaze of Gregs. The constable smirked at Kitty, and she stared back at him belligerently. But Ella stood like a statue, eyes fixed on the entrance to the tent. Her hands were trembling and she clasped them tightly together, at the same time schooling her legs to remain upright. Everything seemed to hinge on the next few moments, her life suspended. She wanted to scream with the frustration of waiting, but something inside her was telling her: I must not show it. I must not let them see …

That's one of the things that attracted me to you, a voice said in her head, a voice from the past. *You are so cold, so frozen. You don't feel anything very much, do you?*

And Ella heard her own silent reply: *But I'm not like that.' Can't you see? I'm frightened and lonely. Can't you see?*

The laird's daughter, the voice went on, measured and self-satisfied. *You're every inch the laird's daughter, wife.*

'Mrs Seaton?' Kitty was tugging at her arm. Ella blinked and brought the girl back into focus. 'Mrs Seaton? He's coming.'

For a moment Ella didn't know what she was talking about. And then she simultaneously shook off Kitty's hand and the strange voice in her head, and turned to face the man she had come to see. Now! she thought. He knows me!

But as soon as their eyes met, she knew she was a stranger to him, just as he was a stranger to her. A sick disappointment gripped her. It took all her strength not to drop to her knees at Mr Gilbert's feet.

'Ma'am?' He looked concerned – a handsome man, middle-aged, with strength and decency in his eyes. 'My clerk tells me you have been misplaced.'

Ella heard her own voice as if coming from a long way away. 'Yes, sir. I had hoped ... I had hoped you may have some recollection of me.' It sounded foolish and presumptuous now that they were face to face.

But Mr Gilbert smiled and shook his head sadly. 'I believe, ma'am, if we had ever met I would have remembered you. Still, all is not lost I will make certain enquiries. Something may well come to light. You are not ... eh, destitute?' And his gaze slipped unobtrusively over her, assessing her situation with all the ease of vast experience.

'No, sir. I have found ... friends.'

'Ah.' His eyes shifted, perhaps a little reluctantly, towards the licensing tent and the growing, restive crowd of prospective miners. 'My apologies, ma'am, but I have my duties to perform. The men find enough to object to in paying for their licences, without making them wait overlong for the privilege.' He glanced at his clerk. 'In the meantime, I shall do my utmost to assist you. In fact, I have just the man ... Lieutenant!' He half turned, calling over his shoulder, and then smiled at Ella. 'You are fortunate, ma'am, that this very day we have been assigned a new officer. He comes very highly recommended. "A man of the utmost integrity", weren't they the governor's words?' And he glanced at his clerk for confirmation.

The clerk agreed in a low murmur, but there was something in his face that made Ella think he did not concur with Governor La Trobe's glowing praise.

'Sir?'

The voice made her look up. And freeze.

Beside her Kitty choked on an indrawn breath, but Ella didn't hear her. She was wondering how she could bear any more today. Fainting would be an easy way out, but Ella was quite determined not to show any weakness in front of Lieutenant Moggs.

He looked just as spick and span as he had last time she saw him, and his boots were dark mirrors. He had recognised her too. She watched his body stiffen, like a hound scenting its quarry, and then his eyes blazed with satisfaction. 'Well, Mrs Seaton!' It was more of a challenge than a greeting.

Mr Gilbert looked from one to the other of them, puzzled. 'Have you met?'

'Indeed we have,' Moggs replied in a gratingly jovial voice. 'At Carlsruhe. I know all about this lady's plight.'

Mr Gilbert half smiled. 'Then it appears I have made a wise choice,' he said quietly. 'I am going to leave this lady in your capable hands, Lieutenant Moggs. As you know, she has lost her memory. Where were you found, ma'am? Seaton's Lagoon, was it? And before that you were seen travelling south through Bush Inn and Sawpit Gully? Yes, quite possibly you originated from the Bendigo diggings. But Lieutenant Moggs will sort it out for you.'

Moggs hastened to reassure him. 'I am more than willing to assist Mrs Seaton, sir. Indeed, I feel that I am just the man for the task.'

For the past few minutes Ella had felt as if she were caught in an ever quickening whirlpool, sucked under by forces far stronger than herself. But now she struggled to the surface. 'Mr Gilbert

... please, I must speak with you. This man ... this man ...'

But the commissioner's clerk was murmuring into his ear, and there were voices growing louder from the licensing tent. Ella's audience was at an end. 'Good day to you, ma'am!' the commissioner called as he walked away. 'And good luck!'

'But, sir! Please!'

He was gone. She could have run after him, but she didn't. Why should he believe her when he had read such good reports of Moggs from La Trobe? Mr Gilbert was a busy man, a man with much on his mind, and her problem was minor in comparison. What did the Bendigo authorities care if one woman, more or less, was misplaced on the gold-fields? They were concerned with the more lofty matters of gold licences or the lack thereof. Order, that was what the camp dealt in. The human face of the diggings was not its concern.

'How providential, Mrs Seaton,' mocked the cold, clipped voice of Lieutenant Moggs.

Well, at least he had remembered her name this time, Ella thought grimly.

Moggs was looking over her head, his eyes searching the camp, and again there was something of the hunter in his action. Ella watched him, saying nothing, making him ask. 'Where is your man?'

'I don't know who you mean.'

But Kitty butted in. 'If you're askin' about Adam, he's buying himself a gold licence so he can't be arrested by the likes of you!'

'So. He is here, then,' Moggs said softly, indifferent to her hostility. 'That's good news.' He sounded pleased, but there was no mistaking the cold danger in his eyes.

Kitty must have sensed it too, for her cheeks turned into two brilliant spots of colour. She cried out, 'He hasn't done nothing wrong!'

Moggs ignored her, concentrating on Ella. 'Our commissioner has asked me to be of assistance to you, Mrs Seaton. He trusts my judgment in this matter. And my judgment tells me that the best thing I can do for you is to remove you from the unhealthy influence of your servant ... Wasn't that what you called him at Sawpit Gully? You appear to have fallen in with very bad company, Mrs Seaton.'

'I'm not going anywhere with you,' Ella whispered in a voice that sounded rusty.

'Well, the choice is yours ... but not for long perhaps.' Moggs watched for her reaction, and when Ella refused to show her fear of him, raised an eyebrow.

'I will tell Mr Gilbert what you have said,' she burst out. 'I will tell him you have no intention of helping me.'

Moggs pretended surprise. 'But I have just said I will help you, Mrs Seaton. And as for Mr Gilbert changing his opinion of me, why should he? I hardly think he will take the word of a nameless slut over that of a gentleman and officer of the Queen.'

Ella opened her mouth to answer him but nothing came out.

'Come on,' Kitty pulled at her arm. 'Come *on*.'

'Yes, you can go now,' Moggs said behind them. 'But I mean to do my duty by you, Mrs Seaton. Tell Adam that! Tell him I'll be watching him ... like an eaglehawk.'

Kitty pulled her along, her fingers making bruises on Ella's arm. 'Bastard,' she muttered furiously. 'Arrogant bloody bastard.' But she shivered as if she were cold.

'I thought we'd left him behind,' Ella said breathlessly, her head spinning. 'It was unpleasant ... unfortunate ... but it was over. His men were talking of him taking up a new post, but I never imagined ... And now he's here, on Bendigo, and he sees himself as Adam's Nemesis.'

'Well, I don't know what that is,' Kitty retorted, 'but I do know that we'd better warn Adam to keep out of his way.'

'Perhaps he won't be staying. Perhaps Mr Gilbert will realise what he is and send him back to Carlsruhe.'

But there was no conviction in Ella's voice, and Kitty didn't even bother to answer.

By the time Adam returned to the cart, Ella's headache was so bad she had to shade her eyes from the winter sun, which from its position showed the time was well past midday.

He looked out of sorts, and rolled his eyes when Kitty asked how he'd gone. 'I stood in line and waited me turn,' he said heavily.

Kitty giggled, twirling a chestnut curl around her finger.

Adam smiled back wryly, his gaze searching out Ella's. But she wouldn't meet it directly – she felt too disappointed and too vulnerable. She answered his question before he could ask.

'Mr Gilbert didn't know me.'

'I'm sorry,' Adam murmured in what was no

doubt meant to be a comforting voice.

Ella didn't believe him. He's glad I've had another setback, she thought angrily. He wants me to be abandoned and forgotten. He wants me for himself.

'We saw Lieutenant Moggs.'

Adam looked at Kitty sharply, his face gone blank.

'He said to tell you he'll be watchin' you,' she added, trying to make a joke of it. But her eyes were scared as she waited for his reaction.

Adam laughed.

'He can't do nothin' to you,' Kitty went on, angry for his sake. 'You haven't broken any laws.'

'No.' He smiled at her and patted his pocket 'I've got me licence right here, if he wants to come and take a look at it.'

Kitty's fears of Moggs seemed to ease when Adam took them so lightly. But Ella noticed that although he joked with the girl, he seemed distracted as they climbed aboard the cart. She wondered whether he was thinking of Eben and Nancy Ure, and wishing he had run with them when he had the chance.

The five-mile-long road to Eaglehawk Gully was well-worn, and certainly much busier than that to Paddy's Gully. Groups of miners struggled along, bent double with their gear, or pushing laden barrows. A gig bounced by, a woman in a black dress and bonnet driving, with two small children beside her.

There *were* women here, if one looked hard enough, but it was the men who dominated. They lived rough, transient lives, ready at the drop of a hat to gather together their sparse belongings and move on to the next rush.

Bess took them through areas of the diggings that looked as if they had been turned upside down - or inside out! Mounds of yellow clay lay on the surface, scars upon the once tranquil land, while only tree stumps remained of once lush forests. Thick stands of ironbarks still blanketed the rough hills around Ironbark, giving it its name, and the place had the reputation of a bushrangers' hideout. The names along the way rang in Ella's head like a song: Ironbark, New Chum Gully, Long Gully, Derwent Gully, Maiden Gully, California Gully, Peg Leg Gully ... and the most famous of them all, Eaglehawk Gully.

Eaglehawk Gully was a thriving place; the clank and bang and rattle of men working reverberated throughout. There didn't seem to be a single inch of ground to spare. The rush here was at its peak, and every week thousands of miners arrived, their heads filled with tales of instant wealth. Peg Leg Gully turned out to be as rich and overcrowded as Eaglehawk.

They moved on as the afternoon closed in, and the wind strengthened and blew cold against Ella's aching head.

The sun was low in the sky when Adam finally found his spot. It was one of the lesser gullies running into California Gully.

'Midnight Gully,' Adam told them with a grin.

There were already a couple of stores in evidence, as well as various tradesmen, but when Kitty pointed that out, Adam promised her they would still do well.

Midnight Gully was a wide strip of ground between two gentle slopes. As yet it still retained something of an unspoiled air, although there were the usual holes and corresponding mounds of earth. They found a slight rise on which to make a camp, and Adam pulled Bess up with a weary 'Whoa!'.

Ella sat a moment in the cart, feeling as if she were still moving. There was an old grey box tree growing further up the rise, its branches outstretched towards the sinking sun, its blue-green leaves making dark shadows against streaks of pink and mauve in the sky.

She listened to the breeze whispering around her, and felt weak tears sting her eyes.

I was foolish to pin any hopes on Mr Gilbert. I should have learned from Mrs Weatherby. But I so longed to have this puzzle at an end.

'Tomorrow we'll set up the tarpaulin and fly our flag,' Adam was saying.

'Have you got a flag?' Kitty asked him in delight.

Adam searched in the back of the cart and found what he was looking for. A yellow rectangle with an 'A' sewn on it. 'I had it made in Melbourne,' he said with a self-conscious grin.

Kitty laughed.

Ella began to climb down from the cart, and then changed her mind. Her headache was a dull, sick thudding in her temples, and her legs seemed to be made of sand.

As if from a long way away, she heard Kitty say, 'What's up with 'er?'

And Adam's reply, 'She's had a bad day.'

'She just doesn't want to do any of the work,' Kitty returned scornfully. 'If it were up to her ladyship there, we'd all starve to death.'

'Mutton and damper?' Ella retorted wearily. 'We may as well.'

'What?' Kitty rounded on her, ready for a fight.

But Adam defused the situation, sending Kitty to check on the prices of the other stores. She went, sulky, but not quite willing to refuse a request from Adam. Suddenly Ella felt sorry for the girl, wishing her less transparent, less in love.

'Have you had a bad day, Mrs Seaton?'

It was asked quietly and with genuine concern. The tears that had stung her eyes, and which she had held back for so long, began to trickle out from beneath her closed lids.

'Yes.'

'Here, I'll help you down.'

She felt his arms around her, and slipped forward heavily against him. He caught his breath at the suddenness of her descent, but steadied himself, supporting her. He was so solid, she thought, all hard flesh and muscle. Surely nothing could ever shake him.

'I don't think I can stand up,' she whispered.

She felt his fingers brush her temple, where the bruise still showed. For once they felt cool, soothing against her hot skin. She thought she heard him sigh.

'You've got a fever, Mrs Seaton.'

Once started, the tears wouldn't stop. *You're so cold, so frozen. You don't feel anything very much, do you?* The voice intruded again on her misery. Panic whirled up inside her. She heard her own voice, as if from a distance. 'Do you think me cold, Adam?'

'You don't feel cold to me, Cinderella.'

'No ... no, I mean,' she cleared her throat. 'I mean,

do you think me cold … as a woman.'

She wanted to see his face, but her eyelids seemed to be glued shut. His fingers brushed her brow again - for a moment she thought she felt them tremble, and was shocked.

'You're like fire in me arms.'

Consciousness was going. Her body clung to Adam's, but in her mind Ella was back at the bleak place where she had been found, Seaton's Lagoon. She was a bird, flying over the water, gliding across its surface in long, sweeping arcs. The cold air ruffled her feathers.

The dark shadow fell over her suddenly, crowding out the light. She looked up, just as the eagle came out of the sun, swift as thought There was an instant for her to register that it had a face … Lieutenant Moggs's face.

And then it was upon her.

Ella cried out, and Adam pulled her closer. But she didn't feel Adam. She felt the strong talons, squeezing her, as the eagle flapped its great wings and took her away.

CHAPTER 14

'*HAPPY BIRTHDAY, WIFE!*'

The mare was grey, and she loved it from the moment she saw it. So much so that she forgot herself, and thanked him warmly.

'She comes of pure stock: the finest in New South Wales.'

She stroked the silken nose. 'You are most generous.' And it was true, he was - it was not his money he denied her, it was his affection. Sometimes when she was with him, she felt as if she were walking on glass - delicate, fine glass, but oh, so cruel. One wrong step and she would be cut...

'You are my wife,' he said now, and there was pride in his voice. The pride of ownership, of possession.

Her words tumbled out before she could stop them. 'I wonder sometimes ... I wonder why you chose to marry me.'

He was silent. No reassurances that he loved her, no teasing laughter and strong hugs. He was silent.

But it was too late to back down now - she would have an answer.

'Why did you marry me?'

His eyes were cold, with a hint of boredom. 'I wanted an heir.'

She raised her eyebrows at his bluntness. 'Is that the only reason?'

'The chief one.' He went on slowly, and she knew he was finally speaking the truth. 'I wanted beauty, and you had that, and you came from a good family, though they'd run through their money. Your father was pleased with my offer, wasn't he?'

'Yes.'

'And so he should have been!' He pursed his lips. 'I've made something of myself here in Sydney. I wanted the best when it came to a wife, but I knew those rich dukes and whatnots back home would look down on me. So I found someone poor enough to be grateful for the offer.'

Her heart was thudding inside her, but she didn't let him see her agitation. She was humiliated by what he had told her, but again she didn't let him see it.

He was watching her. 'Look at you! Proud, by God, and so cold, so frozen. You don't feel anything very much, do you?'

Only because you make me so! her heart cried. I'm not really like that! Can't you see? I'm frightened and lonely. But she composed her face, lifted her chin, and made herself into the cold woman.

'Oh, there's nothing wrong in it!' he reassured her. 'I didn't want passion ... I couldn't have borne passion in my wife. You 're perfect just the way you are. The laird's daughter ... every inch the laird's daughter...'

He did not want passion in his wife. Her throat was dry with misery and anger. Of course he would not want passion in his wife! Passion was for her, that other woman whose existence Catherine, in her pity and kindness, had disclosed to her.

She made her voice polite, indifferent; her only defense. 'I think I shall go in now.'

He smiled at her, a reflex without emotion, and she smelled the peppermint on his breath. 'Most certainly, *wife!'*

As she went to move away he spoke again, only now all trace of good humour had gone from his voice. Indeed there was a hint of something menacing.

'The whole of Sydney thinks you're a queen, did you know that? Half of them are frightened of you and the other half are envious. They think I spoil you, and maybe I do. But it reflects on me, you see. I want my wife to be the best, just as I want everything I own to be the best.'

'I'm glad I please you,' she whispered.

'Oh, you do, you do. But you'll please me more when you give me an heir. A legal heir. I've given you a life you'd never have had if you'd stayed with your father - gambled it away, didn't he?'

She stiffened at the insult, but he only smirked.

'An heir, wife, that's what I want. A legal heir - I've got plenty o' the other sort. You give me that, and I'll be happy with you.'

She felt as if the sun had gone in. His cold eyes blazed. 'And if I don't?' she asked, and immediately wished the words unsaid.

'Then God help you, wife,' he said between his teeth. 'God help you indeed!'

Had she spoken?

There was a voice inside her head, but she wasn't sure whether or not it was her own. Half asleep and half awake, she searched for the sound. But there was only the deep croaking of a frog, out in the darkness.

'Here, drink this.' Kitty, her voice tired and patient.

Ella drank from the mug: cool, sweet water.

'Adam's gone to fetch the doctor,' Kitty went on. 'Been gone a while now. They're hard to get hold of, them doctors. I'll say that about old Doctor Rawlins, you could always get him out if you had a bit of cash. This lot here, they're either too busy or too scared to come.'

There was a shout outside in the darkness, followed by the murmur of men, and a woman's deep laughter.

Kitty flicked a scornful look in the direction of the noise. 'There's a coffee shop across the road from us - or that's what they're callin' it. Plenty o' customers. The woman, Mrs Jardine her name is, came up here earlier, asking if she could help. I don't suppose she meant it,but at least she asked, I'll give 'er that.'

Ella let Kitty's voice wash over her. She felt disorientated. Where was the sky? Above her, where the stars normally shone, was a dense sort of blackness. And then she realised that Adam had rigged up a piece of canvas over two poles, with a crossbeam, so that it hung down to the ground like a tent.

She could see through the narrow opening at the front, where someone had made a fire. It looked cheerful enough, crackling and leaping, but Ella couldn't feel the heat. She shivered, and heard her teeth chatter. Her whole body was shaking with a cold that had seeped deep into her bones.

'Here.' Kitty piled another blanket on top, briskly tucking it around her. 'Adam won't be much longer. Do you want some more water?'

Ella shook her head. She tried to hold herself

still, but the violent shivering continued. Perhaps she was dying? Did that mean she would never now find her husband, never know who she was? She would be buried here, on the Bendigo diggings, in borrowed clothes and with a borrowed name.

The gleam of a lantern caught her eye, bobbing along the gully. Gradually it drew closer, and she heard the rattle and bump of a horse-drawn vehicle. It came to a stop at the bottom of the rise.

'Here he is.' Kitty sounded relieved. She ducked outside the tent, and Ella heard voices. The flap opened again, and a stranger holding a lantern entered. He was dressed rather oddly, in a shabby black coat and a black top hat. Ella thought it a strange outfit to be wearing, calling on people in the middle of the night.

He set the lantern down, its brightness filling the tent, and then he removed his hat and knelt down beside her. He smelt, Ella thought, like something that had been left out in the rain and then not properly dried. A musty, unpleasant smell, underlaid with peppermint and carbolic. The black coat, she noticed, was frayed at the cuffs, and there was a button missing. His hair was so flattened against his skull, it looked as if it might be glued on.

He was peering at her; he seemed to advance and retreat, wavering slightly at the edges. He had a bag with him, which looked impressive. He opened it and took out an apparatus which he used to listen to her heart.

There was something about him that tugged at Ella's memory. Was it the smell, the peppermint smell?

'How long has she been like this?' he was asking in a serious voice that matched his long, serious face.

'Since late afternoon,' Adam answered. 'I tried two doctors before I found you, but they wouldn't come.'

The man muttered something about too much work and too few qualified for it. He was checking her pulse, and gazing into her eyes.

'Delirium?' he muttered. 'Fever, too, chills. Headache?'

Ella nodded. 'I had a headache,' she whispered huskily. 'But it's not so bad now.'

'Vomiting, purging? No? Well, that's something then.' He turned to look at Adam where he stood silhouetted in the tent opening, against the fire. 'I've seen plenty of patients since I came to the diggings. I've treated everything from dysentery to blisters.' He gave Ella another long look. 'She seems in a rather weakened state. It's possible that what would normally have been just a mild fever has become rather more dangerous. I've found most of the diggers suffer from mild fever most of the time – they think it's just one of the hazards of the goldfields.'

'Is it catching?' Kitty whispered anxiously.

The doctor looked at her sideways. 'That depends. She may have contracted it from the food she ate, the water she drank, or simply by wearing damp clothing.'

As you obviously do, Ella thought to herself.

The doctor leaned towards her. He pressed at the fading bruise on her temple until she winced. 'You said she'd had a bump on the head? Well, even that may have had something to do with it. I've found if a person is not hale and hearty when they arrive on the diggings, they're more likely to fall ill. The goldfields are not conducive to good health, sir!' The brief flash of humour was gone almost as soon as it appeared. 'What has she been eating? Has she been sleeping outdoors?'

Adam told him.

The doctor sighed. 'Well, I've heard worse. But if she's to get well, she needs better food. Fresh vege-tables, milk, eggs ...' It was said without much hope that it would be complied with. Fresh food was a rare commodity on the diggings where the stan-dard fare consisted of boiled mutton and stewed tea. 'And she needs to be kept warm and rested, at least until the fever passes. Then I'd better take another look at her.'

Kitty muttered something about some people thinking money grew on trees.

'I'll leave some pills,' he went on, ignoring Kitty, 'and give her plenty of good water to drink. When she's well enough, you can try broth. I'll make up a tonic, to help build her up. You can collect that in the morning.'

'How much is it?' Kitty asked sharply.

'Be quiet, Kitty.' Adam sounded tired and irrita-ble, but his words lacked sting. 'I'll come and get it first thing,' he told the doctor.

The man looked at him for a moment, as if assessing whether or not he was wasting his time. He must have thought not, for he said, 'I've seen worse than this on the diggings, worse by far. And in many cases the patient lets it go, hoping to recover without wasting money on a "quack".

When they finally have to admit defeat and call a doctor, it's too late.' This was said with a certain bitter acceptance. 'You've done the right thing in not wasting any time. If you take my advice about the food and rest, she'll pull through.'

He was gone. Kitty glared at his retreating back. 'How much did he charge to come out?'

'A pound,' Adam replied wryly. 'I had to go down to Long Gully for him.' He put his hand on Ella's forehead. His fingers were fire on ice. 'Has she said anything?'

'No. That is, nothin' that made any sense. Somethin' about a grey mare.'

There was a silence. 'Where am I going to get fresh vegetables?' Adam asked wearily.

'Prayer,' Kitty replied with solemn mockery. Then, so quietly she must have thought Ella couldn't hear her, 'Is she goin' to die, Adam?'

'Not if I can help it,' he said.

———◆———

The pine forest was dense and dark; the pungent smell filled her head. She ran, her bare feet floating above the ground. As she passed each straight, rough trunk, she brushed it with tingling fingers. High above, the moon was following, peeping at her through the branches, sharing in her game of hide and seek.

She was a child again, without care, selfish in her enjoyment of life. The tall man with the cold eyes, and the journey across the ocean to a new land and a new life, were yet to come. Being the laird's eldest daughter was sometimes a suffocating position. So much expected of her, so many eyes upon her. Once, in Inverness, she had seen a lion in a cage, and she still remembered the sleek powerful beauty of it and the restless anger in its eyes. In some way she didn't understand, it reminded her of herself.

Behind her, the voices were calling, the torches were flaring. But she stood alone in the clearing in the pine forest and gazed up at the moon, and dreamed of being free.

———◆———

The silence was so deep, it almost had a sound of its own. Ella lay quite still, listening to it She was comfortable, in a wrung-out sort of way. Indeed, she felt too weak even to lift her hand and brush aside the strand of hair that was tickling her cheek. The headache had gone, leaving her head echoey, like an enormous empty drum.

It was still dark, but she had a feeling dawn was close. Something about the added chill in the air spoke of morning, and beyond the opening in the makeshift tent she could see the faintest glow along the horizon. As she lay watching, some birds started to sing, answered by a dog or two. Wolf followed with a few loud woofs. A voice from somewhere outside groaned and muttered, and then a bottle was thrown, smashing noisily near Ella's side of the tent

'Haven't you got a bloody bed to go to?' Adam shouted, his voice so loud and close, Ella jumped. He must have felt her movement, because instantly he was beside her. He peered down into her eyes, his own creased with concern and lack of sleep.

'Oh God, I'm sorry, Cinderella. I forgot where I was.'

He stooped awkwardly over her, cupping her face in his hands, smoothing back her hair. He looked so worried that Ella smiled. And then he groaned and buried his face against her breast.

It was nice, lying in Adam's arms. 'Adam ...' Her voice sounded husky and unused. She cleared her throat. 'Adam, do you ever dream?'

He lifted his head slightly and stared at her, and then he sighed. 'When I'm awake, I dream of being a moleskin squatter.' His voice rumbled in his throat. 'But when I'm asleep, I dream of you.'

'I'm too much trouble for you,' she whispered. 'You should have left me at Seaton's Lagoon.'

He shook his head slowly.

Suddenly she was so tired, almost too tired to keep her eyes open. Her voice sounded high and childlike. 'How do I know you're not like him? You only want me because I'm the laird's daughter. Not for myself, not for me.'

She tried to turn her head away but he held her firm. His mouth covered hers in a long, warm kiss. When at last he lifted his lips from hers, he said, 'I love you. Believe that.'

She tried to read his eyes, but all she could see was the warmth filling them, reaching out to her. Encompassing her.

With an effort she lifted her hand to touch his cheek. He caught it in strong fingers, and then she felt his breath on her skin as he bent to kiss her, one for each eyelid. She was asleep before he had finished.

By the time Ella awoke again it was well into morning. The sun was shining, though the air was cold. She could see a white cloud puff from Kitty's mouth each time she spoke. The girl was further down the rise, near the road.

Adam had turned the tarpaulin into a large, square tentlike structure, and there was now a large group of people outside it, mostly miners with their hands jammed into their pockets, but also a couple of women with shawls pulled over their hair, one with a baby on her hip.

Kitty was busy measuring out flour, sugar, rice and oats. One of the women wanted some cloth – her finger pointed imperiously – and Adam produced a wicked-looking knife from the sheath on his belt and used it to slice off a length.

The store was open.

Ella heaved herself up so that she could see better. Her head was swimming and black spots danced before her eyes, but she ignored both. Now she had a view all the way down the rise to the bottom – where Adam had his store set up, and beyond, to the road that ran through Midnight Gully. A bullock dray was labouring past, the great beasts with their heads bowed as they heaved the laden vehicle along the slippery surface. The very ground seemed to shake with their passing.

On the other side of the road were more tents, one of them with the words *Coffee Shop* painted prominently on the side. Ella narrowed her eyes at it, and yes, there was the telltale glint of broken glass on the hard, pebble-strewn ground. So that was the sly grog shanty. It looked quiet enough at the moment; perhaps custom was slow at this time of the day. Most of the miners would be working, anyway, if they were sincere in their desire to strike it rich.

A man in a drab coat and bright yellow neckerchief had appeared at the back of the crowd around Adam's store. His arms were folded and his face was drawn down in an expression of angry annoyance. Adam's success did not appear to have pleased everyone.

As Ella watched, the man pushed his way towards Adam. He was gesticulating, pointing at the store, and then back down the road. Adam smiled and shrugged, as if it had nothing to do with him. The man went on, his arms waving more furiously. But Adam wouldn't be drawn, and eventually the man stormed off, shoving his way rudely through the crowd while Wolf ran barking after him.

'I told him the other store owners wouldn't like it,' Ella murmured.

Her head had stopped swimming, although she still felt weak and shaky. As if she wasn't really there. But the scene before her intrigued her, and she wanted to see more of it. Slowly, taking her time, Ella managed to manoeuvre herself closer to the entrance of the tent. Once there, she made herself comfortable against a bundle of clothing, and waited until the world stopped waltzing.

She could see right up the gully now, to the juncture of California Gully. Miners were at their work, heads popping up and down from holes in the ground. Roughly made windlasses creaked as buckets of wash dirt were hauled to the surface, to be puddled or shovelled into cradles. Ella sat and watched the goings on for a long time. Occasionally she dozed, waking suddenly to watch again.

There was Kitty, her pretty face thin with concentration. To her, every purchase was a battle of wits. She bullied and cajoled, and usually won. Then she would turn to catch Adam's eye, grinning from ear to ear.

Adam's methods were different to Kitty's. He was so amiable, his customers' faces mirroring his easy smile, that they thought they had had the best of him even when they had not. As Ella watched, he laughed at something someone said and, turning slightly, caught sight of her in the tent. She saw him lean towards Kitty and murmur some instruction which made Kitty's mouth tighten. And then he was walking up the rise towards her.

Ella had a moment to look at him as a stranger might, to admire the broad shoulders and strong, square body. She noted his scuffed, worn boots, his mud-stained moleskins, his shabby jacket. He still made her think of a tinker, with his wide, smiling mouth that could say whatever you wanted it to, and his dark, clever eyes that saw everything and betrayed nothing.

Suddenly her observation was no longer dispassionate. That feeling was back again, fanned to life within her, where before had been nothing but cold ashes.

'How are you feeling?' he asked, but his eyes were saying other things.

Ella tried to smile. 'I'm alive.'

'I've got something for you.' He crouched down before her, smiling, and stretched out his cupped hands. Ella blinked at the small, grubby objects.

'Potatoes!' she whispered. 'Where on earth did

you get them?'

Adam gave her a wink as an answer. 'I'll put them in the pot tonight.' A crease appeared between his brows. 'Do you think they're fresh enough, Cinderella?'

'I think they're wonderful.'

'I got that tonic for you from the doctor, to build your strength. And there was a woman selling goat's milk along the way, so I bought some of that an' all.'

Suddenly Ella found it difficult to meet his eyes. 'How much did all this cost you, Adam?'

He shrugged as if that was unimportant. 'I'm a businessman now, Mrs Seaton. I can afford things like doctors and medicine.'

'Thank you.'

He hesitated, as if he wanted to say more, but in the end all he did was lay the potatoes in her lap, and leave her to her thoughts.

Her head still felt as if it were floating, but the headache was definitely gone and if the fever wasn't, it was now bearable. Probably the doctor was right. It was just a case of poor food and living rough, and the fact that she was not hardened to either. And yet, if she were so soft, so cosseted, why had she set out to Melbourne on her grey mare with only one servant to protect her? What had happened to cause her to attempt such a desperate feat?

If only she could remember!

She knew she dreamed. Usually the dreams passed from her when she woke, although the emotions they stirred remained. Fear, happiness, loss ... Someone had called her the laird's daughter, but she did not know who. She was a Scotswoman who had travelled thousands of miles to the other side of the world. Why? Who had brought her? Her husband? Then where was he now?

Ella closed her eyes. The feverish chills began to shiver up her arms and legs. She moved restlessly, and felt something roll off her lap. It was one of Adam's potatoes.

They were small. The leavings of the crop, brought out to sell on the goldfields for far in excess of their normal price. But Adam had found them, and paid God knew what for them, and presented them to her.

He loved her.

The words were like a patch of calm in a whirling maelstrom of unanswered questions. She clung on to them, as she would a life raft, and caught her breath. There was a long struggle ahead, she knew it, and perhaps she would not make the shore. But for now, here was a chance to rest and gather her strength. And she knew she must take it.

———

'Margaret Catchpole,' Catherine's husky voice murmured. 'Heard of her, have you?' Warm, clever eyes surveyed her from the shadows, a mixture of mockery and pity in their depths.

She shook her head. She was grateful for Catherine's visit. She was always grateful to see Catherine. She had no real friends apart from her sister by marriage - none she could speak to openly. Catherine knew how unhappy she was, and Catherine sympathized.

It was still a lovely face - she was younger than her brother - but it was the strength of character that attracted attention. Pale, watchful eyes and a smile as if she knew everything. Perhaps she did, despite the fact that she had been as ill-educated as her brother. Like him, she had learned a certain veneer of sophistication, to which their great wealth had added the final gloss.

'Margaret Catchpole,' the husky voice said again, this time with a sigh. 'There was a book come out, not so long ago. I never read it,' with a sharp look, as if she could read. 'From what I heard it was all lies, all romance … well, most o' it. But it was a good tale.'

'Did you know her? Margaret Catchpole, I mean?'

Catherine shook her head. 'I heard of her from a woman I knew when I first came to Sydney, long ago. She knew her, or said she did. Told me all about her. It's a fine tale, one you might enjoy. Perhaps it would cheer you,' and Catherine reached over to press her hand, that same mixture of mockery and pity in her pale eyes.

'Yes, perhaps it might.'

Catherine settled herself more comfortably in her chair. 'Well,' she began, softly, winding a spell, 'when Margaret was young, she loved a man … a highwayman. He was bad, nothing but trouble for poor Margaret. But you know the way it goes. That sort are like magnets, drawing poor silly girls to them. He left her, this highwayman, and her life went on. But one day … one day, he sent word. He needed her, and her love was still strong. So she went. She dressed herself up as a boy and "borrowed" her master's horse, and she rode away to be with him.'

The story was thrilling. Rapt, she listened to that soft voice. Catherine's pale eyes gleamed.

'She was caught, of course, and punished. Sent to New South Wales, and suffered all the pain that went with it. But she bore it, and rose above it, and ended her days content. What do you think of that?'

'I think it is a good story.'

Catherine cocked her head to one side. 'Men,' she said softly. 'Selfish creatures. I've known a few, and had my heart broken by them. They're not worth it, darling.'

Tears stung her eyes. 'Aren't they?'

Catherine shook her head. 'Not a bit. But it's a good tale, isn't it? Can you imagine loving a man so much you'd run off with him and leave everything, every single thing?'

'No. No, I can't imagine that.'

The little clock on the mantel ticked softly, ticking away the minutes. She felt her heart ticking within her, ticking away her life. Suddenly she wished she was Margaret Catchpole. She wished she could up and steal a horse and ride away - not so much to a lover - where would she find such a man - but away, just away.

Catherine was watching her face, reading her.

She put up her hand, to shield her thoughts, pretending that the glare from the window was hurting her eyes. 'Why did you never marry?' she asked.

Catherine smiled at her, and winked in a very unladylike manner. 'I did, in a way. But it didn't last. These things never last. And now my brother says I must be respectable.' She sighed as if respectable were exhausting, but her eyes were sparkling.

She knew she should be shocked, but instead she began to laugh. It was so good to laugh, 'Oh Catherine,' she gasped, 'I do love you!'

Catherine nodded at her gently. 'I know you do, darling, I know you do.'

CHAPTER 15

———◆———

THROUGHOUT THE NEXT FEW DAYS, Ella slept, waking in snatches to drink water or the broth Kitty had made - as well as the potatoes, Adam had somehow obtained a cabbage, some onions and a few withered-looking apples.

At first Ella's chills and temperature returned at regular intervals, but gradually the attacks weakened their hold, and then stopped altogether. Ella's body healed itself in the warmth of the canvas cave, while outside the thin walls of her sanctuary, life in Midnight Gully went on.

Adam and Kitty worked the store, quickly running out of the more popular items, like flour and sugar and canvas. When they were able, during the day, they would take it in turns to walk up the rise to see how Ella was.

'Feelin' better, are you?' Kitty asked, hands on her hips.

'Yes, I am, thanks to you.' Ella gave her a warm smile of gratitude.

Kitty didn't seem to know how to react, glaring suspiciously, and then shifting uneasily from foot to foot. At last she contented herself with a noncommittal shrug, gazing off into the distance.

'We've done all right today,' she said. 'Adam's made a bag o' money, and he says he'll pay me for me time.'

'And so he should. You're working just as hard as him. He probably wouldn't have done half as well without you.'

Again Kitty glanced at her suspiciously, and then a smile transformed her face as she realised the truth of it.

'What will he do when he's sold everything?' Ella asked curiously.

'He said he'd find a bullock driver to go down to Melbourne and bring up another load. Bullocks are a better bet in the mud than horses.' She said it knowledgeably, as if she had thought of it herself. 'And there're always people hawkin' stuff on the goldfields. Stuff they can't sell themselves. He can buy a bit here and there.'

They had obviously been discussing it. Ella felt a stab of something like jealousy, and told herself not to be ridiculous. And then the jealousy turned to depression. It's because I've been ill, she thought, but knew it wasn't that. The truth was, Kitty's words had only reaffirmed what Ella already knew. That she and Adam were ideally suited to each other. In her mind's eye, she could see them together, working in the store. She saw time passing and the tarpaulin changing to a slab hut, and then something more solid and prosperous. She could see Adam, in a frock coat, tipping his hat to the grander customers. Behind him, Kitty was bobbing a curtsey. A plumper and more content Kitty. She could see several children, with Adam's fair hair and Kitty's blue eyes, peeping out from behind their mother's skirts ...

'I said, do you need somethin' before I get back?'

Kitty repeated the question impatiently, eyes narrowed to disguise her concern.

For a moment Ella was disorientated, then she shook her head. 'I still have water, thank you, and I'm not hungry. I'll lie down again, I think. I'm sorry I can't help you and Adam.'

The girl hesitated, and then shrugged. Behind her at the bottom of the slope, Adam measured out some blue cloth for a woman wearing a clay-splattered skirt and puffing on a pipe.

'Ask Adam to save some of that cloth for us,' Ella murmured, closing her eyes. 'Maybe I can sew some new dresses ... or at least some skirts.' She had noticed, on the journey from the camp to Midnight Gully, that many of the Bendigo women wore skirts topped with tight-fitting jackets.

Kitty looked surprised. 'Can you do that?' Then, remembering it was the enemy she was speaking to, 'Please yourself.' And she sauntered nonchalantly back to the store.

It was different when Adam came. He sat down beside her, his knees drawn up, and watched her face as she spoke.

'Kitty says the store is doing well.'

'So it is. But it'll come to an end soon. I need more stuff coming up from Melbourne.' He moved to rub his chin, then changed his mind when he saw Ella wince. 'Does this bother you, love? Do you want me to shave it off?'

The endearment touched her more than his offer. She smiled into his eyes, letting the warmth of his love enfold her.

'It doesn't matter. What were you saying about a bullock driver?'

'Freight charges are liable to go pretty high if the weather stays wet. There's already talk of goods being sent by sea to the Murray River and then overland south to the Bendigo from there.'

'Wouldn't that take longer?'

'Not if the roads are as bad as they say.' He glanced out of the tent, but Kitty only had one customer, a thin miner with a black and grey streaked beard who was inspecting a pair of boots. By the look on her face, she had met her match in driving hard bargains.

'I meant to speak to you about Lieutenant Moggs,' Ella said at last, reluctantly.

He frowned.

'He seems to think it his duty to bring you to justice, Adam. And whether you're guilty or not doesn't come into it He said ...' She tried to remember exactly what he *had* said, but she had been ill at the time, and it was blurred. 'It's very strange, but I feel as if he is familiar to me. I know him. And yet, I'm almost certain I had not met him before Carlsruhe ...'

'Perhaps he reminds you of someone else.'

There was a thought! Ella stared into space, struck by the possibilities.

'What did he say? Moggs, I mean,' Adam prompted softly.

Ella pushed her hair back, trying to remember the scene at the camp. 'He promised Mr Gilbert that he would help me, but when we were alone he said he believed I had fallen in with bad company and that I should be removed from it. When I said I didn't want to be removed, he hinted that that wouldn't stop him. I told him I would inform Mr

Gilbert, and he replied that Mr Gilbert would be unlikely to take my word over his.' It was all coming back to her now. Ella shivered as she recalled the scene. Moggs had called her a nameless slut, but she didn't think it necessary to repeat that.

Adam had his eyes fixed on her face. His stillness told her more about his feelings than his blank expression.

'Men like Moggs think they're God Almighty,' he said quietly. 'But don't worry, I won't let him take you anywhere you don't want to go.'

'I wish he wasn't here.'

He took her hand in his. 'You did the right thing, standing up to him. He feeds off fear; you can see it in his eyes.'

'I still wish he wasn't here. He hates you, Adam. And if he can get at you through me, then he'll do it. Remember, he has the commissioner's permission ... or near enough to it.'

'Perhaps it won't come to that. You might find out who you are and leave Moggs, and everythin' else, behind.'

He said it evenly, smiling, but she didn't believe it.

'No,' she said simply.

His arms came around her, rough with the need to feel her body against his. He kissed her with the same urgent need, and she felt herself responding. Her lips were tentative at first, but there was nothing tentative about Adam.

'Oh, Cinderella,' he groaned, 'I'm burnin' up with wantin' you. I'm like a boy in love for the first time. I don't know how much longer I can keep me hands off you.'

She lifted his face, and saw the pain and long-ing in his eyes. He leaned his brow against hers. 'You say you're frightened of Lieutenant Moggs,' he murmured. 'It's me you should be scared of.'

'Adam!' It was Kitty, calling from down the slope. She sounded irritated, but was trying to hide it. Evidently she felt Adam had spent long enough with the invalid.

Adam swore softly.

'You had better go.' Ella didn't know whether she was sorry or glad for the interruption.

'Adam!' Now the. irritation was out in the open.

Adam pulled a rueful face, and stood up. He turned to leave the tent, and then remembered something and glanced back at her over his shoul-der. 'Kitty said you wanted some cloth saved, so I put it aside for you. What did you have in mind?'

'I thought I'd make something new to wear.' And she spread her skirts for his inspection. Although Kitty had been busy washing since they set up camp in Midnight Gully, there was only so much one could do.

He smiled at her, but it turned into a grimace when Kitty shouted for a third time. 'You're look-ing better,' he said. 'You must have nine lives, Cinderella.'

When he had gone, Ella lay back on her bed. Maybe not nine lives, she thought, pleased, but cer-tainly two! She'd escaped death by the Lagoon and now here, on the Bendigo diggings. It must mean something. She closed her eyes against the muted twilight of the tent. Her lips still tasted of Adam's kisses, and she wrapped her arms about herself, as if to hold the feeling of him to her.

'You should be scared of me,' he had said. And she was scared. Not that he would hurt her, she didn't believe Adam would ever hurt her, not physically. But when he held her ... kissed her, she felt weakened. Something in her reached out to him, and found a match. It strengthened her in some way, and yet at the same time, it made her weaker. He was drawing her away from her goal, the mystery of her past; and she wanted to resist... and she wanted to give in.

———————

Mrs Jardine was one of those larger than life figures Ella had expected to meet on the gold-fields. She was of immense proportions, a middle-aged woman with long, black, stringy hair. The first time she saw her, Ella was resting in the tent, viewing Midnight Gully with half closed eyes. Mrs Jardine was standing in the entrance to her coffee shop, filling it entirely. As Ella watched, she lifted the hem of her skirts, disclosing tiny feet in black boots, and picked her way daintily over the rough ground to Adam's store.

Mrs Jardine made straight for Adam, but Kitty, seeing her intention, casually intercepted her. Ella smiled to herself; the girl reminded her of a small terrier, jealously guarding her master.

Mrs Jardine didn't seem bothered. She exchanged a few words, laughing a deep, gruff laugh, and then turned up the slope in Ella's direction. Slowly she picked her way to the tent, and peered, puffing, through the opening. Her eyes were small and black, like currants.

'Ah, you're awake then!' she beamed. 'They said you was sleeping, but I said I'd take a look anyhow. How do you feel, my duck? You look a bit peaky still. Knocked it out of you, did it?' And she clicked her tongue, shaking her head.

At closer quarters, Mrs Jardine's fleshy face was as white and doughy as an unbaked loaf, but there was something warming in her smile. Ella felt herself soften towards the infamous hostess of the Midnight Gully Coffee Shop.

'I've a nice little drop of something,' the woman went on, with a broad, meaningful wink. 'I'll bring it up later. Put roses in your cheeks, that will, my duck.'

Ella thanked her, and asked politely how long Mrs Jardine had been resident in Midnight Gully.

The little black eyes squeezed nearly shut in the effort of memory. 'Two months, it'd be. We came just after the camp moved back to Bendigo from Bullock Creek. They was out there because of the drought, there bein' no water to be had on Bendigo for love nor money!' And she gave a rumbling laugh, deep in her throat 'Not that you'd think it now, when it won't stop rainin'.'

Indeed, it was difficult to believe that not long ago the Bendigo diggings had been all but deserted because of the lack of water. The government camp had moved to Bullock Creek, and resided there until the rain made it possible to return.

Mrs Jardine was continuing the conversation, exclaiming about the numbers of miners who arrived each day to take part in the rush. 'Naughton has a smile from one ear to the other,' she added, with a certain wry humour.

'Naughton?'

'Naughton Jardine, my husband. Not much of a joker, is Naughton. He's a serious businessman. You'd be surprised how much call there is for hot coffee here in Midnight Gully.' She gave Ella another broad wink.

'You do seem to have plenty of customers, Mrs Jardine.'

The little black eyes were surveying her now with open curiosity. 'How'd you come to be part of those two out there? You don't seem to fit, somehow.'

It crossed Ella's mind that once she may have thought Mrs Jardine impertinent, but those days were gone. Ella smiled, and recounted to Mrs Jardine her brief but very busy past history, naturally omitting her dealings with Eben and Mrs Ure and Lieutenant Moggs. The big woman listened with rapt attention, only interrupting to ask what the servant, Ned, looked like.

'I thought I might o' seen him ... Ned, I mean,' Mrs Jardine said thoughtfully. 'Plenty o' men come through our place, all with a story to tell.'

'I know he has dark hair, and he's small of stature,' Ella murmured. 'That's all, I'm afraid. Oh, yes, he's a Scot, like me.'

Mrs Jardine waved a plump hand. 'Never mind. I'll keep him in mind whenever a new customer comes along, and I'll tell Naughton about it, too. Likes a mystery, does Naughton.' She laughed again, with that wry humorous note that puzzled Ella.

'You've been very kind.'

'I have, haven't I?' Mrs Jardine agreed. And with a smile and a nod, she tiptoed back down the slope to her coffee shop.

Ella must have slept, for when she woke again it was evening, and some parrots were screeching in the grey box tree. The sun was setting in a glorious pink and mauve and pale blue sky, awash with fat, white clouds. There was a smell of eucalyptus wood burning and food cooking, and the sounds of the diggings settling down for another night. Across the road at the Jardines', Ella could see miners gathering, eager for their cups of 'coffee'.

She remembered then that this was Saturday night, a big night on the goldfields, for tomorrow was Sunday, the Sabbath day, the day of rest, and a miner could be fined for breaking it. Therefore Saturday night was looked upon as the culmination of a week's hard effort, a time to celebrate ... or commiserate.

Kitty peeped into the tent and Ella sat up, pushing her hair out of her eyes. She must look a sight, she thought suddenly. She almost wished she was back at Nancy Ure's, if only for the bath and the bed.

'Hungry?' Kitty asked.

Ella thought of mutton and damper, and hesitated.

'Adam's bought us some eggs to have with the ham,' Kitty said, reluctantly. Perhaps she had hoped Ella would refuse so that she could have her share.

'Ham and eggs?' Ella whispered.

Kitty smiled grudgingly. 'Thought that would wake you up. You want some, then?'

'Yes, please.'

Ella crawled outside, stretching her cramped limbs. 'Where's Adam?' she asked, glancing around.

Kitty appeared to be on her own by the fire.

'He's gone out. He's lookin' for a bullock driver that don't charge an arm an' a leg to cart his stuff up from Melbourne.'

'When will he be back?'

Kitty shrugged. 'When he gets what he wants. That's Adam for you, he knows what he wants, and he goes out to get it.' She said it quietly, proudly, as if he were already her man. Suddenly she looked up at Ella, her face shadowed in the fading light. 'I know he loves you ... or thinks he does. I know that. But you're not the right woman for him, and you don't really want him anyway. You've got your husband, and some posh home, somewhere. You'd never be happy with just Adam. But I would, 'cause Adam's all I want.'

There was something very dignified in Kitty's little speech. Ella didn't want to argue with her – Kitty had been good to her since her illness – but neither did she want to believe that what Kitty said was true.

'Surely it's for Adam to say what or whom he wants – ' she began reasonably.

Kitty's face hardened. 'Oh, you're leavin' it to him, are you? Make me sick, you do! I've seen you lookin' at him ... smilin' at him ... teasin' him with just enough to keep him hopin' you'll give him what he wants. But you won't, *your ladyship*. The truth is, you just like to have him runnin' round in circles, tryin' to please you. He's another like your what's his name ... Ned! That's all Adam is to you – a bloody servant'

'No, that's not true.' But her voice sounded weak.

'Oh, it is! You're enjoyin' yourself no end, bein'

treated like a queen. But as soon as you remember who you are, you'll be off. You'll have forgotten his name in a week!'

'I will never forget Adam.' She said the words firmly. But her mind was asking: Are you sure, are you sure? Perhaps she's right and you are just using him, using his feelings for you, to make your life easier. Perhaps you think you can be content with someone like him, but when the chance comes for better, won't you be tempted? Won't you?

'I will never forget him,' she said again, but her voice was shaking.

Kitty made an impatient movement of her hand and turned away to stare down at the Jardines'. The size of the group in front of the coffee shop had grown, their voices getting rowdier by the moment. 'Got any tumble-down, Mrs Jardine?' one of them shouted, and there was general laughter.

'It's not fair,' the girl whispered at last, her voice choked with anger or tears. 'You're allowed to sit up here like a bloody queen. He won't let you lift a bloody finger in case it hurts. While I...I...' But she couldn't finish, her voice gave out She bit her bottom lip savagely, but Ella could see it quivering.

She's young, she told herself. Her life has hardened her, but underneath all that, she's still a young girl. And she sees me taking what she wants so desperately, and thinks, without me here, Adam would turn to her. And perhaps he would.

'I think you're right,' Ella said at last, and now she sounded cold. Herself, again. 'I think you and Adam would deal well together. But things do not always fall neatly into place like a child's puzzle. People are more complicated. I may go and Adam may still not love you. Life isn't so simple, Kitty.'

'Why don't you just go!' Kitty gasped furiously.

'Because I have no where *to* go.'

The girl turned to stare at her, and saw the truth of it. But she rallied, lifting her chin, her face pale and determined. 'I won't give up,' she said. 'You'll leave, I know it, and when you go, I'll be here waitin'.'

'You'll be waitin' for what?' a loud voice asked. Adam appeared on the edge of the fire light, his eyes moving curiously from one to the other.

Kitty flushed a fiery red. 'Nothin',' she muttered. 'It was nothin'.' And her glance at Ella was a warning to stay silent.

Kitty began to cook their meal. The ham and eggs smelled like ambrosia, and several of the miners about the Jardines' tent called out pleadingly to be allowed to share the repast.

'How much were the eggs?' Kitty asked sharply, her embarrassment forgotten in contemplation of financial matters.

Adam smiled at her. 'I reckon if I had a necklace made out of 'em, I'd be a rich man.'

'Did you find a bullock driver?' Ella asked.

'Aye. He'll be setting off in a day or two, but I don't know when he'll be back. He says that there're so many drays and the like bogged in the mud along the Bendigo road, a man could walk all the way and never touch ground.'

Kitty served up the meal, dividing it carefully, and then, with a defiant look at Ella, gave Adam an extra egg. They ate in silence, savouring each mouthful. To follow, there was a jar of preserved plums in brandy syrup so strong it made Ella's head spin.

'Lucky the traps didn't spot this one,' Kitty laughed, as she leaned back, replete. 'You'd be arrested for sly grogging.'

Across the road, candle flames danced inside the Jardines' tent, and someone struck up a tune on a fiddle. The music soared briefly and then settled into a jig, to shouts of approval from the occupants.

'Mrs Jardine said they'd found a fiddler to play a tune or two for the customers,' Kitty informed them.

'Won't the police come and close them down?' asked Ella, palming a piece of ham back behind her, where Wolf waited. He snapped it up gratefully.

'Aye, well, that's what they're paid to do by the governor,' Adam answered her with a frown, obviously not fooled by Wolf's innocent stare. 'When they get a conviction, the arresting police get half of the fine for themselves. It's supposed to spur 'em on, and I bet it does! There're arrests made for the flimsiest reasons. But it's still not enough to stop the bribes. Plenty of money changes hands to make certain Mrs Jardine and her like aren't touched when there's a sly-grog raid on.'

Ella wondered whether Lieutenant Moggs took bribes. It seemed unlikely. He would consider a bribe beneath him.

'What's tumble-down?' she asked, remembering the miner's shout earlier.

'God knows. Some devil's brew. Rum and tobacco, maybe. Imagine that in your belly! Still,' he shrugged, 'I suppose it helps some of them to forget what they've left behind ... or what waits for them in the morning.'

Kitty gave a snort of derision. 'The miners used to come down to Sawpit Gully and spend their money fast as they made it. If I struck it rich, I wouldn't waste it on drink.'

'What would you do with *your* fortune then, Kitty?' Adam was smiling that indulgent smile he saved just for her.

She didn't look at him. Suddenly she was shy, and it was the shyness that brought the note of bravado to her voice. 'I'd buy myself a fine house and fine clothes, and I'd travel around in a fine carriage with blood horses. And all the gentlemen would tip their hats to me, but they'd know ...' she smiled to herself. 'They'd know that they had no hope of winnin' me because I was beyond their reach.'

He smiled back. 'That sounds as good an ambition as any.'

Kitty looked at him then, her heart in her eyes. 'Would you lift your hat to me, Adam?' she asked him.

'Aye, I would.'

He'd pleased her. Ella watched his face, wondering yet again whether Kitty was right. If Ella wasn't here, would Adam turn to Kitty? She moved restlessly.

'Mrs Seaton?' Adam was speaking to her. She looked up, startled, and met his eyes across the fire. 'I asked you what *you'd* do, if you had a fortune to spend?'

'How do we know she hasn't got one already?' Kitty muttered.

Ella ignored her, trying to concentrate on Adam's question. But they were both watching her, waiting to hear her answer, waiting to pounce. 'I'd have ham and eggs every night,' she joked at last, and saw Adam's half smile as he looked away, and Kitty's roll of the eyes.

'What about you, Adam?' Ella asked quickly. 'What would you do?'

The fire crackled, flaring suddenly as a log split in half and slipped further into the heart of it. Adam leaned forward, his eyes half shut against the light. 'Maybe I'd eat ham and eggs with you, Mrs Seaton ... or maybe I'd ride with Kitty in her carriage.'

Kitty laughed, but Ella caught her breath. He had heard them! She knew it as if he had told her himself. He had stood in the darkness and listened as they argued over him. She tried to remember exactly what they had said, and was not comforted.

Suddenly he yawned and stretched. 'I think I'll go to bed, ladies. Unless you want to accompany me in a jig at the Jardines'?'

Kitty flushed and shook her head. 'Not likely,' she told him scornfully, as if she had never worked in such a place herself once. The silence grew, and she rose to her feet, glancing at Ella. 'Maybe we should go to bed, too, Mrs Seaton?'

Ella nodded. 'Yes. I'll come in a moment.'

The girl hesitated, but there was nothing she could do, short of ordering Ella to bed. She murmured her goodnights and went inside the tent. They heard her rustling about, lighting the candle, making ready for sleep.

'You could do worse than Kitty, you know,' Ella told him softly. 'She works hard, and she's very pretty, and she respects you. What more could a man ask?'

'You mean a man like me?' Adam retorted, just as softly. 'Are you matchmaking now?'

'I know you overheard, Adam. I was trying to explain what it was all about – '

'I know what it was about,' he shot back at her. 'And Kitty was right, wasn't she? You're usin' me for the convenience of it. A bit here, a bit there, just to keep me happy. And then, when your chance comes up, you're off, back home.'

There was a bitterness in his voice that shocked her. She shivered, despite the fire. 'No …'

'Yes!' He stopped the shout just in time, and the word sounded strangled.

'Are you comin' to bed, Mrs Seaton, or will I blow out the candle?' Kitty's voice came muffled from the tent.

Ella stood up. 'I'm coming, Kitty.'

Adam looked away, into the fire. His back had a rigid look that tore at her. Ella opened her mouth, and then closed it again. What could she say? Only, 'Goodnight, Adam,' and quietly she left him.

CHAPTER 16

SUNDAY DAWNED DULL. THE FAT white clouds of yesterday had turned grey and threatening, covering the sky. There was a humid, close feel to the air that spoke of more rain.

Ella was still listless from the fever, but definitely on the mend. She lay a moment, listening to Kitty's quiet breathing, and trying to go back to sleep. But it was no use. She had had so much sleep lately her body was urging her to get up, to begin to use her muscles again.

Outside the tent the diggings were quiet. The vast areas of claims lay idle, awaiting Monday. The miners usually spent their Sundays reading, writing letters, or else preparing for the work week ahead by washing their clothes, cleaning their tents, baking, and making the small repairs that otherwise never got done.

Across the road at the Midnight Gully Coffee Shop empty bottles lay on the ground. A miner was sprawled against the side of the tent, mouth wide open, either asleep or unconscious. The sounds of celebration had gone on long into the night, although the fiddler had stopped abruptly shortly before midnight.

By the time Kitty and Adam rose, Ella had lit the fire, cooked breakfast and had the tea brewing.

Kitty grunted her thanks as she took her plate, suspicious at this new turn of events. Adam was more complimentary, if one ignored the cynical gleam in his eyes. 'I can see you've all the housewifely skills a woman needs,' he pronounced seriously. 'Fire-lighting and frying mutton chops, boiling water in a billy – '

'I don't expect special treatment,' Ella said quietly. 'I want to help, just as Kitty does, just as you do.'

Adam gave her a questioning look, and took a mouthful. 'It's good,' he told her, rather muffled. 'As far as I'm concerned you can cook every morning. What do you think, Kitty?'

Kitty bent over her plate, refusing to be drawn. 'Quiet, isn't it?' she murmured, changing the subject.

'I heard there was a preacher down at Golden Point,' Adam said, 'if you feel like singin' hymns.'

Kitty shot him a disbelieving look.

'Or there's a bare-fist fight in Ironbark Gully. I thought I might go over there and take a look.'

Kitty brightened. 'That sounds better!'

Adam smiled. 'Sorry, it's men only.'

Kitty made a sound of disgust. 'Why are all the interestin' things for the men?'

Ella shuddered. 'Do you really think it interesting, to see grown men bloody each other with their bare fists?'

'I like it,' Kitty declared, lifting her chin. 'There was a fight at Sawpit Gully once, and the winner came into Mrs Ure's to shout everyone a drink. He had muscles on his muscles, that one.' She shivered with pleasure at the memory.

'Like a man with a bit o' brawn, do you, Kitty?'

Adam asked her mock seriously.

'I do.' Kitty let her eyes slide over him. 'And you're just about perfect, Adam.'

He laughed aloud. Kitty gave him a saucy smile, collected the bucket and sauntered off to fetch the water.

'She's certainly bold,' Ella said, not sure whether she should be amused or not.

Adam gazed after her, a grin still playing on his mouth. 'She is, isn't she?'

'You wouldn't - ' but she bit her lip, realising what she was about to ask, and knowing she had no right to ask it.

'I wouldn't what?'

'It doesn't matter.' She stood up, shaking out her skirts. 'I'll clean up if you want to go to your fight. You don't want to miss any blood, do you?'

'Maybe I'll go a few rounds meself.'

She stared down at him in absolute horror.

'It's a good way to make a bit of money,' he explained, obviously amused by her reaction. 'What's a bruise or two if you come away a richer man?'

Ella moved to pick up the plates, and put them down again. He was on his feet, hands gripping hers. 'You're shaking,' he murmured, frowning down at her fingers. 'Why are you shaking?'

Ella pulled away angrily. 'Why do you think, you stupid man?'

He stared blankly, and then slowly his eyes widened with amazed delight. 'Is it because you don't want to see me hurt, is that it?'

Ella thought of denying it, but there didn't seem much point. 'Yes,' she whispered.

'I've been hurt before.'

She looked up at him, thinking of Frenchy's knife. 'I know.'

'And I'll probably be hurt again,' he went on thoughtfully. 'I'm not the sort to hold back for fear of a – '

'A bruise or two! I know,' she muttered.

'You wouldn't want me to hide behind your skirts, would you?' And when she wouldn't answer, 'I won't fight anyone today. But ... I am what I am, Ella.'

'I know what you are, Adam.'

You're as cunning as a tinker, she thought, and you're a liar, and your friends and relatives leave much to be desired. But that was only one side of the coin. Turn it over, and there was Adam's other face ... his kindness, his charm, and his bravery.

'Good.' Before she realised what he meant to do, he had wrapped his arms about her and given her a brief squeeze – just to show her how strong he really was. She felt her ribs creak.

Behind them, Kitty marched up the rise with the bucket, her face as grim as death.

Kitty and Ella did what washing they were able to – most of their clothing was on their backs –tidied the tent and the store, and made damper. And then, with the day stretching ahead of her, Ella took out the bolt of blue serge Adam had saved from the store. Kitty still hadn't spoken to her, but she refused to let it bother her. She left the girl to her silent sulks, and set herself up outside the tent, laying out the cloth to cut.

She had already decided to make a new skirt for herself and, if Kitty asked her nicely, one for her too. The girl was pretending to ignore her, but each time Ella turned her back, she could feel Kitty's eyes, watching. It was only a matter of time before curiosity overcame the sullens.

'Can you really sew?' The tone of voice was scornful, but it was a start.

Ella raised her eyebrows in surprise. 'Why, yes. Can't you?'

Colour flooded the girl's face. 'My ma was too sick and too poor to do more than patch up what we had. And there wasn't much call for sewin' dresses at Mrs Ure's. I mended a sheet here and there, that was all.'

'No, Mrs Ure didn't need to make her own clothes, did she?' Ella replied wryly. 'She had enough silks and satins to clothe a duchess!'

Kitty smiled reluctantly. 'I never saw her in any of 'em. She used to dress up in her room, when Eben came to call.' And she giggled at the thought.

'Had Eben been visiting her for very long?' Ella asked curiously.

Kitty shrugged. 'A few months. They had an arrangement about the customers. You know all that.'

'That they used to rob the choicest ones? Yes, I know. A charming pair.'

'You don't want to meet up with her again, Mrs Seaton,' Kitty said quietly. 'When she found out you'd been passin' yourself off as Adam's wife, she went off her head. Threatened to do things to you I'd never heard of before! But Eben quietened her down, and Adam kept sayin' he was sorry. In the end, she believed him, even though she probably knew he was lyin'. He's a good liar, is Adam, don't you think?'

Ella concentrated on her stitching. 'I didn't realise you knew about Adam pretending I was his wife. It was for Eben's benefit, when we met him in the Black Forest.'

Kitty snorted in disgust 'Gawd, it's a sorry thing when you can't even trust your own brother!'

'What do you think of Eben?'

The girl considered the question seriously. 'I think he's a smilin' devil. Adam ... well, Adam has that same way with him, but Eben's different ... darker, somehow. He frightened me, when he came to Sawpit Gully. I used to make sure I was never alone with him.'

That seemed to tally with what Ella herself thought. She glanced up at Kitty and smiled. 'Come here and let me measure you,' she said, taking up some cord. 'Then I'll show you how to cut out some cloth and sew it for yourself.'

Kitty hesitated, but it was only for a moment. It was too good an opportunity to miss, and she was no fool.

They worked in companionable silence together, as the morning drew on. There was a sticky feel to the air, a clamminess that warned of a storm brewing.

'I didn't think someone like you'd know how to do this,' Kitty murmured, frowning over her stitching.

Ella pulled a thoughtful face. 'I don't remember my own circumstances ... but learning to sew has always been a part of learning to run a household.'

Around noon Mrs Jardine tiptoed up the rise in her black boots. They had already seen her husband picking up telltale bottles from around the coffee shop. He had tucked them under his meaty arm before carrying them around to his wagon for disposal in the bush. Naughton was as big as his wife, but surly. He gave the two women a long, unsmiling look before turning away. Mrs Jardine, however, was full of smiles.

'Phew! Feels like a storm, don't it?' She fanned her damp face with her hand, and Ella could see big, damp circles under the arms of her dress. 'Have you heard our fiddler?' she went on. 'Good, in't he?'

'He's loud,' Kitty replied shortly.

Mrs Jardine laughed her deep laugh. 'He only lasted till midnight, and then he passed out cold. That's the trouble with the Irish, they play like angels but they drink like devils.'

Ella smiled at that, but Kitty refused to be amused, pretending disdain.

'Where's Adam?' Mrs Jardine went on.

'He went to see a bare-fist fight,' Kitty answered reluctantly.

'Havin' a bet, is he? Well, good luck to him. Tell him if he wins, he can come down and have a bottle o' brandy on me.' And she left them with an airy wave of her plump hand.

Adam returned in the early afternoon, whistling to himself and looking pleased. Kitty jumped up and ran halfway down the rise to meet him. Ella watched the girl edging as close to him as she possibly could without actually climbing inside his clothes, and gazing up into his eyes as he spoke. They laughed, and Kitty put up a hand to press his shoulder, her fingers closing on the stuff of his jacket in a manner that was both proprietorial and an invitation.

Adam looked down at Kitty, and for a moment his face went still. Ella had the uncomfortable feeling that he wanted to kiss her, and perhaps if Ella hadn't been there he would have. A shiver ran over her skin, as if she had been dunked in icy water. And then Adam had removed Kitty's hand, and turned towards the Jardines'. Kitty trailed back up to the tent, a self-satisfied smile on her face.

'He won some money,' she said smugly, settling herself on the log they used as a seat.

Ella nodded. She didn't trust herself to speak.

'He's gone over to Mrs Jardine's to get that brandy. Maybe I should go and join him.'

'I thought you didn't approve of places like that anymore.' Ella couldn't resist the jibe.

'Well,' Kitty tossed her head, 'Adam'd be there to look after me, wouldn't he?' But she didn't go.

When Adam returned, he brought the bottle of brandy with him, and slipped it inside the tent. Ella murmured something congratulatory, without looking up, and he laughed and said he'd always been lucky with picking winners. Kitty showed him her sewing, setting a few stitches for his inspection.

During the remainder of the afternoon, Adam busied himself with the jobs he hadn't had a chance to do during the week. He took Bess for a gallop and, when he returned, inspected the cart and the traces and harness for signs of wear.

Adam had been keeping the proceeds from the store on his person, and sleeping guard with Wolf in the store at night. It was necessary to take both money and gold in payment for goods – the miners often preferred to spend their gold rather than risk sending it down to Melbourne. In any case, Adam now had a sizable amount in his possession, and he decided it would be safer for it to be kept inside the tent.

'Do you want us to sleep on it, Adam?' Kitty asked.

But he shook his head. 'I've heard of thieves cutting a hole in the back of a tent and slipping their hands in to feel about for anything they can lift. And some of them are so bloody good at it, they can take gold from under your pillow without waking you up.'

In the end, Adam decided to dig a hole in the hard ground in the approximate centre of the tent. He put the money and gold into a thick waterproof bag, tied it, and placed the bag into the hole. Once the soil had been returned, and stamped down, the hiding place was invisible to anyone who didn't know it was there.

Adam viewed it with satisfaction. 'Should be safe enough until I need some to pay the bullock driver.' Wolf snuffled over the hiding place, but Adam pushed him playfully away. 'You'll get your share,' he teased. 'A bone so big we'll need a barrow to carry it in!'

It was late afternoon now. The coming storm had brought an early darkness, and the humidity had only increased as the light faded. Adam fastened down the store tarpaulin, securing it as best he could over the few boxes and parcels that remained. He hobbled Bess, and pulled the cart up behind the tent. Wolf was allowed inside, with

Kitty, Ella and Adam.

A peculiar stillness fell over the diggings as the storm gathered force. Far off lightning flickered, followed by a drum roll of thunder. Adam had lit candles to give them some light, and Kitty and Ella sewed on, glancing uneasily towards the entrance. The flashes of lightning drew closer, until they could see the jagged streak of it across the brooding sky. Thunder followed at its heels, growling over the hills of Bendigo.

Suddenly wind gusted up, plucking at the tent. The candles flickered wildly and went out. Adam pulled the flap across the opening, fastening it tightly. Outside, canvas creaked and slapped and the wind moaned. Ella could smell the rain before it reached them. A brief, heavy shower, so loud it drowned out their voices. The thunder came again, directly overhead, crashing around them.

Kitty shrieked and clapped her hands over her ears. Ella, more startled by the girl's terror than the storm, put her arm around Kitty's narrow waist and held on to her. Adam leaned towards them, his face eerie in the half-light.

'I'd better go out and see how Bess is.'

Wolf, beside him, whined and pressed closer.

Ella nodded, as another explosion of thunder reverberated around them. 'Be careful!' she cried, but although he nodded, she doubted he could hear her. It was her expression he was answering rather than her words.

Adam undid the tent flap, and the wind hurled itself in, splattering them with rain. Ella jumped up to refasten it behind him. Outside, the world had become a wild, untamed place. Rain thudded down like a curtain. Something blew against the side of the tent and stayed there, indenting the canvas slightly. Voices were shouting, faint and ineffectual against the storm, and a horse screamed in terror.

Ella and Kitty huddled together, and Wolf put back his head and howled. Everything was chaos. And then there was a terrible groaning, splintering sound at the rear of the tent, which filled the air, blotting out everything else. Something huge fell with a rush of air and crashed to the ground. The whole gully seemed to rock beneath their feet Kitty screamed again, and Ella jumped up, ready to run for her life.

'Let me in!'

Adam was hammering against the front of the tent. Stumbling over Wolf, Ella fumbled at the fastening and flung it open.

Adam appeared before her, water dripping down his nose and off his chin, and his hair wet and flattened to his skull. He shouted something into her face, something that sounded like 'danger', but the wind whipped it away before she could make sense of it.

'Bess? Is Bess all right?' she gasped.

'Can't get near her!' he shouted. 'Too dangerous when she's frightened like this!'

He was coming into the tent, his clothing sopping. Behind him, Ella could see rain running in rivulets down the rise, like miniature rivers, to the road below. Someone was following Adam. Ella stared blankly at the boy, with his white, exhausted face and lank, black hair. It was only when he looked up at her, and she saw the clear green of his eyes that she recognised David Marr.

Adam had been shouting 'David', not 'danger'.

'He was outside,' he explained.

Kitty had recognised David, too, and with a gasp came forward. 'You're all wet!' she cried, as if she were surprised by it. 'Take off your jacket... you, too, Adam.'

She tried to spread the clothing around to dry, but it was impossible. They were huddled together in the confined space, like miners trapped under-ground, awaiting rescue.

'What was that noise we heard outside?' Ella asked, leaning towards Adam to be heard.

He leaned against her, and she felt the chill of his wet skin through her dress. 'The tree. One of the branches split off. Smashed the cart to pieces.' He met her shocked look with a wry grin. 'Better that than the tent, Cinderella.'

Ella shuddered. A branch! If it had struck the tent, it was doubtful whether she and Kitty would have survived. She resisted the temptation to bur-row into Adam's chest like a frightened animal. The tent had developed a leak now, and water was dripping steadily onto Wolf's head. The dog gazed long-sufferingly into Ella's eyes.

'Have you found your brother?' Kitty's voice came spasmodically above the wind and rain.

David Marr shook his head. He seemed bewil-dered, as if he had blundered into a nightmare.

'What about your father?' Adam asked the ques-tion this time. 'Where's he?'

The boy said nothing, staring at his hands where they hung limply between his knees. His mouth began to tremble, and he bit his lips to stop it. 'My father died two nights ago. He was buried this morning.'

There was a dreadful silence. Kitty was the first to recover. 'Oh Gawd,' she gasped in a stricken voice. 'I'm that sorry. Here, you have something to drink. You look done in.'

David watched her pour a good few fingers of Adam's brandy into a mug, and when she handed it to him, drank it down without protest. The stuff caught his breath, making him choke, but after a few more minutes the colour began to return to his white face and the lost look faded from his eyes. As if on cue, the roar of the storm receded to allow David to tell his story.

Mr Marr, whom Ella had thought looked so ill on the journey up Big Hill, had taken a turn for the worse after their arrival on Bendigo. It had been David alone who searched for his brother, and who finally came to the conclusion he was not here, and may even have headed east to the Ovens field. Undecided as to what to do for the best, David had set up camp in Sailor's Gully, north of Eaglehawk. He doubted his father could go on traipsing about the countryside, and he dared not leave him to fend for himself.

David had staked a claim, but Mr Marr was too ill to help work it. Fearful of his father's deteriorating condition, David had found a doctor willing to come. The doctor had mixed some medicine, but it had done no good –David's father had lost consciousness soon after and never regained it.

David finished speaking and lapsed into silence. Outside, the rain fell softly and placidly to the ground, hardly recognisable as the uncontrolled beast of earlier.

'What are you going to do now?' Ella asked him gently.

The boy shook his head. The thought of the future suddenly seemed to overwhelm him. 'I don't know,' he whispered. 'I'd go after my brother, but I don't know where he is. And I ... I don't like to leave my father, somehow, even though I know he's ... gone.'

Ella's heart ached for him. She knew what it was to be alone, none better! She looked at Adam, hoping he would have some solution, but he was gazing up at the roof of the tent where a big drip of water was just about to fall.

'What's the ground like, where you staked your claim?' he asked slowly. 'Anyone finding any gold there?'

David looked confused. 'I ... I think so. I didn't really have a chance to find out But that doesn't mean – '

'No, that doesn't mean your claim isn't a good one,' Adam agreed. He rubbed his chin thoughtfully, and Ella shuddered. Her movement caught his eye, and he frowned, and then laughed and took his hand away. 'The storm's almost past now,' he said. 'Perhaps we'd better take a look at the damage.'

Tentatively, one by one, they left the safety of the tent. The sky had lightened considerably, as if it were dawn again rather than evening. The ground was sodden and muddy, and covered with wind-blown debris. A huge branch off the grey box lay across Adam's cart in a tangle of twigs and bedraggled leaves. What was left of the tree stood forlorn, a great jagged wound down one side of the trunk.

When Ella was finally able to take her eyes off the more personal devastation of the tree and the cart, she realised they were not alone in their ill fortune. The tarpaulin over the store seemed secure enough, but all about them in Midnight Gully miners were scrounging for lost and broken belongings. Tents had been ripped, or strewn about the gully, and nearly every claim had several inches of water in the bottom. Across the road – now a muddy creek –the Jardines appeared to be in one piece, although the red painted sign on the side of their tent had begun to run in streaks down the canvas.

'You'd better get back to your camp while it's still light,' Adam said to David Marr. 'I'll come over there in the morning and take a look at your claim. It might be worth workin', who knows.'

The boy took a shaking breath, his smile shy and grateful. 'Thank you, sir.'

'Well, then,' and Adam smiled back, 'that's settled.'

Ella smiled, too, with relief. She should have known Adam would come to David's rescue. Another lame duck, she told herself with weary humour. Adam seemed to collect them.

'How did you find us?' Kitty was asking David, busy wrapping up a parcel of food for him to take back with him. 'You could 'ave been blown to pieces out there!'

David hesitated, and a faint colour rose in his cheeks. 'After my father and I left you at Big Hill, we were on our way to Eaglehawk. We met a Mr Morris. He said he knew Mrs Seaton.' He blushed even more, and Ella wondered what the self-righteous Mr Morris had said about her. Nothing complimentary, she supposed, after what she had said to him in parting at Five Mile Creek!

'I met Mr Morris again when I went to get the doctor for my father. He said he'd heard you'd set up a store in Midnight Gully. I don't know how he knew, but he seemed pretty certain of it.'

'Mr Morris, well, well!' Adam smiled as if they had been the best of friends, but Ella saw the gleam in his eyes.

'I thought of you,' David went on, painfully, 'when my father died. I remembered how kind you'd been. I don't know that I expected you to do anything ... I wasn't thinking properly ... I just wanted a friendly face.' He smiled at Ella, but his eyes shifted to Kitty, and the expression in them told its own story.

The sun was dying, staining the sky pink. The air felt sharp and fresh, as if the storm had made the earth new again. Ella took a deep breath, and sensed her return to full good health. David waved to them, and began the walk back to Sailor's Gully. But his shoulders appeared less bowed and his stride had a determined swing to it.

Two miners dressed in Melbourne finery rode furiously by, mud splattering from under their horses' hooves. Mrs Jardine, out picking up debris near her tent, shook her fist angrily at their departing backs.

'Can you help Kitty with the store tomorrow?' Adam asked Ella. 'It would only be for an hour or two, and there's not that much left to sell. I don't expect you'll be rushed off your feet'

'Of course I'll help.'

'Good.' He looked at her, then away, then back

again. He grinned.

'What is it?' Ella asked suspiciously.

'I was just thinkin' of our friend Morris. The Bendigo diggings is a big place. Fancy him knowing exactly where to find you.'

'You think it's funny, don't you?' Ella folded her arms. 'He warned me against you, you know. He wanted me to leave you, and travel with him.'

The laughter faded from his face. 'I know. He was so good at looking after you, he nearly got you raped in the Black Forest, remember?'

'I'm not going to search him out, if that's what you think.'

'I should bloody hope not.'

They glared at each other, bubbling with resentment, and something more.

Behind them, Kitty cleared her throat. 'If you're both finished,' she said dryly, 'perhaps we'd better take a look around for Bess. She seems to have disappeared.'

They never found her. Some of the miners had seen her go past, galloping like a young filly with the wind in her mane, the storm crackling all around her. They'd half thought it was some illusion created by the lightning and thunder, until Adam came looking for her.

But a horse, a good horse, was a prized possession on the diggings, and if you were lucky enough for one to come your way you accepted it and didn't ask questions.

'I hope whoever the bastard is looks after her,' Adam said, when he came back at last. He looked tired and drawn, but more than that. He looked upset.

'You haven't given up yet, have you?' Ella asked, handing him his plate. She and Kitty had eaten long before and had been waiting for Adam's return.

'No, of course not.' But she could see in his eyes that he held little hope for recovering Bess. 'I'll have to get another cart, too. That one's only good for firewood now. Hasn't been the best of days for me, has it?'

'Have you got enough money?' Kitty asked anxiously. 'It'd be cheaper to get a cart and horse up from Melbourne rather than pay gold-field prices.'

Ella stared at her, amazed at her lack of sensitivity. Couldn't she see that Adam had thought more of Bess than just a piece of property? But evidently Kitty could not. A horse was just a horse to her.

'It'd take too long,' Adam said shortly. He leaned back and closed his eyes. 'Tomorrow I'll go over to Sailor's Gully first, and then have another look for Bess. You're in charge of the store, Kitty.'

Kitty quivered with pleasure that he trusted her. 'I won't let you down, Adam,' she promised him.

Adam smiled, his eyes still shut. 'I know you won't.'

————◆————

'Darling?'

She wondered how long Catherine had been standing there, calling her. It must have been some time, for she looked concerned.

'Are you all right?'

Yes, yes, of course.' She straightened, pretending she had been dozing in the chair by the fire rather than staring into space. Thinking. The Margaret Catchpole story had so caught her imagination, she found herself going over and over it in her mind.

Sheer foolhardiness, to do what she did. To take a horse and just ride, leaving everything behind.

'I wish I could do that.'

She hadn't realised she had spoken aloud until Catherine's eyes narrowed. 'What's that?'

'Nothing, it's nothing.' She stood up, smoothing her skirts. The cloth was a fine wool, a dark blue that suited her colouring. She glanced in the ornate mirror above the mantelpiece, and knew she looked her best. Fair hair in smooth wings either side of her face, her skin clear, her eyes … sad.

'I wish …' she whispered, and did not know what she wished. Only that somehow she could escape. But that was impossible, and especially impossible now. He would never let her go.

Her hands moved down to her waist and folded there, as though she could feel the child growing within. So tiny, so new. The doctor thought no more than two months. Such a long time yet to go before it could be safely born into the world.

An heir.

She had done her duty. She should be pleased, she should be happy.

But the eyes that gazed back at her from the mirror remained sad, and behind her Catherine looked on.

CHAPTER 17

FOR THREE DAYS ADAM WENT to work on
David Marr's claim in Sailor's Gully and Ella
and Kitty looked after the store. Business was hardly
brisk. A few customers wandered over, inspecting
what was left. Someone bought a pick, but complained it was too blunt; someone else bought a
length of rope, but said it was too short; and the last
two blankets were sold to a woman with a coughing child, who said they were too thin.

On the first day, Ella tried to imitate Kitty in
making the right noises when a price was mentioned, but as the hours slipped by she gave up.
Something inside Kitty drove her to beat down the
tentative offers of her customers as if it were a fight
to the death. Ella just didn't feel the same passion.

'Takes a bit of practice,' said Kitty, with a superior
smile.

'I don't think practice would make any difference.'

But Kitty only looked more superior, surveying
Midnight Gully as though she owned it.

The place was thriving again after the storm. Most
of the miners had put their tents back together,
although wet bedding and clothing flapped in
the breeze. More clouds were gathering along the
horizon, but they looked like ordinary rain clouds

rather than thunder heads.

'Wonder how Adam's doin'?' Kitty murmured.

He answered her himself, when he returned that evening. 'Not so good.' There was gold to be had in Sailor's Gully, but David's claim had so far produced nothing. They had only dug down about two feet – the ground was hard and stony despite the rain – but tomorrow they hoped to make better progress.

'I had another look around for Bess,' he added, watching the steam rise off his tea. 'No one's seen her, and if they have, they're not sayin' so. She's gone.'

'You'll have a whole team of horses one day,' Kitty said, trying to cheer him up. 'You can drive 'em round and round the goldfield.'

He laughed, but Ella knew it was only to please Kitty. 'I'm sorry,' she whispered, when Kitty had turned away to fetch something. 'Perhaps she'll turn up ...'

He looked at her, and then reached out as if to touch her cheek. 'No, she's gone.'

'Your hands!' Ella caught them, staring in distress. Blisters formed an arch across his palms, and there were a couple on his thumbs for good measure. 'You can't work with hands like this!'

But he laughed again, this time in genuine amusement. 'I didn't realise I'd gone so soft until I started diggin'. Another day or two and I'll be right.' His fingers squeezed hers, and then released them. He stretched and yawned, groaning as sore muscles protested. 'I think I'll go to bed, ladies. David and me have got a few more feet to go before we bottom that hole.'

On the second day, business at the store was even quieter. Across the road, Mrs Jardine served her customers cups of 'coffee', a smirk on her face. Kitty watched her with narrowed eyes.

'I'd like to see that place burnt to the ground,' she muttered.

Ella gave her a curious look. 'Don't you like her? She seems pleasant enough, even though she's breaking the law.'

'I don't trust her.' Kitty's voice was hard. 'She smiles and jokes, but ...' She shook her head, unwilling or unable to explain. 'And as for 'im, Naughton. He's a right surly bastard.'

Ella wouldn't have used those words, but she agreed with the sentiment. They had not exchanged one word with Naughton since they had been here, and any attempts by them at polite friendliness had been met with Naughton's sizable back.

By lunch time, Kitty was yawning. She nodded her head down the gully. 'At least *he'll* be happy we're almost sold out,' she said, meaning the other store owner, who had protested so strongly when Adam first set up. 'That is, until Adam gets his new stuff in!'

Adam had paid the bullock driver this morning. A red-headed chap with a scar across his cheek, he had taken the money and listened to instructions. Ella wondered that Adam trusted him – he didn't look too trustworthy to her – but she supposed he knew what he was doing.

'Does Adam know when the driver will return from Melbourne?'

'Depends on the road. Pretty bad, they say.' Kitty

yawned again. 'I think I'll put on the billy for a cup o' tea. You want one?'

'Thank you.'

They left the store and walked up to the tent where they would have a clear view of any customers arriving. Kitty busied herself making the tea, and Ella took the opportunity to do some more of her sewing. It would be pleasant, she thought, to have something new to wear, even if it was only blue serge. What do I normally wear? she asked herself idly. Do I change for the afternoon, and again in the evening? Do I have a riding habit and a walking outfit?

'Mrs Seaton!'

The hissed call brought Ella's head up. Kitty had risen to her feet and was staring down into the gully.

'Look there!'

Ella obliged, standing up to see better. The scene looked normal to her: miners were working at their claims, and those who had stopped for their midday meal were sitting and eating, or taking a final puff on their pipes.

'There!' Kitty repeated impatiently, her finger stiff and straight.

And at last she saw. A party of police troopers were moving slowly along the road from the direction of California Gully.

At their head an officer rode a showy chestnut horse. He moved with a rigid, military air, not bothering to glance back at his men, just expecting them to follow. Even from this distance, Ella could see that his braided uniform was immaculate.

She froze.

'It's Moggs, isn't it?' Kitty said beside her.

'Yes, I think it is.'

Some of the miners had been alerted now to the troopers' arrival, and turned to stare. The familiar cry of, 'Joe, Joe!' went up as a warning that the troopers were at their sport of 'digger hunting'. The police began to spread out, stopping by each claim and demanding to see those precious pieces of paper.

Grudgingly, the miners with licences complied, while those without were arrested. The troopers moved on down the gully, fanning out in a rough line to cover the whole area as best they could, and hopefully driving the defaulters before them. One escaped, dodging into his tent and lying low in there, but another was pursued and caught, and soon had his wrists handcuffed. As the search drew nearer, Ella watched the crocodile of handcuffed men grow longer.

Moggs shouted orders, turning on his horse, eyes everywhere. His men ran at his bidding, like terriers in search of rabbits, even following hapless miners down into their holes if they refused to come up.

'I got me licence!' one man shouted as he was dragged over to join the unlucky rest. 'It's in me tent!'

But the police just laughed. 'Oh yeah, sure it is.'

'It is, it is. Just let me go and fetch it.' The man was almost weeping. Everyone knew the fine for failure to produce a licence was five pounds, or else ten days in the log lock-up. A miner could lose his claim, his belongings, everything, unless he had a mate to take care of it. And some mates were even less trustworthy than the police.

Moggs rode up on his horse, and his men stopped laughing. 'What is it?' he snapped.

'Says his licence's in his tent,' one of them explained with a sneer.

Moggs's shoulders twitched with impatience. 'Tie him up with the rest, and get on with your job.'

But the miner wasn't so easily disposed of. 'Let me go! I told you, I got a licence! Bloody Joes!'

Moggs's horse reared, but Moggs held it with an iron fist. His face looked fleshless with anger. 'I'd rather be a Joe than scum like you, grovelling in the dirt!'

The miner turned white with fear or anger, Ella wasn't sure which. Suddenly he wrenched himself free of the restraining arms of the police and began to run. The cheers of his fellows filled the air.

The troopers were in disarray. But Moggs was as cool as ever. He reached down to his saddle holster and slid out the carbine. 'Halt!' he shouted. But the man, if he heard, had no intention of stopping. He ran on, around holes and hillocks, to the delight of the watchers. Moggs lifted the carbine to his shoulder, sighted, and fired.

There was a choked scream, and the escapee fell face forward onto the ground. And lay there, still.

Briefly, shock held everyone both speechless and motionless as Moggs calmly replaced his carbine. And then a growl of anger rose from dozens of throats. The miners moved forward. The police, uneasy now and outnumbered, looked to Moggs for instructions.

He lifted his chin, letting his cold gaze travel over

them, each face remembered. He felt no danger, Ella was certain of it. He did not believe rabble such as this were capable of outsmarting such as he.

'The man was trying to escape,' he said, with absolute self-assurance. 'I called for him to halt, but he ignored my order. It was my duty to stop him.' Voices rose in fury, but Moggs's soared above them all. 'Let it serve as a warning to anyone else who wants to flout the law!'

They knew they couldn't win. The law, and the camp, were on Moggs's side. When a voice from near the fallen man called, 'It's gone through his shoulder. He's alive!' there seemed no point in continuing the fight. A number of miners began walking slowly back to their claims, and more followed. They were sullen, but beaten. The incident had done nothing to improve relations between the camp and the diggings. Ella had the feeling it was just one more skirmish in a long-running war.

The wounded man had been carried across to the Jardines' coffee shop, where he was beginning to come round. Naughton was harnessing his horse to his wagon; ready to make the journey to the doctor. It was the first time Ella had ever seen him bestir himself on another's behalf.

'What sort of place is this?' a voice asked, more bewildered than angry. 'How can we tolerate such brutality? We're ordinary men, come here to work. We don't want trouble. What right have they to shoot us for the lack of a piece of paper?'

'They've no right!' Kitty yelled. 'They've no right, the bastards!'

Ella nearly jumped out of her skin. 'Be quiet!' she told Kitty furiously and looked to Moggs to see if he had heard. Her heart sank. The words, or at least the sense of them, had carried. She saw Moggs turn and look up the rise towards them. Fear gripped her with sharp claws.

Kitty caught her breath in dismay, but disguised it with her usual bravado. 'I'm not afraid of him,' she said loudly, as if saying it would make it true.

Moggs had paused to give further orders to his men, but now he spurred his horse off the road, ignoring the mutterings of the miners he left behind. He proceeded up the rise, past Adam's store, towards the tent.

Kitty said something insulting, but too quietly for Moggs to hear. The chestnut horse sidled towards them, eyes rolling, thoroughly unnerved by all that had happened. But Lieutenant Moggs didn't seem in the least unnerved. He stared down at them triumphantly.

'Mrs Seaton and her little friend! I knew it was only a matter of time until we met again. I half expected you to visit the camp to see what progress I had made in regard to your problem.'

'I have been ill,' Ella replied stonily.

He pretended concern. 'Indeed? I have heard the diggings is a very unhealthy place. Luckily, I am blessed with excellent health.'

Ella sensed the retort on the tip of Kitty's tongue, and jabbed her hard in the ribs with her elbow. Moggs saw, and raised his eyebrows. He turned and looked back down the gully where his men were busy tethering the last of their prisoners to the crocodile ready for the long march back to the camp.

'A good afternoon's work, wouldn't you say?'

'No, I bloody wouldn't!' Kitty burst out, rubbing her bruised ribs.

Moggs let his gaze rest briefly on her, and then drift away as if she were nothing. Ella saw her mouth drop open at the insult. 'Where is he, Mrs Seaton? Hiding?' His voice had lost even the veneer of politeness.

'Adam has no reason to hide,' Kitty muttered, near to tears. Ella reached out and caught her arm, squeezing it hard in comfort and warning.

'Adam is a law-abiding citizen,' she said quietly. 'There is no reason for you to pursue him, Lieutenant Moggs.'

Moggs smiled unpleasantly, the harsh lines deepening from his nose to his lips. 'Well, that is a matter of opinion, isn't it, madam? Because of him I left my previous post at Carlsruhe with a less than perfect record. I am not a man who likes to be thought of as second rate.'

'I understood Mr Gilbert was very pleased to have you here,' Ella began.

Anger seemed to tighten his skin, accentuating the bones beneath, and making his face sharp and vicious. 'Gilbert! He sees himself as a friend of the ordinary man. What he fails to realise is that, if one is in charge, one has no friends.' Suddenly he leaned forward towards her, and despite herself Ella took a step back. That amused him. 'Perhaps you will inform your man that I have some information he may be interested in. Very reliable information, I might add.'

'What information?' Kitty sneered, but her voice shook.

'It concerns a meeting he had in the Black Forest. Do you remember the meeting I'm speaking of, Mrs Seaton?'

Ella said nothing, refusing to look away from that cruel face.

'Ask him for me how it is that he and Eben were such friends in the Black Forest, and yet in Sawpit Gully became complete strangers. I'd be very interested to hear his answer.'

He smiled into her eyes. Ella still said nothing, and his smile faded. 'If I were you, Mrs Seaton, I'd leave Midnight Gully and find safer lodgings.'

With a brutal kick of his heels, Moggs sent his horse galloping back down the rise to the road. His men and their prisoners fell into line behind him.

'Gawd,' Kitty breathed.

Ella tried to think, but she couldn't, her mind was numb. The incident filled her with a mixture of fear and foreboding. Moggs had threatened her, and threatened Adam. She felt as if she should do something, but she didn't know what.

———◆———

'He was just throwing his weight around,' said Adam. 'Doesn't mean nothing.'

Kitty pretended to believe him, because she wanted to. Ella wished she could believe him too. But she couldn't. She opened her mouth to protest, but Adam caught her eye and shook his head slightly. So she bit her tongue, and said no more in front of Kitty.

They ate their meal and Adam told them about David's claim. They had dug down to five feet now, and the ground was just as hard.

'Found a pennyweight of gold,' he said wearily. 'Probably about three shillings worth.'

Ella wondered aloud if David should come and camp here with them, but Adam thought it was better if he remained in Sailor's Gully to keep an eye on the claim. 'Not that there's much to guard! But if there is something worth finding in there, I'd hate a midnight miner to get it.'

'How is David managing?' Ella asked.

'He's all right Hands a bit sore, but he's a strong lad.'

Adam was tired, and soon went to his bed down in the store, Wolf trotting behind him. But Ella's unease persisted. It was all very well for Adam to refuse to discuss it, but Ella doubted he understood the full implications of Moggs's words. She tossed and turned, and eventually, when Kitty was asleep, crawled out into the cold to try and make him see sense.

Ella folded her arms about herself, listening to the Jardines' Irish fiddler. The music was quick and light, and played havoc with her senses. She closed her eyes and pretended she was dancing, around and around, skirts swinging and feet tapping. The noise from the coffee shop rose and fell, and sometimes she could hear Mrs Jardine's gruff laughter. Kitty might say she distrusted Mrs Jardine, but Ella found herself liking her. She had seen Mrs Jardine give food to one or two of the more needy cases in Midnight Gully, and even pay for a doctor to visit a man who could not afford it.

Ella sighed, and opened her eyes. I'm dithering, she admitted to herself. I need to speak to Adam, I need to make him understand the danger he is in.

With a firm, determined tread, she made her way towards the store.

Her eyes had already adjusted to the dark, and she walked without stumbling on the stony ground. But when she reached the store, she paused again, leaning her hand lightly against the rough tarpaulin. Wolf growled, making her start. He was peering out at her from the shadows, but when he saw it was her, he wagged his tail. Ella put out her hand towards him, and at the same time heard the loud, ominous click of a pistol being cocked.

'Adam!' she gasped. 'It's me, don't shoot!'

She heard him swear softly to himself. 'I thought you were a midnight miner,' he said in a rough, sleepy voice. 'What are you doing out here? Don't you know it's dangerous to be creeping around in the dark?'

Across the road at the Jardines', the music stopped abruptly, followed by a jeering shout. The Irish fiddler had passed out

'I wanted to talk to you,' Ella said softly, 'but not in front of Kitty. She's frightened enough as it is.'

She could hear Adam moving, and then he appeared in front of her, fully dressed. He slipped the pistol back into his belt. 'I didn't think anything much could frighten Kitty,' he replied evenly.

'Lieutenant Moggs could.'

He sighed. 'Is that what you've come to talk about, Mrs Seaton?'

'He hates you, Adam. And he blames you for the debacle at Sawpit Gully. He wanted to leave Carlsruhe and take up his post here with a perfect record, and because he didn't, it's your fault.'

Adam made a scornful sound. 'He likes to frighten

me women, but only when I'm not around. He's the sort that would run a mile if he thought he might lose a fight. Wouldn't want blood on his nice uniform.'

But Ella knew that wasn't true, and she was certain Adam knew it too. 'What about the man he shot? Mrs Jardine says he has a broken collarbone. But it was the *way* Moggs did it, Adam ... the *way* he aimed and fired, and put his gun away. There was no *passion* in it, no *feeling*. He might have been shooting at bulls' eyes.'

Adam shrugged. 'It's his job.'

'And is it his job to arrest you, now that he knows about the Black Forest? About Eben? He knows you were lying!'

'He always did know I was lyin', he just couldn't prove it.'

'What about this person he says gave him the information?'

'Aye, well ...' Adam took a step out of the store and looked up at the sky. 'I think I know who that is, and I can deal with it.'

She froze, staring at him, but he wouldn't meet her eyes. 'You mean like you dealt with Doctor Rawlins?'

'No.' He caught her arm, giving it a little shake. 'No, I don't mean that.'

'It's Mr Morris, isn't it?'

'More than likely.'

'That's what Moggs will expect you to do, Adam. That's why he told me about it He wants you to go and confront Morris, and then he'll catch you in the act.' She sounded breathless, desperate.

He laughed. 'I'll just be visiting an old friend for

a talk, that's all.'

Ella tried to read his face in the darkness, but he was smiling, unmoved, and she knew he had no intention of telling her what he really planned. 'Why don't you leave here... there are other gold-fields.'

That wiped the smile off his face. 'What, and run away? I'm not runnin' away from him.'

'Eben ran away.'

Adam's eyes narrowed. 'Well I'm not Eben.'

'No, you're a stubborn fool,' she told him angrily, 'and I'm going back to bed!' He didn't answer her, but as she turned away, she thought she heard him curse softly.

———◆———

David's claim bottomed the next morning, but all their hard work was for nothing. David came back to Midnight Gully with Adam at noon and they sat gloomily drinking tea.

'I can face the fact that there was no gold in our claim,' David murmured, 'but it really galls me that thirty yards away they were digging out nuggets as big as eggs.'

'That's the luck of it,' Adam said. 'I've heard o' men thinkin' they've bottomed their claim, and abandoning it, only to have someone else come along, dig a bit deeper, and find a jeweller's shop.'

'Then I should try again?' David asked, frowning. 'I should stake another claim, and then another, until I find gold?'

Adam shrugged. 'Gold mining isn't an easy way to make a fortune, not in most cases, anyway. You have to work for it. That's why so many of them give up and go home. Too hard. But if you stick it out long enough, the chances have to get better.'

David thought about that. 'You sound like my father,' he said wearily.

Kitty looked startled, her mouth slightly ajar. Ella realised that the girl hadn't considered the eight-year age difference between herself and Adam before; nor the fact that David was so much closer to her own age.

'We'll decide what to do tomorrow,' Adam declared. 'In the morning I'll come over and we'll take a look around. Maybe even go further over towards White Horse Gully, and see what's happening there. I heard they'd had some good finds … almost as good as Peg Leg.'

'All right' David managed a smile.

Kitty, watching him, still appeared lost in thought. Perhaps she's finally seeing what's been under her nose for the last three days, Ella told herself. David Marr had possibilities. He was not as good a prospect as Adam, perhaps, but there were compensations. He was educated, he was younger … and he was infatuated with her. It would be a pleasant change for Kitty to be the one pulling the strings.

'I'll take you over to Long Gully to see that doctor,' Adam said, interrupting Ella's thoughts.

She blinked at him. 'Doctor? But I'm better now.'

'He said he wanted to see you again, better or not.'

'You can't afford it.'

Adam laughed. 'Yes, I can. Come on. It's a bit of a walk, can you manage it?'

She was tempted to say she couldn't, but she suspected Adam would only fetch the doctor out to her. Reluctantly, she rose to her feet.

'David, you stay here with Kitty. Can you do that for me?' Adam gave David an earnest look, as if he were entrusting him with something very precious.

David nodded, glanced sideways at the girl, and blushed. 'Yes, yes, of course. I'll look after Miss ... Kitty.'

Kitty laughed at his gaucheness, but Ella could see she was flattered.

'It won't work you know,' she murmured, as they walked down the rise to the road.

Adam gave her an innocent stare.

'It's you she wants.'

Adam grinned. 'She doesn't know what she wants yet, Cinderella.'

They walked on in silence. The wind was bitterly cold today and it pierced Ella's clothing like needles. There was snow falling somewhere and the breeze was coming straight from it on to the Bendigo diggings.

'I wish I had that red woollen cloak right now,' she said. 'The one I was wearing when I left ... wherever I left.'

He was watching her, a smile twitching the corners of his lips. 'Maybe Ned's wearing it.'

It shouldn't have been funny, but it was. She laughed back at him, surprised that she could. Today, for some reason, such things did not seem so serious. She was just glad to be alive.

California Gully was a hive of activity. Although not generally considered one of the richer gullies, it had its devotees. There were the usual stores lining the route, and Adam narrowed his eyes, taking in anything that might be of later use to him. They stepped aside for a wagon laden with wood for shoring up mines. Another rumbled by, full of carcasses to be sold to the goldfields' butchers, the noisome load pursued by dogs and flies.

The rush was still strong at Long Gully, but not as strong as the area around Eaglehawk – that was El Dorado, and wondrous tales were being told about it. The doctor's tent was about halfway along the gully, and emblazoned with his name: *Doctor Fletcher*. Ella saw his horse and gig enclosed in a small, fenced yard at the back.

A cluster of patients waited outside the tent. One of them, on roughly made crutches, had a wound on his leg, while another had a dirty bandage around his head, and yet another sat coughing in a truly excruciating manner.

'I don't need to see him,' Ella begged. 'Really, Adam, I'm perfectly all right.'

'I don't care, I'm not takin' any chances. Not with you.'

She saw the self-mockery in his eyes, as if he thought himself a fool for admitting what he felt but wasn't able to help it.

Ella cleared her throat. 'Perhaps you'd better show him those blisters then. They look sore.' And, indeed, some had burst and become quite red and watery. She had heard often enough how easy it was to become ill on the goldfields, and infected blisters was one of the main culprits.

Adam looked down at his hands and grimaced. 'Aye, well, maybe.'

'Are you really going to keep digging until you

find gold? I thought you didn't intend to be a miner any more, after California?'

He sighed. 'I thought so too, but I don't see much point in sittin' idle, waiting for the stuff for the store to arrive from Melbourne. I might as well do *something*, and I know mining. Anyway, with David to help it's not so bad.'

'Not so good either?' she mocked, glancing at his hands.

'I like it when you worry about me.'

But there was a smile in his eyes, and she was able to answer with, 'Someone has to,' and not feel foolish.

Eventually their turn came. Doctor Fletcher beckoned them across, his face as serious as Ella remembered. She ducked her head under the entrance to the tent and found it was roomy enough inside. The walls were lined with green baize, and there was a small table and two chairs, as well as a stretcher bed against the wall on one side. Ella saw a large cupboard containing jars full of the doctor's cures. The place smelt of Doctor Fletcher's musty coat, and aniseed.

'So, you're completely recovered,' Doctor Fletcher was saying. 'No more fever, chills? Head-aches? Well, then.' He pressed her temple, where the bruise was now only a faint yellow discoloration. 'If you continue to take good care of yourself, Mrs Seaton, I won't expect to see you back again.'

Ella smiled, relieved to hear him say what she had already known herself. She nudged Adam with her elbow. He sighed, gave her a long-suffering look reminiscent of Wolf, and held out his hands.

Doctor Fletcher tut-tutted. 'They'll need to be

cleaned and dressed. I'd like a pound for every infected blister I've seen in the last six months.'

It took only a few moments, but was painful nonetheless. When they left the doctor's tent, Adam's hands were bandaged and his expression was grim. 'Bloody robbery,' he muttered. 'A shilling a blister.'

'Doctor Fletcher said that an infected blister can poison your whole body and make you very sick indeed,' Ella reminded him self-righteously.

He made a sound that suggested he doubted the truth of that.

'I wouldn't want you to fall ill, Adam,' she went on.

He looked at her out of the corner of his eye. 'Wouldn't you?'

'No!'

'Well that's something anyway.'

They walked on in silence. The air was even colder than before, and the sun hung low in the sky. They would only just make it back to Midnight Gully before darkness, Ella thought, with a glance about her. Already the diggings were settling down to evening pursuits - eating and smoking and talking over the day's events. Wolf, trotting beside them with his tail wagging, stopped and stared as another dog barked a challenge, and then pretended he hadn't heard after all. Ella smiled to herself. Wolf looked vicious, but only to those who didn't know him.

Ella wondered how David and Kitty were getting on alone together. Was Adam right, would Kitty decide to fall in love with David? Surely the girl was not so fickle! And yet, she was young. The young seemed to fall in and out of love all the time.

Had Ella been in and out of love, when she was as young as Kitty?

No.

Even without the benefit of memory, Ella knew she had never been like that. Her heart felt untouched, whole within her, as if she had never given it to anyone. The words came back to her, '*cold, frozen*'. Perhaps she had always been so.

Was her heart still untouched?

She glanced at Adam, beside her. She liked the feeling of having him there, she liked the knowledge that if she turned her head and smiled, he would smile back. She liked the warmth that she saw in his eyes whenever they looked into hers. She liked the feeling that he cared about her, that he would protect her from the unknown and rather frightening world she found herself cast adrift in. Did that mean she was still untouched? Or had the frozen woman begun to thaw?

It was when they reached the junction, where California Gully ran into Midnight Gully that they first saw the smoke. It was like a funnel in the sky, drifting, black, with puffs of grey. Adam frowned. 'Looks like it's comin' from the Jardines'.' Without looking at her, he quickened his step. 'You'd better stay here,' he yelled, beginning to run.

His eyes must have been better than hers. Ella peered desperately ahead through the twilight, trying to see the source of the smoke. Her side was aching, but she ignored it, trying and failing to match Adam's long strides. 'Is it the Jardines'?' she gasped out.

'No,' he said. 'No, it isn't.' And there was something about his voice ...

The thick smoke was beginning to thin. Whatever had been set alight was burning itself out. And Ella was close enough now to see exactly what *was* burning.

It was Adam's dreams which were alight.

CHAPTER 18

———◆———

ELLA FORGOT THE PAIN IN her side. Ahead of her, she could see that the tent ... the store ... both were burning. The tent had fallen in upon itself, charred and smouldering, but the store was still well alight, fed by the contents. As she watched, a flame licked hungrily into the air.

People were gathered on the road – Ella could see the Jardines – but they weren't trying to put out the fire, the troopers were making sure of that. Ella saw their uniforms among the crowd as they kept order.

An officer was seated on his horse halfway up the slope. Kitty was kneeling on the ground before him. She appeared to be crying, and as Ella watched, she lifted her head and screamed out her rage at him.

'Come back!' Ella cried. 'Moggs is here. Adam, come back!'

But Adam was too far ahead, Wolf running beside him. Ella could only follow, half crying from the stitch in her side. She saw the crowd catch sight of Adam and give way to let him through. She saw Moggs turn his head sharply, his face a dark blur against the sky. And then Kitty was screaming out his name.

'Adam, Adam, they fired it ... they fired it!'

Adam had reached her now, and he put his arms

around her. Kitty buried her face against his shoulder, and he held her a moment, trying to comfort her. But Ella could see his rigid back and knew how angry he was. He looked up and spoke to Moggs, but she was too far away to hear what he said.

The crowd heard though, and raised their voices in jeering support.

Moggs steadied his horse. 'Take him!' he shouted angrily. Two of the troopers ran forward to grab Adam, but he shrugged them off, and took a running leap at Moggs. The horse panicked, rearing up, while Moggs fought to stay in the saddle. Adam got his hand to the officer's boot, intending to pull him down, but Moggs had guessed what he meant to do. He kicked out savagely, striking Adam full in the face. Adam fell back, dropping to his knees, clasping his head in his hands.

Ella groaned, and the crowd groaned with her. Her legs were barely holding her up, but she was almost there. The crowd parted for her, and she stumbled through to the front.

Kitty, screeching, was being held back by a trooper. Adam, too, was being dragged to his feet. And then Wolf made a sound Ella would never forget. Emulating his master, the dog crept towards Moggs. But again Moggs was ready. He had his pistol out. Behind her, there was a chaos of men shouting and women screaming, but it seemed to Ella that there was no sound at all. She watched in silence as Wolf gathered his strength, his teeth bared and deadly, and sprang. She could see, even as Wolf launched himself into space, that it was too late. Moggs fired. Wolf's big body struck the side of Moggs's horse, already dying. The force sent the dog catapulting backwards onto the ground. Ella felt the thump of his landing.

The sting of the fire was in her nostrils. The store was still burning, but the tent was just a blackened mess. Her eyes blurred with tears of rage and help-lessness. Without realising what she was doing, Ella began to walk up the rise.

'We have information that you are selling alcoholic liquor,' Moggs was saying. He looked unmoved, but there was a wildness in his eyes. 'My men searched your tent and found a bottle of brandy.'

'Half a bloody bottle!' Kitty shouted at Adam, her face streaked with soot and tears.

Adam didn't answer.

'It is enough,' Moggs snapped. He wiped his lips with the back of his hand, and Ella saw that it was shaking. 'I have acted within the law. I fired your possessions, and now I am arresting you.'

Adam still had his back to Ella. He was stand-ing so quietly within the grip of the troopers, she thought he must be in shock. A few feet away lay Wolf, his thick coat bloody. Ella caught her breath on a sob.

Suddenly Moggs lifted his voice. 'Let this be a lesson to you all!' he shouted. 'Now go home!' And he nodded to his men to begin dispersing the crowd.

There were mutters and an anonymous voice retorted that it was Moggs who should be burnt. But the police were watching and the group broke up. Ella caught a glimpse of the Jardines melting into the growing darkness. Although she did not blame them for what had happened, there was a bitter taste in her mouth that it was Adam who was being punished.

Moggs straightened his jacket and smoothed his cuffs, waiting until the road began to empty. He gave Adam a grim smile. 'Bring him.'

Ella came to life.

'No,' she gasped. And then, in a shout, 'Adam!' She ran forward, catching hold of him, and felt rough hands pulling her back.

'Here, let 'im go now,' a deep voice warned. 'Stand back there, mum.'

Adam tugged against the restraining hold on him, and managed to get one of his arms free. He found Ella, dragging her in against him. She felt his cheek against hers, and his quick breath. 'There'll be a fine to pay,' he murmured thickly. 'Money ... you'll need the money.'

'Yes, yes,' she was holding on to him as tightly as she could, but still felt herself being prised away.

'Otherwise it's the lock-up ... Melbourne, maybe.'

'I won't let that happen.' She tried to look at him then, and felt the skin of her cheek sticking to his. There was blood. It was running from his nose and there was a gash on his cheekbone. His bottom lip had begun to swell.

'Oh Adam,' she breathed. 'Oh Adam,' hysteria rising in her voice.

'Don't let him see,' he whispered furiously, his eyes as wild as Moggs's. 'Don't give him the satisfaction.'

They had her now, the grip on her arms making her powerless to do anything but watch as handcuffs were fastened about Adam's wrists. She saw him flinch. But he was still looking at her, as if by looking only at her, he could bear what they were doing to him. One of the troopers passed a rope through his bound wrists and then he was jerked around and down the slope towards the horses. Ella watched his back, watched him trip and only just regain his footing, watched the trooper fasten Adam's rope to his stirrup.

'Very touching,' said Moggs, with distaste.

Adam had asked her not to show Moggs her pain, and she wouldn't. Slowly, carefully, she turned to face him. 'You know Adam wasn't selling sly grog.'

'That's a decision for the magistrate to make, Mrs Seaton.'

'You've arrested an innocent man – '

'Oh, innocent!' Moggs sneered. His horse danced nervously, but he held it. Suddenly his voice was ugly. 'There's nothing innocent about him. He may not have lit that fire at Sawpit Gully but he knew about it, probably planned it to happen when it did so that he couldn't be blamed. He knew what was happening at Mrs Ure's inn, too. He was a party to that. Eben, the bushranger, is his brother! Did you know that, Mrs Seaton? Runs in the family, doesn't it? Now, tell me again that he's innocent'

'You don't understand ...' Ella began, and then closed her mouth. There was nothing she could say to Moggs to change his mind. He had wanted revenge, and now he had it. She had best save her story for the magistrate in the morning.

'I'd like to stay and chat with you, Mrs Seaton, but I have to get on,' that sneering voice continued. 'It's a long walk back to the camp, and in the dark too. Best not take any chances. Your man might trip over and hurt himself. Or then again he might try and escape.' The thought seemed to surprise him ... please him. 'Do you think he'd stop if I told him to? Or would he prefer to take his chances with the bullet?'

Dazed, Ella wondered if she could possibly have heard him correctly. As she stared up at him, frozen in place, he leaned down towards her. His voice was soft: for her alone.

'Maybe you should have said goodbye to him while you had the chance.'

He was gone, loose stones rattling and then the pounding of his horse's hooves as he galloped to catch his troop on the road to California Gully.

Ella stood and stared after him until Mrs Jardine came, clicking her tongue, and slipped an arm about her shoulders.

'Naughton thought they'd come for us,' she said. 'We've paid out a few sweeteners, but I've heard this Moggs don't take bribes.' And she shook her head in a bewildered fashion. 'What sort of policeman don't take bribes?'

'He hates Adam.' Ella heard her own voice, strange and hoarse.

'Well, from what I've heard, he's not right in the head. Rode a man down on that horse of his when he were at Carlsruhe. That's what they're sayin', any rate. Moggs didn't like what he said, so he rode him down. Saved a bullet, I s'pose.'

Ella shivered. And then, remembering, looked across in the darkness to the pale mound of grey fur that had been Wolf. Tears slid down her cheeks. She went over to touch the cooling body. Wolf's long coat stirred in the breeze, but he would never again lift his head to sniff the air. 'Poor old boy,' she whispered. And then, anguish filling her voice, 'Oh Adam ...'

'Never mind, my duck,' Mrs Jardine murmured behind her. 'Naughton'll see to the dog. He died protectin' his master. I reckon that's as good a way to go as any.'

She was right, Ella supposed, but just at the moment she couldn't see it. She wiped her cheeks, glancing back towards the road, invisible now in the darkness. 'I have to go after Adam. I can't leave him alone with that man.'

'There's naught you can do now,' Mrs Jardine replied firmly. 'You'd never catch them up, and if you did, you'd likely be shot by them or someone else. Adam can look after himself for one night. He'll need you in one piece in the mornin', to get him out o' trouble.'

She was right, Ella knew she was right. But as she turned away it felt like betrayal.

Mrs Jardine coaxed Ella down the rise towards the coffee shop. A group of sympathetic customers was waiting at the door. As she passed, Mrs Jardine murmured something to the dark bulk that was Naughton, and then led Ella around to the back where the Jardines had their own tent.

Ella sat down on the edge of a stout-looking bed – a wooden base raised about a hand's breadth off the ground on thick little legs. Mrs Jardine forced something in a mug between Ella's chattering teeth, and while it burned a trail to her stomach, rubbed Ella's hands in her own plump ones.

'If they charge him with sellin' sly grog, it'll be a fine of fifty quid. Have you got that much?' the big woman asked in practical tones.

Ella tried to think. The money. The secret hiding place. Would it be all right, buried beneath the ground? The fire had burned hot, but quickly. Would the money survive? The thought of money brought another name to mind. Ella looked about her, shock turning to anxiety.

'Kitty?'

'Kitty said she was goin' to find someone called David, over at Sailor's Gully. One o' the boys took her.'

Ella began to stand up, and then sat down again. There was no point in worrying about Kitty. She could obviously take care of herself. If she had gone to David, then that was one less concern for Ella. She must concentrate on getting the money, and paying the fine. Otherwise Adam would be sent down to Melbourne, to serve out his sentence in hard labour.

'Do you have the money?' Mrs Jardine asked again.

Ella looked up at her. There was something sharp and bright in those black currant eyes. Suddenly she wondered whether Kitty was right - was Mrs Jardine really to be trusted? But even as she thought it, she dismissed it. Mrs Jardine had come to her aid tonight, she had been kindness itself. Ella had no reason to doubt her.

'I have *some* money,' she said. 'Adam paid some out ... I'm not sure how much is left.' Some remaining doubt stopped her from giving away its hiding place.

'Well, some is better 'an none,' the gruff voice soothed. 'You lie down, my duck, and have a little sleep. You can't do nothin' more tonight. I'll wake you if Kitty comes back.'

Whatever Mrs Jardine had given her to drink had made her head spin - perhaps it was the infamous tumble-down. Ella gladly lay down and closed her eyes. The pillow beneath her head smelled faintly of a mixture of lavender and rum and tobacco. She felt Mrs Jardine heave herself up and waddle outside. Voices, a soft murmur, and then footsteps moving away. And then nothing.

She lay for some time, empty, trying not to think. But the thoughts were there, each one jostling to be faced. She thought of Adam being pulled along in the darkness behind the trooper's horse. She thought of Moggs riding faster and faster, and laughing when Adam fell. She thought of Moggs taking out his pistol and fixing Adam in his sights, and squeezing the trigger.

When the hand touched her shoulder, she sprang up with a cry, eyes wide and wild. The candle dipped and dived, dancing over Kitty's frightened, dirt-streaked face. The two women stared at each other, and then Kitty put down the candle with a trembling hand and cast herself into Ella's arms.

They clung together, shaking, too tired and too scared to cry. After a moment, Kitty said, 'I went to find David. I thought ... I thought maybe he could help.'

'Why wasn't he here when we got back?' Ella asked. She hadn't even thought of David before, but now she did.

Kitty sighed. 'I sent him away. I said he wasn't my sort.'

Ella bit her lip on a terrible urge to laugh.

'Do you know what he said? When I told him what had happened?' Kitty repeated it slowly, with a certain amount of pleasure. 'He said ... he said if anythin' had happened to me, he'd kill Moggs with his bare hands.'

Ella gave her a squeeze, and released her. 'The money – ' she began.

'We had a look, David and me. It's all right. David said it was deep enough down to be protected, especially 'cause the fire was over so quick.'

So saying, Kitty pressed the grubby bag into her hand. Ella's fingers closed on it, hard, and her eyes stung with tears of relief. With some difficulty, she blinked them back. 'How much is in it, do you know?'

Kitty thought. 'Not quite fifty pound, I think. Is it enough?'

Ella sighed. 'I don't know.' Fifty, Mrs Jardine had said. Would they take a little less?

'We'll get 'im out, won't we?' Kitty whispered, and her blue eyes looked hollow in the candlelight.

She nodded. 'I'll go first thing in the morning. Is David still here?'

Kitty wiped a grimy hand over her equally grimy cheek. 'He's still here; he's sleepin' at our camp – or what's left of it. There might be somethin' left, he said, and he didn't want anyone else to get it.' Kitty went on, 'Mrs Jardine says I can sleep in Naughton's bed tonight.' She rolled her eyes. 'Can't hardly wait.'

Ella smiled despite herself.

She listened to Kitty settling down, her familiar sighs and shufflings. In the darkness, it was almost like being back in their own tent. Almost. The night dragged on. She kept thinking: if it's long and slow for me, how must it seem to Adam?

'I'll never be able to sleep,' she whispered.

And then it was morning.

———◆———

The camp was already astir when Ella and David reached it. Soft rain was falling. Like a veil, it coyly revealed a flag here, a man on horseback there. Clouds covered the hills encircling Bendigo Flat, further hindering visibility.

The journey from Midnight Gully had been long and miserable, even though Naughton Jardine had loaned David his horse and wagon. The constant soft rain soaked Ella's clothing, her hair curled about her face, and she was cold. Even her anger couldn't keep her warm. It had been replaced by a terrible, stomach-clenching dread.

'Please let him be all right,' she whispered to herself, like a prayer. 'Please let him be all right.'

Kitty had not come. She had remained behind in Midnight Gully, raking through the wreckage of the tent and the store, pulling out anything that might be useful. Ella had been surprised when the girl did not insist on accompanying them, but David answered her unspoken question.

'She's afraid.'

I'm afraid, too, Ella thought. But Adam needs me, and I can't let him down.

She realised that, until now, she had been holding herself aloof from being fully involved with Adam and his journey. Even while she kissed him, some part of her had stood aside, intent on her own destiny. But now she had been drawn in, and it was too late to pull back.

She did not even want to.

The log lock-up stood in the upper part of the camp reserve. Square and solid, it was like a small fortress. The tall gum trees and fallen logs that framed it were famous for being used as a temporary holding place. Prisoners were chained to them when the lock-up was full, but no one was chained there this morning.

Ella approached the place, her wet skirts trailing in the mud. Behind her, David looked pale and tired, his dark hair plastered to his head. Although he had not said much to her since they set out this morning, Ella sensed his uncertainty. Whether she wanted to or not, it was Ella who must take the lead.

A policeman stood guard outside the lock-up. He eyed Ella professionally as she approached; he had seen enough to recognise the stricken look she wore. 'Best go and talk with the magistrate, missus,' he informed her, kindly enough.

'I want to see one of the prisoners.'

'There are seven in there, missus, which one do you want?'

'Adam.'

'Oh, 'im.' The eyes changed and shifted away. 'He's Lieutenant Moggs's prisoner.'

'Is he here?'

'They were supposed to 'ave 'ad 'im up before the magistrate first thing this morning, for sellin' grog.' The guard shifted his gun to his left hand, and scratched his buttocks with the right. 'But Captain Foster, he took one look at 'im and said he wasn't fit to be charged.'

'Is he here?' Ella repeated, breathless now. What did he mean, wasn't fit to be charged? Why wouldn't the man meet her eyes?

'Nah.' His gaze flicked to hers, and away again. 'He's under guard in the camp hospital. Got broken ribs, they said, as well as the rest'

The ground shivered beneath her feet She took a step back, as if to leave, and felt David catch her arm in his. The guard's breath was hot and unpleasant on her cheek, his tone confidential. 'Mr Gilbert, he don't like officers 'at throw their weight about. Won't be long before he gets rid o' Moggs.'

'Hey! Hey out there!'

The voice came from close at hand, startling them. Ella looked up, expecting to see that someone new had arrived, but there was no one. The guard turned and growled 'Shut up!' in the direction of the lock-up.

'Hey you! Adam's missus!' The voice called again, a desperate croak. 'Can I 'ave a word with yer? Just one word?'

The guard looked at her consideringly. 'You know 'im? I'll give you a word for a shillin'.'

Ella was tempted to refuse to pay, but David handed over the money contemptuously. The lock-up was even more solid close up, its rough, undressed logs piled one atop the other, the gaps between allowing the weather in. It smelt too. Obviously, there was little attention paid to sanitation. Ella resisted the urge to hold her nose.

'Who is it?' she asked.

A pair of eyes peered at her through one of the larger cracks in the logs. 'Eddie,' the voice answered.

'It's Eddie. Your man Adam, he saved my Mary-anne. Remember?'

'I remember.'

Eddie breathed a sigh of relief. 'They locked me up in here for not havin' a licence. But I've only got a couple o' days to go. They'll let me out if you give the guard a pound or two. "Bail", they call it. I'll pay you back, I swear it. Only get me out. I'm that worried about Maryanne ...'

Ella, recalling Maryanne's bold look, couldn't blame him. She had money, and it seemed churlish not to help the man when it was in her power to do so, especially since she wouldn't have the fifty pounds for Adam's fine anyway.

Beside her, David stooped to meet Eddie's eyes. 'Have you seen Adam?'

Eddie lowered his voice. 'He was in 'ere last night, though I told the guard he should o' been in the 'ospital. Moggs had done 'im over pretty good. He were a bit light-headed ... you know, ramblin' on. He kept sayin' his missus'd come and get him out. They took him down this mornin' to charge him.'

Ella swallowed the lump in her throat. 'The guard said Captain Foster sent him to the hospital instead.'

Eddie gave that some thought. 'Maybe you can get him out. Better if you do! That place is bloody unhealthy. You'll need help though. Get me out, missus ... please.'

It only took a moment, and was easier than Ella had feared. The guard agreed to give Eddie 'bail' for a pound, and Ella handed him the money. He unbolted the door and looked the other way as Eddie came out.

He was dirty and smelly, but he was very grateful. He would have hugged Ella with his good arm if she hadn't moved back abruptly. 'They've got fleas in there as big as frogs,' he muttered, scratching at his chest.

'Where's the hospital?' Ella asked him, quickening her step.

He narrowed his eyes, peering down over the barracks, the gold-licensing office with its accompanying crowd of miners, and the officers' quarters. 'There.'

Ella's expectations hadn't been high, but certainly the smallish, rather tatty canvas structure that was the camp hospital fell short of them.

'The camp traps won't go there,' Eddie was saying gruffly. 'But the prisoners, they ain't got much choice.'

Ella looked at him. Her stomach was fluttering, but she knew the question had to be asked, and she steeled herself to ask it. 'Just how badly was he hurt?'

Eddie pursed his lips. 'His nose were broke, I know that. He said his ribs were hurtin' like hell, so maybe they were broke, too. Moggs said he tried to escape on the way through Ironbark, but Adam told me it were a lie, that Moggs stopped there and sent his men on ahead to check for ambushers. But when they came back, it was Adam who'd been ambushed.'

Rage gripped her, draining her face of what colour she had left. Her pale eyes blazed. 'I'm going to make a complaint to Mr Gilbert.'

Eddie eyed her uneasily. 'What can he do?'

'He'll see that Moggs is punished!'

But Eddie looked dubious, giving his head a good scratch. 'It's Adam's word against Moggs's, far as I can see. I know who I'd be bettin' on.'

'But I can try and make him understand!'

'How do you know it wouldn't just make things worse for Adam?'

David cleared his throat. 'I think it would be best if I went ahead, to see if Adam is still there. I won't ask for him. I'll pretend I'm looking for someone else. Once we know where he is, and how badly hurt he is, we can make a plan. I don't think you have fifty pounds to pay the fine if it comes to a sentence for selling liquor, have you, Mrs Seaton?'

'No,' she whispered.

'Well then ... Will you wait for me here?'

She frowned. 'But – '

Eddie was nodding his head in agreement. 'You go and see the lay o' the land, lad.'

But David hesitated, watching Ella. 'Will you wait here?' he repeated anxiously.

David was right. If there was even the smallest chance of getting Adam free, then it was best they work out a plan, not blunder in and spoil it. Ella sighed and nodded. 'All right, go on.'

David smiled, the hollows under his eyes deep and dark, and set off at a lope towards the hospital. No one stopped him, and Eddie and Ella, watching from the shelter of some trees at the edge of the upper part of the camp, saw him disappear inside.

Ella held her breath, but nothing happened. There were no shouts, no gunshots. Only the soothing hum of life in the camp, and the soft patter of rain on the leaves above.

Beside her, Eddie was scratching his neck with a

single-minded relish. He plucked something from his skin, and held it up between his finger and thumb. 'Big as a frog,' he muttered incredulously to himself.

David was returning, head bent, his hair flopping over his eyes. The rain had stopped briefly, but everything was dripping and the ground squelched under his boots. He met Ella's eyes, his own very green.

'He's there, but there's a guard on the door.'

'Is he all right?' she whispered, and then thought how ridiculous the words. He wouldn't be in the hospital if he was all right.

David's mouth tightened, making him look older. 'He was asleep. I pretended I was looking for my ... my father,' and he glanced away, uncomfortable. 'One other thing. There's been a typhoid scare, though the doctor was trying to play it down, but it's keeping them pretty busy. Too busy to worry much about what I was doing.' He hesitated, and then went on. 'The patient opposite Adam was dead, and Doctor McCrea was just finishing with him - signing some official papers and so on. I heard him talking to the hospital attendant. He said the man's brother was coming to collect the body this afternoon.'

Eddie's eyes brightened and he laughed softly. 'You've done well, lad. Did you get his name ... the dead man's, I mean?'

David nodded and, for the first time today, he smiled. 'It was Fortune.'

CHAPTER 19

———◆———

THERE WAS A GUARD AT the door, sheltering from the rain. Ella would not have known he was there had David not warned her. He stood up, presenting her with a face whose deep lines spoke mutely of brutality. Any vague thoughts she had had of appealing to the man's compassion vanished.

'What do you want?' the guard asked, his eyes flicking from Eddie to Ella and sliding slowly down her body.

'My husband,' she whispered, her skin crawling. 'I want to see my husband.'

'Who's he?' The guard jerked his head at Eddie.

'My husband's brother.' She said it quickly, breathlessly, but the guard seemed to believe her. Perhaps she was a better liar than she thought.

'What's yer husband's name?' Again that lecherous look, his eyes fixing on her bosom.

Ella felt as if he had touched her; she wanted to squirm and fold her arms around herself.

'Fortune. Mr Fortune.'

That brought the eyes back to hers. 'Oh yeah. Well, he's over there, but I don't reckon as he'll have much to say to yer. He's dead.'

If she had been unprepared, such cruelty would have sent her into a faint. As it was, his callousness made her go white as snow. Eddie caught her around the waist with his arm, glowering furiously at the guard.

'We know he's dead,' he hissed. 'We're here to collect him for burial. His widda just wanted to see him one more time.'

The guard shrugged, unmoved. 'Hey!' he shouted into the tent.

The attendant, a thin stick of a man, looked up impatiently, a harassed expression on his weary face. 'What is it?'

'They've come to get the stiff,' he said, and smirked.

The attendant clicked his tongue. 'Doctor McCrea's gone out. There's been another case of typhoid over in - ' but he bit his lip, remembering in time that this was to be kept quiet

The doctor had gone? This was a stroke of luck they hadn't counted on.

'I thought the doc had finished with him anyway,' the guard replied laconically.

The attendant frowned. Ella sensed he was just being officious. 'Oh, very well!' he said at last. 'I've enough to do for the living without worrying about the dead.' And, with an irritable wave of his hand, he returned to his current patient.

The guard smirked again. 'Over there,' he said, nodding towards one side of the tent. Eddie glared at the guard's impervious face and, taking Ella's elbow in a protective hold, led her down the narrow aisle between the beds.

The camp hospital was full, and as far as Ella could see, all the patients were men. The beds were stretchers, narrow and uncomfortable looking.

Underfoot was bare earth, while a variety of pails and bowls were set about for slops, used dressings, soiled bedding and other equally unpleasant things. Someone was currently using what looked like a cooking pot to vomit in. As Eddie had said, one would not stay here through choice.

Mr Fortune was a long shape covered with a blanket. Ella and Eddie stood a moment, uncertain how to proceed. The guard was watching them lazily from the doorway.

'We'd better 'ave a quick look,' Eddie whispered. 'Make it good.' He reached out and, at Ella's nod, slowly lowered the blanket from the dead man's face.

In death, Mr Fortune looked peaceful enough, although his skin had a nasty grey tinge. It was difficult to judge his exact age, but Ella thought late forties. He had lost a good deal of hair, and his scalp shone dully, as though it had been polished with a cloth. Eddie nudged her, and Ella remembered that this man was supposed to be her beloved husband. She put a hand to her eyes with a soft cry, and pretending to be overcome with grief, turned away.

Behind her, on a bed close against the wall, was Adam.

He was lying on his side, his back to her, apparently asleep. But there was no doubt in her mind that it was Adam – she knew him instantly. He was naked from the waist up, apart from the numerous bandages strapped tightly around his torso. His arm, flung across the blanket, was bright with the colours of the mermaid tattoo.

With her hand still across her face, Ella risked a glance through her fingers towards the door. The guard had stepped outside to light his pipe. The smoke from it lay around him like a cloak. Now was the moment.

She reached out and touched Adam's bare shoulder. His skin was warm and alive, and twitched slightly under her fingers. 'Adam?' she whispered. Eddie, pretending to be deep in contemplation of his dead brother, stepped between Ella and the front of the tent, so that she was hidden from the guard's view if he should turn back.

Adam groaned.

'Adam?'

He turned his face towards her.

For an instant the ground moved beneath her feet, as if she stood on the deck of a sailing ship. One of Adam's eyes was so bruised and swollen it was closed, the other blurred and bloodshot. The cut on his cheekbone did not look as bad as it had last night, but his nose was bruised and puffy, dried blood not quite wiped clean from around it. His lower lip was cut and swollen out, and there was a livid bruise on his jaw. Ella knew in her heart it was Adam, but her mind rejected this stranger.

Behind her, Eddie made a sound in his throat. Ella could make no sound; tears blurred her vision. She put out her hand to touch his face, and then was afraid to in case she hurt him. Her hand hovered in mid-air, and it was Adam who reached up and grasped it in his. His fingers trembled, and her awareness of such weakness in him, who had always been so strong, nearly undid her completely.

'Oh Adam, what has he done to you?'

He tried to smile, and then changed his mind. 'Rearranged me, it feels like.'

Very gently, she laid her other hand against his cheek. 'Does it hurt?'

'Yes,' he said bluntly, his voice strange and thick, as unfamiliar as his face.

'Moggs has you under guard here in the hospital. Do you remember what happened?'

He sighed. 'Enough.'

'We have a plan to get you out.'

His good eye stared into hers. For a moment something of the old Adam sparkled in it, and then he looked past her to Eddie. 'How did he get here?'

Eddie answered, barely moving his lips. 'Your missus paid me bail.'

'I want to go and see Mr Gilbert,' Ella said quickly, breathlessly. 'I want to tell him what Moggs has done.'

Adam tried to shake his head. 'No.'

'Yes,' Ella whispered furiously.

But Adam glared at her with his bloodshot eye. 'No. Moggs hasn't finished with me yet. He wants me here, under guard, while he finds Morris and gets him up to the magistrate. He's goin' to have me for murder, or highway robbery at the least. I've got to get out ... Now, what's your plan?'

———◆———

The camp hospital was quiet. The patients were sleeping, or lying miserably on their beds. The attendant had retired to a chair at the back of the tent and was dozing. David had arrived with Jardine's horse and wagon, and Eddie had gone to the door to help him, while Ella waited quietly by Mr Fortune's bed.

David had brought a large square of canvas in which to transport the body, and he carried this awkwardly in with him. The guard watched, his eyes dull with disinterest, and then blinked and sat up straighter.

'I seen you before, didn't I?' he demanded.

David nodded. 'I was looking for my father ... Mr Fortune.'

The guard frowned, as if that wasn't quite how he remembered it. 'That your mother?' he asked, distracted, glancing at Ella.

'Step-mother,' said David.

The guard grinned. 'Lucky you, eh?'

The attendant had looked up at the sound of their conversation, and when he saw David he went to rise. But Eddie waved him back.

'You're right, matey. We can manage.'

The man hesitated, his officious nature struggling with the fact that he was tired and overworked. The latter won, and he subsided again into his chair. Eddie and David made their way to Ella's side, and paused there in a suitably sombre manner. Most of the closer patients were asleep, or pretending to be. No one liked to be reminded of his mortality, especially those already looking death in the face. But an elderly man one bed further up was watching them with sunken but very bright eyes.

Eddie glanced at Ella and shrugged slightly. There was nothing they could do except hope that he would lose interest.

David dropped the canvas, and spread it out in the narrow gap between the two beds. He moved to Mr Fortune's head, while Eddie went to stand at his feet. They looked at Ella.

'Ready?' Eddie asked softly.

She took a breath. Was she ready? Her heart was beating a million times a minute ...

'Come on, Cinderella,' a thick voice said behind her. 'We can't let Moggs beat us.'

She met Eddie's straight gaze and nodded.

With a heave, they lifted Fortune from the bed, ready to lower him to the makeshift shroud on the floor. Everyone was silent.

Until Ella screamed.

The sound was so piercing and heartrending, it seemed to bounce off the walls of the tent, filling it Several patients cried out in fear, and another sat up, shrieking like one demented. Ella reeled down the aisle, sobbing and clutching at her clothing, apparently overcome with grief.

The attendant jumped up, white-faced, and knocked over the pail on the floor beside him. The contents oozed out, accompanied by shouts of anger from the nearer patients. The guard was also on his feet, but his eyes were riveted on Ella - he wasn't interested in anything else. She had begun to tear at her clothing; the buttons from her bodice were popping off in all directions. The cloth gaped open, disclosing her bosom, rounded and white, heaving with emotion. She made as if to run out of the tent, and then appeared to trip, falling heavily against the guard. He gripped her hard around the waist, taking the opportunity to press his body to hers. He smelt of onions and sweat, and Ella thought she was going to begin screaming in earnest.

And then it was over. Eddie came up behind her, removing her from the guard's hold and pulling her into his own. A few murmured words and he had soothed her into half-fainting acquiescence. The guard began to grumble something about 'trouble for us all now!', and indeed men in uniform were running rapidly towards the hospital. The attendant was trying to clean up the mess he had made, while his patients jeered at him. And there, beside Mr Fortune's empty bed, David was gently wrapping the body in its canvas shroud.

'What's goin' on?' a voice demanded. The policemen had reached the tent and were peering about with suspicious eyes.

The guard jerked his head at Ella, who had retreated back down the tent. 'Widda got a bit upset, Sergeant. They've come to fetch the body.' And then he grinned and muttered something sotto voce.

The sergeant looked at him with disgust, gaining Ella's instant approval. 'Whose body is it?'

'Fortune.' The guard leaned back, began to pick at his teeth, and then thought better of it. 'Weren't *very fortunate* for him, were it?'

The sergeant had transferred his interest to Ella and the two men, who had lifted their burden and were now carrying it solemnly between them down the aisle. Ella followed, her hand shielding her face.

The elderly patient was still watching, his bright blue eyes ablaze with excitement. Ella saw them slide to Adam's bed, and rest a moment on the man lying on his side, apparently asleep, and well covered with a blanket. And then he looked back at Ella and grinned, his wrinkled face crumpling up like paper.

'Can't a man get any rest in 'ere!' he called in a feeble, quavering voice, very much at odds with his eyes. 'We're supposed to be sick!'

The attendant glared at him, but the guard laughed. The sergeant made an impatient noise. 'No problems with the prisoner?' he snapped at the guard. 'Checked on him lately, have you?'

Ella felt her blood freeze. Eddie and David were nearly at the door, and she forced herself to follow, one step after another, making her legs work.

'Yeah, had a look a couple o' minutes ago,' lied the guard. 'He's asleep. Moggs had a bit o' fun with him, did he? Commissioner won't like that.'.

The sergeant shrugged. 'Moggs seems to think the man will be hanged in Melbourne anyway, so what's it matter what happens in the meantime?'

Ella's opinion of him plummeted.

They had reached the door, and the police stood aside for them to pass. Outside, the horse and wagon waited. Ella passed between the sergeant and the guard, out into the rain. 'Ma'am,' the sergeant murmured respectfully, while the guard stirred her skirts suggestively with his boot. She nodded her head in reply, but didn't speak.

The rain was heavier than it had been. Drops rattled like bullets onto the canvas covering the body. There was some straw sprinkled over the hard wooden boards of the wagon, and a faint smell of alcohol, left over from Naughton Jardine's illegal forays into the bush. Ella prayed the police wouldn't get too close.

David climbed into the back of the wagon, and helped Eddie manouevre their burden aboard. And then he shook out an old blanket and covered the body completely from prying eyes.

'Don't want him to catch cold now, do we!' the guard called, and laughed at his joke. The sergeant frowned, glancing back into the hospital tent. Ella clenched her teeth to stop them chattering. There was still time for their plan to come undone.

'Hurry up!' she gritted at Eddie.

'It's all right,' Eddie muttered back. 'Better to go slow. If we rush it, they'll get even more edgy. Come on, get up beside David on the seat. I'll ride in the back.'

She was up, her shoulders crawling with the feeling of eyes watching. I won't look, she told herself. I won't look. But in the end, she had to look. She glanced back, pretending she was checking on the contents of the wagon. There *was* someone watching her, but it was only the guard. The policemen were walking briskly in the opposite direction.

David shook the reins, and the horse pulled hard, hooves digging into the muddy ground. The wagon began to move, and then they were off, quickening their pace as they rolled towards the camp entrance.

'We did it!' Eddie said.

'Not yet,' Ella whispered. She shivered, and pulled her bodice together with shaking fingers. But already the gate was before them, and then they were through it and out into Camp Street. And they really had done it.

They drove on, along the creek, not really sure where they were going. They hadn't thought that far. Fine plotters we are! Ella told herself, holding in laughter.

At last Eddie called for them to stop. David

pulled up on a side track which led to a smith, who appeared to be flat out sharpening picks. A couple of miners glanced at them incuriously, their faces streaked with rain and mud, and then went back to puddling their wash-dirt.

Ella hoisted up her skirts and climbed into the back of the wagon. She pulled at the blanket, her fingers shaking, but Eddie was already doing the same. Beneath, the body was tightly wrapped in the canvas. Eddie found the end and gave it a tug. It parted, disclosing a white, bruised face.

'I think I'm going to be sick,' Adam gasped, taking a deep breath of fresh air. 'Are we away?'

Ella had thought he looked bad in the dim light of the hospital tent, but out here he looked ten times worse.

Eddie sat back on his haunches, eyes moving about him nervously. 'We can only stop a minute. They might be on to us ... that guard might've decided he'd better take a look at his prisoner after all. Or Moggs might've come back.'

But Ella wasn't listening. She was looking down at Adam, her heart pounding. She didn't know whether to feel happy that he had escaped or angry that he'd been hurt. The rain was tumbling down and drops fell onto his upturned face. She reached out, brushing them away with trembling fingers, and then smoothed his damp, tangled hair back from his eyes. His skin felt hot and feverish and her stomach dropped.

'Tell David to take me to Paddy's Gully,' he whispered, in that thick, stranger's voice.

'But – '

'He's right,' Eddie muttered behind her. 'Midnight Gully ain't safe: Moggs will be lookin' for him as soon as he knows he's gone. And the first place he'll go is Midnight Gully.' His eyes met Ella's with a hint of grim amusement. 'He'll probably search the whole diggings, but it'll take a while for him to get around to Paddy's.'

What they were saying was true, but Midnight Gully had been, if only for a short while, home. It was more difficult than she had thought it would be to give it up, and especially for Paddy's Gully, that dark, deserted place ... But they had no choice.

'Yes,' she said, 'we'll go to Paddy's Gully.'

Adam was looking up at her. His face was so bruised and swollen. She hardly knew how to read it. Even his good eye was bloodshot. But she sensed he was about to say something she wasn't going to like.

'I don't want you with me.'

'Adam!'

'I thought you'd be safe with me, but now I know you're safer without me.'

'No.'

'I can't look after you any more.'

'Not very grateful, is he?' Eddie muttered. 'She's just saved your skin, matey.'

Adam turned his face away. Despite the swelling, she could see that his nose was no longer as straight as it had been, but flattened on the bridge where it had been broken. He had been hurt, and not just physically. He was a hunted man – Moggs was not the sort to forgive and forget. Adam must know that. Perhaps he expected to be recaptured and taken down to Melbourne, and hanged.

Ella leaned over him, and rested her cheek gently

against his. 'I don't need to be looked after,' she told him in a firm voice. 'I'm here with you because I want to be. If Moggs finds you, then he finds me too. I'm not leaving you now.'

She heard him release his breath in a sigh. As if he was too weary to argue with her, but knew he must. 'I don't want you with me,' he repeated.

Ella touched his lips and smiled. 'I don't believe you.'

'How can I make you understand, woman?' He closed his eye. 'You've got your man to find, Mrs Seaton. What about him?'

Ella gave a laugh that was close to crying. 'My man's right here, Adam. You're my man now.'

CHAPTER 20

———————

PADDY'S GULLY HADN'T CHANGED. DAVID urged the horse down the slippery, narrow track, the wagon tilting dangerously as they half skidded, half rolled to their destination. Eddie, so calm and reassuring until now, had become increasingly edgy. Suddenly he lifted his head, as Wolf used to when he had a scent, and peered up the slope towards a single, battered-looking tent. And Ella had her first inkling as to what was bothering him.

The tent looked deserted. Only the thin trail of smoke from the campfire outside suggested that there was still someone living in it. 'Wait here. I'll go and see if Maryanne's at home.' Eddie jumped down from the wagon and began to climb the slope.

David gave Ella a questioning look. 'He thinks she might have found herself someone else while he was gone,' she explained.

David appeared to find this rather puzzling.

After a moment he said, 'I'm worried about Kitty. What if Lieutenant Moggs goes searching for Adam in Midnight Gully and takes it out on Kitty when he can't find him?'

Ella had already thought of that, but had not wanted to mention it aloud in front of the boy.

'Mrs Jardine is there,' she reminded David. 'I can't believe she would allow anything to happen to Kitty.'

But David knew Kitty better than Ella realised. 'Do you think Kitty would really follow Mrs Jardine's advice?'

Ella smiled wearily. 'We'll just have to hope so.'

Eddie had reached his tent and, with barely a pause, ducked through the opening. Ella and David held their breath. There was a screech like a hundred banshees, followed by a shout of rage. The tent jumped, and began to rock from side to side as if someone were dancing around inside it. A man came flying out, his red shirt flapping around his white legs – like some huge, clumsy bird making its first flight – and sprawled onto the muddy ground some way down the slope. Eddie loomed in the entrance behind him, clutching trousers and boots to his chest, and flung them after the half-naked man.

Maryanne was still shrieking inside the tent, and now she appeared behind Eddie in her petticoats, her dark hair wild about her white face. Eddie turned and shouted something at her. The would-be lover took this opportunity to scramble to his feet, collect his scattered belongings, and make his escape. Maryanne let out a wail, and then began to cry. Eddie kept berating her, and she kept crying. It had the appearance of a well-rehearsed scene.

'This has happened before,' Ella said.

David frowned, shaking his head in disgust. 'How could he live with a woman who takes another man as soon as his back's turned?'

Ella didn't know the answer, but she did know that love made some people accept behaviour they would otherwise abhor. And despite her faithlessness, Eddie loved his wife.

The argument had apparently been resolved. Maryanne was clutching the front of Eddie's shirt, gazing up into his face like a bitch that has just savaged a whole flock of sheep but wants her master to forgive her. And Eddie was gazing down at her, doing just that.

Ella nudged David. 'Come on, let's get Adam into the tent. He has a fever, I think, and being out in the rain isn't helping him.'

By the time David had maneuvered the wagon up the slope, Eddie had straightened up the tent and Maryanne was busy boiling water over the fire. Her face was still pale but now it looked transformed - as if she had had some profound life-changing experience. She had a certain beauty, Ella acknowledged, with those great dark eyes, the cloud of dark hair, and her air of fragility. Perhaps she couldn't help what she did, any more than Eddie could help loving her.

By the time they had eased Adam to the tail of the wagon, he was sick and shaky. David and Eddie helped him down onto his feet, taking most of his weight themselves. He groaned, his ribs hurting from their grip, and then pressed his mouth into a hard line and allowed himself to be half carried into the tent and placed onto the bed. It was none too clean, but Ella tried not to look too closely.

Adam lay on his back, trying to catch his breath, his bruised face twisted with pain. Ella moved to pull the blankets up over his chest, and then stopped, staring down at him. In the camp hospital, she had only seen his face. Now she saw the rest of him. The bandages covered most of his back and chest, strapped as they were around his ribs, but elsewhere livid bruises stood out clearly. Rage flared up inside her again and her hands trembled as she eased the blanket over him and tucked him in.

'Have you got any brandy?' he whispered.

Ella looked back at Maryanne, who was hovering behind her. The other woman nodded and, searching beneath some clothing, found a bottle, uncorked it, and handed it to Adam. Ella helped him to sit up enough to drink. He took a long swig, choked, and then gasped with the pain this caused in his ribs. But it was evidently worth it for a few moments later some colour was back in his cheeks and he seemed to be breathing a little easier.

'Wolf?' he whispered suddenly, eyes closed.

'Dead.' She had thought of lying, but there seemed no point.

He said nothing, keeping still and quiet, but Ella knew how much he was hurting.

David stuck his head into the tent. 'I'm heading off now,' he said. 'If I'm lucky, I'll have the wagon back to Mr Jardine before Moggs gets to Midnight Gully. I'll leave the canvas here with Eddie in case you need some extra shelter.'

'David.' It was Adam's voice, hoarse, but stronger. 'Don't come back here. It's not safe. Take Kitty with you to Sailor's Gully. You'll be all right. Moggs won't know it was you drivin' the wagon, and Naughton Jardine won't tell him. If we need you,

I'll send to Sailor's Gully.'

David glanced at Ella, as if for confirmation, but she said nothing – she just hoped Adam's assessment of Naughton's character was correct. 'Good luck,' David said, suddenly looking very young. Adam managed a half smile. A moment later David was gone, the sound of the horse and wagon moving away towards the road.

Maryanne dug Ella in the ribs with a sharp elbow. 'What happened to 'im?' she asked, dark eyes fixed on Adam. 'Last time I saw 'im he was lookin' like a dream come true; now he's more like a nightmare.'

But Eddie called her out of the tent and Ella didn't have to answer. The rain was pattering onto the canvas roof, soft now, and restful. Was it so short a time ago that they had camped here in Paddy's Gully, and Adam had made his plans? And now those plans were torn apart, and so was Adam.

'Ella,' Adam said beside her. She leaned closer and he opened his good eye, letting his gaze roam slowly over her face and down to her torn bodice.

Ella answered his unspoken question. 'It was to distract the guard. I saw the way he was looking at me.'

'And did it work?'

'Well, you're here, aren't you?'

'Yes, I'm here.' He sounded as if he wasn't sure he liked the idea.

'What happened, Adam? What did Moggs do to you?' She asked in a rush, wondering if he would even answer her.

He was silent for a time, and then he shivered and said, 'Will you lie down with me? I'm cold.'

Concerned, she touched his face, and felt the

clamminess of fever. Ella lay down, sliding her arm about his waist, careful not to put any weight on his ribs. He lay quietly in her embrace for so long she thought he had gone to sleep. But he must have been finding the words to tell her what she had asked, for when he started to speak, he did so with fluency.

'We walked for a good few miles before we stopped. Moggs said that there'd been a few bushrangers around. That they'd been hiding behind the trees and the rocks, waitin' to ambush travellers. He sent his men on to check that there were none there hiding in the dark. He waited until his men were gone, and then he asked me to tell him how I had arranged to have Rawlins's hut burned, and how I knew to warn Eben and Nancy about the troopers coming. I told him I didn't know what he was on about. I said I knew nothin' about any of that. I said ... too much, maybe.' He shrugged, and then caught his breath in pain at the movement. He was silent again, shivering.

Ella pressed closer to his side, trying to warm him, trying to comfort him. 'What then?' she whispered. And now it was not so much that she needed to know, but that she felt he needed to tell her.

'He hit me. Maybe he didn't mean to do it more than once, but once he'd started he couldn't seem to stop. And I suppose I didn't help ... I got in a couple of good swings meself. I reckon his ears are still ringing.'

'You had your wrists bound,' Ella whispered. 'Only a monster would attack a man under those circumstances.'

'Oh no, Moggs isn't a monster,' he burst out bitterly. 'He's an upholder of the law. He's protecting the citizens of Victoria from a convict's bastard like me.' His breath fanned her cheek softly. 'Don't cry for me, love. I'll live.'

'I'm not crying for you,' she sobbed. 'I'm crying because I'm so angry.' But the tears kept filling her eyes and overflowing down her cheeks. Adam kissed her eyelids, and then her mouth, his lips salty. 'My love,' he murmured. 'My brave love.'

They lay so close, their faces were almost touching. He sighed. 'I wanted to be a moleskin squatter ... another Ollie McLeod.' And his voice was bitter with dreams lost and hopes shattered.

'Go to sleep now, Adam,' she said gently, smoothing back his hair.

He smiled, and winced when it pulled on his lip. 'Stay with me a bit,' he murmured, already drifting off. He was asleep before she could answer.

Ella lay watching him. She knew that the bruises and the broken bones would heal. But God knew what might be hurt inside him ... perhaps it had been a mistake taking him from the hospital. How long did he have to recover here in the primitive conditions of Paddy's Gully? Before Lieutenant Moggs found them again.

———◆———

'Word's out!'

Eddie, his level gaze glittering with excitement, sat down beside Ella at the campfire. He had been down to the store at Golden Point where one was sure of hearing all the latest news.

Morning had cleared the rain, and brought a few

rays of weak sunshine. But the diggings were a sea of mud and slush, making progress on foot or by hoof difficult.

'What word?' Maryanne asked, pausing in stirring the large pot of soup she had bubbling over the campfire.

'That a prisoner under guard has escaped from the camp hospital.' And he grinned to himself. 'They've given out his name, and what he looks like, and a list o' all the things he's supposed to have done.'

'Do they know who helped him?' Maryanne's eyes were dark with fear and excitement.

'Two men and a woman, they're sayin'. They're callin' the woman Mrs Seaton. Fair hair, blue eyes,' Eddie glanced at Ella out of the corner of his eye. 'An accomplice they're callin' you, Ella.' He laughed, smacking his thigh with his hand.

Ella felt her nerves begin to jangle. Her name and description were being broadcast far and wide. Moggs would know they must be close by, that Adam wasn't yet able to travel. It would only be a matter of time before he found them.

Eddie read her mind. 'How is he?' he asked, nodding his head in the direction of the tent

'Better than I had hoped,' Ella said cautiously. 'The fever's still there, but no worse. It's his ribs I'm concerned about, they hurt every time he breathes.'

Eddie shrugged, and said as one who knew, 'Broken ribs don't stop yer, as long as you keep 'em strapped. He'll have to leave here, you know that?'

'Yes, I know.' She lifted her chin. 'Where will we go?'

He stared into the distance, while Maryanne

lazily stirred her soup. Further across the slope the five miners were still camped - the Scots cook, Hans, and the rest of the men Ella remembered from last time.

'You'd be better out of Victoria,' Eddie said at last. 'Sydney or Adelaide. Maybe even Vandemon. Once you're out of Victoria, Moggs won't be able to touch yer without their say so. You can stand and thumb yer noses at him, and watch him burn.'

It sounded easy, but Ella knew it wouldn't be. 'Sydney,' she said without expression. And then, brightening, 'Adam comes from Sydney ... I mean, originally. He must have relatives there.' Eben, she thought, and shuddered. 'Other relatives,' she amended. Suddenly Sydney sounded their best option. But the first and most important thing was to leave Bendigo before Moggs discovered their hiding place.

'It's not safe for us with you here, you know,' Maryanne pointed out. 'Eddie could get into trouble.'

Eddie growled, ready to chastise her, but Ella put a hand on his arm. 'No, no, she's right,' she said quickly. 'You've done enough for us, we mustn't trespass any further on you.' Eddie and Maryanne had even given up their tent and taken refuge under the canvas in which David had carried Adam's 'body' - although Eddie *had* rigged it up to look rather cosy.

Eddie gave Maryanne an angry glare. 'You stay as long as you like, you and Adam!' he told Ella. 'If it weren't for you, I'd still be in that bloody lock-up with the fleas eatin' me alive. And if it weren't for Adam, Maryanne here would be dead and drowned.'

Maryanne smiled to herself, untouched by his jibes, and carried on with her cooking.

'I'll have to let Kitty and David know what's happening,' Ella went on, unwilling to ask more of Eddie but having no option. 'Can you deliver a message for me when the time comes?'

'Course I can!'

She nodded, and stood up. 'I'll just see how Adam is.'

'Soup'll be ready to eat in a minute,' Maryanne called after her cheerily, as if they were old friends.

Adam was awake. If anything, he looked worse this morning. The bruises had ripened into darker, more violent colours, but Ella comforted herself that they would look worse before they got better. He sat up, painfully, with her help, and ate some of the soup. Even that effort seemed to exhaust him, and Ella, who had been planning to speak of their future, said nothing after all. He slept again, not seeming to know or care where he was.

When he awoke the second time, he was stronger, and met her worried look with a wry, painful smile. 'The bastard had fists like rocks.'

Anger for Moggs choked her, but she swallowed it down. She had more important things to discuss. 'Adam ... we can't stay here. Eddie says that the police have put out our names and descriptions – yours and mine. They won't just let it go; they'll search the whole of the diggings until they find us.'

His eyes were closed, but Ella knew he was listening.

'There's Eddie, too,' she went on softly. 'While we're here, he's in danger.'

He took a deep breath. 'You're right, Cinderella. Here ... help me up.'

It took a while, and it was painful, but eventually Adam was on his feet outside the tent. Eddie had hold of one side of him, and Ella the other, his arm over her shoulders. She felt her knees wobbling under the weight of him.

'Help me walk,' Adam said breathlessly.

Eddie gave Ella a doubtful look. 'I've told yer missus you can stay,' he protested.

But Adam cut him short. 'Too dangerous. Moggs means to have me, and he'll be lookin' high and low. You were right,' to Ella. 'He's a man with only one thing on his mind, and that's me dancing at the end of a rope.'

Eddie settled his feet more firmly on the ground. 'We can't do much about you, Adam, but I've been thinkin' we can maybe disguise your missus a bit.'

Ella looked at him questioningly, and he grinned. 'Seems a pity, but we're goin' to have to turn her into a boy.'

Adam laughed, and then groaned when it hurt. 'Here's your chance, love,' he gasped. 'You can be Margaret Catchpole after all.'

'I've got plans for you an' all,' Eddie went on. 'I've got a mate lives up in the bush. He'll hide you for a bit until you can travel.'

Adam sighed. 'Aye, well ... you'd better get hold of him. We need to get out of Paddy's Gully as soon as we can.' Eddie nodded. 'But first things first ... I've got to be able to walk.'

Paddy's Gully was near enough to deserted. The five miners had vanished to work on their claim. But Ella and Maryanne still kept watch, while Eddie walked with Adam. There was a police camp up at Diamond Hill, Eddie said, and though it wasn't usual for the troopers to come riding through this way, one never knew.

When Adam could walk no more, Eddie set him down onto a sawn log that served as a seat. Sweat stood out on his face, despite the chill wind, and he looked very white beneath the stubble and the bruises. Anxiously, Ella wondered again just how seriously he was hurt.

Watching him for a different reason, Maryanne smiled dreamily. 'You've got yourself a tough man there, Ella. Does he take yer to bed tough? I bet he does ... hard and strong, eh?' And she laughed low, her black eyes bold. Ella felt her face go hot and turned away to hide it.

In the afternoon, Maryanne strolled off to the store at Golden Point, her head full of instructions and her fist full of Adam's money. Adam rested in the tent, and Ella could see Eddie was relieved to have his fugitive hidden again.

Eddie lit his pipe and sat down beside her. 'My mate'll be down tonight,' he said. 'He comes down every night for news. I'll get him to take you and Adam back up with him. It'll be dark and quiet; no one'll see, and there'll be plenty o' time.'

Ella nodded, trying not to let him see the doubt in her heart.

'I'll come with yer, to help,' Eddie added kindly. 'An' I'll come up and see you every day, and bring you anythin' you might need. I reckon yer'll have to stay there a week. A week should be long enough.' Something in his eyes said a week was all they had.

'There was somethin' I didn't tell Adam,' Eddie

went on. 'There's a reward out for him ... and it's big enough to make some think twice about their loyalty.'

Ella stared at him.

Eddie took another puff on his pipe. 'Don't worry, I won't give 'im away. But can you trust the boy ... David?'

Ella nodded. 'Yes, we can trust him.' And certainly Kitty could be trusted. That left the Jardines. Ella let her eyes sweep the empty gully, as if expecting to see Moggs come galloping towards her.

Maryanne returned at last, weighed down with packages. Adam, awake again, was helped out to the campfire, and Maryanne and Ella retreated into the tent to effect the disguise. It was some time before Maryanne reappeared, a smile curling her lips, and behind her, nervous and pink with embarrassment, came Ella. She was wearing the clothing Maryanne had bought: moleskins, a blue shirt, a jacket and, on her head, a felt hat.

No one said a word. Eddie was inspecting her with a professional eye, while Adam looked as if he were trying not to laugh. Ella felt her face begin to burn even brighter. She knew the moleskins were too big, only the belt kept them up, but the woollen shirt was loose enough to hide her breasts, and the jacket covered her from neck to mid-thigh. She looked like a lad wearing his father's castoffs. The limp felt hat was the finishing touch. Maryanne had dipped it down to shade her beardless face, and tucked her hair up underneath it.

Actually, Ella thought, male clothing was quite comfortable. It offered her a freedom of movement she had never had before. If it hadn't been so unfamiliar and strange, she would have enjoyed wearing it. It was the way they were all looking at her that made her self-conscious.

At last, Adam cleared his throat. 'What'll I call you?' he asked.

Ella gave him a nervous smile. 'I don't know ... I hadn't thought.'

Maryanne laughed, enjoying their reactions to her handiwork. 'What about Charlie?' she suggested. 'I had a dog called Charlie, once. At least, I thought he were a dog ... but he turned out to be a bitch!'

Ella shot her an uncertain look, but Eddie laughed. 'Of course,' he went on, 'you'd only get away with it at a distance, or in the dark.'

Adam grinned. 'I was thinking the same thing.'

Maryanne pouted, stepping back from Ella to give her a searching look. 'What's wrong with 'er? The clothes are loose enough to hide the curves, ain't they? And I could rub dirt into her skin, and cut off her hair real short so that – '

'No!' The word burst out of Adam. He took a breath, and repeated more moderately, 'No. We'll take the risk.' He patted the log beside him. 'Come here, Charlie.'

Ella walked over and sat down beside him.

He shook his head. 'What is it about the way a woman walks that you can tell she's a woman even in a man's clothes?'

Eddie puffed thoughtfully on his pipe, giving the question his full consideration.

Suddenly Adam reached over and gripped Ella's hand. Surprised, she looked up at him and saw that his eyes were fixed on something further down the gully, where the shadows were already lengthening.

'There're two people coming on foot,' he said quietly. 'Can you see?'

Ella followed his gaze, squinting, but could not see more than two blurred shapes. It was Eddie who answered him.

'Looks like your friend David, and there's a woman with him.'

———◆———

Kitty looked as if she hadn't slept for two nights – and she probably hadn't. David was pale and grim-faced. 'I'm sorry, Adam,' he said, as soon as he was close enough to be heard. 'We had to come. Moggs has been in Midnight Gully, storming around like a madman, demanding to know where you are. It isn't safe for us ... not even in Sailor's Gully.'

Kitty had seen Adam's face now, and was so shocked she couldn't speak. Carefully, she reached out to clasp his hands in hers, gazing up at him with tears in her eyes. 'Oh Gawd, Adam, that bloody bastard. I could kill 'im ...' And she gulped down the urge to cry.

Adam squeezed her fingers, and tried to smile. 'It's all right, Kitty. It's not as bad as it looks, just bruises,' he lied.

Kitty swallowed again, glanced sideways at David and regained something of her composure. 'Moggs was at the Jardines' yesterday after you'd got out of the hospital. David had come back by then and left the wagon. He wanted me to go with him to Sailor's Gully, but I ... I wouldn't.' She coloured. 'I thought I'd be all right. So he went on his own.

When Moggs came, he was like a madman, like David says. I was there, but Naughton Jardine hid me and said he hadn't seen me. I heard him ... Moggs I mean, I heard him say he'd fire everything unless the Jardines told him where you were, Adam. Naughton had hidden all the grog, and he told Moggs he could do what he liked, he didn't know anything about you. Moggs searched for drink, so he could arrest them, but he didn't find nothin'.' She smiled faintly at the memory. And then looked up into Adam's face. 'But that weren't the end of it.' She bit her lip, and Ella saw that the girl was trembling.

'I wanted to go to Sailor's Gully then, but it was gettin' late and Mrs Jardine, she said I should stay till the mornin' and then they'd find me a ride. She said Moggs wouldn't come back now. So I agreed to stay, but ...'She shifted restlessly. 'There was something I didn't like, something odd. After a while I knew I couldn't stay. I got up out o' bed and collected my stuff. I went outside, meaning to start off for Sailor's Gully, dark or not. I got as far as the old grey box, where our camp used to be, and someone grabbed me. It was David.'

David shuffled, looking self-conscious. 'I couldn't leave her,' he said. 'I'd gone back to Sailor's Gully and collected some stuff, then returned to Midnight Gully. I thought I'd keep watch.'

Kitty smiled at him. 'Well, I was glad to see you, Mr Marr. Anyway, as we were standin' there, I heard voices. It was Moggs comin' up the road with a troop o' men. We lay down flat and held our breath, and they didn't see us. Mrs Jardine came out of the tent and stood there, waitin'. I thought

... I don't know what I thought. Maybe that she'd tell them to go. But instead she pointed around to the back where I was sleepin', and Moggs spurred his horse on around there.'

'Mrs Jardine told him where you were?' Ella whispered, shocked and angry. Mrs Jardine, with her smiles and her 'my ducks', had been no friend after all.

'Yes.' Kitty stared a moment into space, remembering. 'It were rainin' but I heard Moggs's shout when he found I were gone. He came back around to Mrs Jardine and he was yellin' at her. She was scared o' him. I heard her yellin' back, telling him that David was over in Sailor's Gully. We knew then we had to get out o' there.'

Kitty shuddered at the memory.

David took up the story. 'I'd left the rest of my stuff at Sailor's Gully, but I couldn't go back for it. We set off straightaway for Paddy's Gully. I thought we'd be here long ago, but there are so many troopers about, we've had to hide and backtrack to keep out of their way. It's taken us all this time to get here.'

Adam patted Kitty's shoulder. 'You did well,' he said firmly.

'They mean to get you, Adam, they really do,' Kitty whispered, her face old with fright and lack of sleep.

Stunned by their revelations, Ella was silent. David was the one who said the words they were all thinking. 'It's not safe here any more, Adam. Mrs Jardine doesn't know where you're hiding ... yet. But she'll work on Naughton, and I let something slip to him,' with a miserable, apologetic glance.

'When I got back to Midnight Gully yesterday with the wagon, he laughed and said the horse was covered in clay up to the hocks, and I answered him that it was like that over Golden Gully way ...' His voice trailed off.

But Adam reassured him with, 'Don't worry. It's all right. You've both done well.'

Eddie came and squatted down beside them, lowering his voice. 'They have to get away from here. It's no good on foot. They'll need two saddle horses, 'an you'll need another two, Adam, when you can ride.'

Surprised, Adam turned to look at him. 'Can you get me some horses?'

Eddie smiled a conspirator's smile. 'See that lot over there?' And he nodded his head in the direction of the camp of the five miners. 'Did you never wonder what they were doin' here, in a place where the gold's just about gone? Well, they're horse thieves. They steal horses, then ride 'em down to Melbourne and sell 'em on. You can make a fortune that way – a lot bloody more than you would from diggin' gold in Paddy's Gully!'

'So that's it! I thought they'd made a big find somewhere in the bush, and were tryin' to keep it a secret. Horse thieves.' And Adam shook his head.

Eddie went on. 'I'll have a word with Hans, he's the best of 'em. He'll have somethin' for you. What sort o' money do you have?'

'Not much in hand, but I've that bullock dray load of stuff comin' up from Melbourne. That'd be worth a bit. They could sell it on for two ... three times as much as I paid.'

Eddie looked uncertain. 'Who's the driver?'

'Johnson, he calls himself. Has a letter he carries around from one of the banks in Melbourne, to say he's an honest man.' Adam raised his eyebrows.

Eddie smiled. 'I know 'im. He'll be takin' the stuff over to Midnight Gully? Well, it sounds promisin'. I'll tell Hans. He's a fair man.'

And true to his word, Eddie set off to speak to the men, who had returned to their camp at sunset and were preparing their meal.

'Can a horse thief be fair?' Ella asked no one in particular.

Kitty eyed her change of costume, as if she had only just noticed it. 'What are you supposed to be?'

'A man ... I think.'

Kitty smiled, the dark hollows deepening under her eyes. 'David told me about what you did ... how Adam got away. You must o' been scared to death.'

Ella reached out to clasp her hands. 'Very nearly.'

Maryanne had heated up her soup - the extra mouths didn't appear to faze her - and was dishing some out to Adam.

'How *is* Adam?' Kitty whispered softly.

'Sore. Too sore to ride yet. We'll have to wait a bit longer; Eddie's going to hide us in the bush.'

Kitty nodded, hesitated, and then said, 'Good luck.' When Ella didn't answer, she added, 'I mean it. I know we've had our differences, but I don't believe in holdin' onto bad feeling. Adam wants you, and ... maybe I was wrong. Maybe you will stay with him.' Kitty sniffed and straightened, and suddenly her eyes narrowed.

'Look at that bitch!'

Startled, Ella turned and looked. Maryanne was

giving David a long, meaningful stare, which he was trying hard to ignore.

'She doesn't mean anything by it,' Ella murmured soothingly. 'She just can't seem to help herself.'

Kitty sat back and glared. Maryanne was handing David his soup now and, as she leaned over, she took the opportunity to rest her hand on his thigh. It proved too much for Kitty.

'Keep your hooks off him!' she shrieked.

David stared at her, shocked, and realising what she had done, Kitty groaned and turned her back. But David's lips had began to twitch, and when Adam chuckled, he did too. That Kitty should think him worth fighting for was probably the highlight of his week.

When Eddie returned he, too, was smiling. 'You're in business, Adam,' he said quietly, and sat down to warm his hands at the fire. 'They're willin' to listen to you about the drayload comin' up from Melbourne, but you'll have to talk to 'em yerself.'

Adam nodded. He looked around at the faces turned to his. 'If I can, I'll get four horses. Two for me and Ella, and two for David and Kitty.' He hesitated, and then stated the obvious. 'We'll have to split up.'

It was Kitty who spoke up first. 'I knew you'd say that,' she said quietly. 'My aunt lives down Geelong way. My brother and sister went to her when Ma and Dad died, but I wouldn't go. I'd only met her once and I hadn't liked her much, but maybe I was a bit of a shock to her, an' all. So I went north instead, lookin' for gold and excitement.' She grimaced and then glanced sideways at David. 'I think I've had enough o' both, just for now. We can go down there, it'll be safe and there'll be work. If ... if David wants to.'

He smiled into her anxious face, and Ella had a feeling David would have gone to the edge of the earth with her and over the other side. 'Gold digging's for men like my brother who've caught the fever and are willing to go anywhere for it. I learned a lot from you in Sailor's Gully, Adam, and one of the things I learned was that gold mining's not for me.'

Kitty's face brightened, but she deliberately quenched the excitement. Perhaps, Ella thought, the girl had had too many disappointments to allow herself to hope for the future.

Maryanne laughed, amused by the young couple, but both Kitty and David ignored her. Eddie caught his wife's hand in his, giving it a warning squeeze, but his glance was indulgent. Then his gaze slid beyond the fire and he smiled.

'Here he is, here's me mate!'

They followed Eddie's smile, and Ella caught her breath in dismay. That emaciated frame, that lank sandy hair, and that smell were all instantly recognisable.

It was Paddy.

CHAPTER 21

———◆———

'HE NEEDS TO REST.'
Ella heard her own voice, hoarse and breathless. Her legs were on fire with the effort of climbing the rough, stony ground, as well as helping to support Adam. She wondered if her back would ever be the same again.

'He needs to rest!' she called louder, and this time Paddy heard her.

She saw the little man turn and then hop back down the rocky slope towards them, catching hold of a young ironbark sapling to slow his descent.

'He's about had it,' Eddie muttered, gasping for breath. 'How far to this place, matey?'

Paddy cocked his head to the side, as if considering the question. 'How far is it from Kinnadoohy to Killadooh? How far is it across Galway Bay? How far can a man from Kerry spit on a clear day? How far – '

'For God's sake just answer the question,' Eddie snapped. 'The man can't go much further.'

Paddy's eyes sparkled in the moonlight, and suddenly Ella wondered if he was quite as silly as he seemed. 'Not far,' he said shortly, and leapt back up the slope like a goat.

Ella sighed, and bent her back to help Adam to his feet again. 'Nearly there,' she murmured. 'Can you manage it?'

'Aye,' he said, but no more. She knew he was saving his breath for the climbing. She tried to imagine what he must be feeling, and bit her lip. If Adam died before they reached the safety of Sydney, then it was Moggs's fault. Moggs would have as good as murdered him.

Ella's mind shied away from such thoughts, moving back, instead, over the last few hours spent in Paddy's Gully.

Hans had come across to Eddie's campfire and shaken Adam's hand. They had sat down and bargained long and hard for the four saddle horses. At the end of it, neither man was completely happy, but Adam now had four reasonable horses, with saddles and bridles, and Hans had the opportunity to make a fortune selling the bullock dray load of goods if and when it arrived from Melbourne.

Afterwards Adam was tired, but trying not to show it. There was still much to get through before he could lay his head down to sleep. David and Kitty packed what little they had so that it could be tied to the saddle. As it was, David had to discard some of his equipment.

'Here, you take these,' and he handed the shovel and pick to Eddie. 'You can sell them.'

Eddie looked like he might refuse, so Maryanne reached out and received the gift instead, brushing her fingers lingering over David's in the process. Kitty glared at her, but this time managed to control herself.

'You'll need money,' Adam said, and pressed something into Kitty's hand.

The girl stared down at her half-open palm, her

face beginning to crumple.

'You'll need it yourself,' David protested, but Adam shook his head.

'You helped save me skin,' he replied evenly. 'Take it with me good wishes.' He smiled then, looking from one to the other. 'It'll give you both a start.'

Kitty had thrown her arms around him, forgetting his ribs. But he had borne it. 'I'll never forget you, Adam,' she said, her voice high and young like the child she was. 'I hope you get away safe and sound.' And then she had pulled away from him, and thrown her arms around Ella.

Taken by surprise, Ella had held her tightly, smoothing the chestnut hair. 'Take care,' she whispered. 'Look after David ... he needs you, Kitty.'

Kitty hadn't replied but she had given Ella a little smile as she stepped back. It was David's turn. He shook Adam's hand and then took Ella's with a shy smile. Ella could find no words adequate enough to thank him for his help; she felt very close to tears, only the knowledge that she still had much to do kept her strong.

Ella's foot slipped on a stone, and she gasped, only just catching her balance. She was back on the side of the steep slope, and it was dark and cold, the air full of dampness and the smell of the forest.

'It's going to snow soon,' Adam murmured in a muffled voice. 'Better find shelter, or we'll freeze to death.'

Ella looked at him, and then at Eddie. Eddie shrugged, or tried to with the burden he was supporting. 'Thinks he's back in California. Let him be ... probably helps him to take his mind off the pain.'

'It snows up here in the Sierra Nevada,' Adam

went on. 'There're wolves here.' And then, his voice puzzled, 'Wolf?'

'It's all right,' Ella murmured. 'You're safe.' She leaned back against a convenient tree, and while Eddie stood in front and hauled Adam up a few more steps, she pushed from behind. Slowly, they were gaining ground. The top of the slope looked closer than it had done. But Paddy was nowhere to be seen. Ella caught her breath, and turned to look back down the way they had come. It was further than she had thought, and there, through the trees, were lights flickering in the gullies of the Bendigo diggings. Ella's eyes strayed south ... David and Kitty would be far away now, and safer with each mile.

'Good luck,' she whispered.

'Nancy?' Adam asked sharply. Ella could see him leaning towards her, as though trying to pierce the darkness. 'You gave me a scare, standin' there in the shadows.' He laughed, a harsh, rasp of a sound. 'Checkin' up, were you? Checkin' up whether I'd earned me money? Well, I did it...I did him. He's down in San Francisco Bay with the fishes now, Nancy. He won't tell tales again.'

I don't want to hear this, Ella thought, her throat tightening. 'Nearly there,' she gasped, and heard Eddie groan as they heaved and pushed Adam the last few steps to the top of the slope. Once there, they all collapsed on the hard ground.

'I did it,' Adam muttered. 'I did him for you, Nancy. I did him. I did him. I – '

Ella put her hand over his mouth and rested her head against his. 'Shhh,' she whispered. 'Nancy's not here. I'm here. I'm here, Adam.'

He made a sound like a sob, and was silent.

'Come on then.' Paddy was back, hopping from foot to foot. 'It's just a bit further now.'

'You said that before,' Eddie muttered, heaving himself to his feet. 'Where is this camp o' yours, matey? Down a wombat hole?'

But Paddy only giggled and kept hopping.

There was a narrow depression running into what Eddie called Chinese scrub: a low, dense sort of bush. They followed this for some way, the moonlight hardly penetrating it and the tall iron-bark trees. The ground here looked so hard and stony, the miners had either given it up as non-gold-bearing or decided there were easier pickings elsewhere.

Adam was silent now, his breath shallow and painful as he stumbled along. Ella doubted he knew where he was, or cared. She didn't want him to talk … she didn't want to know about his past and what he had done. She had thrown her lot in with the man she had come to know on the journey to the Bendigo diggings, not the man he had been. And if she kept telling herself that long enough, perhaps it would become the truth.

Suddenly the depression they were traversing opened out into a shallow sort of basin surrounded by brush and saplings and the tall ironbarks. Even in the darkness, Ella could smell evidence of a campfire.

'Here we are,' Paddy announced, pleased and proud of himself.

Eddie muttered something that sounded obscene. He lowered Adam carefully to the ground so that he was leaning back against a large rock that protruded from the bank. Adam's head lolled onto his chest, and Ella knelt anxiously beside him, slipping off the pack she had been carrying on her back. It had seemed light enough when they started, but now it felt as if there were rocks in it.

Eddie, too, had a pack, and he dropped this to the ground with a groan of relief. 'We'll light a fire and boil up some water,' he said. 'Here, you do that, Ella. I'll see if I can get some shelter up for the two of you.'

Hands shaking with exhaustion, Ella began to assemble some wood for a fire. It all felt damp to her, and though she struggled to get a spark from the tinderbox, none would come. When Paddy reached out and took it from her, she couldn't help, but flinch away from his grubby hand.

'Hair like the moon,' he sighed. In his practised hands, the fire started almost instantly.

As it grew, sending out waves of warmth and light, Ella began to feel better. She could see now that the basin they were in was about six yards across, hidden by a bank of about one yard in height. Paddy had his tent on the far side – a piece of dirty calico, rigged over a pole, and disguised with branches and leaves across the roof so that anyone standing on top of the bank and looking down would think it part of the scrub.

Ella made the tea and Eddie took a bottle from his pack and poured a good measure into Adam's mug. They managed to get him to drink most of it, coaxing and threatening, and then Eddie and Ella helped him into the makeshift tent, pulled off his boots, and covered him with blankets.

Ella felt too weary to do more than sit beside

him, leaning her head in her hands. Eddie crouched beside her. 'Don't look too good, do he?' he asked no one in particular. And then, lowering his voice, 'I'll be up tomorrow some time to see how you're goin'. If he starts spittin' blood, you let me know.'

Ella lifted her head and blinked at him. She felt her stomach muscles begin to knot. 'Spitting blood?' she repeated in a whisper. 'What does it mean, if he spits blood?'

Eddie pursed his lips. 'Means one o' the ribs might have stuck somethin' it shouldn't have,' he replied heavily. He hesitated, and then reached out and squeezed her arm. 'Go to bed yourself, Ella. Paddy'll keep watch. And don't mind his ways ... old Paddy wouldn't hurt no one.'

She tried to thank him but by the time she got the words out, Eddie had gone. She heard his boots crunching away over the rough ground and Paddy hopping after him. And then nothing, silence, apart from Adam's harsh breathing.

Ella lay down beside him, fumbling to pull the blankets over herself as well, and was instantly asleep.

———◆———

The water was still as glass. Ella heard her own voice, screaming and screaming. Ned was there, his eyes wild and dark, trying to help her, even though he must know they would kill him too. His mouth was open, a black cavern. She saw the blood on his face. These men thought it was funny to murder someone. They were laughing as they caught Ned up and threw him into the lagoon. He was like a rag doll, legs and arms limp and helpless, spi-

ralling outwards, his head hanging. He made a big splash, and the ripples spread out, bouncing along the shoreline. But soon, even they had stopped, and there was nothing to show where Ned had vanished. Nothing to show that he had ever existed.

———◆———

The sun was rising. Ella watched it, a pale ball floating through the mist. That same mist hung in the trees and floated above the ground so that the world seemed white. Ghostly.

Her body was aching from last night's effort, her muscles protesting from even the slightest movement. So she lay still, letting her thoughts drift like the mist. The dream was still with her, but this time not just the sense of it. All of it.

Ned was dead, murdered at Seaton's Lagoon. She had been looking for a man who no longer existed.

Beside her, Adam moved ... and groaned. Ella lifted herself awkwardly onto her elbow and peered into his face. It was even more colourful than yesterday, the bits that weren't bruised were white and drawn with pain and exhaustion. Gently, she touched his cheek.

'It's all right, we're safe. We're at Paddy's camp. How are you feeling?'

He smiled crookedly without opening his eyes.

'Foolish question.' She laughed at herself. 'Do you want something to drink or eat?'

He shook his head.

'Then go back to sleep. It's early yet.'

The mist swirled on the ground outside the tent, caught in a brief, sharp breeze. Paddy's thin, grubby face appeared in the opening and made Ella jump. Adam's eyes opened, but when he saw Paddy he only groaned and shut them again.

'I'm boilin' the billy, me lady,' the little man announced with a grin. 'Tea'll be ready directly.'

'Thank you, Paddy,' Ella managed.

He nodded, and tiptoed away.

'We're at the mercy of an empty-head,' Adam sighed heavily.

But Ella shook her head. 'I don't think so,' she said with growing conviction. 'I think Paddy's rather clever ... in his way.'

Adam was silent, and she knew he had fallen asleep again. She watched him with worried eyes. How could he possibly be well enough to leave this place in a week? He looked as if he should be in a proper bed with proper food and care, instead of ... this! And with the reward being offered for his capture, perhaps Adam didn't even have a week to recover. Money was enough to sway some people's conscience, and it only needed one hint, one word, and Adam was lost.

Ella climbed painfully from the tent and stretched muscles that she had not thought she owned and wished she didn't. She tidied herself as best she could, relieved herself among the Chinese scrub, and made her way over to Paddy's fire.

The little man grinned up at her, showing several gaps where his teeth should be. His skin had a grey, greasy look to it, as though it were coated in several months of dirt and grime. His odour had not improved overnight. But Ella sat down and took the mug he handed to her and thanked him.

The silence was broken by a whip bird, its call

reverberating through the bush. Somewhere far away, the faint sound of an axe rang among the hills. But here they were hidden, secret.

'What is this place called?' she asked Paddy curiously, sipping the hot tea.

He gave her his empty grin. 'It don't have a name,' he said. 'Just like me.'

She frowned. 'But your name's Paddy, isn't it?'

He shook his head. 'They call me that because I'm Irish. They call all the Irish Paddy. I've been Paddy so long, I've forgot what I used to be. Mikey knew me name, but Mikey's gone.' He looked up, brightening. 'Have you seen Mikey? I left him at Kilmore, and we was goin' to meet up, but – '

Ella shook her head. 'No. I haven't seen Mikey. I'm sorry.'

The little man shrugged and stared into the fire.

Ella looked around at his camp site. There was little enough here, apart from the calico shelter and a sack of what she assumed was clothing or food. A haunch of mutton hung from a high tree branch, looking like it smelt. Her nose twitched with distaste. She tried to decide exactly where they were, but Paddy had taken them up and down so often last night, she was completely lost. She hoped Eddie could find them again.

'What's *your* name, me lady?' Paddy was watching her, the sparkle back in his eye.

Ella smiled at him and said, her voice suddenly wistful, 'We have that in common, I'm afraid, Paddy. You see, I don't remember my name either.'

He cocked an eyebrow. 'You don't? Well that's too bad, it is. If Mikey was here, he could help you.' He sighed and lost his sparkle. 'But Mikey isn't here, is he?'

Pity filled Ella for this lost little man. She leaned forward, almost, but not quite, touching his hand. 'No, Paddy,' she said gently. 'Mikey isn't here.'

———◆———

Eddie came in the late afternoon, but there was no news. Moggs was still searching, but as yet Paddy's Gully was untouched. Adam had slept most of the day, and Ella had left him alone. If sleep was what he needed, then he should have it. Eddie stayed for only a short time, but his visit lifted Ella's spirits.

After he had gone, she searched through the packs and found a pot and various ingredients and began to make a stew. All the time Paddy watched her, his eyes sharp and birdlike with interest. While the meal was simmering on the edge of the fire, Ella found flour and water and some dripping and began to knead it together for Johnny cake.

'Eddie says that that Moggs is wantin' to lay his hands on your man there,' Paddy said.

Ella looked up at him, her hands stilling. 'That's right.'

Paddy nodded, but he didn't say any more, and Ella went on with her cooking.

Adam was able to eat some of the stew, and a few bites of the Johnny cake. He looked so drawn and ill, Ella was tempted to throw caution to the winds and fetch a doctor ... or else give themselves up to the authorities so that he could get some proper treatment. Perhaps, if it hadn't been for Moggs, she would have done that. But she was fearful that once Lieutenant Moggs laid hands on him again, he would finish what he had begun in Midnight Gully. And she knew, without him telling her, that Adam would rather die here in the bush than in a gaol cell.

So she lay beside him in the darkness, trying to sleep, while possums snarled and rustled in the trees above.

———◆———

The next two days were unchanging in their routine. Adam slept and ate while Ella stayed at his side. Paddy came and went. Ella watched him threading his way through the trees before vanishing into the shadows. If he did have a secret claim somewhere here, she would never have been able to find it And yet he didn't live like someone who had struck it rich. He was a recluse, mourning his lost friend.

Eddie came each day, arriving puffing, and glancing nervously behind him.

'Troopers've been through the Gully,' he said on the second day. 'I had to scarper ... matter of not havin' a licence,' he explained wryly. 'Maryanne said they was rude ... searched the tent and threw everythin' about.'

'How long do you think they will look before they give up?' Ella asked anxiously.

Eddie shrugged. 'Depends on the dancin' master, I reckon. Maybe a couple more days. Then he'll probably tell Moggs to drop it. Whether Moggs does drop it, now that's somethin' else again.'

He never would, Ella thought. Adam had made

a fool of him at Sawpit Gully, and he had wreaked revenge. Now Adam had made a fool of him again. He would never give up the hunt.

'How is he?' Eddie asked, glancing towards the tent where Adam slept.

Ella sighed. 'All he does is sleep.'

Eddie frowned. 'Well, see how he is tomorrow. If he's still sleepin', I might have to get someone up to see to him.'

'Do you mean there might be something else wrong with him?'

'Well, I've seen men with wounds to the head sleep like that. Go into a deep sleep like, and never wake up.'

'Oh Lord, do you think – '

But Eddie reassured her. 'Wait until tomorrow. Probably just needs the rest. You won't get much o' that once you're on the road,' he added wryly.

But Ella had been mulling over this. 'I don't think Adam can travel overland to Sydney. It's too far. Is there some other way we can get there? By sea, perhaps?'

Eddie nodded thoughtfully. 'You can go down to Melbourne ... take the back ways, like, away from the main road. They have ships out o' Melbourne to Sydney all the time. You could maybe get a place on one o' them. The trip to Sydney takes about two weeks, I've heard, or less if the weather's good. Once you sell the horses, you should have enough for the fare.'

Ella let out her breath in relief. 'That sounds perfect. We'll do that. When will Hans have the horses ready?'

'They're ready now. I'll bring them up to yer

when Adam can travel.' He heaved himself up, brushing down the seat of his moleskins. 'I'd better get back now. Maryanne worries if I'm gone too long.'

Ella doubted that, but didn't say so. A man was entitled to his illusions.

Remembering what Eddie had said about men slipping into a deep sleep and dying, Ella shook Adam awake for his evening meal, despite his protests. She helped him to sit up, with his back against the rock in the bank. He ate silently and mechanically, listening while she spoke of Eddie's visit and Paddy's secret forays into the bush. But he wasn't really interested; he seemed to have withdrawn into himself. It was through frustration rather than anything else that she began to talk about the dream.

'I had a dream the other night. I dreamed of Seaton's Lagoon, and Ned. He's still there, Adam. He's dead.'

For a moment he just kept eating. And then, as if the words had only just sunk in, stopped and looked up at her. 'Dead?' he repeated, his voice husky with lack of use. He frowned, trying to think. 'I didn't see anyone there, dead or otherwise.'

'They threw him into the water. He was dead. I know it.'

He opened his mouth, and closed it again. His eyes showed sympathy before he looked away.

'I don't know why I'm not dead, too,' Ella went on, more to herself than Adam. 'Surely, I was meant to die too? Perhaps someone came along ... you thought that might have happened, didn't you? Perhaps the ... the men left me, hoping I would die from the blow to my head. They left me, and rode away.'

'Don't think about it,' he muttered wearily.

She glared at him. 'I *have* to think about it. I want to know why it happened, and why I was riding south with Ned in the first place, and who I am, and what I am. I want to know, Adam!'

He still wouldn't meet her eyes. 'I know you do,' he said softly. 'But you have to face the fact, Cinderella, that maybe you never will.'

'I wanted to ask you whether you saw anything else at Seaton's Lagoon,' she went on firmly. 'I wanted to ask you again.'

'I told you – '

'I know you told me, but you lie to me sometimes, Adam.'

Now she had his attention. Those dark eyes were looking straight into hers, and she saw the flicker in their depths. As if, for a brief moment, she had caught hold of a slippery fish.

'I know you lie, but I know that's part of what you are. Maybe you do it through kindness, maybe you think you're protecting me ... or maybe you have other reasons. I don't know.'

'I wasn't lyin' about Seaton's Lagoon,' he said quietly. 'There was nothing there.'

'Well ...' She took a deep breath, and her voice came out sharply. 'You killed a man, didn't you?'

The flicker was there again, hiding in his eyes.

'On the way up here,' she went on. 'You were delirious. You were talking about California, about Nancy. You killed a man for her. You told me you'd never killed anyone. You lied.'

'Yes,' he said. 'I lied. It's not somethin' you tell a woman you love, is it? Not when you want her to trust you ... when she needs to trust you to survive.'

'I trusted you with Doctor Rawlins's warning, and he.was nearly murdered. Perhaps I would have been better off if the police had arrested Eben and Nancy.'

'And me?' he finished for her, with an ironic twist of his lips.

'Perhaps you are guilty.'

'No,' he said. 'I didn't fire Rawlins's hut. Nancy would have seen to that. And I knew nothing of their business at Sawpit Gully until Eben told me. I only went there for your sake, and because I thought the risk was worth it. I made a mistake on that count, but I wasn't to know that. If I'm guilty of anything, it's the fact that Eben's me brother, and I feel I've got to look after him, like he used to look after me.'

'And Nancy?'

He moved impatiently. 'You know about her, I've told you.'

'But you didn't tell me you killed a man for her.'

His face creased with pain, and she was tempted to tell him to go back to the tent, to go to sleep, to forget she had asked him. But it was too late for that.

'You've seen Nancy,' he said softly. 'There's something about her, something sharp and bright, that attracts. She made me feel like a big man, bein' with her. I looked after her place, sorted out the trouble. She liked a man who could use his fists. You don't know what it was like, runnin' with the Sydney Ducks. They didn't have any laws but the ones they made themselves. Certain parts of San Francisco were near enough to owned by them.'

'Who was the man you killed?'

Her question brought him back to the present. He gave her a look that was almost amused, complimenting her on her tenacity.

'Just a customer. Nancy said he was going to the authorities, that he knew things about her, that he would bring her down. The Yankees were quick to hang their prisoners ... sometimes before they even got to court. Nancy convinced me she was frightened of being arrested and hanged. It was him or her, she said. She asked me ... she begged me.'

He took a breath. 'It's not like you think. I didn't go there meaning to kill him. I wanted to talk, to threaten. But he wouldn't talk. He told me things about Nancy I didn't want to hear, and wouldn't believe ... then. I hit him, and he hit back. It still might of been all right but he had a knife. One of those big bowie knives the miners in California liked to flash around. When he took it out, things got simple. It was him or me.'

'And you won?'

'I won. Afterwards ... I threw the body into the Bay. I told Nancy I'd done as she wanted me to. But after that, I didn't feel the same about her. I saw something dark in her, like a shadow. I saw the way she brought out that shadow in others, until all the good in them was sucked out. So I left San Francisco and I went up into the hills looking for gold. And I didn't see her again until Sawpit Gully.'

Ella searched his eyes, but they were clear. 'I'm glad you told me. If we're going to be together, I need to know the truth about you.'

He laughed, and then rubbed his ribs uncomfortably. 'These bloody things still hurt.'

'What about the rest of you?'

He felt his face, treating his nose gingerly.

'Not so bad. The ribs are the worst.'

'Eddie said we can ride down to Melbourne and take passage on a boat to Sydney. It would be quicker and more comfortable.'

He thought about that, and she sensed some of the tension go out of him. 'Aye, we could do that. Maybe stop at Tea-tree Station on the way.' And, when she looked puzzled, 'That's where me friend Harvey works, love. He'll give us shelter for a day or two. When can Eddie bring the horses up here?'

'He said any time.'

He felt his ribs again. 'I'll give it another couple of days. But I don't want to push our luck. There's a reward out, is there?'

Ella blinked. 'How did you know?'

He laughed more easily this time. 'Stands to reason, Mrs Seaton.' He stretched his arms, carefully, and smiled at her. 'I feel better for that bit of confession, do you know that? Maybe those as say it's good for the soul are right.'

Ella smiled back at him. 'Maybe they are.'

CHAPTER 22

———◆———

WHEN EDDIE CAME TO VISIT the next day, Ella could see that he was a worried man. At first he spoke of Adam and did they have enough food and how was Paddy?

'Adam seems to be a much better,' Ella admitted, 'and we have plenty to eat, and we hardly see Paddy, apart from early morning and at night-time.'

Adam had been resting in the tent, but at the sound of Eddie's voice he came out, slowly, walking as if he were picking his way over hot coals. Eddie's face filled with relief at the sight of him.

'Moggs's been down in Paddy's Gully again,' he blurted out. 'Askin' Hans and his friends have they seen anyone of your description, have they seen a woman with fair hair and blue eyes. Hans told 'em no, or so he said to me.' But Eddie was uneasy. How far did one trust one's friends when there was a reward involved?

'How much are they askin' for me?' Adam asked curiously, easing himself down with extreme caution against his favourite rock.

Eddie raised his eyebrows, and told him.

Adam whistled. 'If I wasn't keen to stay out of gaol, I'd turn meself in!' he declared.

But Ella couldn't laugh. 'Do you think someone will give us away?' she asked Eddie.

'I think you should leave in the mornin'.' And he gave Adam a questioning look.

Adam felt his ribs carefully. 'I could ride tomorrow, if I have to. I've a friend between here and Melbourne who'll hide us if I'm not fit to go on.'

Eddie nodded. 'All right then. I'll get Hans to deliver the horses and I'll bring 'em up first thing in the mornin'.'

He stood up. He still seemed edgy and nervous. 'I'd best get back to Maryanne. She's been actin' queer ... I reckon she's got her eye on someone.'

Ella stared at him in dismay. 'How can you live with her when you can't trust her?' she burst out, and then was sorry when she saw his face.

'She's always been like that,' he sighed. 'One day I'll probably wring 'er neck. But the truth is, she'd be lost without me. And I'd be lost without 'er.'

He nodded at them, avoiding their eyes, and vanished back into the bush.

'I shouldn't have said that,' Ella murmured uncomfortably. 'It's none of my business.'

Adam stretched out his legs, as though rediscovering the muscles. 'I take it you'd have a dim view of me if I looked elsewhere, Cinderella?'

'Not if it was just looking.'

He laughed, and then stretched again. 'I'm feeling better,' he said softly. 'I'm just warning you, so that you can stay out of me way.'

His meaning took a moment to make sense to her. 'Oh,' she murmured.

'Oh,' he mocked gently. 'That one part of me that Moggs didn't stick his boot into, and its workin' perfectly.'

She didn't know how to answer his teasing. In

the end it seemed wiser to ignore it.

———•———

Long shadows were creeping over the bush when Paddy returned. Birds twittered and rustled, readying themselves for the night. A grey wallaby jumped softly through the undergrowth, stopped with ears twitching when it saw Adam and Ella, and then bounded away into invisibility.

'Find any colour, Paddy?' Adam called out as the little man came into sight.

Paddy shook his head, but his eyes flicked intelligently to Adam and away again. 'No gold up here,' he said flatly.

'If you say so.'

Paddy's face looked as though it wanted to smile, but he wouldn't let it. 'You've made a recovery?' he asked, setting down his pick and shovel and giving Adam the full benefit of his black stare.

Adam patted his sides and grinned. 'I'm beginning to feel like meself again, yes. Eddie says he'll be bringing up the horses in the mornin' so that we can be off.' He hesitated, his smile softening. 'You've been good to us, Paddy. Is there somethin' I can do for you to show our thanks?'

The little man looked surprised, and then shy. He shook his head. 'I've everythin' I want here, thank you, sir. Eddie keeps me in the know, about t'ings goin' on down on the diggings, and I've me work to do. I want everyt'ink right for when Mikey comes. If you see him, could you tell him I'm waitin'?'

Adam nodded seriously. 'We'll tell him that,

Paddy.'

They ate their meal, listening to the night. A mopoke owl called its eerie call and flew off in pursuit of some small prey with a whoosh of its wings. Paddy sat back, drinking brandy from a bottle and staring into the fire. Adam closed his eyes, resting his head back against the rock, while Ella sat close beside him thinking of tomorrow.

'What will you do when we get to Sydney?' she asked him softly, unwilling to break the comfortable silence but needing to know.

Adam smiled, eyes still closed. 'I wish me ma was still alive. If she was, I'd go and find her. I'd knock on the door and she'd look at me and pretend she didn't care whether I was home or not. But I'd see the tears in her eyes. And I'd take your arm in mine, and I'd say, "Here she is ... here's me woman".'

'Would you indeed?' Ella murmured, but she was smiling too. 'What do you think she'd say to that?'

His smile grew. 'She'd look you up and down, and she'd shake her head, and she'd say, "She's no good to you, Adam! Her hands are too soft, and her arms are too scrawny ... she'll never chop your wood and carry your children!"'

Ella pretended to hit him, but he caught her wrists and she felt his returning strength, held in check so he didn't hurt her. He leaned over her, smiling into her eyes. He whispered, 'But I'd look her straight in the eye, and I'd say, "I don't care, ma, she's the one for me."'

Ella felt her insides melting. Like butter in a frypan. How could he do this to her? What power did he have that other men didn't? And then Adam bent his head and took her mouth with his, kissing her with a sort of soft savagery.

'Ahem.' Paddy cleared his throat tactfully. 'I t'ink I'll be goin' to bed now.' And he was gone, the flap of calico pulled firmly across.

Adam lifted an eyebrow, and said, 'It's just like being back with Kitty.'

The thought of Kitty sobered them both. 'I wonder where they are?' Ella asked. 'Are they safe, do you think?'

'They're safe, or we would have heard otherwise. David and Kitty will be fine. She'll run rings around him, and he'll love it.'

He smoothed back her hair, tucking a truant strand into the neat plait she was wearing down her back. 'I liked Kitty,' he said softly, 'she was something worth savin' from Nancy Ure. But I didn't love her.'

'Didn't you?' Ella teased.

He grinned, and wrapped an arm around her waist to pull her in against him, only wincing slightly as she was pressed against his ribs. 'It was you kept pushing her at me, love. *I* was trying to keep me distance.'

'Oh, really?'

He kissed her, lips trailing over her cheek towards her mouth. Her hands went out to push him away, but she didn't have the strength. Her lips parted in anticipation. She closed her eyes.

He didn't move. Ella felt his breathing quicken against her skin. She opened her eyes. He was staring beyond her, past the fire, past Paddy's tent, towards the edge of the darkness. He looked as if he were seeing a ghost.

'Mrs Seaton,' said a familiar, hated voice, 'if you

would move away ... slowly. I have a gun pointed at you, and I won't hesitate to fire.'

Ella turned around, her head giddy, her mouth dry. Lieutenant Moggs was standing in the faint outer glow of the campfire, on top of the bank. His boots shone with the reflection of flames. His face, with the light shining up into it, was full of shadows and lines. He looked what he was: a hard and cruel man.

'I've been hunting you for some days now,' Moggs went on, speaking in a clipped, conversational voice, as if this was a normal evening for him. 'I knew you couldn't be far away. Very clever, to find such a place,' and he glanced about him, the gun pointing steadily at Adam. 'It was the reward that did it, of course. I always find that a criminal's friends tend to fade away when money is involved.'

The circle of firelight was like a little world within the darkness. Moggs's gun caught the light and he took a step forward until he stood on the very edge of the bank. Ella saw that his smile was more like a grimace, a tight stretching of the lips. There was murder in his eyes and, Ella had no doubt, in his heart too.

'It's men like you give the Joes a bad name,' Adam said at last in an even voice. Ella turned to look at him and saw the determined line of his mouth and the bitter hatred in his eyes. If he had to die, it would be on his terms.

'Adam,' she whispered, warning him to take care.

But he tightened his arm around her, and said, 'He's alone, love. He didn't want his men here to see what he's going to do.'

Ella turned and stared at Moggs in horror.

Moggs said nothing; the gun remained steady.

'Now that I think on it, he sent his men off last time,' Adam went on slowly, 'when he beat me, me with me hands bound. Maybe that was the only way he could win. And this time, he needs a gun to help him out.'

Moggs moved restlessly – a stone rattled down the bank. He looked enormous, the firelight gleamed on the braid of his jacket and the soft shining leather of his belt. Ella wondered what sort of world had made a man like this, so certain of his own importance that he took the law into his own hands. He meant to kill Adam … and most likely her too.

She shivered, and felt Adam's arm tighten about her again. She wondered if he meant to try and wrest the gun from Moggs, and decided that would be pointless and Adam must know it. Moggs was standing much higher than them, and had a clear view of everything they were doing. He would shoot Adam first, and then Ella.

'Your insults don't affect me,' Moggs said sharply. 'I am doing my duty, that's all. I'm ridding the colony of scum, men like you who don't deserve to live.'

'Oh, so this isn't anything to do with Sawpit Gully? Or me escape from the hospital?' Adam had raised his voice, startling Ella, but his arm remained tight around her.

Moggs's hand twitched. Ella could see what it was costing him not to lose control. Adam was goading him, daring him to shoot.

Suddenly the mopoke cried out again from its place in the tree, making Ella gasp with fright.

Moggs's hand jerked up, and at the same moment Ella saw what Adam had already seen. A shadow moved behind him. Paddy's grim face in the firelight. He swung the thick clublike branch in his hands with all his might.

It caught Moggs's shoulder, then glanced off. Moggs cried out furiously, clutching at his arm, but he still held the gun. He spun around, just as Paddy swung the branch again, this time catching him on the head with a sound like wood splitting. Moggs crumpled at the knees and went down, falling forward onto his face.

Paddy was breathing heavily, and his eyes were wild as he lifted the branch again, high above his head. But Adam was there, reaching up to take it from him. 'Leave it now, matey,' he murmured, 'leave it to Adam now.' Paddy blinked, as bewildered as a possum in daylight, and let go.

'I heard him, and I went out t'back way,' he burbled, wiping his hands on the front of his shirt. 'Went out t'back of me tent. I've got two ways out, in case o' the Joes. Went out t'back.' His hands moved faster and faster, as though they were so dirty he could not wipe them clean.

'It's all right,' Adam said. 'You did well, you did very well.' He tossed the branch far into the bush, and bent down, removing Moggs's gun and handing it back to Ella. She took it gingerly, laying it down on the ground as if it might go off. Moggs still hadn't moved. His face was turned towards Ella, and it looked pale but still and peaceful. There seemed to be no blood. She expected his eyes to open at any moment, she expected him to spring up.

'We must go,' she burst out, cutting through Paddy's murmurings. 'He'll wake up in a moment. Adam!'

But Adam, kneeling on Moggs's other side, shook his head. 'He won't be wakin' up, Cinderella.' He held up his hand, and she saw the blood, bright and shiny, smeared on his fingers.

She didn't stand up; she couldn't trust her legs. She crawled over to him on her hands and knees, and stared at the mess that was the other side of Moggs's head. And turned away and was sick.

'Oh Jesus, oh Jesus,' Paddy was muttering.

'Come here, now,' Adam was saying, 'come here,' and he caught Paddy by the shoulders and shook him, hard. The little man stopped speaking, his mouth hanging half open. 'Go down and get Eddie for me. Will you do that? Can I trust you? Are you me mate now, Paddy, will you do that for me?'

Paddy stared at him, and a sudden spark came into his eyes. 'Mikey?' he whispered. 'Is it you, Mikey, is it you indeed?'

'Go on,' Adam said awkwardly, 'go now. Get Eddie for me.'

The little man backed away into the darkness, and then turned and ran. They heard him crashing through the bush, and the crackle and rattle of his progress, until gradually the silence returned.

Ella had been as sick as it was possible to be, and now sat, shaking and cold, her back against Adam's favourite rock. 'He's dead,' she said, and it wasn't a question.

'Aye, and I didn't lay a finger on him, though I wanted to ... He would have killed you, you know that, Ella? Me first, then you. Potted you without feeling anything but pleasure in it.' Anger darkened his eyes, and he closed them. 'What now?' he asked himself, struggling to think. 'I'll be blamed for his murder, I know that. We'll find a way out though. I'll not be hanged for him dead any more than I'd be hanged for him alive.'

'What can we do?' Ella whispered.

'We'll get rid of the body and then we'll leave. If he told anyone where he was going, they won't find a thing. But I don't think he told anyone. He came up here alone so that he could kill me.'

'Who told him?' Her words seemed to startle him. He opened his eyes and stared at her.

The Jardines? she thought. Perhaps the reward had been too much for Naughton's integrity, such as it was. And yet how did he know exactly where Adam was hiding? This was a place known only to three others ... Eddie, Maryanne and Paddy. It couldn't have been Paddy ... but the other two? Eddie ...

Ella's eyes widened, but Adam had reached the same conclusion.

'And I've sent Paddy down to fetch Eddie,' he whispered. 'Come on!'

He bent down to grasp Moggs's arm, beginning to drag him. 'Help me with him.'

She realised then what he meant, and began to shake her head.

'Help me!' he ordered.

Slowly Ella got to her feet and went over to the bank. Adam broke off what he was doing to reach out and take her hand, pulling her up beside him. And then, together, they bent to grasp Moggs's arms. He was heavier than she could have imagined. His head lolled and bumped against the ground, as they dragged him into the scrub. Ella was sick again but there was nothing left in her stomach so she only retched miserably. Adam was sweating, his breath coming in gasps, and he stood up to take a rest.

It was only then they heard the sound of running feet, fast approaching.

For someone just risen from his sickbed, Adam moved like lightening. He rolled the body over and over until it came to a rest in the Chinese bush out of the firelight. And then he grabbed Ella and pulled her down with him, flat onto the ground.

'Where's the pistol?' he hissed.

'I put it down.'

He pushed himself up on his hands as if about to make a dash to fetch it. But it was too late. Eddie, with Paddy close behind him, had burst into the camp site. Eddie stopped, puffing from the exertion of his run, his head turning. 'Where are they?' he managed, as Paddy came up beside him.

Paddy frowned, peering into the shadows. 'They was here, right here,' he whispered. 'Do you think the trap's taken 'em away?'

Eddie made a sound of despair, or anger, and took a step towards the tents. 'Adam!' he called. The name rang around them, loud and echoing. As if in answer, the mopoke's strange cry came again. Paddy crossed himself, muttering, and then he spied the pistol.

'Look, that belonged to the trap!' he breathed.

Eddie bent and picked it up, turning it over in his hands. He sniffed it cautiously, and said, 'Hasn't been fired.' Slowly he straightened, glancing about intently now, trying to pierce the shadows.

'Adam!' he called. 'I know you're out there. You don't trust me, do you? Is that it? You've had time to think now, haven't you, and you're thinkin' that it must've been Paddy or me that give you away to Moggs.'

Ella held her breath, watching him. Her hands felt stiff and dirty, as if touching Moggs's body had soiled them. She wanted to wash them, or wipe them on her shirt as Paddy had done, over and over and over.

'I've got his bulldog here, look!' Eddie called, and held the pistol up. 'If you think I'm goin' to use it to bark at yer, you're wrong. Here,' and he handed the pistol to Paddy, who took it and slipped it into his belt. 'And I've said nothin' to anyone. You saved Maryanne's life, and that means I owe you mine.' He sighed, as though all his pride had left him. 'It were Maryanne what told the traps, Adam, when Moggs came round that last time. She was askìn' him about the reward, teasin' like she does. I don't think she really meant to tell him. She didn't know what he were like.'

His shoulders slumped and he shook his head miserably. 'I don't believe she really meant to tell him,' he repeated. 'But he saw she knew somethin' and he scared her bad. He said he'd hurt her ... or me. She had to tell him.' He paused. 'I didn't know about it until now, when Paddy came, and she broke down an' told me. I knew she was actin' queer, but I thought she was gettin' the itch again ... I thought there was another man.' His voice lifted and broke on the last word.

Ella's heart went out to him, even as her fury rose

at Maryanne's perfidy. Beside her, Adam let out his breath in a long sigh and pushed himself to his feet.

'All right,' he said, and Eddie's head swung round in the direction of his voice. His face lit up with such relief, Ella could no longer doubt his innocence. 'All right, Eddie. We've a dead police lieutenant up here, and we need to hide him.'

Eddie's white face looked even whiter, but he swallowed his moment of fear and nodded. 'I'll get Hans to fetch the saddle horses,' he said quietly. 'We can use one o' them to take the body down to one o' the abandoned holes. Not Paddy's Gully, that's too close for comfort. Don't you worry, Adam, I'll find him a fittin' restin' place.'

Adam walked over to the edge of the bank where Moggs had stood so short a time ago. Ella got slowly to her feet and followed him. 'We need to go tonight,' Adam said. 'Moggs might have told someone else ... or maybe Maryanne did.'

Eddie looked miserable again, not meeting his eyes. 'I'll leave her,' he said. 'God help me, I'll leave her this time.' But his voice was weak, despite the bravado in it, and no one believed him.

Hans came with the horses and they wrapped the body in a blanket. Ella and Paddy didn't go with them. Her last sight of that 'gentleman', Lieutenant Moggs, was his shiny boots dangling from the end of the blanket as the horse was led away.

She didn't ask where they meant to hide him, or how. She didn't want to add that to the nightmares she knew she would have in the weeks ... the years, to come.

Paddy's dark, grubby face looked ghastly in the firelight. The little man seemed to have aged years. Ella felt sorry for him. Lieutenant Moggs's grudge had been against Adam and herself, not Paddy, and now Paddy had been drawn into it.

'We'll be leaving soon,' she murmured in an attempt to soothe. 'You'll have your camp to yourself again, Paddy. No more excitement.'

Her smile was weak, but he responded to it. 'I'm used to bein' on me own now,' he muttered. 'I'm used to bein' without Mikey. He's dead, ain't he?'

The dark eyes were clear and lucid, peering into hers. Ella opened her mouth to lie, and then found she couldn't. 'Yes, Paddy, I believe he must be.'

The little man nodded.

'Had you been a friend of Mikey's for long?' Ella asked, as much to distract her mind from what was happening with Adam.

He grinned at her. 'He was me brother-in-law, me lady. I married his sister, you see.'

Ella was shocked, and unable to hide it. Paddy giggled at her expression.

'You're not believin' me, are you? Well, I *was* married once. She had hair like the moon, like yours. Fine and soft and pale, like finest silk through me fingers. She died.'

He looked away, and she felt the ache of his pain and loneliness.

'I lived with Mikey after that. It got to feel sometimes as if I was married to *him*,' He giggled. 'It was Mikey heard o' the gold rush and decided we could make our fortunes. So we took a steerage passage on a ship that had more water in it than out and came to Victoria. And now Mikey's dead and I'm on me own.'

'You have Eddie,' she reminded him.

A log slipped and fell, crackling with flames. Smoke blew in a haze, taking sparks into the black sky. Paddy peered at her, suddenly intent. 'Eddie's woman's got dark hair, black hair, like her heart. Not like yours, me lady.'

He rose to his feet, and Ella looked up at him nervously as he came towards her. He stopped beside her, looking down into her face, while Ella's pity struggled with her revulsion.

'Can I touch your hair, me lady? Would you allow me that privilege?'

Ella stared up at him, seeing the stringy, sandy hair and beard, and the grime ingrained in the pores of his skin. She didn't want him to touch her. She couldn't bear him to touch her ... And then she saw the tear. It had oozed from the corner of his eye and was rolling down his cheek, making a paler track in the dirt. Ella met his gaze again, and now she saw past the outer shell of the recluse to the shattered human being within.

'Yes,' she whispered. 'You can touch my hair, Paddy.'

Paddy put out his hand, his fingers trembling, and brushed against her hair. Ella closed her eyes, and felt his fingers, so gentle, smoothing the silky strands. And then he sighed, a deep sigh, as if his very soul were sighing. 'Like the moon,' he whispered.

Ella opened her eyes and saw that a second tear had joined the first.

It was well after midnight by the time the men

returned, and Adam looked utterly done in. Ella made him lie down in the tent, while Eddie, Hans and Paddy sat by the fire, talking in low voices. They seemed to think it would be some time before Moggs was discovered, and when he was, Ella and Adam would be long gone.

'Head over Kilmore way,' Eddie told her. That'll keep yer off the main road. Take yer time ... Adam's not in any fit state to run a race.'

'Yes.'

'Look after 'im,' Eddie added, his smile crooked. 'And yerself.' He looked like he had aged ten years tonight.

'You too, Eddie. And thank you, thank you all for your help,' and her weary smile encompassed Hans and Paddy.

Eddie's smile slipped away and suddenly he was very serious. 'You're on yer own now, Ella. And with Adam hurt, it's all up to you.'

'We'll get there,' Ella replied confidently, jamming her shaking hands between her moleskin-covered knees.

'Maybe you'll be seein' Mikey?'

Paddy was looking at her intently. Ella, startled, glanced at Eddie. 'Mikey?' he asked quietly. 'Now then, Paddy, you know in yer heart Mikey's dead.'

But Paddy giggled. 'I've somethin' for him. I'll fetch it out.' He was gone, darting into his tent. Eddie raised his eyebrows at Ella.

'He's not as daft as yer think,' he whispered. 'Comes and goes, like, in his mind. He told me once he was a teacher. He has books in that tent o' his with words long enough to hang a man with!'

Ella smiled despite herself. Paddy, an educated

man? She felt sad that he had come to this. And yet, perhaps he was perfectly happy with his lot. In the town, he might be locked away and called mad. Here, he was free to be as eccentric as he liked.

'Here it is then!'

Paddy was standing before her, holding out a small dark bottle. 'The leprechauns gave me this to give to Mikey,' he said. 'Being as he won't come here now. You'll give it to him, won't you? If you see him?'

Hesitantly, Ella took it. The weight belied the size of the thing, and she tightened her grip. 'What if I don't see him?' she asked awkwardly.

Paddy veiled his eyes with his eyelids. 'Well, if Mikey doesn't want it, I reckon as you can have it, me lady.'

She thanked him, wondering if this was part of the act or if Paddy's brief moment of sanity was already at an end.

Eddie was laughing and slapping Paddy on the back. 'You're a fine one to talk about leprechauns,' he said. 'I reckon you're one yerself.'

Paddy giggled, and danced a little jig, holding out the hem of his jacket like a skirt. But as he turned, his black eyes caught Ella's, just for a moment, and gleamed with a deep intelligence.

THE DARK
DREAM

CHAPTER 23

———◆———

THE BUSH HAD A SAMENESS to it, despite the changing terrain. The same rough, twisted trunks, the same grey leaves dripping with rain. The whole world was raining, soft as mist, and the horses' hooves were muted on the soft, muddy ground.

They had started out from Bendigo just before dawn. Adam, tired and pale, had hardly said a word as he climbed into the saddle. Eddie waved them goodbye, with Paddy at his side - Hans had long since returned to his warm bed. Their faces faded into the rain, and were gone.

The sun rose wan and sickly through the trees, while a crow sat, black feathers gleaming, giving its melancholy cry. They circled Big Hill to the east, travelling through open, undulating country, magnificently treed, almost parklike. Once, Ella heard the sound of a gun being fired, but it was far away and of no immediate concern.

Adam seemed to hear nothing, see nothing, his whole being concentrated on riding.

They stopped at midday for food and drink and a short rest. But Adam, despite his haggard looks and weary body, was keen to get on. 'We haven't put the Bendigo far enough behind us yet,' he said.

'Do you think they'll find Lieutenant Moggs's body soon?' She asked it softly, almost unwillingly. Until this moment she had concentrated on riding, on following Adam's back, and had closed her mind to all the fears and terrors of yesterday. But now Moggs intruded again and she saw his face as he stood over them with his pistol, ready to kill them both because of his own warped sense of pride.

'No.' He answered her question. 'Not in a week, and probably not in a month. It's well hidden.'

She nodded, feeling the sickness rising in her throat. If she asked him, she knew he would tell her what he and Eddie and Hans had done, and why. But she didn't ask. Some things were best not to know. She would have nightmares enough without knowing the final moments of Lieutenant Moggs.

By late afternoon Adam was swaying in his saddle, in imminent danger of falling off. 'We'll stop now,' Ella announced.

But he shook his head. 'Just a bit further. There's a creek up there ... I can see the way the trees are growin' along the line of it. We'll stop up there.'

She sighed, but didn't argue. In front of them the land dipped down towards the narrow creek, which cut a path between curving hillsides. It was green and lovely, and Ella was so engrossed in the scenery, she didn't notice Adam's horse stumble until it was too late. Either through weakness or weariness, his fingers lost their hold and he fell heavily to the ground.

Ella pulled her own mount up hard and was

down, running back to him, her fear hammering so loudly in her ears it blotted out the sounds of the bush and the water. Adam was already trying to get up when she reached him. His face was white.

'Give me your arm,' he gasped. Ella bent down so that he could slide his arm about her shoulders and, with some tugging and heaving, got him back onto his feet. Still with his arm over her shoulders taking some of his weight, she began to help him towards the shelter of a large boulder set against the hillside. When they were almost there he stopped, leaning heavily against her.

'I need a moment,' he whispered.

Ella felt his legs sagging under him. 'Adam! Come here ... sit here ...' She managed to get him the last couple of steps and into the shelter of the boulder. He collapsed onto the rough ground, his head between his knees. Ella bent over him, frantic, not knowing what to do.

Gradually, the colour returned to his face and he seemed to recover himself. Slowly, he sat up and leaned his head back against the pitted surface of the boulder towering above them.

'Where are you hurt?' Ella asked, half frightened to hear his answer.

Adam tried to smile. 'Everywhere.' Then, with an impatient shake of his head. 'Nowhere new, love. Everything that was already hurtin' just jarred a bit, that's all.'

Should she believe him? She had a suspicion that he wouldn't tell her, even if some new injury had been done to him. Well, after they had eaten, she would insist on inspecting his hurts ... all of them! And then she would be able to judge for herself.

It was a good spot to stop, Ella decided as she went about setting up their camp. The trees gave shelter and the boulder, set in as it was against the hillside and with enough overhanging to shelter them from the weather, made a good spot to pitch their tent. And added to that there was the fast, shallow creek a few yards further down the bank. Ella tethered the horses where they could crop the grass and then she gathered some wood to make a fire.

Everything was so wet. Twice she nearly had a spark, only to have it flicker and die. But on the third try, the flames darted through the twigs and leaves and caught, sending up a choking spiral of smoke. Ella sat back, coughing and wiping her streaming eyes.

The rain began to patter softly in the trees above them, and the air was suddenly full of eucalyptus smoke and the fresh, sharp smell of the earth. When the fire was burning brightly, Ella went to the horses to remove their gear. She felt only slightly sore from the long ride - indeed she had enjoyed being on a horse again. There was something of freedom in the act of riding, as if she could go anywhere, do anything ... as if she were in charge of her own destiny.

Well, I'm not, she reminded herself irritably. I'm running and hiding. My name and description have been handed out all over the Bendigo gold-field, and now I'm likely to be charged with the murder of a police lieutenant. Hardly freedom!

When Ella had removed their packs from the two horses and placed them in the shelter of the boul-der, she added some more wood to the fire, making sure it wouldn't smother. Then she set about finding a warm blanket. I should have done this first, she thought, giving Adam an anxious glance. He was sitting where she had left him, very still, as though conserving his strength ... or holding in his pain. She brought the blanket over to him and wrapped it around him, gently.

'Sorry,' he murmured, as if it were his fault.

She managed a smile. 'I don't mind. Makes a nice change, me looking after you.'

'Aye.' He smiled back. 'But it's only temporary, Mrs Seaton.'

The creek was swollen with rain, but able to be crossed. Ella clambered over some large rocks, slippery with green and brown moss, and filled the billy. Everything dripped with moisture. Even me, Ella thought wryly, as she wiped a raindrop from the tip of her nose.

When the billy had boiled, she made tea, and poured in a good measure of brandy before bringing the mug to Adam.

He sipped, closing his eyes, savouring the warmth. The bruise around his eye had turned a nice shade of yellow, and the cut on his cheek was all but healed. Although his nose looked less swollen, it would never be the same again.

'How far is Tea-tree Station?' she asked him, setting aside her own mug.

Adam blinked and shook his head slightly as if to capture his thoughts. 'Two days' ride ... more.'

Two days, she thought grimly, was too much for Adam. He had come as far as he could. Search or no search, police or no police, they had no option but to stay here until he was fit enough to resume the journey.

Ella took a deep breath, and made her voice firm. 'We will stay here tomorrow, Adam. You need to build up your strength. We have the voyage to Sydney, remember, as well as the ride to Tea-tree Station.'

Adam's eyes opened and she saw his strong will struggling against the weakness of his body. It was his look of failure when he realised his will wasn't strong enough that brought the tears stinging to Ella's eyes.

They didn't eat much, far too tired to bother with the mechanics of chewing and swallowing.

Afterwards, following Adam's instructions, Ella set up their tent close to the boulder. It was snug and comfortable enough, once she had filled it with their blankets and belongings.

Ella was tempted to delay the inspection of Adam's ribs, despite her earlier determination, as he was shaking with tiredness. But her real concern that he had hurt himself seriously when he fell from his horse overcame her compassion. She lit the candle, helped him to strip off his jacket, and then eased the shirt over his head. Ella knelt before him, looking doubtfully at the now rather grubby bandages that covered most of his chest.

Slowly, as gently as she could, she began to unwrap them. Adam didn't speak, and his eyes were closed. But she heard his quick breathing, as though he were trying to still the pain in his ribs by breathing as shallowly as possible. When at last she had finished, Ella sat back and inspected her handiwork.

The bruising was spectacular. The entire rib area

was a collage, with colours ranging from deepest mauve to almost orange. She ran her fingertip down his breastbone and felt him tense, waiting.

'Would I be able to see if your lungs were damaged?' she asked, remembering what Eddie had said about spitting blood.

Adam shrugged, and then winced.

Intently, Ella watched him breathe, but couldn't see anything unnatural in the rise and fall of his chest. There was no area more bruised than another, or indeed any fresh bruising or swelling. She touched him again, and knew in her heart it was because she wanted to rather than because she needed to. His skin was so warm, despite the chill of the evening. She just had to look at him to know the physical strength of him ... and marvel at the gentleness that went with it. Unable to resist, Ella ran her fingers over contours of muscle and bone, and then down the long puckered scar on his left side.

Watching her, Adam gingerly traced the old wound for himself. 'When Frenchy cut me,' he said quietly, 'it was a real mess. I was lucky to pull through.' His fingers found hers, closing on them strongly. 'I like it when you touch me.'

I like touching you, Ella thought. But she did not say it aloud - she still felt awkward admitting such a thing, constrained by the rules of a past she could not even remember.

She squeezed his hand and withdrew her own. 'You have a scratch or two I should clean.' Her voice was matter-of-fact. 'Lie down. I won't be long.'

With a groan, he lay back onto the blankets.

'Don't worry,' he said, a gleam in his eyes that had been missing all day. 'Just patch me up enough to get me to Tea-Tree Station. Harvey'll do the rest.'

Would he? Ella wondered, as she crawled out of the tent to boil more water. She had only met Harvey briefly but she found it difficult to imagine him playing nurse.

When she was done, Ella rewrapped Adam's ribs as near as possible to the way they had been wrapped at the camp hospital by Doctor McCrea. Adam said nothing as she worked, but she knew it must be painful.

'I'm sorry if I'm hurting you,' she said at last. She felt as though she wanted to cry, but she held her face rigid, refusing to let herself give in to emotion. Adam didn't need weakness, he needed strength, he needed to lean on her as she had leaned on him all this time. He needed ... he needed ... But after all her face crumpled, and she turned away abruptly, trying to hide the tears.

'It's all right,' he whispered, and she felt his hand on her shoulder. 'I'll live. They thought I was goin' to die after Frenchy got me with his knife, but I didn't. And Moggs did his best to kill me, too, but I didn't die.'

'Not yet,' she replied tartly, but she was comforted.

'We'll be at Tea-tree Station in a couple of days and – '

'No!' She turned back to him, wiping angrily at her cheeks. 'We're not moving from this spot until you're well again. We're staying right here. I mean it, Adam.'

He frowned. 'This land has got to belong to

someone. They could order us off it, or send for the joes.'

'I don't care. If they order us off, then we'll go, but until they do, we're staying right here.'

He met her angry, frightened eyes, and she watched him debating whether or not he could persuade her. At last he sighed, and a familiar grin curled his mouth. 'All right, Mrs Seaton. We'll stay one more day. But that's all.' His eyes narrowed. 'Now come here and lie beside me.'

I shouldn't, Ella thought. He's hurt, and he needs to be left to sleep. I should go back outside to check the fire and the horses and ... But already she was crawling over to lie down beside him, very carefully. He put his arm around her, pulling her closer, until she was a mere extension of him. She felt his sigh of contentment stir her hair.

Soon, the soft, evenness of his breathing told her he was asleep. Ella lifted her hand and touched his cheek; his beard felt rough against her fingers. 'I won't lose you,' she whispered. 'You're all I have now.'

———•———

When Ella woke, it was very early. She lifted the canvas flap and peered outside. The sky had cleared, and the sun was even trying to shine, sparkling off the damp grass and gleaming on the leaves. A bird sang a slow, melodic song.

Behind her, Adam was still asleep, lying sprawled within his nest of blankets. Ella raised herself up onto one elbow, watching him in silence. Overnight, some of the haggardness had smoothed out of his face and he seemed more relaxed. As she gazed at him, a frown passed swiftly over his forehead and was gone, and then his fingers twitched.

He was dreaming, and she wondered about what. Ella's thoughts turned to her own dreams. She closed her eyes and shivered, remembering how Ned had been murdered at Seaton's Lagoon. She wondered if her past would begin to return, now that she knew about Ned. Surely Ned's death was the terrible event that had been preventing her from remembering?

Cautiously, Ella probed her memory to see what she would find. Still only a deep, deep tunnel. Ella thought of it as a well. When she looked down it, she saw nothing – it was so deep ... not even a glimmer of light illuminated the secrets at the bottom.

'Good morning.'

Ella started, and opened her eyes. Adam was awake, and watching her. And smiling.

She felt her own lips smiling back. 'Good morning.'

He reached up, hesitated, and then slid his hand around to her nape, gently pulling her face down to his. She supposed she should resist, but she didn't want to. And then his breath was hot against her throat and his lips were touching where his breath had been and resistance was the last thing on her mind.

Ella shuddered, and lost her balance, falling across him. He groaned, and she clambered up onto her knees, gasping with embarrassment at her own clumsiness and the fear that she may have hurt him. 'I'm sorry! Oh Adam, I'm sorry – '

He caught the hands that were fumbling all over him, squeezing them tightly in his, and she saw that his face was alight with laughter. 'It's all right. I'm all right. You just took me by surprise.'

When he saw the stunned look on her face, he laughed aloud. Angrily she tried to pull away, but he held her, and the laughter died in his eyes. 'Come back here,' he said softly, 'and this time, be gentle with me, Cinderella.'

She didn't know what to do. She was certain that no one had ever spoken to her like this before, and she was certain, if they had, she would have turned and run in the opposite direction. Her legs *were* trembling, but she knew it was towards Adam she wanted to run.

Adam eased himself up until he was sitting beside her. His fingers were gentle as he smoothed the loose curls of hair against her cheek. He bent forward and began to nibble at her jaw. A pulse was leaping in her throat, and he put his lips to it. She caught her breath and, as if the sound had drawn his attention, his mouth moved to hover over hers.

He kissed her softly. He explored her face with his lips as if he were blind. By the time he had finished, Ella was gasping. His hands found their way under her jacket, and he tugged the woollen shirt from inside her moleskins until it hung loose about her hips. He slid his hands beneath it and up, over her narrow waist, over her ribs, to the swell of her breasts.

Ella closed her eyes, taken by surprise by the wave of pleasure his touch brought her.

'Will I stop?' he breathed.

Unable to speak, she shook her head. She heard

the smile in his voice. 'Your skin's so smooth.' Gently he cupped the soft, rounded flesh in his palms, as though accustoming himself to the feel of her. She bit her lip, but he felt her shiver. 'You like that?' he whispered. 'You like me to touch you there ... and there?'

'Oh yes ...'

'This isn't how I wanted it to be,' he said, and there was a note of sadness in his voice, mingling with the familiar humour. 'I dreamed of us dining on oysters and champagne, with white wax candles burning hot. And afterwards, when you were all warm and ready, I'd lay you down on the soft feather mattress and love you like I've dreamed of doing since I first saw you.'

Surprised, Ella met his eyes. He looked faintly embarrassed by the admission, but sincere. He wanted no quick, rough coupling.

'You're too ill,' she began sensibly, if a little breathlessly.

But Adam only smiled, and began to unbuckle her belt. 'It hurts when I breathe, love. I might as well do somethin' that makes the hurting worthwhile.'

He kissed her mouth, while his warm, scarred fingers caressed the tender skin of her belly and thighs. She felt him press her legs gently apart, making her aware of how vulnerable she was in such a position, and yet how much she wanted him to touch her there.

'Adam ...'

'You want me?' He said it as a question, but it was not. He knew she wanted him, he could feel that she wanted him.

He pressed her down onto the blankets, and now his mouth was hot and hard on hers. She no longer knew or cared if this was hurting him. His body came down over hers, and then he was inside her, and the wonderful strangeness and yet familiarity of it made her catch her breath.

Somewhere in her past was a vague memory of discomfort and fear. She thought: I've done this before. But never like this. This is a foreign country to me.

And then all thought fled. Adam was stirring feelings in her she had not known were there. She felt as wild and free as the storm that had lashed Midnight Gully. If she had ever been a frozen woman, then Adam had melted her.

He nuzzled her shoulder, bending his head to taste her breasts. Something was gathering force inside her. She felt it, surprised that it was there at all, and then terrified that it would stop before she was ready for it to stop. But Adam's mouth was on hers again, and his body moved with hers, and suddenly whatever he had stirred within her took hold, lifting her high and flinging her far.

———

'Love?' He whispered the word, his fingers gentle as he stroked her face. Ella looked up at him, where he still lay above her, and smiled, her whole soul laid open for his perusal. 'Have you never felt that before?' he asked her, a mingling of surprise and male arrogance in his voice.

Ella shook her head, and then was embarrassed; she felt herself beginning to withdraw. But Adam kissed her lips, forcing her back from her retreat. 'Never,' she admitted at last. 'I would have remembered.'

'But you were no virgin,' he murmured, as if to himself. His mouth tightened. 'If I had a woman like you for me wife, I'd treat her like gold.'

'But I'm not your wife,' Ella said softly. And then she shivered.

He began to kiss her again, but she felt his arms trembling and all her anxiety returned. 'Lie down,' she insisted, and pressed him down.

This time he didn't resist, but lay on his back, grinning lazily up at her. 'Can we try that tonic again, ma'am, in a little while?'

She smiled back at him.

'I've never met a woman like you,' he began, and then frowned at the triteness of his words. 'I mean, well … I'm not the same man I was before, I can't ever be the same again.'

Ella knew then that his life had been as transformed as hers. Not just from their love-making of a moment ago, but by their very meeting. 'I can't ever be the same again, either,' she told him, repeating his words like a vow. 'And I don't want to be.'

After a little while, his eyelids flickered, and he fell asleep. But Ella remained wide awake.

I love him, Ella thought, and there was pleasure in thinking it.

And guilt.

Because somewhere, she had a husband, perhaps even now searching for her, and grieving at her loss. And she was here, with a man she had only known a matter of weeks, her body tingling from his … and already wanting him again.

CHAPTER 24

———◆———

*T*HE THOUGHT OF THE BABY *soothed her,
blunting the edge of desperation and loneliness she
often felt. She allowed her hands to stray to the growing
roundness of her belly, and thought: Here is my future.*

*But already there were doubts of that. Her husband
had endless plans to make his heir in the same mould
as him. 'I'll start teaching him the business as soon as
he can walk! Then he'll be ready to take over when he's
grown.'*

'What about school - an education ?' she ventured.

*But he gave her a frigid look. 'I'll give him what edu-
cation he needs, wife.'*

*It seemed as if her presence was not required. She was
merely the vehicle by which the child was manufactured
- like a machine - and when it was born, she would no
longer be relevant.*

Unless, of course, he wanted another.

*But she would never ask him. She had learned to bite
her tongue. There was something secretive about him,
something forbidding. Something dangerous.*

*He was proud of her. She saw that, and sometimes
there was a sort of comfort in it. But it was her breeding
he was proud of, her background, her poise. As a person,*

as a woman, she did not exist for him. He didn't visit her bedroom any more, and she was glad of that. There had never been pleasure in his visits and now she did not have to dread the tap on her door and what followed.

He was visiting someone else's room now. Catherine knew. Catherine knew everything. She loved her brother, she said, but she had come to love his wife, too.

'You must look after yourself, now that you are carrying a child,' Catherine told her, her clever eyes seeing everything and knowing everything.

'I intend to look after myself.'

'You've given my brother something she cannot,' Catherine added, lowering her voice. 'She's jealous of that.'

There was a silence, to mark this new step forward in their relationship.

'Is she?' She tightened her lips, but the question spilled through them anyway. 'Why doesn't he put her aside if she cannot give him what he wants?'

Catherine turned to look out of the tall windows, where leafy English trees drooped in the hot Australian sun. 'She seems to hold him in her hand, for all his strength and his power. She makes o' him a little boy.'

Her cold husband begging, pleading, like a child … 'Who is she?' she whispered. A shiver ran over the flesh of her arms, making goose bumps.

Catherine sighed wearily. 'I don't know. It's as if he's under a spell … was before he went home and married you.'

Shocked, she stared. 'Why did he marry me then?'

Catherine smiled sadly. 'It's obvious, darling. She is … unsuitable.'

A convict woman, she thought. Someone he could not be seen with in public, in case his rich clientele objected.

She felt Catherine's hand, warm and strong, clasp hers.

'You are carrying the heir,' she reminded her. 'He will never abandon you while you carry his child.'

'Sometimes, I wish I could ride away … do you remember the story you told? I want to escape this place. I have never been free, not at home and not here. Now I am twenty-five, and I want to be free of it.'

Catherine shook her head. 'None of us are that. Even I have ropes that bind me.'

'Why do you stay?' And then, quickly, 'Not that I am wishing you away, Catherine! I would never wish that.'

The pale eyes narrowed. When at last she spoke, it was in a soft voice, as if someone might overhear her. 'I left my home because of a shame, a secret shame. There was a man,' she smiled a half smile. 'My brother followed me. By the time he arrived in Sydney, I was low and falling lower. I had no money and no friends, and I did things to stay alive.'

She stopped, remembering. 'I won't tell you o' my life then, darling. It's not for your ears. My brother pulled me back from all that, and I'll love him whatever he is or whatever he does because of it.

'He saw ways to make money, in those places where I had been. I helped him run an inn, and watched him learn the dark side o' Sydneyton, as I had. But he was observin' us all like a boy with a jar o' ants. He watched and learned, and when it was time, he began to buy up the grog houses and the shanties, the places where there was money to be made, if you had the stomach for it. And he had the stomach, darling, and now he's a rich man.'

'Is that when he met her?' she whispered.

Catherine's eyes lost their warmth. Her face seemed suddenly old and careworn. 'Perhaps.'

'Sometimes I think I will follow him, and confront her. I would like to see her, this woman, who can turn *his coldness to fire.' She was bitter and humiliated, and could not hide it.*

Catherine reached for her hand, squeezing it hard. 'Don't do that,' she said. 'Don't ever do that.'

And it was a warning.

———————

The nap had refreshed Ella. She woke in the afternoon with renewed vigor. Outside the tent, the air was cool but full of sunlight. The urge that had been nibbling at her ever since she first saw the fresh, clean creek, was suddenly too strong to resist.

Ella pulled off her boots and moleskins quickly, before she could change her mind. The billowing shirt she left on, for modesty rather than convenience. Cautiously, her toes curling with the cold, she picked her way over the smooth, mossy rocks into the creek. The water came up to mid-calf and was so cold it made her catch her breath. She splashed herself, the icy trickles running down her bare legs and making her gasp. She had never felt as clean as she did now from the fresh water. Her skin tingled, coming alive. She bent over to wash her face, feeling her woollen shirt damp and clinging. That was when she sensed that someone was watching her.

She looked up sharply.

Adam stood on the rise above the creek, one hand resting against a tree trunk. He was wearing his trousers and he'd stopped to pull on his boots, but that was all. He was gazing down at her with rapt attention.

Ella lifted her hands, as if to cover herself, but

somehow the expression on his face made such a thing seem unnecessary between them. Adam came down the slope towards her, but he didn't stop on the edge of the creek – he walked straight into it. The water rose up over his boots and soaked the bottoms of his moleskins.

'Adam!' Ella cried out, in laughter and dismay. 'You'll catch cold!'

'I doubt that,' he retorted, and an echo of her laughter gleamed in his eyes. 'Do you know what you look like, standin' there?'

'Adam – '

He stopped her with his mouth. His hands cupped her hips, pressing her body against his. She thought: He's right about not catching a cold. He was hot all over, and hard with wanting her. She let her mouth open before his, giving herself willingly. Her cold flesh caught fire from his.

'You're like ice,' he whispered, his fingers caressing the chilled skin beneath the shirt. 'Come back to the tent and I'll dry you.'

Inside the tent, it was like twilight, the air soft and filtered. By now Ella's body was shaking with cold. The wonderful alive feeling had given way to numbness. Adam pulled the shirt over her head, and she huddled her arms about herself, teeth chattering, wondering how she could ever have found the creek revitalising.

'Perhaps it wasn't a g-g-good idea after a-a-all,' she managed.

Adam grinned. 'No, perhaps it wasn't. But you'll feel better in a moment.' He picked up a blanket and began to dry her. The cloth was rough against her skin, and he rubbed her all over until she glowed. Soon he was using his hands instead of the blanket, and she squirmed in his arms, all trace of coldness gone. He was teasing her, prolonging the excitement, enjoying her loss of control.

Ella watched his wide mouth begin to smile. It was a mouth made to smile. And to kiss.

Between kisses, Adam managed to remove his moleskins. Ella had not seen him completely naked before, and the sight of his strong body excited her in a new way.

'You're like a silky,' she whispered. 'All sleek and hard and irresistible.'

'What's a silky?' Adam asked.

'A fairy tale. A magical creature.' Her voice grew dreamy. 'A silky is a seal which can change into a man. And when he comes up out of the sea, he's so fine and so irresistible, no woman is safe from him. And when he finds the one he wants, he carries her back into the sea with him.'

Adam smiled, but his dark eyes were glowing. 'Is that how you see me, Ella? A magical creature?'

And in that moment Ella believed her own fantasy. She simply couldn't look away from him. Slowly he drew her in against him so that her legs straddled him, her thighs resting on his. It seemed natural to have him inside her. And there he held her, drowning in her eyes. 'I'd come out of the sea for you,' he whispered. 'I'd come out of hell itself.' And then he was rocking her in his embrace, until she lost herself completely and became only a part of him.

Shortly after dawn, they were packed up and ready to set out. Adam, Ella thought with a certain smugness, looked better than he had in days.

The horses picked their careful way through the creek and galloped up the other side. Ella turned her head for one more glance of that idyllic spot, but it was already hidden in the trees. Sadness filled her, and she knew that she would remember their time here forever.

They rode throughout the day, pausing for a rest at noon, and then off again. Clouds lumbered in from the west, but at this stage only threatened. The rain held off until darkness, when they made their camp in a bleak and lonely spot. And then the wind blew, trying to tear the tent apart, while the horses stood stoically in the meagre shelter of a stunted tree.

They were both very tired, and fell asleep huddled together under the blankets while the rain fell heavily and water seeped through the roof at an ever-increasing rate. By morning, they were both wet and stiff with cold.

'We're getting close to Tea-tree Station,' Adam soothed. 'Harvey'll shelter us for a night or two.'

Harvey, with his toothless smile and his terrible thirst for rum. Somehow, despite his discovery of her at Seaton's Lagoon, Ella couldn't build much faith in Harvey. But there seemed little alternative. At least Adam appeared prepared to rest a while when he reached Tea-tree Station. If only the weather would improve!

But it didn't.

The sky glowered over them for an hour or two, as though its mood was darkening, and then it opened up on them and wept continuously. What hadn't been wet before was wet now. There was nothing for it but to continue on.

They stopped again to give themselves and the horses a rest. Adam wouldn't eat more than a few bites of damper, although the tea seemed to revive him. It was obviously an effort for him to climb back into the saddle. Ella herself felt so weary she could have lain down on the ground and slept for days. But if Adam could climb back into the saddle, then so could she.

They rode on until the hours joined into one, endless and dreary. Eventually the light began to go. Ella could hardly see ahead, and Adam was squinting into the distance. And then suddenly he lifted his head, as Wolf used to, as if he had caught the scent of something familiar. His voice was full of relief. 'There it is.'

Ella felt dizzy with excitement. She peered in the same direction as Adam, but she couldn't see anything special, certainly no signs of habitation. 'How do you know?' she asked him anxiously.

Adam turned. 'I recognise that hill over there. That's a valley to the side. Harvey has his shepherd's hut down there.' He gave a sudden, violent shiver.

'Adam – '

'I'm all right'

'You don't look all right,' she retorted.

He wiped the rain off his face, and managed a grin. 'I've been better. Is that what you want to hear?'

It wasn't really what she wanted to hear, but at least they were in reach of safety and shelter. And

Harvey, she added to herself with a grimace.

They rode on in silence. The hill, which seemed so close, took forever to reach. Ella's body was aching with weariness, but she pushed on. And quite suddenly the hill loomed beside them. Adam, with an effort, spurred his horse.

There was a valley opening up before them, just as he'd said, and within its folds flickered a single light.

Ella found herself laughing with relief, although her eyes were wet with tears. Digging her heels into the weary horse, she sent it galloping down into the valley after Adam. Somewhere along the way she passed him, and so it was Ella who was first to reach the hut.

A man came out, disturbed by the barking of the dogs and the nervous whinnying of the horse. He was carrying a primitive-looking lamp and, in the light of it, Ella saw that even though it was nearly night, he wore a hat. Beneath it, his face was gaunt and hollow with shadows.

'Harvey,' Ella whispered, and smiled at him as though he were the most wonderful sight in the world.

'Hey, matey, yer trespassin'!' Harvey shouted in the gravelly voice she remembered. 'Yer on Tea-tree Station, not the diggin's!'

'I know!' she managed to shout back. She slid down from her horse, and found her legs had no bones in them. She had to cling to the saddle for a moment to prevent herself from falling in a heap on the muddy ground.

Harvey was frowning at her, puzzled at the incongruity of her woman's voice and male clothing. And then his eyes moved beyond her to the man who had just reached them. Adam was swaying on his horse, trying to catch his breath. Harvey took a step, and then another, lifting the lamp so that he could peer into Adam's face.

'Adam?' he burst out. 'Gawd, what's wrong with you, matey? Looks like you've been in a fight.'

'I have,' Adam replied in a hoarse voice. 'Is it all right if we stay a couple o' days, Harvey? We're just about done in.'

An understatement, Ella thought wryly.

Harvey glanced at Ella, and then subjected her to the same inspection with the lamp. His eyes widened. 'Hey! You're the one without the shoes, the one from Seaton's Lagoon.'

Ella laughed, feeling a strange joy that someone ... *anyone* should recognise her. 'Yes. I'm the one you found at Seaton's Lagoon.' She pushed herself away from the horse, her legs able to hold her now. Adam was still mounted, and she knew he would need the support of a strong arm to walk to the hut. 'Can you help us?' she asked Harvey. 'Adam's been ill... and he's in trouble.'

She saw something in Harvey's eyes flicker, something old and wise, and then he was grinning toothlessly. 'Aye well, Adam's always in trouble,' he replied laconically. 'Come on, me friend, let's get you into a warm bed.' He took hold of Adam's reins and led the horse across to the yard.

The shepherd's hut, which had looked like the answer to Ella's prayers from a distance, was rather a disappointment closer to hand. There was a railed yard in ill-repair and propped up in several places. The horse was the one Ella remembered, and still as ugly. Sheep bleated out in the darkness - Harvey's charges - but apart from them and the dogs, the valley was deserted.

'Are you here alone?' Ella asked curiously as Harvey prepared to help Adam down.

'I used to have a mate, but he went to find gold.' Harvey looked surprised that she needed to ask. 'Half the country's gone to find gold. The rest of us just 'ave to carry on best we can.'

Harvey grasped Adam's arm and helped him slide down off the saddle. Adam groaned as he found his feet, and would have buckled, but Harvey's skinny frame was evidently stronger than it looked because he had no trouble in holding Adam upright.

'Careful,' Ella warned. 'He has broken ribs.'

Harvey pulled a face, but merely said, 'Let's get him inside.'

The dogs kept barking, but didn't seemed to want to bite. They were a mangy lot, eyes and teeth gleaming yellow in the lamplight. Ella ignored them, following in Harvey's wake.

The hut consisted of two rooms and was surprisingly clean. The earth floor was swept, and a piece of sacking made do as a mat There was a stretcher bed in the second room and it was onto this that Harvey manoeuvred Adam. Ella came and knelt beside him.

His face looked pinched with exhaustion, and probably pain. 'Just need a bit of a breather,' he muttered, and closed his eyes.

'Can you send for a doctor?' Ella asked more sharply than she meant.

Harvey snorted. 'The nearest doctor's in Melbourne. I can look after him. He probably just needs a bloody good sleep. A couple o' days in bed an' he'll be right. He's a tough one is Adam.'

'He likes to think so,' she muttered.

Harvey gave her one of his gummy grins. 'Looks like someone took a dislike to him.'

'You could say that,' said Ella. 'No doubt he'll tell you himself.'

Harvey nodded. 'We'd better get his gear off. It's wet enough to swim fish in.'

Together, awkwardly, they stripped Adam of his clothing. He neither protested nor seemed much aware of what they were doing. The bandages were grubby now, and damp with rain and sweat.

Harvey clicked his tongue, shaking his head. 'Don't hold much with them things. Had broken ribs meself once, and I reckon the bandages hurt worse 'an the ribs. We'll take 'em off.'

Ella opened her mouth to protest, and closed it again. Perhaps he was right, who was she to argue? And Adam *had* been complaining about the tight wrappings.

Harvey began to unwrap the bandages, his hands surprisingly gentle. Watching him, Ella felt a sudden, overwhelming sense of relief. Harvey knew what he was doing. Adam was right after all.

Harvey poked and prodded the bruised area, causing Adam to groan and push at his hands. But Harvey ignored him, continuing his examination. Then he placed his ear carefully against Adam's chest and listened to him breathing for a long time.

Ella watched anxiously, trying to read the unreadable expression on the man's gaunt face. 'Is something wrong ... inside, I mean?' she asked at last, unable to stay silent any longer.

Harvey shook his head. 'Don't think so. Sounds all right to me.'

Ella's shoulders slumped with relief, and Harvey straightened and gave her a sharp look. 'What are you doin' here with Adam?'

She was too weary to prevaricate. 'We've been together since you found me at Seaton's Lagoon.'

Harvey's eyes narrowed in surprise, and then he grinned. 'Well, it were a lucky thing for yer both, the evenin' I rode that way, eh?'

There was no disputing that. She cleared her throat. 'How long have you known Adam?' she asked, as much to lighten the conversation as from curiosity.

'I've known him since he was a lad. We both come from Sydneyton, ma'am. We both worked for a man called Ollie McLeod.'

Ella looked at him in amazement. 'He's spoken of Ollie McLeod.'

Harvey pulled a face that made him look even more grotesque. 'I bet he 'as. Ollie never liked Adam. The lad was too bright by half, and his ma brought him up to look every man, no matter how high and mighty, straight in the eye.' He hesitated. 'Ollie McLeod's the owner of Tea-tree Station. He owns two properties in Victoria, this one and another up north, on the Campaspe River. I came down here to manage Tea-tree about four years ago, but I weren't much good at it. Took to drinkin' a bit more than I should 've. I ended up out here, shepherdin'. But it's all right, if yer like yer own company.' Harvey was a man who had plummeted in the world, but he seemed philosophical about it.

The fact that Harvey and Adam knew each other

so well surprised Ella – and again that name, Ollie McLeod. His tentacles reached out even this far.

'Adam knew you were here at Tea-tree Station?'

'Aye, he knew. When he came back from California and sailed into Melbourne, he thought o' me. He had news for me, about his ma.'

'That she was dead?'

Harvey flicked her a look and then nodded. 'I knew his ma – we were close at one time. I were sad to hear she were gone. The night that we came across you, Adam'd been out to visit me and was headed back to the Melbourne road. I was goin' with him ... I needed a drink.'

He said it matter-of-factly. There was no subterfuge with Harvey.

'First time I've ever known Adam to take up with a woman as dresses as a man. This a new thing with him, is it?'

'There was a reason,' Ella replied coldly, and then blushed.

Harvey grinned.

Ella followed him into the other room. The fire was alight in the hearth and Harvey set a large pot of stew on to warm, as well as boiling water for tea. Ella drank gratefully of the hot brew, not realising until now that she too was cold and wet. Harvey glanced at her over his shoulder. 'If you want to wrap yerself in this blanket, you can dry yer clothes beside the fire here. I'll just bring in yer gear and see to the horses.'

Ella realised she had forgotten both in the need to get Adam to warmth and safety. She also realised Harvey was giving her a chance to undress in privacy.

When he returned, Ella was well wrapped in the blanket, her wet clothing already steaming. Harvey poured warm water into a mug and added some dried leaves rather like tea leaves but with a bitter aroma. 'Good for near anythin', this medicine,' he told Ella confidently. 'A hawker sold it to me. He were part gypsy and knew all about it.'

Ella sniffed it uncertainly, and thought it smelled a little like sage. 'Do you really think he needs gypsy medicine?' she began cautiously.

But Harvey carried the mug in to Adam, hoisted him into a half-sitting position and began to pour the stuff down his throat before Ella could protest further. Adam coughed and spluttered, and shoved the mug away with surprising strength.

One bloodshot eye opened and glared at Harvey, who smiled at him in a friendly fashion. 'There yer are, Adam. That'll fix yer up in no time.'

'Or kill me,' he muttered. He glanced at Ella, and away again. 'Don't believe anything he tells you,' he warned.

Harvey grinned. 'Sounds like yer feelin' better already.'

———◆———

They stayed at Tea-tree Station for three days, and during that time Adam finally began to mend.

'The Lord loves a sinner,' Harvey said piously, and then spoiled it by grinning his toothless grin.

During the day Harvey was out with his sheep. 'I 'ave to look out for anythin' that could harm 'em. Not that there's much these days. The blacks an' the wild dogs're all gone. Ollie McLeod saw to that.'

By late afternoon Harvey was always back at the hut preparing the evening meal. Ella had tried to help but Harvey preferred his own way of doing things. 'I'm used to bein' on me own,' he told her. 'Last time I went down to Melbourne, the noise drove me half crazy. I was glad to get back here.'

'But you lived in Sydney once,' Ella reminded him.

'Aye, I were a wild boy then. But I've got used to me own company now.'

When they were alone, Ella asked Adam about his time in Sydney with Harvey. 'Harvey looked out for me,' he told her. 'I remember him hidin' me down in the cellar at The Jolly Roger after I'd given some lip to two whalers upstairs.'

'The Jolly Roger?'

'It's a ... a place in Sydney. Ollie McLeod owned it, but Harvey ran it.'

'What sort of place?' Ella asked curiously, wondering why Adam's face suddenly looked so blank.

'Just a place.'

Suspicion struck her. She narrowed her eyes. 'Not a cat-house?'

He blinked, and then laughed. 'Aye, a cat-house! Where did you hear that?'

'From Kitty.'

He tried to look stern, but couldn't quite manage it. 'Well ... Harvey ran it. But it was respectable enough, as these things go.'

'Indeed! You sound as if you know all about them.'

He gave her his innocent look. 'I was only a lad at the time.'

Ella hesitated, and then decided to let the subject lie. She knew from experience that Adam would never tell her anything he didn't want her to know. 'Did Ollie McLeod own many cat-houses?'

His smile told her he was aware she had decided to let him off. 'Aye, all over Sydney. He owned drinking dens, pawn shops ... anything that made money. He owned a couple o' ships. And land ... lots of land.'

'And he owns Tea-tree Station?'

Adam grimaced. 'We'll be gone tomorrow. I don't expect to run into him, although Harvey says he was down here a month or so ago, checking up on things. He likes doin' that - arriving suddenly, so he can catch everybody napping. I'll be glad to get off his land.'

'Why do you hate him? I can understand dislike, Adam, but your feelings seem ... excessive.'

Adam hesitated, and Ella realised he was deciding whether or not to tell her the truth. When he looked up at her, the expression in his eyes was a mixture of bitterness and bewilderment. 'I found out something about him, from ma. Something I couldn't believe at first. I dismissed it, and tried to forget it. But it played on me so much ... ma was dead then, and I couldn't ask her any more questions. No one else knew the truth of it, apart from Ollie McLeod. One day I couldn't stand it any more - I went and asked him.'

Adam stared at the wall opposite him. A flicker of sunlight from the narrow window played over his still face. 'He looked at me like I was something that'd gone off. Rotten meat, maybe. I knew then it was true, but that it meant nothin' to him. And now I hate him.'

Ella touched his arm gently. 'What was it you learned, Adam?'

He glanced at her, and found a smile. 'Ma was feeling maudlin. She knew she was dyin' by then. She said to me, "If only your father'd taken you in hand.""

'"Me father was a sailor," I reminded her, laughing. But she gave me a look, as if I knew nothing. '"No," she said. "Your father's Ollie McLeod. I met him here in Sydneyton - he came to see me every Friday. But when he knew you were on the way, he didn't come no more.""

Again Adam paused, remembering. 'He paid her off. And later, when she asked ... begged, he gave me some work. But I reckon it was only to have her beholden to him. To lord it over her, the way he liked to lord it over everyone. I never meant anything to him. I was a convict's bastard. I was nothin' ...'

It explained the bitterness she had sometimes sensed in him. And his single-minded ambition to outshine Oliver McLeod.

'Does Eben know?' Ella asked finally.

Adam shook his head. 'Eben believed what ma told us when we were little lads. I was a man grown when she told me the truth.'

'Why hadn't she told you before?'

'She said I wasn't the only by-blow Ollie had. He'd never acknowledged any of them. So she thought it was better I didn't know. In case I expected somethin' of him. Better I make me own life. Ollie'd come from nothin' and she believed I could too.'

'Does Harvey know?'

Adam shrugged. 'He might o' guessed. He and me ma were pretty thick at one time.'

'You're Oliver McLeod's son.' The son of one of the most powerful men in Sydney. Despite his hatred of his father, must not Adam sometimes dream of what might have been? Ella herself had wondered what Adam could have become, with education, with opportunities ... Different certainly, but would she still have loved him as much?

'I don't think of it so much now,' Adam went on quietly. 'When I went to California I was full of it. I wanted to come back rich so I could go up to Ollie and say: "See, I don't need you." But after a few days up to me waist in freezing water, lookin' for gold, I knew if I was going to do it, it had to be for meself, not Ollie.'

She leaned forward and kissed his lips softly. 'I'm glad I found you.'

'I thought *I* found *you*,' he whispered, and pulled her into his arms.

———————

The only other thing of any importance that occurred while they were at Tea-tree Station concerned the bottle given to Ella by Paddy.

She had found it, forgotten, at the bottom of her pack, and brought it to show Adam. 'We'll never see Mikey to give him this,' she said, a little guiltily. 'I shouldn't have taken it.'

'Didn't he say you could have it if Mikey didn't want it?' Adam retorted. 'Perhaps he wanted you to have it all along.'

'Why would he want me to have it?'

Adam gave her a crooked smile, and took the bottle from her hands, weighing it thoughtfully. It was dark, opaque, and the stopper was old and stuck fast. He wrestled with it for quite some moments before it came free. And then he tilted the bottle over his palm.

The gold dust ran out like nectar, gleaming softly and seductively, filling his cupped hand. Ella couldn't speak a word.

'It was for you all along, love,' Adam murmured. 'He just didn't want the others to get suspicious. I don't know if Paddy's got a mine, but he's been doin' some panning somewhere.'

'I never thanked him,' she whispered. 'I should have been kinder to him.' She had given him so little, and Paddy, in return, had given her so much.

But Adam wasn't listening. 'There's enough in here to give us both a start, Ella. That's all we need ... a start.'

CHAPTER 25

*S*HE HAD ALMOST DIED.
Death had brushed her cheek with icy fingers. But he hadn't taken her. For some reason she had been spared. And so she lay in her soft bed, in the hushed silence of her sick room.

It had happened so suddenly. One moment she was carrying the child, and the next ... the blood, and the pain. And now she lay in her soft bed, empty.

Catherine sat with her, stroking her hair as if she were a little girl. 'There'll be other babies.'

But Ella wondered if she could go through this again. Her husband had married her to give him an heir, and she had failed him. He had never loved her.

'There, there, darling,' Catherine murmured.

And she clung to that warm, loving voice as if it were a lifeline.

Melbourne was busier than Ella had ever imagined. The gold rush had turned a village of muddy streets - more like ploughed fields, really - into a boom town. Ella saw miners in cabbage-tree hats and clay-covered boots swaggering in the streets. One pair was nonchalantly wiping the mud off their boots with bank notes. New arrivals gazed at them in utter fascination. 'Gold,' they were saying.

'Gold!' Until the very air seemed to buzz with it.

Shop windows displayed artistic tableaus of shovels, picks, pistols and other digging paraphernalia; some even had piles of gold nuggets to add authenticity. One wooden building, crammed between two others, proclaimed itself an *American Barber's Shop*, and flew the flag of that country above the door. Further down the street, a tavern flew a Union Jack just as proudly. Two men in loose tunics and trousers, with long pigtails down their backs, stood silently waiting their turn at a water cart. The Chinese were so very different from everyone else that Ella turned to stare.

Persons of all classes and dress went about their business. The streets were full of vehicles and horses, churning in the mud. Pedestrians had to use long bridgelike planks to cross from one side of the street to the other. A carriage and four horses, with one of the famous wedding parties aboard, clattered by at full pelt. They had all the trimmings: the bride in her white lace and orange blossom, the groom with his white kid gloves and a bottle of champagne in one hand.

'Are they really married, or just pretending?' Ella asked Adam.

'Could be either. It's the show they like. When they've gone from poverty to riches with one swing of their picks, it goes to their heads.'

Channelling her thoughts along more practical lines, Ella wondered where she and Adam were going to stay while they were in Melbourne. The place was full to bursting, and Adam told her that the inns were so crowded they were using the stables as additional lodgings, charging extra for straw!

For those with no other option, there was unoc-
cupied or waste ground on which to pitch tents ...
the rest walked the streets, and often slept in them.

Ella, in her male attire, had begun to feel very
comfortable. It was so much easier to travel about
as a man. As long as she remembered to slouch
and keep her head bowed, no one looked hard
enough to recognise that she was a woman. It was
like being invisible. Perhaps that was why Margaret
Catchpole had done it - she had become invisible
...for a little while.

Adam led Ella up Bourke Street, past shops selling
tin pans, kettles, mining tools and clothing. Where
Bourke Street intersected with Queen Street,
and for some way beyond, were the horse-deal-
ing yards. The air bubbled with deals being struck,
while sharp-eyed men gauged the size of their customers' purses.

'I'll only be a moment.' Adam had dismounted,
and now handed her his horse's reins to hold. 'I
want to see the lie of the land.'

He walked over to a group engaged in an auction. Ella saw him speaking to one man here and
another man there. He moved on to other groups,
conversing briefly in each. Ella's eyes wandered
over the busy, noisy yards. Some of the livestock
on sale looked rather suspect. One old nag, leaning against the railings, seemed in danger of falling
over, while another appeared completely unbroken, rolling wicked eyes.

Suddenly it occurred to her that her own mare
might be here - the one she had ridden south with
Ned and lost at Seaton's Lagoon. She intensified
her study of the busy scene, but could see no grey

mare. As her eyes shifted about, they were held momentarily. She had a glimpse of black hair and beard. But it was gone too swiftly.

And then Adam had returned to her side, and she forgot everything else.

'This'll take a while,' he said, resting his hand on her knee. He inspected her pale face. 'You look done in. I'll get us a room first, then I can come back.' He winked at her. 'Sellin' horses takes a certain amount of cunning.'

Ella gave him a doubtful glance. 'Surely rooms are rather difficult to find?'

Adam looked smug. 'I've just heard about one that's empty.'

The inn was only a short distance away, still in Bourke Street. Inside, the proprietor left his rowdy customers to ask their business. His quick eyes took in at a glance that they were from the gold fields.

'A room? Well, you're in luck, sirs. I do 'ave one as it 'appens.'

Ella stared at Adam in amazement, but he only smiled. The proprietor was busy finding the key, and boasting that his wife had just changed the linen for the week.

'Do they only change it once a week?' Ella whispered to Adam appalled.

'Probably only once a month,' he retorted. 'He's havin' us on.'

They climbed the creaky staircase, one following behind the other because it was so narrow. 'I thought you said rooms were hard to get,' Ella said to Adam, as they reached the head of the stairs.

He gave her one of his innocent looks. 'Usually they are. It just so happened the man who'd paid for this one didn't need it anymore.'

'Didn't need it?' She was really puzzled now, and the speculative expression in his eyes made her uneasy. 'Why not?'

'Well ... he died.'

'You mean, he died in our bed!' she squeaked.

'Aye. Died in the night. They only found him late this morning. Not a mark on him, and hadn't been sick a day in his life. He was a friend of one of the men I was talking to at the horse yards. He said he didn't think the room had been taken yet ... people are funny about sleepin' on a dead man's sheets.'

'I'm not surprised.' Ella shivered. 'No wonder the landlord made such a fuss about having changed them!'

'Should I have said no?' he was watching her, ready to turn back down the stairs if that was what she wanted.

Ella sighed and shook her head. Anything was better than sleeping on the street. Even a dead man's bed. Anyway, she told herself firmly, he was probably a perfectly respectable fellow, who had just had the misfortune to...to die. She swallowed. 'I hope he was a *nice* man,' she murmured, and frowned at Adam when he laughed.

The room was small but it contained a reasonable-sized bed, a wash-stand and a chair. A narrow window overlooked Bourke Street, and Ella could see across to the signal on Flagstaff Hill with its flying pennants announcing which ships were in port.

'Will you be all right?' Adam was already at the door.

Ella glanced at the bed, but it looked innocent enough. No imprints of bodies in the mattress, no suspicious stains on the quilt. In fact, it was probably the cleanest room in the inn! 'Yes, of course I'll be all right.'

'I'll unload our gear and get someone to carry it up. Maybe I can sell the tent and a few other things we won't be needing again.'

'Could you ask them to send up some hot water? I'd like to have a wash.'

'I thought you liked cold water ... the colder the better.'

She felt a curl in her stomach. 'You won't be long, will you?' she asked in a soft, low voice.

The laughter left his eyes, replaced by something even warmer. 'You can be sure of it,' he told her with certainty, and closed the door.

The hot water arrived in due course, and Ella washed herself thoroughly and then brushed her hair free of dust and debris. Finally, she shook her clothing until it was as clean as was possible in the circumstances. She was tempted to climb into bed and wait for Adam there. The wantonness of such an action made her blush, but she would still have done it had it not been for the fact that a man had lately died there. Perhaps when Adam returned she would be able to put that from her mind. But not yet.

The sounds of the inn drifted up to her, waxing and waning. Now and again a horse galloped wildly past as a prospective buyer from the horse yards tried before he bought

The day was ending, gusts of cold rain rattling against the narrow window, when Adam finally returned. He shivered as he closed the door, and when Ella flung herself into his arms, his clothing felt chilled and his lips were cold.

She helped him off with his jacket. But before she could fold it, he had slipped his arms about her and pulled her down onto the bed. She tried to protest, but he kissed her, rolling her over so that she was beneath him.

'I missed you,' he said, smiling down at her.

'Did you?' she whispered.

Bending his head, he took her mouth in a long, passionate kiss. And then he was undressing her, and she was undressing him. She didn't even give the dead man a thought, for they were celebrating life and not death as Adam spent himself in her body, and she clung to him as if she would never let him go.

A long time later, Adam pulled her more firmly against his side and said, 'I got a decent price for the horses.'

'I'm glad,' Ella murmured, her eyes closed. Her face was resting in the warm hollow of his shoulder. Her hand slipped across the muscle of his chest and stopped above his heart to feel it beating.

'It's enough to get us to Sydney, at any rate. I'll find us a passage tomorrow. The sooner we're on our way the better.'

'Will I be a woman again?' she asked. 'I quite enjoy being a man.'

He laughed. 'I think it's safer for you to be a man, at least until we get to Sydney. If anyone's looking for the lovely Mrs Seaton, they'll find only old Fred with his bandy legs and smelly- Ow!'

She had pinched him.

Adam gave a mock growl and pinioned her hands above her head. But whatever he meant to do, he changed his mind and kissed her instead.

'Did you see a grey mare at the yard?' Ella asked finally and a little breathlessly.

He touched her brow very gently, smoothing away the frown. 'No. I didn't see Bess either.' His voice was casual, but she knew him too well to be fooled. And then the memory of Bess and Adam's attempts to start a store sent her thoughts from the past into the future.

'Adam, what do you mean to do once we reach Sydney?'

'Perhaps I'll buy another cart and horse and head off for the Turon diggings.'

Ella stared at him in disbelief. 'You mean ... you mean, you *liked* being in that cart, with Bess, and the rain and the ... the mud and...'

He laughed, doubling over with mirth. 'Oh, Cinderella!' he gasped at last. 'Your face ...' He took a breath, cleared his throat, and wiped away his tears. He grew serious. 'No, love. It wasn't so much that I liked it. But I was me own man, do you see? I answered to no one.'

'I see.' And she did. He was an independent man. But could she do all that again? Ride in a cart, through the rain and mud? Could she sleep in a tent, on the hard ground, and eat mutton and damper and stewed tea?

His breath brushed her cheek, and she turned and found him very close to her, his eyes searching hers. 'I'm not asking you to do that,' he said very softly. 'I'd never ask you to do that again.'

'You don't have to,' she retorted, her voice sharp

to hide the tears. 'I'd do it anyway. I'd do anything to be with you.'

Adam had expected her to refuse him, and her answer took him by surprise. For a long moment he did nothing apart from stare at her, seeking the truth behind her words. And when he realised she meant what she said, he smiled. It was a smile full of love and pride, and it took her breath away.

The pounding on the door came so suddenly and so loudly it sounded like gunshots.

Ella jumped, half sitting up, and Adam swore and leapt out of bed, pulling on his moleskins. 'If it's the Joes,' he hissed at her urgently, 'we're from Tea-tree Station, in town on a binge.'

The pounding came again, making the whole door frame rattle as if it would cave in. Ella felt Adam's hands painfully tight on her arms and realised he was standing over her, speaking to her. 'Ella!' he said, and shook her urgently. 'Listen to me. I said, if I let 'em take me, they might leave you be.'

She shook her head violently.

'Ella–'

And then a voice came muffled through the wood. 'Adam, boyo, let me in!'

It was more like a low growl than a voice, but Ella recognised it. Shock held her tongue, but she turned to Adam with wide eyes. He was staring blankly at the door. 'I meant to tell you ... at the horse dealers' yard ... I thought I saw Eben. I thought I was wrong. Oh Adam, don't let him in!'

But he met her anxious eyes and smiled wryly. 'How can I do that, Ella? He's me brother.' He took a deep breath and went to open the door.

Eben stood in the passageway, big and dark, with his wolf's smile gleaming through his black beard. He was wearing a brown coat and breeches, both well made, with a yellow silk scarf at his throat, and high-cut black riding boots on his feet. He looked like a miner who had struck it rich and wanted every man to know it.

'What are you doing here?' Adam asked sharply, standing in the doorway and effectively blocking Eben's entry. He was wearing only his moleskins, his fair hair straggling untidily about his shoulders. The bruising on his ribs had begun to blend into his sun-browned skin.

'Is that any way to greet yer brother,' Eben retorted, still grinning. His gaze slipped over Adam's head to Ella, huddled in the bed. His grin grew even more wolfish. 'Hello there, Adam's wife.'

She said nothing.

'What are you doing here?' Adam asked again, but there was a new urgency in his voice, as if he sensed something wrong.

'Nancy and me, we've been up north,' Eben answered him conversationally. 'Thought we'd go overland to Sydney.'

'Why didn't you then?'

Eben winked. With a sudden movement, he pushed Adam hard on the shoulders. Adam fell back involuntarily, letting his brother into the room. 'Gettin' slow, boyo,' Eben mocked. 'Or are you just tired out?' He strode across the room, glancing about in a curious fashion, before coming to a halt beside the bed.

Adam followed him, and faced him, frowning. He was standing in the wan light of the narrow window, and for the first time Eben seemed to notice his brother's bruises. 'You been in a fight or something? You look different.'

Adam shook his head impatiently. 'There was some trouble, but it's all fixed now. Are you going to tell me why you didn't go overland to Sydney, Ebenezer?'

'Why? Aye, well, something happened. A bit o' luck, you might say. We came across a station, up on the Campaspe River, called Lochlyn.' He looked intently at Ella as he said it, but she did not move. 'They was in a terrible state up there. Seems the lady of the house was a bit touched. Sweet as an angel, they said she was. But her and the master had a bit o' a to-do, and she bolted. Cleared right out. When we got there, they'd been lookin' for her for weeks and hadn't got scent o' her. It was like she'd died and gone to heaven.'

Suddenly the bed was not so warm. Ella felt a coldness creeping over her, numbing her, like some awful paralysis. Lochlyn, he had said. Lochlyn. It rang in her head like a poem or a song. She reached up to push her hair out of her eyes, and found her hand was trembling.

'The people at Lochlyn told us that the lady's husband had left and gone back to Sydney. They'd both come down from Sydney, you see, and he had pressing business back there. He'd left the finding of his wife to them, and they hadn't found her.'

'Is this getting us anywhere?' Adam asked evenly. He was watching his brother, but Ella knew his attention was on her, sensing her fright and her growing awareness of what was to come.

'Patience now, brother! I'm gettin' to the point.

It's better if I tell you everything, so's you'll under-stand me point o' view. Where was I? Oh, yes, the husband wanted his wife found. But he didn't want no fuss. He didn't want it spread about that his wife had bolted – embarrassing for him, I reckon. He wants her found, but quiet like, and returned to him. And he'll pay well for any information.'

Eben turned and looked at Ella, and his dark eyes locked with hers. At the corner of her vision, she sensed Adam's step closer, but she couldn't look away from Eben.

'What was this lady's name?' She heard her own voice, like that of a stranger.

Eben tucked his fingers into his belt and leaned back on his heels, completely at ease. But Ella had seen Adam do that and she knew it was a front. Eben was not easy at all.

'They said it was Mrs McLeod. Eleanor McLeod.' He grinned. 'And do you know a funny thing, Adam's wife? She looks just like you.'

The paralysis had taken over her whole body, and Ella knew she could not move a muscle. From far away, she heard Adam say, sharp and hard: 'McLeod?'

Eben turned to him with a laugh. 'Aye, I thought that too, little brother. Ollie McLeod! And this is Ollie McLeod's wife. Now there's a man with some brass! Think what he'll pay to have his wife back, all safe and quiet like?'

But he was watching Adam carefully, and Adam knew it. He said nothing.

'So Nancy and me,' Eben went on, 'when we heard, we just set off back the way we'd come, boyo, to find you and your *wife*.'

'You don't know it's me,' Ella burst out. But her

voice sounded small. The darkness within her was churning around and around. Mrs McLeod, Mrs Ollie McLeod, Eleanor McLeod. No wonder the name Adam had given her pleased her. It was so close to her real name.

And then, the thought she had been shielding herself from, the worst thought of all: I am the wife of Adam's father.

She put her head in her hands. She felt ill. 'Oh God,' she whispered. Adam's hand closed on her shoulder, and she tried to concentrate on the feel of it, steadying herself, as if she were Maryanne down a hole, drowning, and he were trying to save her.

Eben laughed. 'We know it's you,' he answered her. 'Even if you don't remember it. Nancy told me you'd lost your past, Adam's wife. Only you're not Adam's wife, are you? You're Ollie McLeod's wife.'

'Maybe she just looks like this Eleanor,' Adam began, and there was a desperate note in his voice Ella had never heard before.

Eben sighed. 'Just listen, will you, Adam? Now I only know your wife's story from what Nancy's told me. Maybe I'm wrong ... but here goes.' He began to tick off the points on his fingers. 'Your wife here was travellin' south from the direction of Bendigo. Mrs McLeod was travellin' south from Lochlyn on the Campaspe, which is north o' Bendigo. Your wife had a servant with her called Ned. Mrs McLeod left with a servant called Ned. Your wife had a red cloak. Mrs McLeod was wearin' a red cloak when she left. Your wife was ridin' a grey mare. Mrs McLeod was ridin' a grey mare ...' He gave up on his fingers. 'Seems like pretty good odds to me, brother.'

Adam said nothing, but his hand, still resting proprietarily against the bare flesh of Ella's shoulder, spoke for him.

'I know it's a bit of a blow,' Eben went on, sympathetically. 'I'd be pissed off if I found out me wife was already shackled to someone else. And she's a sweet armful, too.' He sighed.

Ella felt sicker than ever. He was pretending he cared, but he didn't. She already knew what he was going to say, but still she asked the question. 'What are you going to do?'

'What are *we* going to do?' a voice echoed from the doorway.

Startled they all looked up into Nancy Ure's vicious black eyes. Like Eben, she was dressed well. She wore a dark green woollen skirt and a tight, dark red jacket. The bonnet on her head was red too, giving her an almost jaunty air. Only her eyes gave her away for what she was.

'What are we going to do?' Nancy repeated, sounding amused. 'Why, we're going to take you home to your husband, me lady!'

'No.'

Ella and Adam spoke the word at the same time.

'Oh come now, Adam,' Nancy sighed, and walked towards him with a distinct sway to her hips. 'You can be in this with us if you want. We're not greedy, are we, Eben? We'll share the reward. Why do you want to make trouble for yourself? They're plenty of other sluts in the sea.'

'No.' He said it quietly enough, but he meant it.

Nancy's mouth tightened with anger. Eben interrupted before she could give vent to it. 'You're a wanted man yerself, Adam,' he reminded his brother quietly. 'We found out that much while we were lookin' for you. The traps on Bendigo are runnin' around like ants in a thunderstorm because o' you. There was even some talk o' murder.'

Adam's hand tightened on Ella's shoulder, but his face betrayed nothing. 'What's a bit o' talk?' he said dismissively. 'There was some talk in Sawpit Gully that Nancy tried to burn a man to death.'

Nancy shrugged impatiently. 'As you said what's talk? I'm not interested in that.'

'I gave you the warning that night at Sawpit Gully,' Adam went on. 'I stayed behind. Are you tellin' me now that that counts for nothing with you?'

Eben shifted uncomfortably. 'He did stay behind, Nance,' he murmured. But Nancy shot him a furious look and he said no more.

'You owed me that, Adam, for what you'd done to me. This is different.'

'Like hell it is!'

'She's Oliver McLeod's wife – '

'She's *my* wife.'

Nancy opened her mouth, and closed it again. But she didn't back down before the anger in his eyes.

'I saw you at the horse yard, didn't I?' Ella said suddenly, watching Eben.

The big man nodded, and grinned at Nancy. 'She's the brains! When we'd got to Bendigo and asked around and couldn't find you, I would 've given up. But Nancy worked it all out. She kept at them Jardines until they told her what she wanted to know. And then she asked in Golden Gully, and kept askin' until she found them friends o' yours.

When they heard I was your brother, they couldn't tell us enough. We knew you were going to Melbourne then, and that you'd probably go slow. So we rode quick. Nancy said you'd have to sell the horses to get money to pay for the boat. So we set a watch on the horse yards, and waited. And here we are.'

Adam shook his head. 'Just as well the police aren't as smart as you, Nancy. I'd be dancin' at the end of a rope.' There was a note of wry humour in his voice.

Nancy smiled back. 'I know you, Adam, that's all. I know how your mind goes. It's easy, when you know how someone's mind goes.'

His smile turned down. 'Then you'll know I'm not going to let you take Ella.'

Nancy was still smiling. 'You can bring her to Sydney yourself. I'm offerin' you that, Adam. You can travel with her ... use her ... say goodbye, like.'

'No.'

Nancy sighed and shook her head; her smile had finally vanished. 'Well, I'm sorry for that.' Her eyes flicked back over his shoulder.

Suddenly Ella knew what was coming. Eben moved, one hard swing to Adam's head. Whatever it was he had in his hand, it had the desired effect. Ella opened her mouth to scream, but it was already too late. Nancy was on her. The other woman's strong fingers pressed against her mouth so hard her lips cut against her teeth. Beside the bed, Adam lay on the floor, unmoving.

Ella began to struggle even more furiously, but Nancy held her, enjoying the cruelty of her hold. 'He's not dead,' she hissed. 'But he will be if you scream. Do you hear me? If you scream, we'll *have* to kill him.'

That was when the fight went out of her.

Nancy knew it and, with a sound of disgust, let her go. Eben had stooped down to check on his brother, and now he straightened. 'He's out to it. But it won't be for long – he's got a head like a rock.' His dark eyes slid to Ella. 'We've got to get her out o' here before he wakes up fightin'.'

'I'm not going anywhere without Adam,' Ella announced, her voice shaking. She tasted salty blood from her cut lips and wiped it away impatiently with the back of her hand.

'Yes you are,' Nancy retorted. 'An' when we're outside, if you start screamin', or tryin' to get away, we'll send word to the police where he is. Don't you think they'd be interested to hear that piece of information, me ladyship?'

There must be a way out, Ella thought. There must be something I can do. Her mind darted back and forth, searching for that solution. And Nancy just stood there and waited, watching her, enjoying seeing the trap closing, watching Ella run out of hope. As soon as Ella dropped her head into her hands, the other woman set to work.

'Get dressed!' she snapped and, picking up Ella's discarded clothing, threw it at her.

Slowly, her fingers still numb and clumsy, Ella began to pull on her woollen shirt and trousers. She hardly knew what she was doing. All she could think was that she was leaving him, and there was nothing she could do to stop it. They were taking her back to her past, the past she had longed for so passionately ever since she awoke at Seaton's

Lagoon.

Only now she didn't want to go.

Once out of the bed and dressed, Ella knelt by Adam's side. He was breathing steadily, as if he was asleep. She put her hand on his face and absorbed his warmth. She felt as if to leave him was to die. Like the man who had had this room before them, her heart would simply stop. But if she didn't go quietly with Eben and Nancy, it was Adam who would die. Nancy had said so, and Ella believed her.

'Come on,' Eben pulled her arm, though not roughly. 'There's a schooner sailin' for Sydney at high tide. You're in luck, Mrs McLeod. If we'd had to let that one go, we'd have had to wait three more days and - '

But she didn't care about that. 'What about Adam?' she asked, cutting him short.

'He'll be all right. He'll come round in a little while. Have a bit of a headache, but that's all. He'll have to wait three days to follow ... if he wants to. By then it'll be too late.'

No rescue at the final moment then. No fairy-tale ending. Adam would come to and she would be gone, and he would know that he could never catch them in time. She would be back with her husband, where she belonged.

And yet, in her head, Ella heard Adam's voice.

I'd come from the sea for you. I'd come back from hell itself...

CHAPTER 26

———◆———

*T*HE DOCTOR HESITATED, WATCHING HER, *and then decided upon a soothing tone. 'You need rest and quiet, Mrs McLeod. I think it best if you disassociate yourself from the places you ...er, you associate with this tragedy.'*

Beside her, Ollie said nothing, but his mouth tightened impatiently. He was bored with doctors and illness - he was never ill himself and found it tiresome in others.

'She can go to Lochlyn,' he said abruptly.

'Lochlyn?' the doctor asked curiously, glancing at the wife to see how she was taking this. But she just sat, mutely, as if they were discussing someone else.

'Lochlyn is a property I own in the Port Phillip District . . . or Victoria, as they call themselves these days,' Ollie explained shortly. That's distant enough from painful associations, I trust?' with a frigid stare at the other man.

'Yes, yes, of course.' The doctor closed his bag, sensing he had said as much as he would be allowed to. 'So, you will be accompanying Mrs McLeod, sir?'

McLeod frowned at the impertinence of such a question. 'I'll stay for a short time. I do an annual inspection of my properties anyway. While my wife's at Lochlyn, I'll be travelling about the countryside.'

'Of course, of course,' the doctor murmured.

'You haven't told me the most important thing,' Ollie

went on, cold eyes hard. 'Will there be any more children, or is my wife now useless to me?'

The doctor stared at him. He had known Ollie McLeod was a plain-speaking man, but this was more than that.

'With rest and care,' he replied, tight-lipped, 'I believe your wife will be able to bear another child.'

Ollie grunted, and the doctor allowed McLeod to usher him from the room. The muffled sound of his footsteps retreated into silence.

Eleanor looked up at last at her husband. He met her eyes, speculative, without emotion. She knew he was calculating how long it would be before he could come to her room again …

Suddenly she was afraid. Perspiration broke out, beading her skin. She had lost her child and nearly died. And none of it mattered to Ollie McLeod. All he cared for was his business, and himself, and her.

'I'm glad she can't give you children,' she whispered, in a voice that chilled even her own blood. 'That makes us even.'

'What are you saying, woman?' Ollie demanded, his accent thicker than usual. 'Are you out of your senses?'

But Ella stared back at him, and watched his face go pale.

———◆———

The schooner *Fair Maid* moved slowly down the narrow channel towards The Rip, and the sea beyond. The grey sky did not bode well for smooth sailing, but the sea was flat, if sullen. Gulls wheeled, seeking fish in the newly churned, milky water. The captain ordered up an extra sail, to catch any faint breeze that might hasten them on their way.

The *Fair Maid* was one of the regular traders plying between Melbourne and Sydney, and had lately arrived with a cargo of cedar and wine. At sixty-five tons, she also carried passengers, as well as the occasional prisoner bound for trial in Sydney. Eben, Nancy and Ella had gone aboard almost immediately, stopping only briefly to collect their luggage and for Ella to change into one of Nancy's dresses.

'You're my sister,' Nancy had instructed her. 'Eben is our brother. Can you remember that?'

Ella hadn't answered, and Nancy had pushed her face closer, threateningly.

'It's not too late to send word to the traps,' she whispered.

So Ella had nodded and gone with them as quietly as a lamb.

Nancy and Ella shared a cabin, with a bunk each and enough room to turn around ... just. Eben slept in the steerage quarters. Their masquerade as brother and sisters seemed hardly necessary. No one was particularly interested, and besides, Nancy kept Ella apart as much as possible.

The captain was a big man with a black moustache rather like a paintbrush. His crew seemed somewhat in awe of him, and went about their work with quick and quiet efficiency. Perhaps it was that awe which had kept them aboard the schooner when so many other sailors had deserted for the goldfields. Ella had seen many ships deserted of crew, riding idle in the bay - clippers, barques, whalers, even steamers.

Ahead, that aptly named narrow entrance to Port Phillip Bay, The Rip, lay calm and relatively harmless. Today Ella found it difficult to believe that many ships travelled from far ports, only to founder here so close to their destination. But she had heard from Nancy just how dangerous The Rip could be.

'When the tide's running, it can take a ship and draw it onto the rocks without the crew bein' able to do a thing about it,' she had said, with relish. 'There're reefs under the water like shark's teeth, ready to rip the bottom out.'

Nancy had been trying to frighten her, she knew that. But now, as she looked out over The Rip and beyond to the sea, Ella couldn't help but remember her words.

Deliberately, she turned and looked the other way, far down the bay, where Melbourne drowned in a dream of gold. Adam was back there, and her heart ached as the cold wind dried her tears. Should she have fought and struggled? Should she have ignored Nancy's warnings, and tried to remain with Adam? But Nancy was not to be taken lightly – she knew now that Nancy was capable of anything.

In her mind, Ella saw Adam coming to, and finding her gone. He would search, and his search would take him to the port and the *Fair Maid*, and by then Ella would be far away.

And it would be three more days before Adam could follow her.

'I'll be with my husband by then,' Ella whispered into the salt wind.

Ollie McLeod ... Why could she not remember him? What had they argued about at Lochlyn? Why had she bolted? Why had he left before she was found, and returned to Sydney? Why had he asked for her to be found without a fuss - any other husband would have raised a hue and cry all over the country! Still so many unanswered questions. More than before when she had known nothing of her past... Unease caught at her, tugging like the freshening breeze at her hair. I will know soon enough. I will know everything, soon enough.

———◆———

They made quick time. The sullen sky had foreshadowed blustering winds and squalls, which pushed Fair Maid up the coast like a sleek bird. Ella was meant to keep to her cabin anyway, but the weather conditions made that ordeal much easier. Only occasionally was she allowed to venture out on deck, with Nancy or Eben at her side, to feel the tug of the cold ocean beneath her and the sting of spray in her face. When Nancy went out alone, she locked the cabin door behind her.

The other passengers were not an overly curious lot. Eben described them to her: a newly married couple who blushed every time he met them face to face, a middle-aged couple who appeared to have fallen on hard times and resented it, and a merchant on business. Nancy and Eben and Ella aroused no particular comment, apart from the usual questions about where they were from and where they were going. Nancy dealt with these inquiries. They were going home to Sydney, she said, and her black stare offered no further encouragement. Most of the passengers withdrew at this point. The wife fallen on hard times was the only one who didn't.

'You have a family in Sydney?' she asked of Nancy, with a nervous laugh. 'Surely, you have a husband waiting for you there? And your sister ... so pretty. I cannot believe all the gentlemen are not sighing for her return.'

She was silly, but Ella could feel it in her heart to be sorry for her as Nancy smiled a wicked smile. 'I'm a brothel keeper,' she replied. 'My "sister" here is my latest acquisition. An' I reckon you're right about those gentlemen!'

The woman looked at Ella, shocked beyond words, and backed away. She did not speak to them again, and every time she passed them thereafter she turned her face the other way.

It wasn't so bad during the days - Ella could get through the days - but she dreaded the nights. Then she was alone with Nancy in their cabin, and it was Nancy's pleasure to torment her. The torture wasn't physical, Nancy was too clever for that. She used words to make Ella's life a misery.

'I want to tell you a bedtime story,' was how she would begin. And then she would go on, her voice winding a story around Ella despite her determination not to listen. Ella never replied to her, she had sworn she never would. She pretended she didn't hear, that she didn't care, and hoped that perhaps Nancy would stop.

'He don't want *you*,' Nancy laughed one night. 'He never wanted *you*. It's me he dreams of at night. Me and San Francisco, and the inn by the waterfront. He was my man then. He wanted to please me. And oh, he did ... he did.'

Ella had sworn to herself she would never answer

Nancy's jibes, but this time she couldn't help it. The words spilled out of her, unstoppable, into the darkness where Nancy lay.

'Dreams?' she said. 'He doesn't have dreams about you. He has nightmares! He killed a man for you, he told me so. He hates you for it. He hated you then, and he hates you now.'

The waves slapped against the hull and the schooner creaked like an old woman rather than a fair maid. A sailor pounded across the deck above, hurrying about his business. But Ella heard none of that, all she was aware of was Nancy's silence.

'You're frightened,' Nancy said at last, and her voice was soft and almost sweet. 'You don't understand. You think love is like what he feels for you ... but your love is like brandy that's been watered down. He don't feel that for me, I grant you. What he feels for me is stronger, so strong it's sometimes near enough to hate. But it's love all the same.'

Ella said nothing, and this time the silence went on unbroken. It's not true, she thought calmly. I know it's not true. When he held me and made love to me, it was something wonderful. He doesn't love her. He *can't* love her.

But Nancy Ure's words hurt her all the same, and frightened her. And now she couldn't rid herself of them. Whenever she thought of Adam, she thought of Nancy.

———◆———

She was in a dark place.
Not the pine forest this time, but the long and narrow passage with the jewelled carpet of red and green and

black. Her bare feet touched its softness, its luxury, but she did not feel comforted. Before her, the light shone from the doorway, and the voices whispered and hummed.

Were they singing?

She was still at Lochlyn. Ollie had been south on business, but he was back again, preparing for his return to Sydney. She had been sleeping and for some reason had awoken and heard sounds. The homestead was dark, apart from the light spilling from the doorway.

She walked on.

What were they saying? She wanted to hear, she was desperate to hear! But at the same time she was afraid. There was a sick feeling in her stomach, and her palms were sweating.

Secrets . . .

———◆———

Of the two of them, Nancy and Eben, Ella preferred Eben. He said little enough to her, but what he did say was not threatening. Ella did not fool herself into thinking Eben was her friend. He, too, was dangerous, but she did not think he was quite in Nancy's league.

One morning, when he accompanied her up onto the deck, she made up her mind to ask him some questions which had been preying on her mind ever since she learned her true identity.

'Did the people at Lochlyn say why I had run away?'

Eben leaned against the railing, watching her with half-closed eyes.

'I can't remember, you see,' she went on, in a gentle voice meant to elicit sympathy. 'It makes it very difficult.'

'I wouldn't worry too much about it, Mrs McLeod. Ollie must want yer back pretty bad to be offerin' a reward. An' we won't tell him about Adam, so he'll never know.'

Ella bit her lip. Adam's name was enough to cause her a stab of longing. But Eben thought she was only concerned about her reputation.

He moved closer to her, dropping his voice.

'If Ollie McLeod knew his wife'd been with another man, he'd have him gelded. I don't want me brother hurt. Do you?'

'Of course not,' she retorted, shaken.

He looked at her a moment, and then gave his wolfish grin. 'Adam wouldn't 'ave been too happy when he woke up and found you'd flown. Did he really think he could keep yer? Keep Ollie McLeod's wife?'

Ella said nothing, staring stubbornly beyond him. The coastline was perfectly visible today, with the rise of mountains further inland.

'Tell me about Ollie McLeod,' she pleaded softly.

'Tell yer what?'

'Anything. You know more than me. You must know how I came to marry him … didn't you ask questions at Lochlyn? Adam didn't even know he was married.'

He looked away from her candid gaze, suddenly uncomfortable. 'Ollie came out to New South Wales around twenty-five year ago and since then he's spent his time draggin' himself to the top o' the pile. The weddin' happened while Adam and me were away. Ollie took a trip over to Scotland to look over some bloodstock for his stables, and found himself a wife while he was there. Seems he'd already had a bit of a tour of Sydneyton, but nothin' took his fancy. He 'ad to have breeding as well as beauty, he said. So he went to find a lady. Aye, a real lady.'

Ella didn't know whether she should be flattered or frightened by the look he was giving her.

'So, he's not young.'

'Not as young as Adam, no,' Eben admitted wryly. 'But he's vigorous enough. He runs his business himself, and they say he hardly sleeps, and even when he does, he has one eye open!'

'Why did he leave me at Lochlyn? I don't under-stand that. It seems like a … a punishment.'

'Well…' Eben cleared his throat, and stared out to sea.

'What happened?' Ella insisted.

'There was a child,' Eben said awkwardly.

Ella felt herself go still, her throat closing so that her voice came out strained and harsh. 'I have a child?' But Eben shook his head. 'No. It were born too soon and died. You were sick from it. *They* said, at Lochlyn, you turned a bit touched … in the head, like. The doctor wanted you to have a holiday, so Ollie took you south with him when he came to look over his properties.'

Tears welled into her eyes. She tried to take in what he had told her. That Ollie McLeod had as much as bought her, like one of his horses. That she had had a child, which had died. That she had been so ill they had considered her touched. Ella thought back over her journey north with Adam – the harsh conditions and the harsh people. A feel-ing of pride filled her. I've changed, she thought.

I'm a different woman to the one who allowed herself to be sold to Ollie McLeod.

And this time I'll fight him.

She realised Eben was watching her, reading her expressions. She cleared her throat. 'This is all very strange. You've given my past back to me, and I'm grateful. But some of it will take a little getting used to.'

Eben laughed sharply. 'Aye, I bet it will!' He handed Ella a handkerchief and she blew her nose. So much had happened to her, and although now she knew what had happened, she still didn't remember it! Suddenly she felt weak with longing ... she wanted to tell Adam, she wanted to be held in his arms and comforted and loved. She wanted him to call her Mrs Seaton, in that respectful voice, with his dark eyes telling her what he would really like to do ...

'Don't be too hard on Nancy.'

The words took a moment to make sense, and then Ella looked up at Eben in amazement. 'Hard on Nancy?' she repeated blankly.

'She has a bitter tongue, I know, but that's only because – '

Ella's voice rose, drowning his out. 'Nancy is an evil woman! At night she ... she tells the most atrocious lies!' More tears stung her eyes, but she blinked them angrily away.

Eben frowned. 'She's had a bad time of it,' he growled. 'She started out respectable enough, and then she married a bad 'un, who took her to San Francisco. When he died, she had to be worse than the rest to keep her head above water. She took a real shine to Adam ... I know, I was there. He has his own way of tellin' the story, no doubt, but I know. Nancy had her heart set on him, and he walked away from her.'

'I won't believe any of that,' Ella said firmly, while underneath her heart was pounding. 'She tried to kill Doctor Rawlins at Sawpit Gully. If he hadn't been called out to a patient, he would be dead now!'

'He informed on her.' Eben gave her a narrow look.

'She was robbing her guests, with your help! You were both breaking the law!'

Eben glowered at her, but he could see the truth of her words, and eventually smiled sheepishly. 'Well, that's fair enough, I can't deny it.'

'And what about Adam? Would Nancy have killed him if she had to? You say she was fond of him. She has a very strange way of showing it!'

'She wouldn't really 'ave hurt him,' Eben muttered.

'I don't believe that, and I don't think you really do either. How long will it be before you do something she doesn't like? What then? Do you think she won't treat you in the same way she treated Doctor Rawlins, and Adam?'

Eben's face was grim, and Ella knew she had made him think of things he did not wish to.

'Let me go,' she whispered suddenly, urgently. 'When we get to Sydney, let me escape. Nancy'll never know. Adam'll find me, I know he will ...'

But he was staring at her in open-mouthed amazement. 'Let yer go? You *are* touched in the head! Come on.' He took her arm in a hard grip. 'You've had enough air for today.' And he hurried her below.

Ollie had taken his sister out riding. Ella, although not well enough for that, felt able to stroll alone in the sweet autumn, watching the station work. It was a long time since she had made such an effort and she was proud of herself.

She thought, life here at Lochlyn homestead moves onward. Everything moves onward, and so must I. She was beginning to feel herself gaining strength in body and mind. She was beginning to turn her eyes from their inward gaze to the outside world.

Catherine helped. She was always sympathetic, always ready to spend her time with Ella. And Ella had grown to love her and depend upon her more than ever. The two women had become almost inseparable, and Ella felt that Ollie looked upon her, his wife, more fondly because of it.

She strolled on, lifting her face to the crisp air. The sound of horses surprised her, and she turned to look. Two young men had ridden in and were dismounting. She hadn't seen them before. She was almost certain that they were strangers. And yet when they strode past her, looking her way, one of them tipped his hat.

'Mrs McLeod,' he said respectfully, but his eyes were corrupt.

Sydney sprawled, white buildings clustered on the hillsides and in the hollows, interspersed with greenery. Larger piles of official buildings stood above businesses and dwellings. Flags flew and the sound of drums rattled out over the water. Ships

waited at anchor or unloaded on the busy wharfs.
As they drew closer, Ella saw that Circular Quay
swarmed with life beneath the shadow of tall
warehouses. A fitful sun shone over the town, flat-
tering it. The craggy, crowded ridge known as the
Rocks looked like a quaint fishing village, some of
its houses perched on the rock face so precariously
they seemed about to drop down into the water.

On one side of Ella, Nancy stared ahead, while
on the other side, Eben lit his cigar with a celebra-
tory air. The voyage from Melbourne had given
Ella time to grow accustomed to many things. She
had accepted that she was Ollie McLeod's wife and
that she had suffered a tragedy. Although she could
not remember, she had accepted, and so that had
enabled her to move forward and concentrate on
her present predicament.

On the dock, a boy was minding a horse. The
animal was restive, the thin legs stamping, the wild
eyes rolling. Ella felt something inside her tense in
sympathy – a hard coil of apprehension.

I am coming home, she told herself. Ollie
McLeod is here, somewhere, and very soon I will
meet him face to face. And I am ready to do so.

Nancy gripped her arm, and Ella realised they
were about to leave the schooner and go ashore.
Their luggage had been loaded into the boat, and
Nancy and Ella followed, with Eben close on
their heels. From the railing above them, the other
passengers watched them leave with expressions
ranging from speculation to relief.

The little boat glided over silver water so smooth
it was like polished glass. All about them other
boats, large and small, were on the move. Light-

ers plied their trade from the bigger ships, while little steamers ploughed back and forth. Emigrant ships rocked gently off Dawes Point, their cargoes already discharged into Sydney, probably bound for the goldfields beyond.

Now that they were so close to their goal, Nancy and Eben grew edgy. Ella saw them watching her, murmuring secrets she could not hear. She supposed she should be frightened but she did not think they would hurt her. They were too greedy for the reward.

Once ashore, Eben found them a cab and they travelled up George Street in style. Despite her apprehension, Ella looked about with interest. George Street, at least, appeared to be lively and full of business. Inns, taverns, shops and offices lined their way, the buildings a mixture of stone and timber, some with ornate verandahs. Like Melbourne there was evidence of the gold rush. The shops displayed the same mining gear and nuggets, and miners swaggered in the universal uniform of moleskins and red woollen shirts.

Eben didn't watch the scenery, he was too tense. He showed it by a series of little movements he repeated over and over again. He adjusted his belt, he smoothed his sleeves, he scratched his nose. Nancy watched him silently, but her black eyes betrayed her contempt.

She doesn't love him, Ella thought. She's using him for her own ends. And I think he knows it, and hopes if he does what she wants she will turn to him eventually. But I don't think she will. Nancy Ure has no softness in her, no compassion, and no gratitude. Adam was right, she preys upon others, sucking all that is good from them.

The cab turned a corner into a narrow lane and thereafter entered a confusing labyrinth. Ella held her breath as the driver twisted and turned his vehicle between buildings that looked as if they had been built at the beginning of time. Now and again she would see the entrance to a dark little courtyard, or some narrow, tunnel-like passage between the houses, where faces peered out at them like rats, waiting for the night. This was a different Sydney from the wharves and George Street with all their noise and bustle. This was Sydney's old face, a stark reminder of a grim past.

'What is this place?' Ella asked, bewildered.

Nancy smiled at her from the shadows. 'This is the Rocks, me ladyship.'

Ella stared. 'But I thought you were taking me home!'

Nancy snorted at her naivete. 'Did you think we'd just turn up at Ollie McLeod's door and hand you over? We'll make sure of that reward before we let him near you.'

Of course! She should have realised they would keep her hidden until a deal was struck. Nancy would trust no one. Nancy would take her time, make sure she got as much money as was possible, before she allowed Ella to be returned to her husband.

There's time for Adam to reach me then! The thought was so loud and frantic, Ella was certain the other two must have heard it. Three days, they had said, before the next ship left Melbourne bound for Sydney. She didn't allow herself to think of the vagaries of the weather. If she could just stay here for three more days, Adam would have a chance of finding her.

Nancy Ure was watching her.

Ella wondered nervously if she could read her thoughts. Anything was possible with Nancy. Ella schooled her face to be expressionless.

'Is it all like this ... the Rocks, I mean?' she asked a little breathlessly.

Nancy laughed scornfully and turned away. The squalor of their surroundings did not seem to affect her at all.

Eben searched in his pocket for another cigar. 'Not all o' it, Mrs McLeod. The nobs 'ave moved in, further up the hill. But make no mistake, there are parts here where you wouldn't walk at night, even if you 'ad an armed guard. So don't go thinkin' you can take a stroll and find yer way home by yerself. You'd never make it.'

The cab slowed to turn yet another corner, and Ella saw one cottage perched up above them on a rocky shelf, looking as if it might tumble down at any moment. Grubby children ran past shrieking and vanished into a dingy looking house.

The cab had negotiated the corner, and they were now in a narrow lane which ended abruptly at a set of stone stairs. The driver drew his horse to a halt. 'This is it, sir!' he called out 'The Shipwreck. I wouldn't have brought you here, but for the fact that you're a gentleman. Nasty place, this. Not very nice for the ladies. Do you want me to wait?'

Nancy laughed. 'A gentleman!' she said in a loud whisper. 'Well, at least we didn't have to walk in the filth.'

Eben gave her a grin, and jumped out. 'No, boyo,

no need to wait. Here's a bit extra, though, for yer trouble. And I've another guinea here if you help with the luggage.' Nancy rolled her eyes as he reached up to hand her down. Ella followed, and at once saw what Nancy had meant about the filth. The lane was paved, but the gutter running down the centre of it was obviously inadequate. Refuse lay along the walls of the buildings either side, washed into untidy heaps by the rain. But it hadn't washed away the smell – Ella's nose twitched – damp and decay, supplemented with stale urine.

Ella turned her face determinedly upwards, towards The Shipwreck Inn. She saw then that the steep stairs were the only way of reaching it, for the two-storey inn had been set into a sheer rock face about thirty feet high. It had been built of the same stone, too, so that if one didn't know better, one would have thought it had grown out of the rock.

Narrow windows of warped glass peered down at them blindly, reflecting the cloudy sky. The only sign of life was a few items of washing hanging limply from a single balcony. The name of the place was printed starkly above the door: The Shipwreck.

Ella let her eyes travel over it again in fascinated horror. Eben was already leading the way up the stairs, while the cab driver set about unloading their bags under Nancy's direction: Ella hurried after Eben.

'Why do we have to stay here?' she asked, sounding more frightened than she liked.

'Not what you're used to, eh?' he asked her. There was a gleam in his eyes she had never seen before. The ring of his boots echoed down into the lane; the sound was eerie and confusing, as if they were hearing a ghost. It frightened Ella even more than The Shipwreck, and made her incautious.

'No, it isn't what I'm used to! I'm sure Ollie McLeod won't be pleased to hear about this. Look at it,' and she waved her arm to illustrate her point. 'It's the most appalling place I've ever seen – '

Her voice trailed off. Eben had narrowed his eyes at her and something in the way he was standing made her suddenly aware of danger.

'Well, I'm sorry about that,' he snarled. 'But this here was near enough to home for me when I was a lad. To be frank with yer, Adam's wife, what pleases Ollie don't count much with me.'

Eben turned and continued up the stairs, his back very straight.

Slowly, Ella followed, realising she had over-stepped herself. At the top it was high enough to see over the roofs to the mirrorlike waters of the harbour beyond. Ella was sure she could taste the tang of salt on her lips.

Nancy had come up behind her, and now tugged roughly at her arm. But Ella resisted. Adam was somewhere out there, on the ocean, on his way to Sydney.

'Come on!' Nancy hissed impatiently, and dug her fingernails into Ella's arm.

Eben had been pounding on the door and now it opened onto a man with a pipe clamped between his teeth. 'Yer business?' he gritted. His expression was mild, but that did not fool Ella. By the look of his battered face, this man had once been a boxer.

Eben gave a savage smile. 'Don't you remember me, Davey? It's Eben, back from California!'

Davey peered at him suspiciously, and then gave

a broad, ugly grin, pushing the pipe to one corner of his mouth. 'Eben! I didn't know you in that
get-up. You're a rich man then, are you?'

Eben winked his answer. 'We're wantin' to stay a
day or two. That all right?'

Davey was still smiling, but his eyes slid beyond
Eben, to his two companions. 'Aye, that's all right.'

He was plainly wondering why Eben, back from
California and with money in his pockets, wanted
to come and stay at The Shipwreck. But it wasn't
wise to ask questions in a place like this, even Ella
could understand that.

'You'd best go in,' Davey said at last, and stepped
aside.

CHAPTER 27

———◆———

IT WAS LIKE STEPPING INTO night. The room was low and wide, a man-made cavern, with benches and tables about the walls and an oil lamp hanging from the ceiling. A few shrivelled old women sat on stools near the fire, shrouded by the smoke of their pipes. Relics from ships hung on the walls, most of them too dirty to recognise. The place smelt overwhelmingly of rum and tobacco and rotten fish.

Even Nancy was taken aback. 'Shipwrecked is right,' she muttered.

'It's gone down a bit over the years,' Eben murmured, with a note of apology. 'It weren't like this in the old days. Then the place was full of laggers and sharps and their doxies, with the blue bottles outside bangin' on the door. There's a stairway cut into the rock at the back. You used to be able to get to it through a secret door. Many a sneaksman took that way out when the thief-takers were on his scent!'

Nancy didn't appear to be impressed by the picture Eben had just painted, and Ella found most of it incomprehensible.

A man was sitting at a table, a tankard before him. He had the most villainous-looking face Ella had ever seen. It was thin and fallen-in, with a nose so broken it was little more than a bump. His eyes were small, round and bloodshot, and he wore rings in his ears and his scant, greasy hair in a pigtail. When he saw the quality of his customers, he lurched to his feet. His blue shirt and white trousers, both extremely grubby, were still recognisable as the uniform of a seaman.

Eben swung down the room towards him, his boots ringing on the floor. He had to duck his head under the beam that held the lamp. 'Yer still here then, Jacko!' he boomed.

Jacko stopped in his tracks, staring intently at the approaching figure, and then he went bowling forward on bowed legs and threw his arms around Eben's waist – which was about as high as the little man could get. Eben reached down and patted Jacko's head fondly.

The crones at the fire glanced up, but none of them spoke. They were like the witches in *Macbeth*, Ella decided, only worse.

Nancy muttered something under her breath and, gripping Ella's arm, followed Eben down the long room.

'You're back?' Jacko was saying. His words were difficult to understand, probably because of his flattened nose. 'Adam too?'

'No, not Adam. He's away about his own business.'

Jacko nodded darkly. 'Aye, he always were. Thought he were too good for us, did Adam.'

Eben laughed uneasily. 'Nah! Yer wrong there, Jacko. It were the ideas ma put into his head. Yer know he was her favourite.'

Jacko thought a moment. 'Always kept herself

nice, your ma,' he allowed. 'Always smelled o' flowers.'

Eben cleared his throat. 'Aye, well, speakin' o' business, how is it these days?'

Jacko's little eyes grew crafty. 'Well enough. I 'ave me regulars, and the sailors still come by to take a look, more for the sake o' the old days, I reckon. We was famous then, and there's still some as remembers. But things is changin', Eben.' He shook his head sadly. 'The nobs further up the hill, they're buildin' their big houses and when they look down on us, they don't like what they see. Some o' the old places are gone already.'

'They'd never knock down The Shipwreck!' Eben cried, genuinely distressed.

'Good thing if they did,' Nancy muttered.

Both Jacko and Eben glared at her suspiciously, but she gave them an innocent smile.

'Aye, things is changin',' Jacko went on after a pause.

'I bet you still got the touch, eh, Jacko? Can you still lift a purse without a wrinkle, eh? Fingers like fish hooks, this boy.' And Eben gave Jacko a rap on the shoulder that made the little man go pale.

'I don't get much practice,' Jacko gasped when he had caught his breath. His gaze darted to the two women and away. 'You got yourself one o' them harems, have you, Eben?'

Eben grinned. 'If only, boyo, if only! No, the truth of it is-' And he stooped and said something quietly in Jacko's ear. The little man tilted his head to one side, and peered around Eben at the approaching women. He nodded wisely. 'I've just the place.'

Eben smiled down at him, and when he turned

and looked at Nancy and Ella there was something new and crafty in his eyes. Ella glanced at Nancy, and realised that she too was made uneasy by this development. Here at The Shipwreck, Eben was on home ground, among friends. Suddenly it was he who was giving the orders and not Nancy.

Ella wondered what Nancy would do. Would she reassert her authority with a few well-chosen words? Or threaten him with reminders of their crimes at Sawpit Gully?

But Nancy did neither.

Deliberately, slowly, she reached up to remove her hat. Her grey hair had been drawn in to a loose chignon, low at her nape, and it had the effect of softening her sharp features. She shook her head, and the hair came free, cascading over her shoulders. Her slanting black eyes lifted and fixed Eben with a bold look.

'We'll put her ladyship in a room of her own,' she said slyly. 'I've a mind for some privacy. What do you say, Eben?'

Eben looked surprised by this new turn of events, but his grin was as lascivious as the gleam in his eyes. He slapped Jacko on the back so hard the little man nearly collapsed. 'Come on, boyo, let's get upstairs!'

The Shipwreck owned nothing so grand as a staircase. Instead, a trapdoor opened up a hole in the ceiling, with a ladder resting against its lip. Nancy sighed but bundled her green skirts tightly at her knees and, holding them with one hand, climbed nimbly through. Eben watched her slim legs disappear through the hole, and then turned to Ella.

Ella looked up into the darkness. 'I'm sure if you took me to my husband right now, he would pay you well,' she began.

But Eben wasn't interested. 'Up!' he snarled. So Ella bundled her skirts up, too, and did her best.

The loft was like a rabbit warren.

Passages ran everywhere, and the light was so poor she could see no more than a few yards in front of her. She supposed the upper storey had been constructed in the same manner as the room below - long and low. But whereas the room below was open and cave-like, there had been partitions added here to make tiny rooms for guests to sleep in. The builder didn't appear to have considered the need for light or fresh air.

And it stank.

'Fifty years o' filth,' Nancy said quietly, looking about with distaste. 'An' he's happy to be home!'

Eben's head appeared through the hole and he climbed out neatly beside them. However, he couldn't straighten to his full height, the ceiling was too low, and he had to stand with his head and shoulders bowed. Jacko had no such problems.

The little man looked even more villainous in the half-light of the loft. He had brought a lamp with him, and it shone outwards in a pool of yellow. Something scuttled into a corner. Ella peered at the casks and boxes stacked untidily among the dust and grime, and saw the gleam of eyes.

'How many rooms do you have up here?' Nancy was asking.

Jacko frowned with the effort of the calculation. 'Ten. But I keep me bits and pieces up here, too.'

'Your bits an' pieces,' Nancy echoed with barely

concealed mockery. 'Do you really have guests sta-yin' up here?'

The little man nodded his head importantly. 'I 'ave some stay overnight, and I charge good rates for the week. Meals as well,' he added proudly.

Nancy shuddered.

Holding the lamp high, Jacko led them down one of the dark, noisesome passages. Ella stumbled after Nancy, with Eben breathing close behind. It was like being caught in a nightmare, she thought. An endless, dark labyrinth leading nowhere, and with no way out. She had had this dream before, and she didn't much relish it being turned into reality.

Ahead of them Jacko made a sound that could have been satisfaction, or perhaps he was just pass-ing wind. He pushed a door, and a room opened up before them. It was very small and poky, but at least it had a window. The light filtered weakly through the dust and dirt, so Ella was able to pick out a narrow bed, a table with a drunken lean to it, a cracked washing bowl and a slop bucket.

'Ah, this looks like your room.' Nancy was obvi-ously enjoying herself now. 'Does the door lock?'

Jacko nodded, his glance flicking from Nancy to Eben and back again. 'There's a bolt on the out-side.'

'What about the window?' It consisted of several small panes of old glass, warped and bumpy. Nancy strolled over to peer outside, rubbing away the dirt with the tip of her gloved finger.

'She'll never get out there,' Jacko replied. 'Too far to drop. She'd smash her head in.'

Ella went suddenly weak in the legs. She felt

Eben catch her elbow, his fingers warm and strong. For a moment she could almost believe they were Adam's, that it was Adam standing behind her.

But it was Eben's voice which said, impatiently, 'She'll be all right by herself. Show us our room now, Jacko.'

Jacko gave him a wink that Nancy wasn't meant to see, and went back into the passage. Eben followed, his hand on Nancy's waist, and the door closed behind them. Ella heard the bolt squeak as they slid it across, and then their footsteps retreated, merging into the general sounds of the place.

Slowly Ella went across to the window and looked out. The little panes were very dusty, and she wiped her hand across them until she could see outside. The warped glass distorted the view, making it wavy, like a scene under the sea.

Below her were the steep stairs and the shadowy lane, with its air of hopelessness. She could see more lanes and passages and steps, winding between steep tenements and little broken cottages. This must be what the 'nobs' further up the hill saw, when they looked out from their fine houses. The Rocks, spilling down the hillside towards bustling George Street, like a dark river of poverty and evil.

Adam had grown up here. His boyhood had been spent in those vile places. But unlike Eben, they had not seeped into his soul. He had risen above the degradation, partly because of his mother and her belief in him, and partly because of his own strength of character.

Ella lifted her eyes from the tangle of the Rocks and looked outwards across the sagging roofs towards the harbour. Ships rocked at anchor, and

Circular Quay thrived. But her eyes moved on, following the bright water. Away past the bush of the isolated North Shore, past Pinchgut and Garden Islands, towards the sea. This was the direction from which Adam would come. When he came. If he came ...

———◆———

'Get her, get her!' The voice was loud and furious. The two men grabbed her arms, dragging her down the bank towards the water. She screamed, struggling, kicking at them with her bare feet - she had lost her shoes back along the track when she and Ned had tried to outride the bushrangers who had waylaid them along the Melbourne road. And then Ned was there, hitting at them, shouting. They dropped her, and she saw them strike at him. One of them swung his pistol with a crunching blow.

There was silence.

'You've killed Ned,' the younger man whispered. 'Ned weren't supposed to die! Ned were supposed to get away, so's he could tell everyone what had happened to Mrs McLeod! How's he gonna tell 'em now?'

The other man shrugged, his eyes already old in his young face. 'It's too late now. Come on, let's get rid of the body.'

Ella crouched on the bank, stunned and horrified by what she had witnessed. They had killed Ned. But something was wrong beyond that fundamental horror. She recognised them. This was not some meaningless robbery and murder, this was planned, and these were Lochlyn men.

She saw them catch up Ned's body and swung it high, out into the water. The splash was like a slap bringing

Ella out of her shocked inertia. She leapt up and ran, the mud squelching between her toes.

There was never a chance she could outrun them. But still she tried. They were behind her, already swiftly gaining. She fell to her knees just as they reached her, and it was that which saved her life. One of the murderers swung a blow with his pistol, but it glanced off her temple rather than caving in her skull. She went down, and the light went out of her.

There was a sound like horses approaching along the track. But Ella didn't hear. And didn't see the men leave her, careless in their fear of being discovered. She was a child again, running through the dark pines.

———◆———

Ella woke, confused, her body aching from the hard floorboards. She had forsaken the reeking mattress, pulling the blankets off it and onto the floor. They were still dirty but not as dirty as the bed. At least she hoped not.

She had been dreaming, and although, as so many times before, the sense of it escaped her, it had left feelings of weariness and depression.

Beyond her little world the sun had sunk low and was about to set. While she had been sleeping the afternoon had drained away, and now darkness was fast approaching. There appeared to be no lighting out in the laneway, although Ella was sure she had seen gas lights in George Street. Evidently those in charge of such things did not consider this lane to be deserving of a light.

With the darkness came the sounds of fighting and scuffling, echoing up from the maze of streets below. A woman screamed. Downstairs, the voices of the customers rose and fell, and for a time there was the squeal of a fiddle and the heavy stamp of dancing feet. Ella wondered if Nancy and Eben were down there, enjoying themselves. As far as she knew, no one had come to check on her or feed her or ask if she was all right.

They had forgotten her.

She thought of Adam, far out at sea, the wind shrieking in the sails and the waves pounding. He would come, she knew it, just as she knew the sun would eventually rise. He would come for two reasons ... because he loved Ella, and because he hated Ollie McLeod.

The night seemed very long. Things scuttled across the floor, and scratched in the walls. Once she heard footsteps approaching her room, but they turned off at the last moment and went some-where else. The moon came out and shone into her window, a pale stream of light. She watched it move slowly across the room.

I would come out of the sea for you. I'd come out of hell itself.

She repeated the words over and over, like a chant. They were her prayer and her comfort. They were her own moonlight in the blackness.

———◆———

She was in the tunnel again, and her bare toes sank into the carpet runner. Her nightgown swirled about her ankles as she walked, and her hair was loose and tousled from sleep.

I am at Lochlyn, she thought. I am here to get better.

She was walking down the corridor, towards the lighted doorway. And the sounds that had awoken her.

I must find out what they're saying, she told herself. I must know. But somewhere in her mind, a voice was shouting at her to stop, that this was a secret. The sick feeling in her stomach twisted, and for a moment she thought she might vomit.

She had almost reached the doorway, and the light shone out over her bare feet. Inside the room the voices went on, and she strained to hear them, to make sense of them. Why couldn't she make sense of them? She bent her head closer, closer ... and dissolved in a swirl of colour.

'Got yer breakfast here, Mrs McLeod.'

Eben stood in the doorway, a tray in his hands, a sheepish look on his face. He was washed and dressed, and had obviously already eaten his own breakfast.

Ella, who had long since risen, stood up. She felt light-headed from lack of sleep and anxiety; she knew both must show in her shadowed eyes and drawn features.

The food smelt good, and she reached for the tray. Eggs and ham, and some bread fried in the fat. The grease made a sea for them all to swim in, but she didn't mind. She was too hungry to care.

'You eat up now,' Eben said, in what was meant to be a kindly voice. 'I'll fetch you some hot water.'

During the long night she had passed from fear to anger and back again. But all that had gone with the morning. Now she was only tired and longing to be let out, even if it meant going home to Ollie

McLeod.

Eben was watching her eat, looking pleased with himself. Ella thought him a fool. Nancy had won him back to her side by pretending a passion she did not feel. Why couldn't Eben see through her? Didn't he realise she was just using him? Or was he content to be used, as long as he got what he wanted?

'I'll be goin' to see yer husband today.'

That got her attention.

He smiled, and nodded at her look. 'Aye, that's right. Ollie himself. If he agrees to what we want, you'll be home tonight ... or tomorrow, maybe.' He tempered his hasty promise when he saw the flash of hope light up her woebegone face.

Ella forced herself to quash the surge of feeling. 'What if he doesn't agree?' she asked evenly.

Eben pursed his lips. 'Can't see why he won't. Yer his wife, aren't yer? He'd want yer back, wouldn't he?' Such a thing obviously had not occurred to him, and now he looked puzzled and a little worried.

It had occurred to Ella. Oliver McLeod had said he didn't want her found if it meant a fuss. Did that sound like a husband desperate to have his wife back?

'But what if he doesn't agree?' Ella insisted.

Eben looked down at his boots. She felt his unease, and his weakness. He was a big man, with a loud voice and a violent nature, but inside he was soft as butter. Briefly, she contemplated telling him the truth about Adam's parentage, but decided against it. Eben would tell Nancy, and Nancy would use it for her own gain.

'Will you let me go, Eben?' Her voice had dropped to a pleading whisper. She gazed up into his face intently, trying to mesmerize him into agreeing.

Eben hesitated, but even as he made to answer, two hands slipped around his waist from behind, and Nancy's sharp face peered over his shoulder. 'And why would he let you go, me ladyship?'

Shocked and angry, Ella stared back at her.

'You're worth money to us, one way or another,' Nancy went on. 'If Ollie don't want you, we'll find someone who does.'

'Adam wants me!' Ella burst out.

Nancy laughed, and slipped under Eben's arm to stand in front of him. Her eyes were hard and pitiless. 'Adam hasn't got the money to pay for you, though, has he? And even if he did, he wouldn't waste it. I know him. He's more careful o' his pennies than that.'

Ella knew her face showed the starkness of her despair, and couldn't help it.

Eben shifted uneasily. 'Maybe he could raise enough to – '

'No.' Nancy's reply was quiet, but it was final.

She smiled after the fact, to soften it, looking up into his eyes. But neither of them were in any doubt that she meant it.

Eben smiled back, stroking her cheek with his thumb. 'Aye, well,' he sighed and then shrugged off the moment of weakness. 'Eat up, Mrs McLeod! I'll get Jacko to fetch up that water. Are yer comin', Nance?'

Nancy, still smiling, shook her head. 'I'll come down in a moment. You go ahead.'

Again he hesitated, flicking a look at Ella and away. But he had no intention of antagonising Nancy, and with a brief nod of his head, he turned and vanished into the shadows.

Nancy remained where she was. It was as if she were feeding off Ella's misery, gaining pleasure from it. As Ella watched her, tense and waiting, she walked over to the window and peered out.

'Adam told me somethin' when he was at Sawpit Gully.' Nancy stood on her tiptoes, as if something outside interested her and she wanted to see it better. 'Do you want to hear what he said?'

'Not particularly.' Ella's voice was cold. That's better, she thought.

'He said that it was a good thing you'd lost your memory, 'cause if you'd remembered, you'd have known he was one of the men that attacked you at Seaton's Lagoon.' She turned then, the light slanting across her cheek, and smiled. 'He rode after you and knocked you down, and left you for dead. He needed the money, he said. That was all.'

Ella's legs were shaking and she pressed them hard together. 'You are a wicked and evil woman,' she said, her voice trembling. 'Why do you tell these lies? Does it matter so much to you that Adam loves me and not you? Is that why you're trying to poison his memory for me? But you can't. I know he loves me, I know it in my heart. And I know he'll come after me.'

Nancy's mouth was still smiling, but now it was rigid, more like a snarl. 'If he comes to Sydney, it'll be for me, not you.'

Ella shook her head slowly.

'Yes.' The smile had vanished altogether now.

Nancy gripped her hands into fists, and the muscles of her throat strained into cords. 'Yes!'

Someone made a small sound. Shocked and speechless from Nancy's words, Ella turned and saw Jacko standing patiently in the doorway. He was holding a jug and basin, the steam rising off the hot water. Nancy stared at him as if she didn't know him, and then she pushed him aside and hurried after Eben.

Jacko rocked on his bow legs, almost dropped the water and then regained his balance. His villainous face split into an admiring grin. 'Got the devil in her that one!'

Ella sat down heavily on the side of the bed and didn't dispute it.

'Eben said as you wanted some water. Got some soap an' all.' The cake was thin and greasy, and looked as if it had been well used. But Ella thanked him for this kindness.

Jacko set the water down on the drunken table, and then closed and bolted the door behind him.

The water helped. Ella washed herself all over and, after shaking out her clothes, dressed again. She felt better for it. Beyond the window, the lane was still shadowy and damp from a brief, early shower. The sky was glum, and clouds hung low over the rooftops, promising more rain as the day progressed.

Ella shivered, and wished she had something to occupy her time. It would be nice to read or sew. Anything that would take her mind off her present problems. She spent a moment inspecting the room, but apart from the furnishings and the blankets, it was bare. Not even a sheet of yellowing newspaper lined the single drawer in the table.

Ella sighed. Had Eben gone to see Oliver McLeod yet? Was her moment of release from this prison any closer? Ollie McLeod seemed a devious individual and Eben, for all his savagery, was unlikely to be a match for him. She had a feeling Ollie McLeod would tie Eben up in knots. But whereas such a certainty should have pleased her – wouldn't that mean she would be released from The Shipwreck all the sooner? – instead she felt a trembling unease deep within her.

For a long time she stood at the window, staring out. Heavy rain came, sounding on The Shipwreck's roof, and wind gusted against the walls, making them shudder and groan. Out on the harbour, the water was rough and the ships at anchor rolled.

During a lull in the storm, a woman in a thin dress and heavy boots made a dash across the laneway and into one of the houses. Two sailors strode up the stairs to The Shipwreck, and didn't come down again. 'You've come to the wrong place here, my fine gentlemen,' Ella whispered to herself. Jacko would be rubbing his hands together at such pickings.

The rain stopped and the sun shone weakly. Down in the lane, the gleam of water was everywhere. There was a man standing against the wall, in the deep shadow. As her eye slid over him, a movement further up the laneway caught her attention. Eben was returning, and with him a servant in a rough, ill-fitting jacket and cap. Ella watched them climb the stairs to the door of The Shipwreck.

What now? she thought. Was this the reception of a husband for his lost wife? Was this Ollie McLeod's way of welcoming her home?

Nancy's voice sounded, raised and angry, 'See her? Why do you need to see her? We want our money first!'

Eben made a soothing, rumbling noise.

'You should've arranged to see her somewhere else,' Nancy was saying, and now there was contempt in her voice as well as anger. 'Don't you know anything? I should 'ave done it myself!'

They were coming closer.

Ella turned and faced the door, hands clenched at her sides. The door opened. Nancy came in, her face flushed, her black eyes glittering, and gripped Ella's arm in fingers that hurt.

'Here she is!' she announced. 'Look at 'er and look well, 'cause all you'll be doin' is looking if we don't get our reward.'

'Nancy ...' Eben hovered in the shadows beyond the doorway like a huge, ambling bear, but it wasn't Eben who drew Ella's eyes. She was looking at the man in the rough jacket, the servant. He had removed his cap, and his hair was dark and streaked with grey. There was something in his stance, in his manner, that made her think this was no servant after all, despite his dress.

His eyes were fixed upon her, but there was nothing in them to give her a clue to what he was thinking. The long, handsome face was deeply lined about the mouth - she could not imagine it smiling. There was something cruel in the way he held his lips tight closed. Ella's breath felt constricted in her throat: the room was tilting.

Nancy shook her arm roughly. 'Well, is it 'er?' she

cried impatiently. 'Is it Eleanor McLeod?'

A gleam came into the man's pale eyes, but when he spoke it was without emotion. 'It's her. I'll take her now.'

Nancy laughed. 'You won't. We'll have our money first, and then you can come back for her.'

Eben cleared his throat nervously. 'You don't understand, Nancy,' he began tentatively. He was looking at the man before him but his gaze kept slipping away as if he could not hold it steady. Ella realised, with a jolt, that Eben was very much afraid.

'I understand all right,' Nancy retorted. 'Eben can stay here, and I'll go back with you. And you'd better not try anythin', or Eben'll break her neck and you'll never get her back. He's strong enough.'

The man looked up at her, startled, and then he gave a brief humourless laugh.

Ella pressed back against Nancy, for suddenly the room wasn't large enough for her. The air in it had gone bad. 'I won't go with you,' she said, her voice thin.

Ollie McLeod gave her his frigid smile. 'This is the second time I've paid for you, wife. And the last.'

Nancy, her face avid, looked from one to the other. 'This is him then?' she demanded of Eben. 'You never told me this was him.'

Eben shifted uncomfortably. 'He didn't want me to.'

Nancy smiled. 'Well, you've seen her now, Mr McLeod. All you need do is hand over the money and you can 'ave her.'

Ollie McLeod gave her a withering look. 'I don't carry such sums with me. You'll have to come to my house.'

Nancy bowed her head in agreement. There was an expression on her face of something between admiration and awe. This is Ollie McLeod, it seemed to say. This is the most powerful man in Sydney.

He turned back to Ella at the door, a spark of curiosity in his cold eyes. 'I've been told you've forgotten everything. Is it true?'

'Yes,' Ella whispered. Then, in reckless desperation, 'I've made myself a new life now. Let me go.'

'Let you go?' he repeated in astonishment. 'You're my wife, Eleanor. I will never let you go.'

She spun around to the window, and heard the door close behind her. Their steps faded as she gazed blankly through the glass. Ollie McLeod had brought something dark, something evil into the room with him, and it was still here. Her hands, gripping the sill, were shaking.

As she watched, she saw the two of them descend the steps, Ollie McLeod and Nancy Ure. They walked briskly, the wind tugging at the woman's skirts and the edges of her cloak. They passed the building where the man still stood in the shadows, his jacket pulled up around his ears and his hands jammed in his pockets. He was leaning against the stone wall of the house, as though huddled for warmth, his head bowed. He appeared to be sleeping.

As Nancy walked past, she paused and glanced back. But Ollie was already ahead of her, and she turned and hurried to catch him up. The man straightened, staring after them.

It was Adam.

CHAPTER 28

HER FIRST INSTINCT WAS TO scream and shout and bang her fists on the window. But even as the thought crystallised, she knew she couldn't do that. They would hear the noise downstairs and come to investigate.

And yet she couldn't just do nothing. Ella looked around her, and then down. The toes of her boots peeped out from the hem of her skirt. They were the same boots she had worn when dressed as a man - Nancy had not offered to lend her shoes - and they were sturdy and strong. She sat down and removed one.

Adam was still in the laneway, but he was no longer alone. The sailors Ella had seen earlier were standing beside him, deep in conversation. Ella hesitated. Should she go ahead? She was afraid if she didn't that Adam would leave. Perhaps he had sent the sailors in to The Shipwreck to see if she was there? And now they were telling him she wasn't...

Ella took aim with the heel of her boot and cracked the middle pane a resounding blow. It shattered, instantly, with a small, brittle explosion. Pieces scattered across the floor and the bed. Outside, glass fell tinkling onto the stone steps below.

Ella pressed her face as close as she dared to the broken pane and its jagged edges. Cold air hit her with a slap, making her eyes water. She blinked to clear her vision.

Adam was gazing straight at her. She tried to say his name but no sound would come out. He was smiling. She stood and gazed at him, wishing she were small enough to squeeze through the gap she had made in the window and fly down to him. She wanted to tell him all she had learned, and at the same time hold onto him and never let him go.

Suddenly someone was coming towards her door.

Ella stepped back, bumping against the bed, and sat down abruptly. Her hand felt heavy and when she looked down at it she saw she was still holding onto her boot.

The bolt squealed as it was drawn. Fingers shaking, Ella pulled her boot back onto her foot just as the door was flung open.

Eben stood there, breathing thickly. He stared at the window, and then down at the broken glass. A chill breeze seemed to gust into the room through the gap, bringing with it the smell of the sea and the rain.

'What's this?' he asked angrily.

Ella forced her chin up in a courageous, defiant gesture. 'I couldn't breathe, so I opened the window.'

The dark eyes narrowed. Eben stepped to the window and was peering out. Ella, breath held, eyes fixed on the man's back, waited for the cry of recognition, or warning ...

'Did yer think yer could drop from here and get away? If yer weren't dead when yer hit the ground, yer'd be so broken yer soon would be,' he said in a matter-of-fact voice.

'I didn't intend to drop.'

If Adam was still down in the lane, Eben obviously had not recognised him. But Ella only really relaxed when Eben finally turned back to face her. He was frowning and he looked worried.

'Nancy's gone off with Ollie McLeod.'

'I know. I saw her. How long do you think, before ...?'

'Before he comes for yer? Tonight, he said. When it's dark.'

Tonight. It wasn't very long. It must be well past noon now, and the days were short. So little time for Adam to rescue her ... if he could.

Eben touched some of the glass with the toe of his boot, crushing it into the floor. 'She don't know what Ollie McLeod's like. She wouldn't be told. He'll eat 'er up and spit 'er out.'

Ella stared at him. 'Nancy?' she asked, with a touch of disbelief. 'Are you sure you're not just worried she might just take the money and leave you here?'

Eben crushed another shard of glass. 'Nancy wouldn't do that.'

Ella wondered, but said nothing.

'I'll give 'er till dusk,' Eben said to himself, 'and if she's not back – '

'You'll let me go?' Ella whispered hopefully.

He laughed. 'No, I'll not let you go, Adam's wife. I'll think of something, that's all I meant to say.' And he winked at her and closed the door.

Ella gazed after him a moment, at a loss, and then she jumped up and peered anxiously out of the window.

The lane was empty. No sign of Adam or anyone else.

The disappointment was like a physical blow. She leaned against the wall and closed her eyes. He'll be back as soon as he can, she tried to tell herself. But it didn't really help. She was alone again, at the mercy of others, and soon Ollie McLeod would be back for her. Like the darkness, panic was drawing closer. She was afraid she would disgrace herself, and give way to it.

Slowly, wearily, she turned back to the bed. After a moment she lay down, no longer caring about the state of the mattress. The long, sleepless night was catching up with her at last.

———◆———

She was in the pine forest. The tall dark trees leaned over her, and the moon drifted in the faraway sky.

She ran over pine needles rough and dry underfoot. Voices were calling her, calling her name.

'Eleanor! Eleanor!'

She didn't listen. The forest beckoned her, and she ran on. The shadows deepened. Her feet slowed, uncertain. The moon had hidden itself behind a cloud, and suddenly the air had a chill.

Someone stepped out from the shadows. A man with cold eyes and a handsome face. 'Eleanor,' he said sternly. 'Come here at once, wife!'

He stretched out his hand and through the sheer force of his will, she began to obey him. And then a movement distracted her, and she hesitated, turning slightly. Two men stood there, shapes in the darkness. But she knew them. They were the two men who had followed her to Seaton's Lagoon, and murdered Ned, and tried to murder her.

Frozen, she watched them fall in behind her husband, like soldiers behind their captain.

And she understood.

It was her husband who had planned to kill her in that lonely spot. He had fetched her across the seas to be his bride and the mother of his heir, to sit at his side and make him proud. But she had discovered something he had kept hidden for many years, the thing that may even have sent him to Sydney in the first place. His disgrace. And in discovery, she had changed from being his perfect wife, to a threat. A threat to his position, his business, his life.

His plan was to make it seem as if she and Ned had been attacked by bushrangers, and leave only Ned alive to tell the tale. And all of Sydney would mourn - for Ollie, and no one could point the finger of accusation in his direction.

But the plan went wrong.

Ella, backing away from his outstretched hand, turned and ran. The moon came out from behind the cloud and followed her, her enemy now, its brightness giving her no place to hide. An owl swooped close, and she saw it had a woman's smiling face. Her heart beat faster.

The two men were behind her, she could hear them. They were running, gaining ground. They wanted to kill her all over again.

'Get her!' cried Ollie McLeod. 'Get her!' His voice was full of a desperate savagery that made her catch her breath on a sob.

The arm came out of the darkness and pulled her in. Close. A warm chest, someone breathing softly against her ear. 'Quiet now ... quiet now, love.'

They were down in the pine needles - a fallen log, warm and damp. The two killers ran past, silent and deadly, and were gone. After a pause Ollie McLeod stumbled along behind them, puffing and cursing. He stopped beside the hiding place, bending over to catch his breath. Ella pressed closer into those warm arms, and prayed to be made invisible. Ollie McLeod straightened, and the dark shape of his head went still, as if he sensed her close. Above them, the owl hooted softly. And then he moved forward again, slowly, following after his men like a hunter his hounds. And all was silent.

'Ella?' First his voice brushed her cheek, and then her lips. 'Oh Ella, love, I've missed you ..."

———◆———

'Ella? Ella?'

Someone was shaking her awake, gently but firmly. Her eyes shot open, as the sound and smell and feel of him registered in her sleeping mind. She had been dreaming, dreaming of Adam. And he was here.

'Adam?' Her voice was a croaky whisper.

While she had been sleeping the light had begun to fade, and now the figure above her was but a dark shape against the window. He cupped her face in his hands, bending close enough for her to see the gleam of his eyes.

'Oh Ella, love, I've missed you,' he said, and pressed his mouth to hers in a short, savage kiss.

She responded, her arms going up to hold him. 'I knew you'd come,' she said at last.

He grinned. 'Aye, well, we had fair winds. Made it in near record time.'

She touched his cheek, and felt his beard, grown longer since last she saw him. He turned his face and kissed her palm. 'How is your head?'

'Hard, lucky for me.'

He was helping her up, off the bed, his hands still gentle, but she could feel the urgency in him. She saw him glance about, taking in the state of the room and the broken windowpane. The door into the passage was open and the noise from down-stairs floated up. Jacko had a full house this evening.

'How did you find me?' she whispered, standing in the curve of his arm.

'Nancy isn't the only one to know what goes on in a man's mind. I know Eben. I knew he'd come here as soon as he got to Sydney. It was his second home, this place. He'd think he was safe here.'

'He went to see my ... Ollie McLeod,' she blurted out. 'And then they came here, and Nancy went to fetch the reward. Has she come back?'

She felt his eyes on her in the half dark, specu-lative. 'She hasn't come back,' he said quietly. 'But I've friends of me own, and they tell me Ollie McLeod is on his way now and he means business. That's why we've got to get out of here ... if you still want to come with me?'

Ella felt strange, unsettled, as if there were a storm brewing. But it was a storm inside her head rather than outside.

'Ella?' he repeated.

'Yes,' she answered him, 'Yes, of course.'

His fingers squeezed hers. 'Just as well! I've paid Eben a King's ransome for you.'

'You've *paid* him for me?' she gasped, shocked.

He laughed. 'What else could I do? I told him

Ollie McLeod was comin' for you and Nancy had flown with the money and he wouldn't get a penny. He weren't too happy, and when I made an offer he accepted it.'

'How much?' Ella demanded in a strangled voice. She was so angry, she was shaking.

'It was the only way I could get you out,' he said quietly.

'How much?'

He gave her a careful look. 'Fifty pounds.'

Fifty pounds. A horse could cost twenty, if it was a good one. That made fifty pounds a lot of money, but to Ella it was an insult. That he should pay for her at all made him just as bad as Ollie McLeod.

'I'm not letting you pay for me,' she said at last, more calmly. 'I'm not letting anyone pay for me. I belong to myself, and not you and not Ollie McLeod. Do you understand that?'

She had a feeling he was trying to keep a straight face. 'Aye, Mrs Seaton, I understand it perfectly.'

His agreement flattened her. 'Well ... good.'

'Can we go now? Before Ollie arrives and batters down the door to get you?'

The passage was in darkness, only the light shining up from the hole in the floor to guide them. There was a roar of laughter, and a screech from one of the crones. Jacko yelled something incomprehensible which everyone but Ella must have understood, for they roared again.

Even Adam snorted quietly to himself, as if in appreciation.

'Did you come here with Eben?' she asked him suddenly, uneasily.

He glanced at her. 'Not as often as him, no. Ma

worked here, off and on. She came here when she was first sent out, she was assigned to the owner as a skivvy.' He said it with irony. 'Come on, we'd best get out of here before Ollie arrives. I don't want to meet up with him any more than you do.'

'I've already seen him,' she said dully. 'I didn't *know* him, of course, and yet I did. Adam ...he frightens me in a way I can't explain.'

He took her hand in his, squeezing her fingers.

The noise from downstairs increased as they drew closer to the hole in the floor. When they reached it, Adam knelt down and peered through. Over his shoulder, Ella could see the strange shadows thrown by the oil lamp, she smelt the tobacco smoke and the rum, as well as some savoury aroma which she assumed was Jacko's cooking.

Adam looked up at her. 'I'll go down first, just in case Eben's changed his mind. You follow me.'

She thought of arguing but there seemed no point. If Eben was waiting beneath with a weapon, Adam would be better able to fend him off than Ella. She nodded, and watched him begin to descend the ladder. When he reached the bottom, he looked up at her and smiled. His face was so wonderful, she had to blink back tears. Awkwardly, Ella caught up her skirts, bundling them about her legs as she had on the way up, and took her first tentative step onto the ladder. A quick glance down showed her where the next step was, and she began her own descent.

Halfway down, Adam reached up and caught her around the waist, as if to lift her down the rest of the way. And at that moment there was a terrible thudding on the door of The Shipwreck. Ella stiffened, turning to stare as if she could penetrate the heavy wooden door and see who was outside. But she didn't have to see, she knew.

The thudding came again, a demand for admittance. But it took a moment for the noise to penetrate the stupefying fog of rum within. Jacko was busy serving nobblers to his customers, his little eyes even smaller and more bloodshot than Ella remembered. He glanced up and caught sight of her, and the smile he was wearing vanished. He leaned sideways, and Ella realised that Eben was standing there in the shadows.

'Adam,' Ella managed, meaning to warn him. But he already knew, and swung her down off the ladder and set her on her feet. His arm stayed where it was, about her waist.

'I can deal with Eben and Jacko,' he said evenly.

Perhaps he could, thought Ella, but could he deal with all of them? For Jacko's stillness had communicated itself to a number of his confidants, including Davey, and they too were watching Adam with a silence that was more frightening than any shouting.

The banging on the door came again, rattling the frame, and now everyone heard it.

'Blue bottles!' screeched one of the crones by the fire.

There was immediate panic. A number of men by the door, engaged in a game of dice, scattered, and Ella saw one of them slip the dice - no doubt loaded - through the floorboards. A woman in a low-cut blouse and tight skirt threw herself into the arms of a sailor, saying, 'Don't let 'em take me, duck!' and one of the crones slid quietly and drunkenly under her chair.

Jacko held up his hand for silence. 'We'll hear what they want before I let 'em in!' he announced.

The banging on the door was becoming more persistent. Now the whole wall seemed to quiver and shake, and the wooden bar which was holding it didn't look as if it would hold out much longer.

'Who is it?' Jacko shouted, stumping across the room on his bowed legs. 'What do yer want!'

'You've a woman there,' a voice came back faintly but clearly. 'We want her.'

A few titters greeted this request. 'Will I do?' a crone shrieked, and more laughter followed.

There was a narrow door behind the bar, and Adam brushed by Eben to open it. He pushed Ella inside what she assumed was a cupboard, and closed the door behind him. The only light was from gaps in the wall, shining in from the other room.

'They're Ollie McLeod's men,' Adam said softly, grimly.

Ella shivered violently.

Suddenly, behind her, something pushed against the cupboard door, knocking her into Adam's arms. He grabbed her and spun her behind him where it was safe.

It was only Eben.

'It's Ollie McLeod,' he hissed. 'Nancy's taken the money and left me to Ollie.' He was angry, but there was a sound of genuine grievance in his voice. Ella stared at him in amazement. After all he had done – the kidnapping and the threatening and the brutality – Eben could still feel aggrieved by someone else's perfidy!

'Well, at least we know whose side you're on this time,' Adam said evenly.

Eben sighed, and then stepped closer. 'You remember the way out, little brother? Then go! Go now, before I change my mind!'

A voice came from the chaos of the taproom.

'She's here!' it shouted. 'She's in here! Come and get her and leave us alone.'

To Ella's horror, Jacko began trying to lift the beam from its position across the door, while Eben ran to stop him. They struggled.

'Come on,' Adam said grimly, and closed the little door on the scene.

Come on? Ella thought. Where was there to 'come on' to? But when she turned to look behind her, she realised this wasn't a cupboard after all, but a small room. There was a narrow bed against one wall. It probably belonged to Jacko.

Voices were shouting now, making threats Ella didn't try to hear. Women were screeching and men were cursing. Ella thought: Ollie McLeod has come for me, but not as a loving husband. He has come to take me away and finish what he began at Seaton's Lagoon.

Ella blinked, frightened by the clarity of the thought. The whirling blackness was going. Her past was opening before her, like clouds tumbling apart to disclose a clear summer's day. She remembered who she was and what she was ... she remembered her illness and Catherine ... she remembered the desperate struggle at Seaton's Lagoon for her life ... she remembered Ned ...

But there was something still missing: the reason for Ollie's decision that she had to die.

Adam was pulling her towards a small fireplace immediately in front of them. He ducked down, and stood up inside the chimney. 'Come on,' he said, his voice echoing. 'There's a tunnel up in here. You can get out through it, out to the back. There're steps cut into the rockface leading up to the top of the cliff.'

Ella followed him into the chimney, hardly knowing what she did. Her head was humming with so much newfound knowledge. People and places and scenes appeared before her. And she knew them.

'Adam, I remember,' she breathed. 'I remember!'

He spared her a quick glance. 'Do you, love? Come on, put your foot here ... up you go.'

There was a space, out of sight, in the back of the chimney. Ella found herself on her hands and knees in a low brick tunnel which ran back into blackness. As she moved slowly forward, a spider's web wrapped itself around her face. She made a strangled sound, damping down the scream just in time.

'What is it?' Adam was close behind her.

'Nothing ...' She swallowed, reaching up to brush the clinging stuff away. Don't think of it, she told herself. Don't think of anything, except that Ollie is outside, and if he gets you he will finish what he began at Seaton's Lagoon.

Determinedly now, she crawled forward. Dust trickled through the roof and made her cough. More cobwebs tangled in her hair. The floor of the tunnel felt gritty with dirt and disuse, a home only to those insects and animals which loved the darkness. Something soft and quick ran across her fingers. This secret entrance had not been used for a long time.

'Adam ...'

He was right behind her. 'They're in,' he said softly. 'I can hear 'em in the main room. Maybe they think we're trapped and they're in no hurry to have us out. Quick, love!'

She couldn't see a thing. It was so dark she felt as if her eyes were closed when they were wide open. And then her searching hand, stretching before her, found a barrier of rough and splintery timber.

Her heart thudded in terror.

'Adam, it ends here!'

But he wasn't concerned. 'No, no, it's just boarded up. Here, let me through and I'll get us out.'

He squeezed past her, pressing her body against the brick wall of the tunnel. She felt his breath on her face, and his mouth on hers, rough with the passion he had no time to express. And then he was past, and she heard his hands on the timber, pushing and pulling at it.

'Aye, it's been boarded up a while,' he sighed. 'I'll have to try and kick it in. It'll make a bit o' noise. They'll know what we're up to. Let's just hope I can do it quick.'

For a moment they were both quiet, listening. The banging on the front door had ceased. Boots were moving about in the room next door. Jacko's voice was raised, but it sounded more bluster than anger. Surely he knew of the tunnel? Perhaps he was giving them some precious time.

'Ready?' Adam sounded as if he were gritting his teeth. She felt him manouevre himself onto his back so that his knees were bent and the soles of his boots were pressed flat against the wood.

'Adam?' Quickly, as she felt him move to begin.

His groping hand found hers. 'What is it?'

'I've remembered.'

She heard him let his breath out, slowly. 'Do you want to go home with him then?' he asked her at last, in a voice that strove to be matter-of-fact. 'Is that it?'

She loved him then more than ever for what he was willing to do for her. But the memories and the dark horror of them swelled up and filled her. 'No. It was Ollie McLeod's men who attacked Ned and me at Seaton's Lagoon. He wants me dead.'

'Then we'd better get out o' here, hadn't we,' Adam said grimly. And he drew back his legs and kicked out with all his might.

The noise seemed tremendous in such a confined space. Ella shuddered and covered her ears as it reverberated about them, wondering if the roof would fall in. But Adam kicked again and again, quickly and savagely.

The wood splintered. Suddenly light trickled through, full of floating dust. Adam kicked again, deliberately choosing the weakest points, and again the wood gave way.

Boots racketed across Jacko's floor. 'Here!' someone shouted. Fearfully, Ella looked back and saw a light as someone lifted a lamp inside the fireplace. In a moment she and Adam would be outlined perfectly for anyone who wanted to fire a shot.

But Adam was already crawling through the space he had made. His hand gripped Ella's, pulling her after him. Her skirt caught on a jagged piece of wood, and she pulled at it frantically, hearing it tear as she stumbled to her feet.

There wasn't any artificial light out here, but the sky was clear and starry and seemed bright after the blackness of the tunnel. Ella gasped in lung-fuls of the night air, finding it clean and salty after the filth and grime of The Shipwreck. In front of them rose the sheer rockface, while behind was the wooden wall of The Shipwreck, leaning crookedly. There was a narrow gap between the two, but nar-row as it was, it was large enough for a person to pass through.

'Here, take me hand!' Again Adam was reaching back for her, and again Ella gripped his fingers. He took a step up, and Ella saw that there were steps cut into the rock, steep and shallow, curving up towards the cliff top more than twenty feet above them.

Behind them, a light shone through into the tun-nel, its beam pooling out against the cliff face. Ella could hear the sounds of scuffling and scraping, as someone began a hasty pursuit.

Her legs were already trembling, and they had hardly begun their climb. Adam hauled her up after him, sometimes two steps at a time. The cliff top was closer now, and beyond it Ella could see the stars winking at her. Then they were above the roof of The Shipwreck, and beneath them the Rocks dropped away dizzyingly. An occasional light shone softly in the darkness, and there was a faint strain of music.

It was difficult to believe that down there life was going on as normal.

'Look! Up there!' A man's voice, but Ella thought she knew it. The young man with the old eyes, who had murdered Ned and would have murdered her.

She looked back, and saw the shadowy shapes thrown by the light of a hand-held lamp. The man at the front looked up, his face suddenly, clearly visible. She knew it, feared it.

'It's Ollie McLeod,' she whispered. 'He's come for me.'

CHAPTER 29

———•———

'NOT IF I CAN HELP it,' Adam muttered. He was over the top, and with one final lunge, so was Ella. She collapsed onto the ground, and would have stayed there but for Adam pulling her to her feet.

It wasn't a clifftop after all, Ella realised, but a street. Or what passed for a street in the Rocks. A sort of narrow goat track, curling between steps and boulders, with cottages built higgledy-piggledy either side. Some were so old and derelict, it was difficult to imagine anyone living in them.

Something had died close by, and the stench of it filled Ella's nostrils. Even when they had passed by it, the scent of death lingered.

'Do you know where we're going?' Ella gasped as she ran, clinging to Adam's hand as if it were a lifeline.

Incredibly, Adam laughed. 'I know this place better than anyone!'

She remembered then that this was his home. But Ollie, too, knew the Rocks. This was where he had begun his fortune, with Catherine his sister. *I helped him run an inn,* Catherine had said once, *and watched him learn the dark side of Sydneyton.* Ella felt her breath gasping and hurting in her chest as she ran.

Suddenly, behind them, came an explosion. Sharp and short. Something struck a rock beside Ella. Ollie McLeod and his men had pistols.

Adam pulled her around a corner and down some more steps, and then around again. It was darker here. Taller tenements blocked out the light. A group of men was ambling towards them, but broke away when they heard a second shot. Adam didn't slow down. He ran up a ramp cut into the rock, and ducked beneath what looked like someone's front verandah.

There was a strange silence in Ella's head, as though fear had blocked out the sounds of running feet and voices and Adam's heart beating beneath her cheek. They huddled together in the damp darkness. Above, the wood of the verandah floor was rotten, full of gaps and broken boards. There was a slow seep and drip of foul-smelling fluids. Someone walked in the cottage, slowly, as if they were old.

Ella held her breath and turned her head slightly to peer out and down the way they had come. Dark shapes were silhouetted momentarily against the sky, before vanishing down the stairs into the shadows. She heard the scrape of their boots on the rough stone, and the hissed curse of someone nearly falling. The men rushed past the ramp Adam had taken, on down the steep laneway into the heart of the Rocks. And were gone.

Adam moved, but Ella gripped his arm in sharp nails. 'No!' she gasped.

'They're gone,' he murmured.

'No!' How could she explain her fierce certainty that they must not move yet? And then, just as she had known it would, another figure appeared at the top of the stairs.

Adam froze.

The man clattered noisily down the steps and stopped, panting, just opposite the ramp. He bent over at the waist, to catch his breath. Ella could see the shape of his head, the profile of his face.

It was her husband, her enemy.

Voices called out from further ahead, and Ollie McLeod lifted his head. 'Go after them!' he shouted. 'I'll follow!'

Ella felt Adam's arms about her, knew he was warm, and yet she was cold. Something with a thin tail scuttled across the ground nearby. She wanted to scream and knowing it, Adam put his hand over her mouth. A stone rattled out from beneath his boot.

The sound made Ollie turn his head. He stared fixedly at the ramp, as if only just noticing it. Ella watched him straighten and hesitate. He was deciding whether to follow them up to their hiding place or go on, after his men.

The slow steps in the cottage above them sounded again, closer. Ella heard the rattle of a cough, and an old voice, shrill with weary irritation, asked, 'Who's there? Can't you let a body get some sleep!'

Ollie hesitated a moment more, but the words had convinced him. He turned and vanished after his men.

Adam squeezed Ella against him so hard he stopped her breath. 'How did you know?' he whispered.

How did she know? How to explain that fierce tug of warning? How to explain the strange mixture of past and present and future, that she had dreamed in the room at The Shipwreck ...

But he hadn't waited for an answer. He was helping her out from their hiding place and back down the ramp.

She clung to Adam's hand. Soon, they were in a narrow lane which dripped with putrid moisture. A bundle of rags lay against one of the walls, and it was only as they ran past that Ella realised the bundle was a person, either drunk or dead.

Adam led her through an archway into a tiny square hemmed in with bleak, dark houses. He went to the house at the furthermost corner and there was another passage, even narrower than the first. He was breathing quickly, and Ella wondered if his chest was hurting as much as hers. She remembered, belatedly what he had only recently suffered at Moggs's hands.

The place appeared deserted, but Ella could hear something ... the stirring of air, above the rooftops perhaps. It whispered and breathed, as if it were a living thing. Adam led her through the narrow throughway, turning almost sideways so that he could fit. Ahead, a lighter patch showed where the passage ended. The narrow space was oppressive, making her gasp. 'Where are we?'

'I forget its real name. We called it Hangman's Walk.' His voice held its usual trace of humour. 'We called it that because the crimes committed here were usually dealt with by hanging.'

'Do you think my husband's still looking for us?'
'Yes.'

There was no answer to that. She followed Adam, trying not to smell the smells of this place, or imagine what horrors had taken place here. It was only when they were almost at the far end that the shadow appeared, blocking their way out.

Ella felt her breath lock in her throat.

'Who are yer?' The voice was rough and savage, like a dog that has been let run wild.

'We're bein' followed,' Adam replied in the same gruff voice.

'Who by?'

'Blue bottles.'

'What'd yer do?'

'Slit a man's throat for askin' questions.'

They were almost upon the shadow, but Adam didn't pause. He kept walking, quick and determined, his bulk filling the narrow space. The man hovered a moment, hesitant, and then disappeared.

The passage spilled out at the side of yet another lane, only this one was cobbled. There was a lamp on a pole at the far end, and in the wider street beyond it Ella could see moving horses and vehicles and people.

Adam turned to take her hand and tuck it firmly into his arm. His smile was warm enough to thaw some of her fear. Slowly, as if they had all the time in the world, they strolled out into George Street.

Even at this time of the night it was full of noise and movement. A tavern was doing noisy business catering for miners. A troupe of acrobats was performing on one street corner, and passersby were bothered for payment. A couple of miners rode past, wild and drunk, shouting about rivers of gold. A girl with a crimson shawl and equally bright lips watched the passing trade with an experienced eye.

'Where are we going?' Ella asked. She felt as if

everyone they passed knew they were escapees, and her skin prickled from unseen eyes.

'I'll try and get a passage on a ship.'

But the harbour was the first place Ollie McLeod would try when he couldn't find them in the Rocks. The harbour wasn't safe, the Rocks weren't safe, Sydney wasn't safe. Ella's mind spun wildly in a search for sanctuary ... and found a pool of calm. Suddenly she knew where they would be safe.

Ella pulled at Adam's arm until he stopped, turning to face her with a puzzled look.

'I know someone who will help us,' she said. 'She was ... is my friend.'

Adam hesitated, but she sensed he was desperate enough to take a chance.

'Catherine McLeod,' she went on. 'Ollie's sister. She'll help us.'

'Why would she help us?' he demanded.

'She was always sympathetic. I believe she will be now.'

Adam looked behind him, as if expecting to see Ollie and his men bearing down on them. 'Where does she live?' he murmured quietly at last.

'I'll show you,' Ella replied.

———◆———

The house was modest in comparison to Ollie's. It stood overlooking Hyde Park, in an older, established area. The curtained windows threw muted light over the garden trees and shrubs. Ella gazed up at the flat, Georgian facade, knowing she had always felt welcome at Catherine's house. She was certain that Catherine would help her now. Catherine loved Ollie, but she loved Eleanor too. And she would see how impossible and, indeed, how dangerous it was, for Ella to go back to Ollie.

Adam was standing just behind her, but Ella did not touch him or turn to him. She stood alone, trembling, on the verge of some momentous discovery. Here was her past, and she was about to plunge back into it.

But at what cost?

The door knocker was a thistle, bronze and well polished. Ella rested her hand on it, and glanced back at Adam. He gave her an encouraging smile.

'She'll help us,' Ella repeated, but now some of the confidence seemed to have left her voice.

Adam put his hand to his belt. 'I've got a gun,' he said. 'If I don't like the look o' things, I'll get us out, fast.'

Ella nodded, somewhat comforted. Before, she had faced her troubles alone, with only her cold pride as a bolster. Now she had Adam, and he was strong and sure, and he loved her as she loved him. She let the door knocker fall. After the initial clatter, there was a silence, and then light footsteps trembling on marble.

She knew it was marble. She knew what she would see when the door opened. A staircase rising in a curve to a stained-glass window. A row of closed doors gleaming with polish. A small table with a blue vase full of flowers, spilling out, warming the coldest, loneliest heart.

The door opened.

The girl at the door was young and neat, eyes big and frightened under her white cap. Her name was Letty. 'Mrs McLeod!' she gasped, and the healthy colour vanished from her face. And then she saw Adam, and looked even more frightened.

'I wish to see Miss McLeod,' Ella announced, her voice full of the certainty of being obeyed.

'Miss McLeod? But...' The girl glanced over her shoulder.

There was someone in the hall, a woman in a grey dress that belled out about her and swept the marble floor. Dark hair coiled neatly, a face at once familiar and intriguing.

'Eleanor?'

The woman came forward slowly. She rested her hand on the little table, with its blue vase of flowers, and her knuckles shone white. 'Eleanor.' Her voice was a whisper, and shock made her sway, her eyelashes flicking as if she might faint.

Ella rushed forward and held the other woman to keep her from falling. Catherine rested her head on Ella's shoulder and took a great, gulping breath. 'Eleanor,' she gasped. 'We thought ... thank God, oh thank God.' She seemed to gain control of her emotions then. With an effort, she straightened her back and lifted her chin. She was taller than Ella, and regal in bearing. But for all that, her mouth trembled as her pale eyes fixed lovingly on Ella.

Adam's quiet voice was an intrusion. 'Is there somewhere we can talk, Miss McLeod?'

Catherine looked at him as if just noticing him, and her eyes narrowed. Slowly, she took in his broad shoulders and fair hair, his smiling mouth and warm, clever eyes ... the sheer attractiveness of him. And perhaps she understood even then what they had come for.

'Close the door,' she said sharply to the servant

girl. 'We're not to be disturbed. Do you understand that, Letty?'

The girl bobbed obedience.

Catherine led the way into one of the rooms off the hall. Ella followed her across the threshold, and stopped. Tall windows, the trees hidden now by plush red drapes. A mirror hung above the mantel, with gold curling around the frame. It was all so familiar.

Ella turned to Adam, speechless, tears stinging her eyes. She felt his warm fingers grasp hers. Behind them, the maid closed the door.

Catherine was pouring some brandy into glasses. She glanced up with a smile. 'I'm more glad than I can say that you're safe, Eleanor.'

She held out a glass to Adam, and he came forward to take it. The look she gave him was almost antagonistic. 'I know you,' she said. 'You're Frances Hart's son, aren't you? I knew Frances well, in the old days. We worked together at The Shipwreck. She held herself high, but it's a fact that poverty has no favourites, even women like Frances Hart. I was sorry to hear that she'd died.'

Adam gave her a lazy smile. He was leaning back on his feet, looking relaxed and unconcerned, but Ella knew it was a pose both he and Eben affected to disguise their tension.

'Aye, I'm Frances Hart's son.'

'She had a way of telling a story that drew you deep in,' Catherine murmured, and then sighed. 'She was a witch, I used to think, the way she wound a spell.' The pale eyes widened, losing their dreamy vagueness. 'You worked for Ollie, didn't you?'

'I worked for your brother ... off and on, over the years. I've seen you, Miss McLeod. I remember you.'

He said it as if it were a threat, but Catherine only smiled at him, mocking him.

'You did more than work for him, Adam Hart. You're one o' Ollie's bastards. He never took much interest in them usually, but he was fond o' Frances ... more fond o' her than the others.'

Adam's dark eyes shone like granite. 'So fond he allowed her to die with nothin' but the clothes she wore, and be buried in a box her sons made. Aye, I know Ollie McLeod's kind of fondness, Miss McLeod.'

Catherine's smile remained, as if his words touched her not at all. 'You've the look of him, I've always thought so. I used to watch you runnin' your errands, and think, "Lord, but it's Ollie all over again!" You've the same single-minded purpose, the same determination. If Ollie wants something, he'll squash everything flat in his path to get it, and you're the same, aren't you, Adam Hart?'

Adam laughed angrily.

'What is it you want, I wonder?' Catherine went on. 'Money and power? Do you want to hold lives in your hand, like Ollie? Or is it simpler than that?' And she let her eyes wander to Ella.

Ella felt her face colour, even knowing she should show nothing, say nothing. Once, she had been expert at hiding her feelings, at being the cold, proud laird's daughter. But that outer shell had been stripped from her when she was abandoned for dead at Seaton's Lagoon, when she had had to rely upon others for survival. When she had fallen in love with Adam.

She did not want it back. Eleanor McLeod was gone, and could never return.

Catherine sat down. Above her dark head hung a painting writhing with hunting hounds bringing down a wounded stag. It was a brutal work, but Ollie had always liked it.

Adam pressed a glass of brandy into Ella's hand, and bent closer, murmuring, 'Talk to her. You said she'd help us. She doesn't like me, but she'll do it for you. Make her!' And then he'd stepped back, and she was alone, staring into Catherine McLeod's pale, knowing eyes.

'I've been so very worried, darling,' Catherine said quietly, and her voice shook. 'Why did you run off like that from Lochlyn? I knew you were unhappy ... I knew it better than anyone. But you shouldn't have gone alone.'

'I had Ned.'

Catherine shook her head. 'Why didn't you tell me?' she pressed. 'We told each other everything, Eleanor. Why didn't you tell me you meant to run?'

There was something in her insistence that rang false. Her face looked taut with shock and pain, yes, but her pale eyes were lying.

'I don't remember why I ran,' Ella replied slowly. 'After Lochlyn, I was hurt and ... I found Adam. It took me some time to remember my life before that moment, and why I ran is one thing I still don't remember.'

Catherine stared at her. Despite the chill night, there was a line of perspiration above her lips.

Ella took a breath, and went on. 'I can't go back to Ollie, Catherine. I need you to help me. He wants me dead. He tried to kill me when I ran from Lochlyn, and now he's trying again.'

Ella's words were rushed and breathless, but Catherine did not scoff at them as Ella had feared she might. Indeed, she seemed to have expected them, as if she knew already. Her voice went flat and grim.

'I know Ollie's done things he shouldn't have. I've closed my eyes to them, because his business is his own, and because I love him. He's my brother, Eleanor.'

'He'll listen to you. He always wants to please you, Catherine. Can you not help us in this? Whatever he thinks I've done, whatever his reason for wanting me dead, it means nothing to me. I don't want his secrets. I want to go away with Adam. Far, far away.' Suddenly, she realised she was speaking for Adam as well as herself, and glanced questioningly at him.

'As far away as you want.' He smiled into her eyes, answering her.

'You're Ollie's wife,' Catherine reminded her sharply.

'I'm more Adam's wife than I ever was Ollie McLeod's!' cried Ella.

Catherine cocked her head to one side, watching. 'You've changed,' she said quietly, and with a certain sadness. 'I used to think of you as a pampered wee bird, locked in a bonny cage. Now you don't look so well cared for, darling ... and you're free.'

It was so exactly right, that Ella caught her breath. 'Oh Catherine,' she whispered, 'please, please, help me.'

'You don't know what you're asking me to do,' Catherine said harshly, and leaned forward to set the empty glass down. The coil of her hair lay heavy against her nape. Thick, dark hair with a touch of grey. Ella knew it would reach to her waist if it was loosened ...

The memory came without warning, filling her mind. Ella stood, frozen, blind to the present as the scene played itself out within her.

———◆———

She was in the dark passage, and beneath her feet the jewelled carpet runner led her forward towards the doorway. The air whispered secrets.

This was Lochlyn. Lochlyn, the night she fled. She had awoken in the dark homestead and heard voices . . .

The doorway was before her and the light spilled out over her bare feet. She bent her head, straining to hear the voices, to make sense of them. Why couldn't she make sense of them? And then, like a puzzle clicking into place, she knew.

It was a song! A passionate song. A song sung by a man and a woman making love.

Now that Ella knew, she could hear it perfectly - the lower note of the male, the woman's higher pitch. Their combined notes rose, tumbling over each other in a marvellous crescendo. And then dying, fading into whispers and sighs, into silence.

She stepped into the doorway and faced into the room. And felt herself held there like a butterfly on a pin.

The woman lay sprawled on the sofa, her skirts spilling, shimmering, to the floor, framing long legs and the man between them. He was still clothed, as if his passion had been too great to allow for undressing.

It was Ollie, of course it was Ollie.

She was telling herself it was Ollie, even as her eyes moved over the woman, seeing her hand pressing Ollie's face to her bosom in a gesture that was terribly possessive, almost motherly. Seeing the way her long hair fell over them, like a dark wave, streaked with silver foam …

She must have sensed Ella's gaze. She lifted her head, and the pale eyes gleamed through the dark hair. And then they widened, as shocked as Ella's, and yet … resigned. 'I warned you,' they seemed to say. 'I told you how dangerous it would be to pry, darling.'

Ella stood a moment, frozen beyond feeling, and then Ollie's head jerked around, his handsome face twisted with fear and hatred. 'What are you doing here?' he shouted at her. 'How dare you be here!'

As if she were the guilty party.

He was still shouting at her … the foulest abuse. But Ella had fled, running silently on the jewelled carpet, away from Ollie McLeod and his sister.

Long before morning, she and Ned had left Lochlyn forever.

———◆———

'You know, don't you?' Catherine asked softly.

'Yes.' Ella heard her own voice, dead with shock.

'How long had you known … before Lochlyn?'

'Not until that night, when I saw you both. That was why I ran. I thought I could get to Melbourne, find safety … a place to hide.'

Catherine let that pass. 'Ollie thought you already knew,' she went on. 'He was afraid you meant to tell. He said he wanted to talk to you when we got to Lochlyn, make you understand how important it was to keep silent. He told me I had to convince you … that you'd listen to me.'

Ella looked away from those pale eyes, dizzy with the knowledge of what had sent her into flight, what had taken her memory from her until she was able to face it without madness. Ollie and his sister were lovers. It was Catherine he had loved all along. When Catherine had spoken of the other woman in her brother's life, she had been speaking of herself…

'I didn't know until I saw you,' Ella repeated, more for herself than Catherine's benefit. There was a horrible taste in her mouth.

Catherine moved, reaching out towards her with one hand, but Ella turned her face away. The hand fell limply against the arm of the chair. 'I told him you didn't know, that you were ill. I told him you didn't know what you were saying. But he was so afraid … he was always afraid. At the start, Ollie didn't have much to lose. But as time went on, and he grew richer and more powerful, it mattered more. He'd be ruined if anyone found out, and he knew it. But he couldn't leave me … I told him to many times. Oh Eleanor, many, many times!'

'Is that why those men were at Lochlyn?' Ella demanded. 'To make certain I was never able to ruin Ollie?'

Catherine put a hand to her eyes. 'Yes. He told me, afterwards, when you were gone. He knew I'd never o' let him do it.' She lifted her head, white faced and haggard. 'Whatever you think o' me, darling, I was no part o' murder.'

But Ella didn't want to feel sorry for her. She

went on doggedly, brutally. 'So when I ran off with Ned, he sent his men after me. But they made a mess of it, and killed Ned and left me. And Adam found me.'

Catherine smiled a gaunt smile. 'I was glad you were alive. Ollie sent his men back, but it was too late. You'd gone. I prayed for you to run, Eleanor. I prayed for your life, in return for my own ...'

But Ella wouldn't hear her. 'Ollie sent word to Lochlyn that he wanted me back, but without a fuss. Did you know that? He hoped to find me, and finish me. And he very nearly did.'

Catherine shook her head. 'No,' she mouthed, but no sound came out from between her white lips.

'I asked you once why Ollie didn't marry that woman he loved so much, why he had married me instead. And you told me that she was unsuitable. Do you remember?'

'Eleanor, I didn't know what he meant to do!'

'How could you?' Ella spat. 'It was you, all the time it was you – was that why you left Scotland? You said it was because of a man. Was it Ollie even then? Aren't you sickened, Catherine, by what you've done? By what you are?'

Disgust twisted her words and her lips. Revulsion filled her. But as well, there was a feeling of sick betrayal. Catherine had pretended to be her friend when all the time she had been the enemy.

'Eleanor,' whispered Catherine, and her eyes showed the agony within. 'I loved you both, can you not understand that? I love you both.'

'Well I hate you!'

Adam stepped in front of her, and for a moment

she didn't see him. Ella blinked, and his face came into clear focus, his wide mouth, made to smile, the soft darkness of his eyes. 'Stop it,' he murmured. 'She's speaking the truth, Ella. She does love you, and you must forgive her.'

The enormity of what he was asking took her breath away. Her eyes widened, searching his.

'Forgive her,' he repeated. And then he turned and faced Catherine, his voice brisk. 'Help us get a passage out of Sydney. Before Ollie McLeod arrives and finishes what he's begun.'

Catherine stared at him angrily. 'I can protect Eleanor.'

Adam shook his head slowly. 'No you can't, Miss McLeod. Ollie's gone beyond reason. He's after her, and he won't stop. And when he knows about me, he'll have me too. You know that, maybe better than anybody.'

She was silent, struggling with his truth. And then, painfully, she pushed herself up out of the chair. She looked old, her strong face suddenly haggard and drawn. Ella realised then how the strain of the past weeks had aged her. And she knew Adam was right. Catherine must be forgiven for her weakness, and her love.

'Yes, I'll help you,' Catherine said quietly and firmly. 'Ollie has a ship due out on the tide early tomorrow morning. You can take passage on that. *The Gull*, it's called, and the captain is Mr Ingram. I know him. He'll keep your secret, and take you with him.' She looked up, her eyes bright in her white face. 'Do you need money?'

But Adam shook his head. 'We've our own money, thank you. A friend o' ours gave us enough for a new start.'

Catherine nodded, and went to the little desk in the corner. She reached into one of the drawers and took out a pouch. 'There's a ring in this,' she said, turning and holding it out. 'Show it to Captain Ingram. He'll recognise it, and know it comes from me. Tell him I've given you free passage.'

Adam took the pouch.

'Thank you,' Ella whispered. Her wild hatred had gone and in its place was a bewildered sadness.

'You're running after all,' Catherine sighed. 'Like Margaret Catchpole. You're leaving everything behind.'

Ella caught her breath on something between a laugh and a sob. She glanced about at the rich furnishings, the plush room. She was leaving everything behind her, and suddenly she realised how little it all mattered in comparison to what she was running to.

The sound came from outside in the hall. The thud of boots, someone being driven by rage or terror or both. Ella jerked into movement, but Catherine gripped her arm, nails biting into her skin, and shook her head. They heard Letty's voice, trembling with terror.

'Miss McLeod asked not to be disturbed, sir.'

'What! I need to see her now,' ground out Ollie McLeod. Ella heard the mixture of anger and desperation in his deep voice.

Catherine trembled. 'There's a door behind you,' she murmured. 'It leads into the dining room. Wait in there until Ollie is here with me, and then leave.'

Adam took Ella's hand, but she held back. 'What are you going to do?' she whispered frantically.

'What will you tell him?'

Catherine turned and looked at her, and her smile was gentle. 'I won't give you away, darling.'

Ella felt the tears sting her eyes. 'I know that, I know that, Catherine.' Adam tugged on her hand again, but she stood her ground, watching her friend.

Catherine patted her cheek. 'Ollie used to dabble in the gutters of Sydneyton, and it didn't touch him. He said he despised the men he made his money from, their vices made him laugh. But he's changed. He thinks nothing now of killing his enemies to save himself the bother o' a few bribes. And he thinks nothing o' killing his wife, because of what he's done ... we've done. He's become what he used to despise. And I knew it, and I couldn't face it.' Catherine took a deep breath, 'Go now, Eleanor.' She turned away, towards the desk, and Ella realised she had said her goodbye.

Adam was pulling Ella to the door that led into the dining room. She looked back over her shoulder. Catherine had reached deep into one of the pigeonholes, and closed her fingers on an object within, drawing it gently out. Ella saw the dull, deadly gleam of the pistol, before the door closed.

'Adam,' she gasped, but he held her hard in his arms, stopping her struggles.

'Be quiet!' he said, so sharp it shocked her into stillness.

The angry boots marched into the other room, their sound sending Ella's mind catapulting back to Lieutenant Moggs, and suddenly she realised why he had seemed so familiar to her.

'Catherine,' the voice was saying, thick with some

emotion that Ella did not want to understand.

'I know what you've done,' Catherine murmured, in a voice at once loving and scolding. 'Come here to me, Ollie.'

There was a silence, and Ella imagined that great man, Ollie McLeod, burying his face in Catherine's shoulder, her head bent over his ...

Adam led her out into the hall, and then they were hurrying towards the front door. Letty peered at them, wide-eyed, and then bolted up the stairs.

'Catherine has a pistol,' Ella gasped, resisting as he tried to close the door.

'I know.'

'We must do something!'

'There's nothing we can do.'

'I didn't mean her to do this ... I didn't mean this ...' The tears ran down her cheeks. Out in the garden, a twig of winter sweet brushed against her, the strong perfume making her head spin. And then she heard the faint, sharp snap of the pistol. Adam didn't hesitate, but pulled her on, towards the street.

And then she heard the second shot.

———◆———

The moon sailed above, peering around trunks and through branches, as though they were the masts and spars of a ship. She ran, her feet flying over soft pine needles, the faintest breath of air stirring her fair hair.

The moon gazed down upon her, clouds like wisps of dark hair, mouth curved in a gentle smile. Catherine, she thought. Catherine is up there, watching over me.

Her feet ran on, leaving behind the voices calling, and the men chasing, and Moggs's stony-faced fury. Ahead was a clearing, and the moonlight filled it like gold dust. And someone was waiting there for her.

The moonbeams warmed her hands and her arms. She lifted her face and closed her eyes, and felt someone kissing her, soft as misty rain. 'Adam?' she asked aloud. 'Is it you, Adam?'

'It's me,' he whispered, and caught her hand in his.

'Where are you taking me?'

'I'm taking you on a journey.' She could hear the teasing laughter in his voice. 'A great adventure.'

'Will we be happy?' she murmured, thinking of what had been and what was to be.

'Aye, we'll be happy,' said Adam. 'Forever and ever.'

ABOUT THE AUTHOR

KAYE DOBBIE HAS BEEN WRITING professionally ever since she won the Big River short story contest at the age of eighteen. Her career has undergone many changes, including writing Australian historical fiction under the name Lilly Sommers, to romance written as Sara Bennett and published in the US and Australia. Her books have been translated into many languages. She is currently writing under her 'proper' name, Kaye Dobbie, and is published by Harlequin Mira in Australia and Weltbild in Germany. Kaye lives on the central Victorian goldfields with her husband and three very important cats.

Sign up to her Newsletter for the latest.
www.kayedobbie.com
www.facebook.com/KayedobbieAuthor

OTHER BOOKS BY THE AUTHOR

When Shadows Fall
Whispers from the Past
Colours of Gold
Sweet Wattle Creek
Mackenzie Crossing
Willow Tree Bend
Footsteps in an Empty Room